THE MONKEY ON FRIDA'S SHOULDER

THE MONKEY ON
FRIDA'S SHOULDER

by Catherine Barrera

TCU PRESS
Fort Worth, Texas

Library of Congress Cataloging-in-Publication Data

Names: Barrera, Catherine, 1967- author
Title: The monkey on Frida's shoulder / Catherine Barrera.
Description: Fort Worth, Texas : TCU Press, [2026] | Includes
   bibliographical references.
Identifiers: LCCN 2025049180 (print) | LCCN 2025049181 (ebook) | ISBN
   9780875659541 | ISBN 9780875659558 ebook
Subjects: LCSH: Kahlo, Frida--Childhood and youth--Fiction | Rivera, Diego,
   1886-1957--Fiction | Spider monkeys--Fiction | Art and
   revolutions--Mexico--Fiction | Mexico City (Mexico)--Fiction | LCGFT:
   Novels | Magic realist fiction
Classification: LCC PS3602.A777466 M66 2026 (print) | LCC PS3602.A777466
   (ebook)
LC record available at https://lccn.loc.gov/2025049180
LC ebook record available at https://lccn.loc.gov/2025049181

TCU PRESS

TCU Box 298300
Fort Worth, Texas 76129
www.tcupress.com

For my Grandma Cuca. In honor of all your ruby red geraniums stuffed into coffee cans, the hum of the sewing machine that was your livelihood, the kelly green floor boards you painted yourself, and the ever-present aroma of your chicken mole.

CONTENTS

THE BEGINNING AND THE END

Outside of México City
The Town of Coyoacán
Fall 1937

It's dusk when the monkey and the dog walk into the bar.

Shadows are encroaching on the town's Centro, making the buildings list to one side, greedy for the juicy tidbits of gossip that make up their charla at this same time every day. "Psst, you see the way ese pendejo was ogling her from that park bench, so inappropriate, no? And what about that Señora Goya, painted up like a lady of the night just to walk her dog, ja!"

"Shhh," hiss the grackles, disgruntled by the habitually poor timing of such egregious clatter precisely at nesting hour, their peals of rebuke petering out on the tails of the sun.

The neighborhood has grown quiet in a comfortable way. People have packed up their wares and their children and wandered home along the cobblestone streets, now tucked away behind stucco walls painted deep-sea turquoise, fire-engine red, and sunflower yellow—making dinner, gathering around the radio, changing out of their street clothes, and unpacking their burdens until tomorrow.

The bar the monkey and the dog have entered is immune to time, however, as bottles clank, voices scrape, and patrons loose on their feet belt out-of-tune melodies with mismatched lyrics. The smell of fermented agave, grit, and buried dreams hangs in the rafters, trapped in a cloud of cigar smoke that never fully recedes. It's not the most logical place for the two of them to be, but right now it feels like the only place they're safe.

"She's worse than I thought. Es una . . . una . . .," the monkey stammers, searching for the right word. "Well, she's the meanest person in the whole wide world—ever—yeah, that's what she is!" he snorts childishly.

"The UglyFrogMan's the one who drove her to it!" replies the dog, unusually confrontational for her generally mild demeanor.

"Dos reposados," the monkey calls out to the bartender, ignoring the dog's provocation.

Because the pets are regulars here, the bartender has anticipated their order, two tequilas already sliding down the bar in their direction. The monkey, still clumsy in his thumbless-ness even after all this time, claims a sip for himself, and then manages to tip the glass in the dog's direction, the two of them silent as the fire water begins to soothe their pummeled souls. The clock above them continues counting out the seconds, though time has carried no significance since the moment the monkey opened Frida's bedroom door back at the Casa Azul.

"What fools we were, trying to fix her," grimaces the monkey. "'Poor Frida,' we kept telling ourselves. 'First the bus accident, and now this.' Bah, she's been playing us the whole time! Pues, a la mierda todo. I'm done! I never wanna see that hairy, rouge-caked, doped-up face again!"

The monkey downs what's left in his glass, then whistles over the bartender for another round. He and the dog settle in for a long night.

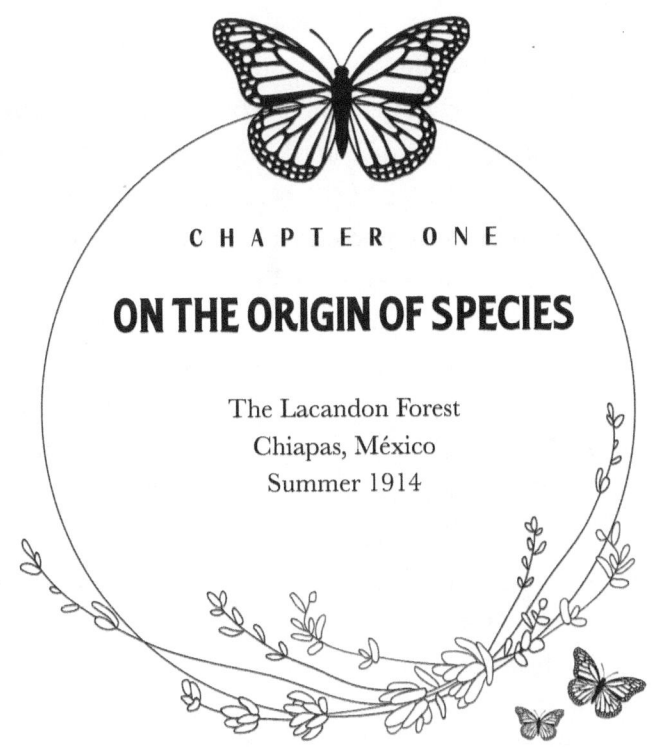

CHAPTER ONE

ON THE ORIGIN OF SPECIES

The Lacandon Forest
Chiapas, México
Summer 1914

During the apex of the seventh moon cycle in the year 1914, somewhere in the eastern jungles of Chiapas, a spider monkey destined for an unordinary life was delivered into the world.

The truth was, he'd seen it coming before the rest of them, that tonight was his fate. There was science on the one hand, gestation periods and all that biological stuff. And then there was that other realm—the perfectly full moon, for example, a misty mosaic in opal and gray, anointed in a sparkling halo of purple and gold, the slight breeze whispering through the treetops, making the leaves dance, and dusting the sweet perfume of the trumpet flower across their canopy, the world so soft and fluid. He felt like he could see them already, his

Troopmates gathered there in a circle around Mamá's nest, each holding a single golden trumpet flower, swaying back and forth in time with her metered breathing. When her body quivered, he could feel their gentle fingertips stroking the top of her head, how her calm was briefly restored. But then, in the next moment, he was in motion again. There came a spasm, and he was being jostled upside down, squeezed and contracted, forced down a tunnel of darkness. Mamá lodged herself more firmly into the mahogany tree, bearing down, sinking into the pain, willing this miracle, pushing her baby out—and into this new world. Far away, the oceans receded to accommodate the moon's brilliant surge, fitting illumination for the occasion.

He exhaled, opening his eyes for the very first time, seeing them there, staring down at him with awe, speechless, proud to be part of this performance, and then, as if it'd been rehearsed a thousand times before, releasing their flowers into the night sky in a single flow, to give praise, solemn and exhilarated at the same time. It was in this silence that he heard everything; this was what home felt like, the immersiveness of their communal love reaching to the core of him.

Vamos derecho, derecho, straight ahead we go
To the trees of our bisabuelos, our sacred refuge every year

Their celebration was interrupted by a chorus from above, a blustery shadow of black and orange shooting down from the night sky, blocking the moon and the stars, and turning their stage pitch black. The monkeys squinted, looking up with a collective gasp at whatever augury was presenting itself. Ah, but there was nothing to fear, they chortled with relief, for it was only a flutter of monarchs, that was all, come to pay tribute to this new life. Tonight was a double blessing, they whispered amongst themselves, for it was well-known among jungle inhabitants far and wide that a flutter appearing at nighttime was a very good omen, indeed.

Swoosh, came the butterflies, funneling down in a single burst and hovering over Mamá. For she had to know what magic she'd brought into this world, on the one hand. And also, she had to know that with this great gift came much responsibility.

Your babe is special, said the matriarch once she'd separated herself from the rest of them. *For he is destined for great things beyond the limits of the jungle, a healer of things great and small. But you must act quickly to prepare him for the challenges that lie ahead. Only you will know how best to accomplish this end. The march of history depends on it.*

He heard, too, of course, though larger adult concerns were still incomprehensible to him at this point, too easily captivated by the romanticism of the moment. For while he was born with an uncanny ability to measure a creature's essence morally speaking, he was, unfortunately, horribly, awkwardly, perpetually flawed when it came to inferring meaning behind everyday details. In this sense, his destiny was predetermined, because invariably, he knew too much, and not nearly enough.

Mamá nodded through a face full of tears, though whether they were the product of joy or fear, he was unsure. Nonetheless, she smiled up at the flutter with gratitude as they departed, and then relief poured over her, limbs slackening and her body growing soft. She pulled him more closely into her chest, kissing his peach fuzz, his body tingling with this love she emitted.

He groped instinctually for her teat with his mouth, finding it, then drawing his first drops of milk. He felt her shudder as her body capitulated to his demand, ceding all control of her power in this world, to be able to share with him, until he could feel her body in his, this maternal nectar the conduit. He took and he took, hungry and intent with a voraciousness that had no end, somehow extracting much more than mere nutrients, siphoning off liquid bits of awareness about her. And though he basked in the consonance that exists between mother and babe, something was giving him pause. He thought he detected a slight mar on the far edge of an otherwise pristine landscape, something that reeked of doubt, perhaps? He stopped sucking for a moment, tempted to chase what he didn't know. But no, not today, not when he'd just been cast into this Edenic setting, meeting his mother and his Troopmates for the very first time. Not today when the moon shone with a heavenly glow, and the monarch butterflies came to offer their blessing, and he'd found this place of deep belonging.

For the next month, the newborn, now called Infant, lay tucked away in his nest with Mamá, allowing her to recover from the birthing, and mother and child the chance to bond. She regaled him with tales of the jungle around them, explaining in her soft, wispy breath that their Troop had taken up residence here centuries ago, that they were a matriarchal society of which she was the current leader, and that one monkey's burden was everyone's to share, all of them working together. He begged her for stories of the personalities that lived among them, delighting in her colorful depictions of wise Bisabuelas, grumpy Tíos, and mischievous Chicos, of jaguars they'd fought off, nest-castles they'd constructed, and bug stew recipes renowned across canopies far beyond the horizon. Oh, how he dreamed of the day he'd be able to join their ranks and become an apprentice to this fairytale he'd been born into. He couldn't imagine fitting any more happiness into his physical frame, so full was his heart in those early days. His dreams were aflush with blue skies and fragrant breezes, with warm embraces and tender kisses, with endless monkey chatter that was often too sophisticated for his young mind, but still wholly translatable, because the most powerful displays of happiness always are.

"Mi'jo," she began cautiously when her time for resting was over, and she'd reassumed her role as the Troop's leader. "It is important you learn to appreciate what the Universe has given us, the bounty of resources that surround us, everything so lush and fertile." She feigned nonchalance, though the tremor in her voice suggested otherwise. She was strapping him face-first to her chest in preparation for the flight ahead as she continued on with the lesson the monarchs had urged her to impart. She suspected what challenges they'd been referring to—the rumors were impossible to ignore, even if there was no confirmation—and the pressing nature of their directive had left her unsettled.

"And though we are welcome to enjoy what we have been given, we mustn't ever take it for granted, or we risk throwing our world out of balance. Each of us has an important role to play, for if the bee neglects to gather the flower's nectar, there is no pollination, and without pollination the flower is destined for extinction, entiendes?" She tapped him gently on the nose; he responded with a gurgling coo. He didn't particularly understand what the bee had to do with the seriousness of the moment, but he could feel her conviction, that all living things had purposes, that they belonged to a larger whole, and if everyone worked toward these ends, he would always be safe.

"¡Vámonos, entonces!" She turned her attention to the Troop now, unleashing the squad of them, an ocean of monkeys spreading out across the canopy like a wave exploding on the shore. Mornings were for foraging, which meant uncovering Nature's hidden delicacies, the kinds overlooked by less mindful passersby, so that it always felt to the monkeys like the supply was their own private reserve—the forest bugs tucked into the cracks of the tree bark, the tiny chayok berries buried behind tangled overgrowth, endlessly layered surprises for the most patient observers.

Still clinging to her underbelly, Infant watched his world unfold in all its glory, his Troopmates testing their findings as they floated along, drooling and belching with pleasure, snickering at their bodies' emanations, commenting on the quality of produce from one cluster of trees to the next, every bite sounding sweeter than the last simply because their mounting satisfaction was being experienced together. The monkeys ate until their bellies were full, and then they stopped. Words like hoarding and profiting didn't exist in their vocabulary. No, it would take the arrival of the TwoLeggers, as the Troop referred to humanity, to introduce them to such concepts. "We'll be back tomorrow anyway." *Burrrrrp. Whooofff. Rear-end scratching.*

On this day, rather than usher them back to their base camp that was the JungleTent, Mamá called the monkeys around, for she had an announcement. She suggested they forego their regular afternoon repose back at the Tent and that, instead, they mark this day with celebration—for Infant's birth, yes, but also for the endless supply of hope their Troop generated. "Wouldn't it be a perfectly fitting tribute," she let her otherwise strict delivery melt into something deviously childlike, "if we were to venture to the EmeraldLagoon?"

Infant was startled by the fevered pitch of their collective response, monkeys leaping higher into the trees, spinning acrobatic feats with their tails from the branches, pumping their chests with clenched fists. This was because the EmeraldLagoon was said to be so magical that it had become the subject of lore among jungle creatures across all corners of the land. It was the cradle of civilization, they relayed to each other through the ages, a place so perfect in its physical presentation that not even an evil thought could be construed while present on its sacred grounds.

"Well, then, off we go!" trumpeted Mamá, signaling them onward with the wave of one hand. The monkeys all knew the route by heart: eighty-five adult swings ahead, straight as the macaw flies, all the way to that juncture point where the foliage dropped off, and a brilliant flash of limestone beach spread out in its place, as if they might be entering another galaxy altogether. Tucked into the crescent mass of rock was the Lagoon itself, shimmering there in the late morning sun, a million tiny prisms of light dancing across the water. The opposite side of the clearing was hemmed in by sheer cliff, pristinely white if not for the rust incursions where tides and currents refused to be forgotten. A waterfall tumbled down one section of the back corner, empowered by the momentum amassed during its cross-isthmus journey, roaring of both its arrival and its goodbyes, having finally been delivered to its ultimate resting place here in this most poetic setting. But by far the Lagoon's most striking feature was the color of the water itself, such a deep and vibrant green that it evaded all conventional categorizations, its emerald-ness mesmerizing, depth-defying, endlessly mysterious, bringing first-time arrivals to their knees, it was reported, even chanting nonsensically at the sky above.

"This is it, Infant!" sang Mamá, pulling him away from her chest, holding him at arm's length now, spinning around on her toes as she gazed into his eyes. "Let us cherish this afternoon, shall we? Try to savor the many wonders the Universe has bestowed upon us, memorize the flavors and the textures, store these images in our hearts . . ."

And there it was again! In the space between her words came that trickle of fear he'd sensed on the night of his birth, and again periodically as her milk took on an increasingly acrid taste.

"There is one more thing I must tell you, mi'jo. I realize this is much to take in. But these are trying times." She pulled him back into her chest, patting his head. He could feel the hastened beat of her heart. That she loved him, he was entirely sure. And that she was trying to hide something from him, he was also entirely sure. He wanted to tell her right then, that he understood more than she could imagine, that he was only one month old, but he was also so much older, that she needn't worry for him, he just needed the details. If she'd just tell him what was wrong, then things would be okay. But he held back because he was afraid he might hurt her somehow, or perhaps startle her into a more frazzled state. Worst of all, he was afraid that what she had to tell him might sabotage the way he saw his perfect world. And so, he said nothing.

"I don't know what our future holds. But I need you to be ready, my son."

He forgot to exhale, his head turning heavy with the cumulative weight of the warning signs, all her awkward hesitations and strained silences.

"The truth is," she paused briefly, "spider monkeys can't swim."

Her pained expression caught him off guard. Was swimming what was preoccupying her?

"I know this is devastating news, Infant. Why, here I've gone and made all this fuss over how sacred the EmeraldLagoon is, only to dash your dreams by telling you it's off-limits. But I need you to be aware of this unfortunate fact. It is important to set realistic expectations so that we're able to direct our efforts to best serve the communal whole, me entiendes?"

He nodded dutifully. But, no, he did not understand. Not one bit. His head was spinning, and he had a thousand pressing questions. Including what did she mean, "realistic expectations"? He'd been able to hear and feel and love while in utero. He felt her emotions and physical sensations as if they were his own. So what ought he to be expecting given his highly unrealistic capabilities? And more importantly, why wasn't she being honest with him? There was more to her grief than swimming alone, he was sure of it. For the very first time in his short life, he felt disappointed by his mother.

"On the other hand, we needn't avoid the water altogether. Did I mention we can go wading? Now, won't that be fun?" she exclaimed with awkward enthusiasm. "Right now, though, I have some things to discuss with the elders. And it's your nap time, little one. But when you're up again, you and I will go wading," she babbled on, doing her best to either assuage or distract him, which, it didn't matter, because it wasn't working. All she was doing was confusing him further with all this ambiguity. "You rest here," she whispered, nestling him into a clump of odd grass sprouted between the rocks. "I'll be right over there, where you can still see me."

"*Waaaa!*" His wail of despair was so raw it surprised even him. Why was she speaking in puzzles? What was he supposed to be afraid of that she wasn't telling him? All he wished for right then was to go back in time, into their nest made for two, to listen to her stories of his ancestors' feats, how they managed through droughts and built their nests to withstand rainstorms, how they fell in love and mourned the dead and reared their young.

"Ay, cariño, no te preocupes." Reacting to his grief, she dropped to her knees, cradling his face into her elbow, then resting her head on his, whispering her greatest truth. "The Universe's most basic rule is that a mother look after her babe. Nothing is more important to me than you, Infant, nothing."

He stopped crying, stunned by the effect of her words, because the confidence had returned to her voice. But what really touched him was that the conviction was melded with a gentleness so pure, he suddenly felt safe again. So that when she wiped a tear from his cheek, settling him back into the grass, then placing one hand gently over his tummy, running her fingers through his fur, he didn't fight back, this time drifting off into what he would come to remember as the most blissful slumber of his life, where everything was good and true, the afternoon passing by in a hazy, dream-like sequence. He thought he felt Mamá swaddling him in her arms, blessing him with her sweetest milk and kisses as soft as velvet. He envisioned himself smiling, trying to express this joy bubbling in his belly, this feeling of being safe and sated, because maybe everything really was fine.

But those were the halcyon days. By the time Infant was halfway through his first trip around the sun, Mamá had become a stranger, tightly coiled and quietly cursing under her breath about enigmas he didn't understand because she'd never shared the details. Her milk went from sour to dry, that vital channel neglected until it became altogether unserviceable.

Meanwhile, as reported by the rodents and birds who happened by, armies of TwoLeggers engaged in the industry they called logging were heading their way, chopping and plowing, laying waste to everything in their path. They were vicious and cold-blooded, it was rumored, armed with tools that had teeth capable of felling entire canopies, and then commanding the horned beasts they'd tied together in pairs to drag away the trunks, leaving nothing but dust and destruction in their wake.

"I saw 'em, just a day's flight from here! I'm not making it up, guys! The term 'eagle eye' doesn't come from nowhere!" insisted HarpyEagle. "I'm not one to gossip, but I'm telling you, the apocalypse is upon us! Beware, the end is near!"

"Well, I heard the reason it's turned permanently dark all hours of the day in some parts is because they stole the sun! Yup, word in the branches is they cut it down from the sky and took it away, can you believe that? How're we supposed to survive without the sun, huh? I just don't see how . . ." YucatanSquirrel chattered away.

As their leader, Mamá listened to the passersby's stories with great attention. When her concerns grew heavy and sleep evaded her, she sat down with the available numbers to do the math. She didn't like what she came up with the first time, so she tried again, and then again, carving figures into the tree bark until her fingers were raw. But it always came back the same: Their time was running out. Left with little other choice, she tucked Infant into his nest on that most forsaken evening, and then she called an emergency meeting at the AgoraCanopy, the monkeys' public arena located in the center of their Tent.

"Monkeys, thank you for coming tonight," she hushed the crowd, albeit in a less-than-authoritative voice. "I'm afraid I come to you with disturbing news. It's all true, what they've been saying about the TwoLeggers. They are indeed coming. And they are coming quickly. I've run the math—*over and over I've run the math*, she whispered to herself—and I can tell you with scientific certainty that they'll be here in just three moons. Which is why I've called this meeting. Because we must act now or be destroyed."

Where there had been whispers and fidgets in the crowd, everything went still.

"I recognize that what I'm about to suggest will sound treasonous, that it flies in the face of everything our Troop has stood for since our dynasty was established here centuries ago. But this time is different; this time our foe is too powerful." She issued a deep sigh, using the pause to try steadying her voice for what came next, the part she'd most been dreading. "As your leader, I advise that we disband immediately, set aside allegiances to our Tent . . ."

Gasp!

¿Qué dijo?

What'd she say?

". . . gather up those closest in bloodline, and run, scatter far and wide—into the highlands, or across the peninsula to the coast, it doesn't matter, just make yourselves scarce and hard to find. And most important of all, act now! There's no time to waste."

Where once they were curious, and then they were afraid, now they were paralyzed with disbelief. How could something so perfect be facing its end? It didn't work that way; when an animal died or a flower wilted, it was to serve some other good, to provide nourishment for a predator, or nectar for a bird, but not this—this was plain antithetical to the way Nature operated!

"Which is why Infant and I leave tonight."

Shwooo, went the air leaving the bubble that had kept the Troop intact for generations, monkeys rising to their feet in protest, because she couldn't ask this of them! She. Just. Couldn't!

"Stop, please! Hear me out!" She was screaming with every gram of her being now, to be heard over their mounting frustration. "Infant came to us in the direst of times. I won't pretend to know why. But what I do know is that his birth was according to the Universe's larger plan, and that, as both your leader and his mother, it is my duty to follow through what She has started: I must rescue our son from the storm that's headed our way. What I know for sure right now is that I must get him to safety, so he can go on to do whatever it is he's destined for. And whatever that turns out to be, I will continue to believe that it has something to do with our Troop, and that the life we built here was not in vain." Her voice tapered off, shoulders slackening, because she had nothing left to hide.

Neither did the crowd, rising to their feet, ready to challenge her directive.

But Mamá was already on the move again, slight and fragile looking, perhaps, but now immune to the mayhem she'd just unleashed and numb to the shattering blow she'd just thrown. It was the only way she could go through with it. In a single flow of motion, she retrieved Infant from their nest, strapping him to her chest, leaping high into the trees, and then floating off into the horizon, soon nothing more than an anonymous silhouette bobbing on the edge of the world, getting smaller and smaller, until she'd disappeared altogether.

CHAPTER TWO

HARD LINES AND SHARP ANGLES:
WHEN THREE WORLDS COLLIDE

Palenque, Chiapas
Fall 1914

It was the third day of their exodus. The scenery continued to sputter by in the same indistinguishable, convulsing waves of limbs and brush Infant had become accustomed to, a nameless anywhere, one more canopy further away from everything familiar. His world had come undone. Because he'd snuck out that night to eavesdrop on his mother's speech at the AgoraCanopy, he knew everything. And while this provided him answers for what had been eating at her, he didn't understand why running was the right choice. Her credo had always been one giant ode to the Universe, for its unlimited ability to adjust and self-repair, so long as everyone did their part. And weren't his

Troopmates doing their part? How could she turn her back on something so perfect? Once again, he felt let down, empty in all the places he used to be so full.

Poor Mamá was faring no better at this point, exhausted and fumbling for branches, sending mother and son tumbling headfirst into canopies below each time she lost hold, then picking them up again, squeezing out a little more, until, at last, she had nothing left to give. Resigned, she lowered them from the treetops to find a resting spot.

"I must go search for food, mi'jo, or we are not long for this Earth. You wait here, where you'll be safe; I won't be long." She patted him a spot in the brush. Infant winced, recollecting that afternoon at the EmeraldLagoon, how she'd comforted him through his first bout of disappointment, so badly had he wanted to believe her. *The Universe's most basic rule is that a mother look after her babe.*

"And don't worry, Infant. We'll find a new nest—a place far away from the loggers, where berries grow as big as the moon, and pygmy owls sing you to sleep." And then she disappeared into the brush in a single flash. How quickly she'd become an expert at that, ja, disappearing whenever things weren't going her way. Well, that was the easy way out, he thought to himself. He'd never do anything like that. *Never. Ever. Ever.* He grimaced through his repulsion.

Infant rolled over onto his back, welcoming the soft breeze on his sweaty, rumpled frontside—apparently, an unfortunate result of days travelling in captivity. It was regenerating, to feel the ground beneath him, reminding him that he was still attached to this Earth, if not his Tent. The sun was high in the sky, its warm rays trickling down through the treetops, kissing his face, making him want for beauty over fear, for living in this moment rather than chasing the lesser of two evils. He took a deep breath, sucking it into his lungs, feeling his extremities tingle with life, reminding him to have faith in the Universe. That's when everything went dark.

Infant shot to sitting. It wasn't nighttime. Was it? So why had the sky gone suddenly dark? When he looked up, he could make out a faint glare that was the sun, now ensconced behind a thick curtain of orange-and-black mosaic. He quickly discerned that what he was witnessing was a flutter of monarchs descending from the heavens, a clarion chorus on their lips so sweet and tender that Infant was stirred to the core. Wait, he knew that sound! Could it be that these were the same butterflies who'd come to Mamá on the night he was born?

Vamos derecho, derecho, straight ahead we go.

To the trees of our bisabuelos, our sacred refuge every year.

Vamos derecho, derecho, homeward bound we go.

A pause, and then, *Vamos derecho, derecho, straight ahead we go . . .*

He stared at the elegance of their collective movement, thousands of vibrating wings performing perfect pirouettes, each in time with the next. *Vamos derecho, derecho,* they glided to the left to avoid a thorny outgrowth, *straight ahead we go,* then corrected course, such aggregate beauty and graceful cohesion. As captivating as their presence was, he knew he had to act fast, that this good omen had appeared to him twice now, and that he'd be a fool not to seek out their guidance. Surely, they'd know what to do about his predicament, how to find Mamá, and maybe even help him convince her they'd taken a wrong turn and they should return to the Jungle Tent immediately.

"*Helloooo?* Down here!" He screamed at the top of his lungs, flailing his arms overhead, an island castaway begging to be rescued. "Please, I'm all alone, help me!"

But it was not fated to be, because in the next moment, the sun burst forth with a blinding surge that made him wince. The flutter was gone. A wave of despair rushed over him, the recognition that he was more alone than he'd ever been. Mamá had cut him off from his Troopmates, and now he wasn't sure if she was coming back, and even the monarchs had ignored his pleas. He imagined he was standing precariously on a thin sliver of land, a giant chasm spreading out around him in every direction, cutting off all escape routes, swallowing the ground whole, then spitting out bits and pieces of fodder as if to mock him. There was nothing left to hold on to; he had to act now. He knew there was a chance Mamá might still come back for him; he also knew there was a chance she might not. Discombobulated by the emotional fireworks going on in his head, and cut off from the warm direction of his Troop, he succumbed to the siren call of anger and disappointment, and he took matters into his own hands.

And so, he scurried into the treetops, reaching for the vine in front of him, and he took a giant leap of faith. The fear plunged into the pit of his stomach as both feet left the safety of the tree, descending along a steep arc from which he couldn't be sure there was an upward force to save him. But the vine held steady, carrying him toward the sky, euphoria and adrenaline surging through his veins. He was an infant, yes, but he was doing this, master of his own ship for the very first time! His heart was pumping with the thrill of it, awakened to this new conviction that as long as he looked forward, everything would be fine. Sure, he thought about Mamá, but it only stirred up the very fear he was trying to escape, and how was that productive for either of them? It was at this point he decided it would be counterproductive to keep wondering about the what-ifs, that the best thing he could do was deliver himself to safety, to be a Jungle Tent survivor—*yeah, a voice to keep the Troop's memory alive, now that was a good idea.*

On and on, he traversed the Lacandon Jungle, floating across the treetops with increasing ease, the birds tweeting their encouragement, the squirrels offering up nuts and berries to keep him fueled, even his nemesis, El Jaguar, wagging his tail from down below, a gesture of silent support for wildlife everywhere.

A week into his treetop travels, Infant came to a churning river, forcing him to abort his flight. He wasn't giving Mamá a whole lot of stock right now, but about the spider-monkeys-can't-swim thing, he didn't have a lot of room for error. Mumbling under his breath, he lowered himself from the trees to assess his options.

"Hello there, young fella! Now, I'm willing to bet you're not from around these parts, are you?" came a voice amongst the reeds. "I know practically everyone out here, and since rarely does a creature venture out this far without an entire army for protection, I have to assume that you're lost?"

"Who's there?" Infant shot back, sinking onto his legs and pivoting left, then right, then back again. He'd proved himself to be a real ace at tree swinging, sure, but he was in uncharted waters here, so to speak.

There was rustling among the water's foliage, and then, gliding slowly to the surface, Cocodrilo revealed himself. "Ta-da, it is I, Carlos Carmen Rodriguez de Cocodrilo. The third, actually. I come from a rather regal line, you see, we've made our presence known over many generations, on account of . . . um, on account of my family's fondness for . . . um . . . for the fauna, yes, that's it." He spoke with the exaggerated enunciation of a nineteenth-century prince from Cádiz, as if to lend proof to his ennobled status. "But, please, everyone around here calls me Cocodrilo." He bit his lip to contain his enthusiasm—well, and also his fangs, lest he frighten off this fine slice of meat.

Infant had never met a crocodile before, but basic instinct told him that this guy could gobble him up in half a second if given a chance. On the other hand, Cocodrilo was in the water, which inferred he could swim. Which Infant had been led to believe he could not.

"Cocodrilo, why, yes, you're right. I am a bit off my mark—it's an unfortunate and tangled story." Infant grimaced, waving one hand contrarily in front of his face. "But I won't bore you with all that." For which Cocodrilo was glad; lunchtime was quickly approaching.

"The truth is, I'm not sure exactly where I'm headed. You've been here a long time. Tell me, what do you know about the outlying area— in terms of suitability for spider monkeys, that is?"

"My, my, you're an adventurous little one, now, aren't you, ja ja." He affected harmless jocularity as he made his way out of the water, inching up the bank toward the monkey. "Yes, I'll gladly disclose all the pertinent residential details, but in just a moment. I'd be remiss if I didn't pause first to thank you for not running off the moment you spotted me. You wouldn't believe the ends the others go to just to avoid me—pretending to 'accidentally' leave me off the list for the FullMoon party? Come on, everyone gets invited to that party as long as they're still breathing. How can I not take offense? I hear what they say behind my back, calling me 'OcosingoOgre' and 'DiabloDientes.' Well, and it hurts, being discounted like that, before they even try to get to know me. I have feelings, too, you know." He cast his gaze downward, doing his best to contain the saliva pooling in the corners of his mouth.

"So, thank you, little monkey," Cocodrilo perked back up. "I consider myself in your debt for your magnanimous gesture today. But okay, then," he clapped his disproportionately small hands in front of his chest, "back to the question at hand. About the neighborhoods in the area—" He paused. "Say, you know what? I just had a brilliant idea! How about, as a token of my gratitude, I give you a tour of the area? To give you an up-close look at what's around here? Oh, I'd be happy to do it! So very, very happy. All you gotta do is hop on my back, and away we go!"

Infant was torn. To accept the offer would be to put himself in grave danger. On the other hand, how else was he going to reach the other side of this gurgling torrent? Not to mention, there was Cocodrilo's shaky self-esteem to consider. Should he turn down the offer, would he be heaping on even more harm? And herein was a big problem: Infant's special awareness of a creature's essence had the tendency to cloud his thought process, causing him to undervalue the real threat involved in certain situations. According to Infant, if Cocodrilo's essence was good, then his faults ought to be viewed within this larger context. Ergo, maybe Cocodrilo did overindulge in his carnivorous cravings from time to time, but this didn't make him inherently evil. The way Infant saw it, it just meant he needed a little help getting straightened out, a friend to share his berries with or to help repair his nest, everyone pitching in what they could for the overall bienestar of the local ecosystem.

And yet, what good was JungleTent philosophy outside of the JungleTent? It was a biological truth that Cocodrilo could rip off his limbs and have no remorse. Infant shuddered as the reality sank in, that he no longer had the luxury of doing what was best for the collective whole by nurturing its individual parts to their full potential. The rules would be different out here, and he was going to have to learn to fight his natural inclinations.

"Mil gracias," he sputtered, dreading the idea of disappointing a fellow living creature. "I think I'm just gonna do a little exploring on my own. I hope you understand?" Infant avoided looking Cocodrilo in the eye, newly aware that in this new environment, even an infant spider monkey had the capacity to do harm to others. Best to speed along this goodbye so that each of them could move on. "I really did enjoy talking with you—Oh, and another thing? I think the friends you do end up making will be real lucky, Cocodrilo!" And with that, Infant offered Cocodrilo a wag of one hand before fleeing into the safety of the trees from whence he'd come.

"Pinche monkey! Friends, shmrends!" Cocodrilo mumbled as he waded back into the river, pushing away from the shore and into the currents, and starting the hunt all over again. Except he was smiling now, not malevolently, but because his heart felt unusually light.

Infant dawdled along the shoreline for the rest of the morning, wondering if he should've accepted Cocodrilo's offer, and after that, whether he should've waited for his mother to return. Just when he was heading down this rabbit hole of regret, he came upon a well-worn path leading back into the jungle's depths. He'd seen the way a succession of jaguars could clear a swath along the jungle floor, but what he was looking at was of an entirely different scope. It was much wider, yes, but more importantly, it had been cleared of all ground cover and then smoothed over until the dirt looked almost polished. Intrigued, he hopped on the trail, loping along a half kilometer or so, until he arrived at a giant clearing amidst the otherwise dense foliage. The space had been leveled of everything organic, a jungle wonderland reduced to a blank, dirt slate. Instinctively, Infant turned up his nose.

Smack in the middle of the open space, or finca, was a large structure composed of hard lines and sharp angles, wholly incongruous to the region. There was no fluidity, no natural curves or dips or bends to the parameters of this edifice, which befuddled Infant. A tree's branches twisted and turned in pursuit of the sun, after all. And only the most foolish monkey would construct a nest with straight lines in mind, as wind and rain currents demanded functionality over artistic taste.

Nonetheless, this rigid structure must've once been grandiose given its physical breadth. It looked to Infant as if three separate nests had been stacked on top of one another, each with a matching horizontal line of equidistantly positioned windows, all of which were enveloped in carved limestone trim. Ionic columns fastened the nests together—at least, more or less so. The truth was, the windows were broken or altogether missing, and the shutters had come unlatched and hung there like displaced nest fodder after a storm had come through. Come to think of it, noted Infant upon closer inspection, the dilapidated frame was listing to one side, as if waiting with bated breath for the next hurricane to blow through, so it could be allowed permission to at last assume its final resting place. Not a creature stirred, not a flower bloomed, and there was no sign of life.

And yet, Infant knew at once that he'd stumbled upon something extraordinary. Because he'd spent the first months of his life watching his Troopmates' weekly NestRepairWorkshop, he knew that branch ends frayed when they got snapped off. Such a factor had to be considered when calibrating the integrity and soundness of the structure that would house one's family, after all. Which was highly relevant right now, because the wood on the structure Infant was looking at was smooth and sharp-edged; only an extraneous tool could've created such neat lines. Perhaps a tool with teeth? Such as the ones rumored to be commanded by the TwoLeggers? The hair on his neck stood on end. He gasped at the realization that he'd come upon the work of those who had altered his life. The TwoLeggers had been here!

Perhaps he should've been scared. But Infant was different. He realized in that instant that if the TwoLeggers were running the world, he'd be a fool not to try to glean a thing or two from them. How else was he going to survive in their world unless he knew something about it? Besides, the place looked abandoned. No harm would befall him if he just poked around a little. And so, down he went.

Between himself and the CasaGrande with the mighty columns and the listing exterior was a row of thatched huts, each identical to the next. Curious, he wandered over, pulling back the tattered curtain, unveiling a dark emptiness, nothing but a few straw mats on the dirt floor, then checking the next hut and finding exactly the same. Which confused him, because whatever could explain such a disparity in living arrangements? Where he came from, a nest was a nest was a nest.

Scratching his head, he ventured on, plodding up the porch steps of the CasaGrande, reaching for the door, then pushing it open when he felt no resistance. With some trepidation, he ventured inside. And ran smack into a thick curtain of spiderwebs that made him cough, batting his hands in front of his face to break free from the tangle. Once he'd succeeded, he paused to let his eyes adjust to the foyer's darkness. That's when the room in front of him lit up, a cone of golden dust sprinkling down through the far window as if the sun's glory was pointing the way. With a nod, he accepted the invitation, stepping across the threshold to meet the rest of his life.

Like the exterior, the quarter's glory days had expired, but hints of its regal past lingered. Though Infant couldn't yet identify the Two-Legger accoutrements he'd come upon, he could appreciate their aura of softness and ease. There was a grand piano on one side of the room, a scattering of damask settees and mahogany end tables on the other. Pewter candlesticks towered above him as he ambled past the central coffee table. Persian rugs as lush as the jungle's undergrowth and life-size portraits of meadowy hillsides awash in wildflowers and sheep made him catch his breath. He named this spot the StatelySittingRoom.

Pick us up, young monkey! came the seductive call. *Sip from our wisdom, why don't you? Go ahead and inebriate yourself on our knowledge! El conocimiento te hará libre, our collective truths will set you free!*

He rushed past the marble fireplace and the porcelain figurines on the mantel, past the carefully laid out formal tea setting resting on the ottoman, over to the voices, until he was standing before a wall of books. Staring down at him were a thousand gold-scripted leather spines, pulsating with an energy that made him shiver with intrigue. He drew one from the bottom shelf, flipping through its pages, soaking up that intoxicating smell of expired tobacco, dried ink, and ripened intellect, pulling the perfume into his gut, holding it there, feeling his heart soar with possibility.

Though he'd never seen a book before, Infant knew how to read. Actually, it turned out he could do far more than that. For even on that first day, Infant was able to take in copious amounts of information—first one volume, then another, and then the next—such that within an hour he was thinking critically about what he was reading, extrapolating from popular theories, and then adding his own spider monkey keenness, ultimately composing highly unique theoretical arguments that were both masterful and convincing. He felt a surging sense of pride, and his confidence was growing—that is, until the ghost appeared and he tipped over onto his behind in surprise.

So, lad, you're here to learn about humanity? Though Infant didn't know it at the time, he was looking at none other than Charles Darwin, blasting in at the *Beagle's* prow, his long white beard flapping in the Pacific breeze. *Well, you've come to the right place! I'm not intending to be boastful, but take a look at my work,* On the Origin of Species. *You can find it over there, on the middle shelf,* he pointed. *It's about survival and adaptability. I suspect you'll find it quite useful in your ventures. Well, I've got to catch this next current if I hope to reach the Galápagos by breeding season! Happy reading,* he called out. *Oh, but do be careful, young primate. I'm afraid there are some maleficent folks out there using my ideas in twisted ways. Tsk, tsk, how unfortunate it is the way the truth can be so easily distorted.*

When he was sure that Darwin was gone, Infant took his time peeling himself off the floor, his head turning on a swivel as he considered what he might've gotten himself into. When nothing outrageous befell him, he crept over to the opposite wall to retrieve the book Darwin had recommended. Slipping it from its spot, Infant clasped the book to his chest, wrapping both arms around the volume and then slowly rocking back and forth with it as if he'd just inherited the royal crown. Well, and since he was there already, why not select a few others, indiscriminately pulling books off the shelf, because who cared what they were about? He had everything to learn.

When their weight surpassed his own, he teetered back to the tree from which he'd descended only a short while ago. First, he lodged his precious books carefully into a nook there, and then he began gathering up an assortment of twigs and branches, constructing himself a temporary nest. Once satisfied with his design, he climbed in, turned over on his back, and he began to read.

Greetings! boomed the second ghost, floating above the wall of books. Infant had returned to the StatelySittingRoom, now sitting cross-legged on the ground, and looked up with a start. He was glad he hadn't been standing this time.

The name is Herbert Spencer. And if what I hear is true, you've already met my friend . . . or . . . er, perhaps better said, my counterpart. He coughed awkwardly into one fist. *Charles Darwin is to whom I'm referring.. The ghost world is abuzz with your arrival, you see. Naturally, I wanted to introduce myself. They say you're interested in human adaptation and progression, is that right? Because you're looking right at the guru of all gurus on those matters!* He paused to laugh, a deep guttural coughing sound that echoed menacingly across the StatelySittingRoom. *As it happens, I've produced something I think you might find interesting. I used Darwin's ideas as my basis, you see, and then I extrapolated beyond plants and animals according to my own research—to consider humans, specifically. That's where my interest lies. I revealed proof that some humans are naturally more capable than others—more civilized, you might say. I recommend you take a look, see what you can learn from what I have to say, eh, amigo?* He shot Infant a patronizing grin, and then he was gone.

Infant remembered Darwin's warning from a few days prior. And while he didn't much care for Spencer's gruff demeanor, out of curiosity, he went ahead and dug up the man's work. What he uncovered was a tome on something called "survival of the fittest." Specifically, the theory provided rationalization for why one sector of humanity should be made to sleep in mud huts, for example, while another was awarded the comfort of the big house. It was who got the big house that continued to befuddle Infant.

And so, back to work he went, building a bibliography ranging from seventeenth-century philosophers to nineteenth-century novelists, until he had the evidence he needed to prove what he had been hoping was untrue: Humanity organized itself hierarchically—which was bad enough, but worse still—based on things as arbitrary as skin melanin levels, sex organs, and the accumulation of circular pieces of gold or silver or whatever metal was in vogue. Put all these variables together, and what you got was this: Humanity was ruled by men who were white and had lots of those metal pieces. Apparently, everyone outside of this norm deserved whatever miserable fate they'd been born into.

It's not that Infant didn't have an opinion; it's that he didn't have a lot of choice. Spider monkeys were significantly lagging when it came to the accumulation of coinage, for starters. He had a penis, true, though he'd yet to find out how his appendage compared to that of a TwoLegger. As for the third and final trait, he was utterly unsure whether his particular "skin tone" might be viewed as an asset or a detriment. Upon considering his predicament more closely, he realized that precisely because he was a monkey, he wasn't predetermined to fit into this TwoLegger caste system. Wasn't it entirely possible that people would no more likely assume he was a tenement dweller than a gentleman of leisure? A denizen of the StatelySittingRoom rather than a thatched hut peon? The thought inspired him, that there was a way through this quagmire that was humanity, if only he turned himself into a true gentleman, the kind who was adored and respected by society at large! How hard could it be? He had all the tools to learn by here in the StatelySittingRoom. Sure, it would take some work, but he'd been known to navigate his way through a challenge or two.

The first thing he did in his quest to become a bourgeois extraordinaire was teach himself sixteen languages, for versatility purposes, because apparently there were plenty of countries on the other side of the Atlantic that had also constructed their national ideologies around the presumed superiority where wealth and whiteness intersected. As his linguistic capabilities expanded, so did his imagination, and he began using his lessons to transport himself to these faraway lands, imagining himself dining on foie gras in the manicured gardens of Versailles or leisurely rowing a boat down the Avon, wooden pipe angled coolly to one side of his mouth. At first, the caricatures he tried on felt awkward, because hadn't he mocked the very inequality he was sampling from? But he justified this as part of the game he'd have to play here on TheOutside, a world that, alas, was not run by spider monkeys.

Before long, a month had gone by, and still, his thirst for knowledge was far from quenched. By now, he was visiting the StatelySittingRoom daily to refresh his collection, but also because he enjoyed the company. For in addition to the authors who ventured forth to boast of their writings' nonpareil value across time and place, the ghosts of the inhabitants who'd once resided here had begun revealing themselves. These ghosts were at first hesitant to show themselves, hiding in the shadows until they'd ascertained that Infant was *"ni bandido ni caníbal, ja ja."* Interestingly, they never engaged directly with Infant—yes, he could stay and observe their goings-on if he really wanted, but they refused to include him in their conversations.

Heavens no, it's a dirty animal! Can you imagine if people back home knew I was socializing with a monkey over here in no man's land? Why, they'd have me sentenced to life in the asylum, ja ja ja!

All of which was fine by Infant; he could learn a lot by observing.

He grew particularly fond of their weekly parties, where the XY chromosome TwoLeggers occupied one corner of the room, reclining majestically in plush armchairs with cigars in hand, pontificating about European politics or Transatlantic shipping prices. Meanwhile, their XX counterparts occupied the far end of the room, where they crowded together in a semicircle around a glass table that was stacked with Bibles and sewing lessons, passing idle gossip behind the mystique of their handheld fans and boasting of their prowess at the piano when called upon.

Infant both admired and was repulsed by them, the way they seemed to be entirely unmarked by worry, impeccably preened in their linen trousers and silk ties, their corseted waists and satin gowns, sipping champagne, showcasing their knowledge of French opera, Austrian balls, German philosophy. All of this while they complained of the unrefinement that surrounded them here in the jungle, the workers who couldn't be bothered to even keep their meager huts clean, and the way the smell of los indios' mere existence had seeped into their china cabinets and linen closets, souring everything that was respectable. Infant struggled to explain how the supposedly most advanced subsection of the supposedly most advanced species on the planet had created a system in which the rules lacked any compassion. And still, he couldn't look away, drawn in by the power of their ostentatious allure, curious about what it might feel like to be on top of the world.

To further his approximation to the folks he aspired to be, Infant amassed a collection of fashion magazines on haute couture he'd found lying about—slightly outdated, perhaps, but certainly more up to speed than his current style choice, which was absolute nudity. He committed an inventory to mind: he'd need a couple of those stylish high-collared vests . . . yes, and a smoking jacket, that would be nice . . . oh, and some ascots wouldn't hurt, a few bowler hats, perhaps? (Interestingly, though he was fully committed to his self-transformation, Infant refused to don pants. Releasing one's bowels was both a biological necessity and a means of retribution against enemies where he came from; pants would only get in the way. He'd no idea who his enemies might be along this journey; best to be prepared. You can take the monkey out of the jungle . . .) And since he currently owned none of these items, nor was there a men's clothing emporium in the vicinity that he was aware of, he'd little other choice but to learn to fashion them himself.

It was a formidable task, indeed, as spider monkeys lack opposable thumbs. But then again, translating Arabic into Olmec was no simple feat either, he reminded himself with a pat on the back. *To be impressive, one must think impressive thoughts,* he'd begun muttering to himself on such occasions when the work ahead seemed insurmountable. And so, he winced through the pin pricks and blistered fingers, and, cursing under his breath, he tossed away countless first attempts he deemed unsatisfactory, doubling down on his efforts until, finally, he'd turned himself into an authentic tailor. Why, he even came up with an altogether new sewing stitch, subsequently referred to as the sin pulga. The technique called for the pinky and fourth finger to be used as one opposing force, and then the middle and index fingers as their counterpart, the result being a looser, more elastic style, which, in turn, meant airier garments, coincidentally befitting the region's climate.

Vamos derecho, derecho. Straight ahead we go . . .

In Infant's dream, he was in Paris, standing behind the counter of his very own tailor shop on the Champs-Élysées, a starched white apron around his waist, pockets stashed with measuring tapes and needles, sketching pencil behind one ear as he explained his concept for the princess's gown. His client's eyes twinkled with appreciation at what he was proposing. That's when he was jolted awake.

To the home of our bisabuelos . . .

No, it couldn't be! He slapped his cheeks to wake himself, shaking the grogginess from his head. It was the flutter. Again.

"What is it? What are you doing here?" He shot from his nest in a single leap, sailing across the canopy to keep up with the monarchs, knowing their inclination to make a flash exit. The sun was just rising, darts of pink and orange dancing between the branches. "Why are you following me?" He looked up, to be sure he was on target, because he didn't want to lose them, not again—

Boom! He hit the ground with a thud. He looked up to see the flutter sailing by, heading toward the end of the tree line in the distance. He'd lost them again. He cursed himself for forgetting that he was in the land of the TwoLeggers now, masters of this utterly counterintuitive masterplan that had chopped up this canopy against its natural physical flow. Luckily, Infant wasn't hurt, standing up now, wiping his hands clean, then giving his rear end a soft pat for having taken the brunt of it.

Because the jungle floor is the last to see the light of day, Infant stumbled through the remaining darkness, nearly taking a second spill. Gratefully, he caught himself with both hands this time, feeling around for what might've caused the stumble. *Ja*, he snickered to himself when he discovered the explanation: It was a book. He must've dropped it on his walk back from the StatelySittingRoom, always trying to carry more than he was capable of, he chided himself.

You okay there? That was quite a fall.

Infant looked up.

Hope I didn't startle you. I know, I know, you're used to seeing us ghost authors in the house. Seeing me out here is probably a little odd, I get it. The thing is, well, that book you're holding? It's mine. I could feel you pick it up—we get a little shock to the back of the head when there's an interested reader. So, of course, I wanted to come find you, to share a little bit about myself. Monkey, I am Sir Arthur Conan Doyle, and I write detective mysteries.

"Oh . . . Um, I'm fine, thank you . . . Sir Conan Doyle." No author ghost had ever stuck around long enough to let him get two words out. He was drawn immediately to this Conan Doyle fellow.

So, I'll get right down to it. My novels, while ostensibly about solving crime, provide important commentary on the relationship between logic and illogic, which I think you should probably add to your list he suggested through twisted lips, *that is, if you want a more balanced understanding of the irrational side of human behavior. One more thing: You must read between the lines—that's where you'll find all the answers.* And then, like the others before him, he disappeared back into the shadows.

Infant flipped open the book, using the rays of sunlight beginning to trickle down to the jungle floor. He felt himself pulled halfway around the world, into the streets of London, where he was tagging along beside Mr. Sherlock Holmes, darting breathlessly through the city's underground opium dens one minute, then upstairs to a glittering ballroom the next, leaving no time for the thief to anticipate an abrupt change of plan. Only when the culprit had been successfully apprehended was Infant aware that the sun was now blazing directly overhead. Rather than take a break, he raced back to the StatelySittingRoom to return the book to its proper place in the collection. And to look for more of the same.

Perhaps it was his deep-seated concern over humanity's moral code that caused Infant to take so fervently to the stories of Sherlock Holmes. He marveled at the sleuth's ability to move in and out of investment clubs, dance halls, and neighborhood taverns without being noticed, a chameleon bent on discovering what social presumptions kept others from seeing. Why shouldn't the opera manager be suspect just as much as the opium den operator, for example? Because he dressed better? Owned a larger bank account? Had whiter skin? Infant admired the way Holmes challenged what the Social Darwinists were preaching—that civilization marched in one direction, and that progress was achievable only when the darker, smaller, weaker were forced into submission.

As he worked his way through the Sherlock Holmes collection, Infant began creating clever escapades in his head featuring a monkey savant, Inspector Infant, who was called upon to solve the most baffling crimes, especially those with a connection to monarch butterflies. The most famous case involved Inspector Infant apprehending the elusive Mister Miser, a London haberdasher. It seemed that Miser had planned to corner the button market, but met his fate on one otherwise sunny afternoon, when the sky had turned suddenly (though strategically) black and orange, thus causing the villain to unwittingly strike a pothole with his motor vehicle, lose control, and crash into a storefront wall. At which point, ten thousand buttons spilled into the street, proof of Miser's culpability. From there, Infant was inspired to look the part, sewing himself an Inverness cape, and later, whittling himself a pipe, though it was more a prop than anything else. He didn't use tobacco; the plant produced the loveliest pink and red flowers, if ever you were patient enough to look for them on a morning's forage with your Troop.

He'd been on the finca for two years when he turned the last page of the last volume in the Holmes series. It was a bittersweet moment, for as grateful as he was for his adventures with Holmes, he was also deeply saddened he'd exhausted the trove. As he was shutting the cover, wondering what came next in his life, an envelope slipped into his lap, postmarked from Germany. With fumbling hands (sans thumbs), he opened it:

Fall, 1906

Dearest Frau,

I hope this letter finds you and Herr well. We worry about you so, stuck there in that dreadfully uncivilized place, no opera or ballet for consolation. Sometimes my dear Dolf jokes, "Wife, what shall become of our friendship if they should turn to voodoo whilst living in the jungle?" Of course, he says this in jest only, dear friend. My only hope is to bring some cheer to your day.

On to more pressing matters . . . I write with good news! A friend of ours here in Nuremberg has a nephew recently arrived in México City! He's reputed to be a fine gentleman, and a connoisseur of photography by trade. How wonderful if you were able to get out of the wilderness for a holiday? I'm forwarding his information, should you be so inclined to call upon him. After your last letter, so full of homesickness, I do encourage it.

Your adoring friend,
Lillian

Señor Guillermo Kahlo Kauffmann
Londres 247
Colonia del Carmen
Coyoacán 041000
Ciudad de México

Infant's heart stopped. What he was reading was an old letter—he could tell by the discoloration of the stationery—written a decade ago, perhaps? But given this glance into the past, could it be that this Herr and Frau were the ghosts who'd presided over all the parties in the StatelySittingRoom? The ones with the refined salon gatherings and pretentious chatter? Was it Herr and Frau who were behind the development of this foolish venture designed with rigidity and sharp edges? The ones who made snide comments about the natives, demanding they sleep on the hard ground outside?

Why they seemed to have abandoned ship so hastily, he'd no idea. And that wasn't his problem at the moment; what was important was that outside of all logical explanation, the butterflies had led him to Sherlock Holmes—first, by encouraging him forward across the Lacandon landscape, and then, by causing him to land smack on his bottom, practically on top of that book. Which had led him to this letter. Ergo, could it not be argued that he was being prodded by the Universe's larger forces to leave the finca, and to go out in search of this Guillermo character? He didn't need any convincing. And so, Infant gathered together a few of his favorite books, his newly designed foppish wardrobe, and his prized sewing supplies, and off to the Ciudad de México he went.

CHAPTER THREE

LA PROSPERIDAD AVOCADO FARM

Outside of Coyoacán
Summer 1916

Once upon a time, there was a farmer who grew arroz and frijol for a livelihood, the same way his father had done, and his grandfather before that, and so on, and so on. It's what his people survived on. Throw some chiles in there, and even the hardiest man could be made full. It didn't make for a fancy life, but they got by fine enough.

But when the proponents of Social Darwinism blasted into the quiet rural town to build a web of railroads, the farmer got to wondering whether he wouldn't be able to get ahead by switching to avocadoes. He'd heard the gringos went crazy for them, and with the trains passing through, he'd be able to get them to el norte before the fruit got even a single brown spot. And so, with peso signs in his eyes, the farmer took his hoe to the rice and beans, and he lopped the crops to the ground. When he was through, he exchanged the hoe for a machete, and he etched "La Prosperidad Avocado Farm" into a spare plank of wood. Then he sauntered out to the edge of his property, and he nailed the sign to a tree there, for all to see.

To his chagrin, the Indians and the comunista workers took up arms soon thereafter—to get their land back, or for the right to unionize. Cual locura, it was all nonsense to the farmer who didn't give two wits about any of it. All he'd ever wanted was to get in on even the smallest piece of whatever windfall was available in this beloved patria of his. But the political tensions turned explosive, the countryside was drenched in blood, and the farmer's land was rendered useless.

"In the name of 'justice' and 'equality' for all," scoffed the farmer. "Pues, now what? How am I supposed to feed my family now?" he screamed at the sky above. "¡Ay, Dios, dígame, por favor!"

Just then, his son approached, a small dog cradled in his arms. "Papi, look what I found! There's a whole litter, up the hill, right by Mami's altar. The rebels must've left them behind. Can I keep this one, Papi, please? I'll take care of her, I promise!"

As despondent as the man was, he smiled down at his child. "You know what? Yes, you can," he said, tousling his son's hair with one hand, the boy's eyes twinkling back. "Just don't go giving her a name like Zapata or Villa or any of the rest of them agitators, you hear me?"

No way he wanted to be a dog breeder—God, his father would turn over in his grave if he knew! But he'd noticed the hope on his son's face, even in the wake of so much destruction. Yep, kids liked dogs, and dogs were cheap. Now this was a real lucrative idea, he was sure of it.

And so, with machete in hand, he walked back out to the edge of his property. This time, he changed the sign to read, "La Prosperidad Puppy Farm."

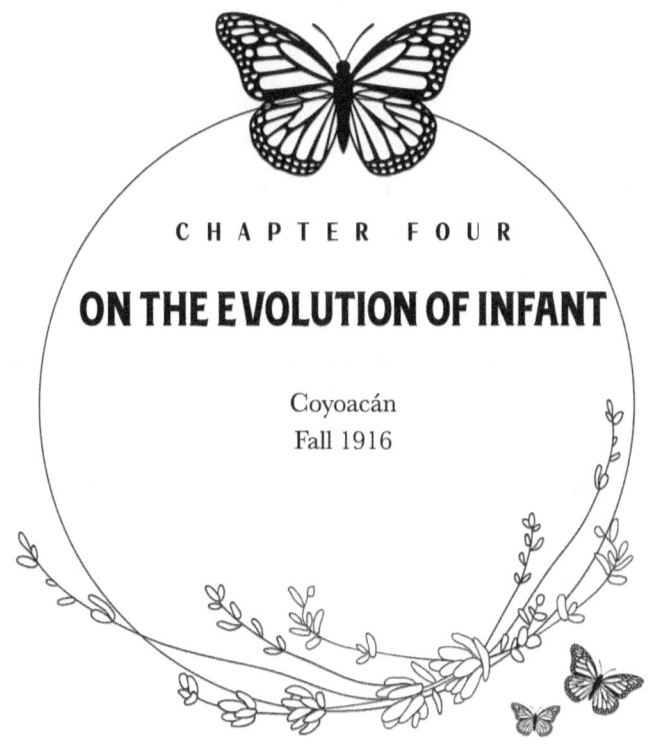

CHAPTER FOUR

ON THE EVOLUTION OF INFANT

Coyoacán
Fall 1916

Half a day into his travels, Infant realized he'd entered a world that was in turmoil. He'd seen nests ripped to pieces by hungry jaguars and blown across entire canopies by unforgiving storms, but nothing could've prepared him for the destruction he was witnessing. He came upon entire villages that had been burned to the ground, roads rendered impassible; the smell of gunpowder never left him alone. There was some kind of a monster here on TheOutside, that was for sure, though he didn't know enough about his surroundings yet to explain the whys. He recognized that he'd need to move forward with the utmost caution and courage. As such, Infant traveled by night to avoid whatever daunting forces had inflicted this magnitude of damage. Sometimes he got lucky, and he'd be able to hitch a ride on the back of some unsuspecting stagecoach, but more often, he was reduced to crawling through tumbleweed thickets and leech-infested swamps that left his knees and elbows shredded and his stomach and back blistered. Day after day, he centimetered his way north, telling himself that his destination was just ahead, one more hill, one more creek bed, it wouldn't be long now.

It turns out he was right. Sticking to the coordinates he'd gleaned from the atlases in the StatelySittingRoom, he arrived at a clearing with a lone building on the horizon. His heart leapt into his throat when he spotted the signature green flag flying from the weather vane there, symbol of the regional train station, that, should it be in operation given the destruction he'd observed in his travels thus far, would usher him to México City! He stood up, brushing the debris from his fur, straightening the collar on his latest creation (a flaxen vest with pleats down the front and buttons fashioned from polished pebbles, a durable choice suitable for such rigorous travel, but also one with modern flair), prepared to make a proper entrance into this next stage of his life.

A lone lightbulb burned from behind a desk inside, and a silhouette moved across the room—evidence of life! He was in luck! It was when he pulled open the depot door that he realized he hadn't made the trip alone, the flutter of monarchs filing in ahead of him in an all-consuming flush that sucked the air out of the room. He paused, rumblings of anger stirring in his gut, because this was his show; he deserved this break! He'd heeded their call, hadn't he? He was pursuing the address they'd planted for him to find, no? He was accepting their nudge; now it was time for him to grow up and forge his own way. The tipping point was imagining himself pulling into México City in an insect-ridden train car.

"Hey, guys?"

Flutter-flutter, they hovered in the uncertainty.

"*Sooooo,*" he began awkwardly, for he loathed disappointing others. "Looks like we're gonna have to sever the ol' ties here, comprenden?" The butterflies continued hovering in place. "As in, today, here. As in, this is goodbye?"

The butterflies stopped fluttering.

"You guys have been real great over the last few months, I mean it. You've kept me pressing forward when I thought about giving up. You've helped me get this far, so thank you." Infant swallowed, steeling himself for the blow he was about to deliver. Gosh, he hated saying no, letting down other living creatures. "It's just that, I can't take you with me—it'd look weird. I really need this Kahlo gentleman to take me seriously. What I'm trying to say is, I like you guys, I really do, and I don't want any bad blood between us. But this is where I have to go it alone, you know what I mean? Go do impressive things with my impressive thoughts?" He held his breath.

Querido Infant, you needn't fret, child, the matriarch separated from the bunch, just the way she'd done on the night he was born. *You're ready now. The time has come for you to take on what the Universe has in store for you. Your gift has always been meant to share; now you must go do so.* And then she cycled back into the monarch flux, signaling them into a single stream, then leading them out the door with a reverberating swoosh.

Vamos derecho, derecho, straight ahead we go . . .

Infant was greatly relieved at the butterflies' amicable reaction, but there was a little melancholy mixed in there, too, because he'd miss them. Their recurring presence in his life had occurred at a formative time. But then again, he reasoned, quick to collect himself before he travelled down a road of regret, he needed to stick to the plan, keep looking forward. Sometimes you had to do things that made you feel uncomfortable here on TheOutside, he reassured himself.

"Excuse me," he said, clearing his throat as he began beckoning the first TwoLegger he'd ever met face to face. Unfortunately, only his forehead reached past the lip of the stall, so that his voice was swallowed up by the wall in front of him.

"Hellloooo?" he tried again, a little louder this time, straining his neck for any extra height and a chance at better acoustics. "Anyone there?"

"Yes? Next!" went the vendor, scanning the length of the counter. "Oh-ho! There you are, little fellow," he chuckled, finally noticing the furrowed brows and hairy hands waving wildly in front of him. For his part, Infant was immensely relieved that the vendor hadn't pulled out one of those tools with teeth the TwoLeggers were reported to wield. And it tickled him greatly to be referred to as "little fellow." It wasn't "gentleman," but neither was it "wretched jungle rat." And he was just getting started.

"One ticket to México City!" he declared with faux assuredness—as much for himself as the vendor—reaching into his satchel and fumbling around for the correct change. He felt a tinge of remorse for having taken the money from a porcelain box in the StatelySitting-Room. But the ghosts there sure as hell weren't lacking for anything, ja, they'd be just fine without the measly sum he'd pocketed for his journey. As he attempted to count out the correct amount, he realized that, without thumbs, transferring objects like paper money could only be carried out in the most unrefined way, in this case, with both palms up, as if he were some pitiful street urchin.

"You sure you want to do that? It's pretty dangerous up there, pal. There's a Revolution going on, you know! All the carrancistas and villistas, they're blowing things up left and right. No order on the roads these days. But it's not up to me," he raised one hand in deference. "Just want you to know what folks are saying, that's all. Hate for something bad to happen to such a little guy like yourself."

Can't be any worse than what I've already been through, Sir; you'd hardly believe me if I told you!

"Yes, Señor, I'm sure. I'm looking for someone . . . or, well, I've received word from a third party that I'm supposed to meet someone—Guillermo is his name, and he lives in México City." Infant saw no need to mention the prognosticating monarchs in all this. "Which is why I'm rather anxious to get there." He made a mental note that once he'd gotten the social and cultural milieus that governed humanity down pat, he would look into why people were so drawn to violence and wars. Really, it made so little sense.

"Okay, then, I won't try to stop you. Here you go, changuito. Váyase con Dios, you have a safe trip!"

"Oh, thank you, Sir, I know I will!" He turned away with a polite nod to the vendor, smiling proudly at the ticket clasped between his palms, and then he climbed aboard the train bound for the nation's capital.

As much as he'd tried preparing himself mentally for the dramatic shifts in landscape ahead of him, it was impossible to have predicted the chaos that was México City. His rural sensibilities were turned upside down. For starters, the depot vendor who'd sent him on his way sure had been right about a war going on. Infant had witnessed it firsthand as the train plowed north—the heaps of cadavers, the shells of buildings rendered unrecognizable, the scorched earth in black and tan. As for the station, hordes of frazzled-looking young men in uniform scrambled around, jumping onto and off of train cars, climbing onto the roofs when there was no vacancy, or clinging to the side windows if that might keep them attached to their method of transportation and this new life they'd been thrown into. The other passengers' murmurs and gossip during the train ride had alerted Infant to the fact that the bulk of the fighting had ceased in the capital, moving mostly to the north, so that was reassuring at least. He didn't have the mental space for politics right now; he had a life to get on with!

And still, Infant had the distinct feeling that even had there not been a war going on, this mayhem was simply the city's natural heartbeat. It felt like time was chronically urgent here—people scurrying about like cockroaches when the lights shut off, beggars and peddlers competing in aggressively raised voices for attention.

"Por favor, tengo hambre, I'm so hungry."

"Te lo doy a cinco, tan barato, I'll give it to you for cheap."

All the while, a monotonous voice droned on in the background, a continuous stream of times and gates, trains arriving and trains departing. Infant's head was spinning. The stench of petrol and horse manure didn't help.

"Excuse me," he squeezed out the words between pants when he reached the curbside, because he'd sprinted through the station like he was being chased by a ravenous jaguar, pouncing on the first driver he came upon, before there was time for any more self-doubt to seep into his consciousness. "I'm going to Coyoacán, do you know it? Would you be willing to take me there? I have an address. Here, let me get it for you, just one second, I know it's here somewhere," he blathered on, fumbling through his satchel for proof of his credibility. "I'm prepared, I know exactly—"

"Para servirle, but of course, Señor. That's why I'm here," smiled the driver, as if there were nothing odd about a monkey with a pleated vest asking to go to Coyoacán. Then he bowed at the waist over one elbow, pulling open the door for Infant to get in. Relieved that he'd yet to be revealed as the fraudulent interloper that he was, Infant jumped into the car, leaning back in his seat, trying to relax now, to regain his façade of gentlemanly composure.

Miraculously, several breaths later, he'd accomplished just that, able at last to take in the urban wonders he'd only read about. They passed entire blocks filled with mom-and-pop shops, or bodegas, their fronts painted in fuchsia, turquoise, and violet, some of them riddled with bullet holes and burn scars, others entirely unscathed, evidence that war had come and gone and chosen its victims indiscriminately. And then there were avenues lined with much taller buildings, flaunting their European designs in steel and marble, flanked by business-men promenading along, leather briefcases in hand as if civil strife were something that didn't exist in their world. The roads were crawl-ing with horses and buggies and cars and dirt-splattered buses carrying old women wrapped in colorful serapes and mothers with small chil-dren in tow. Horns honked, bells tolled, and brakes screeched. It was both exhilarating and utterly humbling for a fellow more accustomed to a landscape of trees and bugs.

So when they got to the house on Londres Street, and Infant stepped out of the car, he felt suddenly small again, his stomach churn-ing. The manufactured environment felt threatening, as if he were put-ting himself at risk with no tree branches he might've escaped into or butterflies to watch over him. He paused to look down the street; as far as he could see there was nothing but an endless matrix of cold, sharp lines, reproducing into more squares and rectangles, repeating the cycle until the rigidity spilled over the horizon. *Impressive thoughts, impressive thoughts,* he prodded himself forward with his head down, a soldier obligated to fulfill the assigned mission. When he reached the address that matched the one on the letter in his satchel, he tapped gently on the door.

"¿Alo? ¿Quién es?"

"Hello, um, yes, buenos. I am Infant. I've come looking for Señor Kahlo, Ma'am . . . to ask him a few questions, er . . . about some ac-quaintances from Nuremberg?" Okay, not perfect, but these human formalities were tricky, the way you had to talk around what you really wanted to say; from what he'd read, that's what it meant to "be polite." Apparently, his message was effective because the door cracked open, exposing one side of an old woman's leathery face.

"Sí, Señor Kahlo is here." The one eye peeking through the slat moved up and down, scanning the visitor. How odd that the monkey could talk, but then again, she'd witnessed stranger things. The curan-dera from her native village knew how to use herbs and small animals to make diseases go away, chickens fly, and spirits rise from the grave. "He's about to take his afternoon tea, if you'd care to join him?" She opened the door wider; Infant slipped inside. And into a whole new world.

The patio was a pantheon of color and sensual allure, an out-of-place oasis hidden behind thick stucco walls. Vines and blooms tumbled from their planters—pops of red, yellow, fuchsia— and hummingbirds danced fitfully from bloom to bloom in search of the sweetest treat. Potted agaves stood like sentries around elevated tree beds, their thin green fingers outlined in the finest calligraphy strokes of neon yellow. Tall and spindly cereus cacti sprouted from every corner, their bristly skin providing contrast to the flushness of the other flora. Bougainvillea dripped from the walls in thick curtains of purple. Birds chirped merrily from the trees, pirouetting along the branches to announce their mating calls. Squirrels darted across walkways, then retreated to their respective tree trunks, scolding each other for trespassing, their cheeks stuffed with their stash. The smell of freshly watered topsoil, the sweetness of the plumeria bloom, and the unscriptedness made Infant shiver with delight. It was everything he was running from, and everything that gave him comfort at the same time.

Conchita, the old woman who'd answered the door, showed him to a small table tucked into one of the garden's nooks. It was surrounded by a cluster of ruby red geraniums as tall as the tabletop itself, each carefully clipped and watered. Guillermo was seated there reading the newspaper, an array of baked goods and a tea kettle set out neatly before him.

"Señor, con permiso, this monkey is here to see you." Guillermo lowered the paper to acknowledge the visitor. "He might know some friends of yours, from Nuremberg? Por eso, I invited him in." Conchita bowed slightly, backing away to give them proper privacy.

"I apologize, Señor Kahlo, for the unplanned visit . . . um, it's just that, well, only a couple days ago did I come into possession of this letter here, and what it reveals is . . . well, of enormous interest to me." *Shit, I'm not good at this! Can you just tell me already why the butterflies sent me here? Or worse, why I chose to believe them in the first place? Ugh!* "It suggests you might know some people I've come to know." *Well, their ghosts, anyway.* "I'm wondering if you wouldn't mind too much, um . . . taking a look at it? Perhaps you know them?" Infant finished, standing there awkwardly with the letter wedged between his palms.

Guillermo was aware he was about to take tea with a talking monkey. But he wasn't at all bothered. In fact, he was rather taken by the young fellow, so well-spoken and finely dressed. *What a stylish vest . . . but how odd he's chosen not to don pants. Oh well, live and let live.* He had a wife and four daughters. The presence of another male around the house was welcome indeed. So he accepted the letter from Infant as he adjusted his reading glasses, turning his attention to its contents, and a brief silence ensued. When he was done, he leaned back in his chair, a genial smile on his face.

"First of all, no guest with a connection to my beloved Germany need apologize for calling on me—at any hour, day or night! Are you hungry? A pan dulce perhaps?" He pointed to the baked goods.

Infant was famished. His first inclination was to hop right up onto the table—bare rear end notwithstanding—and to shovel in as many of the delicacies as possible. On the other hand, he didn't have a lot of faith in how his digestive system might respond to human comestibles, and so, graciously, he declined.

"Fine, then, on to the business at hand. Yes, I believe I did meet this Herr and Frau—"

Infant grabbed the back of the chair where he was standing because this was it. This was the moment he'd been waiting for! Though what he was hoping Guillermo was about to say was entirely unclear. He'd neglected to consider this next part.

"But I'm afraid it was long enough ago that I can't be sure. I don't want to burden you, but so much has happened since then, you see—

my first wife died, leaving me with daughters I'd no capacity to edu-
cate properly, and then, well, I've been in and out of work since the
onset of the Revolution. Plus, there's been Frida's illness to reckon
with, so I just can't seem to keep track of things the way I used to.
I'm sorry. I do hope this news isn't too disappointing?" He furrowed
his thick brow, his woeful expression revealing genuine concern. "If I
might so inquire, why are you looking for them—I mean, if I'm not
being too forward?"

Rats, he should've brought the butterflies with him! Now what?
*Um, because the letter you're holding fell out of a book Sir Arthur Conan Doyle
recommended.*

"Papi, where's my chess set?"

And just like that, he was saved! For now, anyway.

Infant's rescuer was a young girl dressed in a school uniform
composed of the standard blue skirt, white blouse, and knee socks to
match. Somehow, her aura made a mockery of everything proper and
demure. Perhaps it was the devious grin? Or maybe the way she spoke
out of turn, interrupting her father rather than waiting to be called on
first? Infant couldn't help but notice she moved with a limp, her right
leg dragging behind the rest of her like it would have preferred not to
come along for this silly romp in the first place. He couldn't decide if
he was intimidated by whatever trickery she might be hiding from the
rest of the world or if he pitied her for her obvious physical ailment.
Or if two things could be true at the same time.

It was when she got close enough to discern the details of her father's company that her face lit up.

"Oh, Papi, a monkey! Qué precioso, he's so cute! Wait! Papi, did
you do this for *me*?" she accused him playfully, hands on hips, *tap-tap-
tapping* with one foot. "To help me heal?"

Infant watched the way Guillermo fidgeted with the creases in the
letter he was still holding, glancing up with that same furrowed brow,
then back at his hands.

"This is my daughter, Frida. As you can see, she's not shy to ask for what she wants, ja ja," he tried to cover up his unease.

But Infant had already figured out enough to make his next move. He had no direct practice reading humanity's nuances and alternative meanings while in conversation. Of this liability he was keenly aware. On the other hand, he was able to read a creature's essence. In this case, he'd already decided that Guillermo and Frida were good, the same way he knew this to be true of his Troopmates and the butterflies and even Cocodrilo. He found himself drawn to the Kahlos, curious about the complexities that made them seem both compassionate and guarded, naïve and stubborn. So why shouldn't he stay on a bit, help entertain the girl if that's what Guillermo needed, maybe learn a few things about those sneaky nuances and alternative meanings in the process? It seemed like a situation from which all three of them might benefit, come to think of it.

"Hi, Frida, I'm Infant. Your father and I were just discussing, our, er . . . social connections." He laughed through his cringe. "Señor Guillermo, it would be a true honor to recuperate here, just for a few days, if you agree to it? At which point I'll resume my travels. I certainly wouldn't want to impose any more than I already have." Something was clicking, the words were spilling out more smoothly. He relaxed, even puffing out his chest a little, but not too much, because he couldn't afford to get ahead of himself.

"Yes, Infant, we would honor the opportunity to host you! I think it might do us all a great service to have a holiday from the usual. A week, two, stay as long as you like, please! I'm sure Frida will keep you plenty occupied, though, so prepare yourself." He chuckled, a surge of relief pouring over him, because he wouldn't have to disappoint his daughter after all! Not to mention, he'd have more time to get to know this interesting creature, hombre a hombre, maybe even ask him about the fashion statement behind the no-pants rule?

"Oh, yay, Papi, thank you!" And then, she turned to her true focus.

"Vamos, Infant, let's go play! You pick! Papi got me a chess set—do you know how to play chess? I know, I know, chess is for boys. But you'll see, I don't do girl things, it's so *borrr-riinngg*," she said, rolling her eyes. "Or I could show you the neighborhood? There's always something good going on out there—if you like adventure, that is!"

"Frida, querida, easy, easy, you're only just getting back to—"

"So, what do you like, Infant? Come on already, pick something!" She held her arms out to him. Forgetting everything he'd taught himself about steeliness and grit on TheOutside, he jumped straight into them.

And just like that, Infant became Frida's muse and playmate, the duo inseparable from that first day onward. Their friendship was built on juvenile antics, things like peddling mud pies made from monkey dung, ja ja, or blowing milk out their nostrils to get a rise out of Conchita, ja ja. What made their relationship unique, however, was that their play was highly strategized. What appeared to others as simply childish misbehavior was, in fact, steeped in very precise intention. To steal the brassiere from the clothesline of the curmudgeonly neighbor who harassed the neighborhood's waifs just for existing meant constructing a pulley system, which was only feasible, they learned after much trial and error, with the use of Guillermo's fishing pole, Conchita's eggbeater, and the rake from the storage shed. Their camaraderie didn't need articulation. It just happened—an implicit recognition of their shared "otherness," that with their natural wit and heady drive, they would achieve what naysayers said they never could.

In time, nine-year-old Frida revealed that her limp was the result of a bout of polio contracted two years ago, and that she'd suffered from poor health even before that, but she refused to be held back because of some silly medical report. She told Infant that her physical limitations only made her fiercer, fueling her desire to run, jump, swim, dive—all of which she would work to do better than everyone else. He'd see what she meant. She wouldn't be caught dead trying to perfect her curtsy or fine-tuning her penmanship like her peers.

"Those other girls are tontas!" she declared one day. "My life is going to be so much more interesting. Just wait, Infant, you'll see," she snorted, grabbing at her crotch through her skirt.

In those days, Frida couldn't get home from school fast enough. On one afternoon, she dragged Infant into the street, a soccer ball tucked under her arm.

"Vamos, Infant, it's the championship game, you and me against la burguesía—let's destroy them!" she hissed, too young for such venom.

At first, it seemed silly to him, the way she dribbled around invisible opponents and cursed at nonexistent referees. Because he was destined for much bigger things, he reminded himself. What kind of gentleman would be caught running around in circles chasing shadows? And yet, Frida's enthusiasm for life was infectious. Though he tried to fight it, he found it endearing the way that, each time she scored a goal, she'd limp over to the sidewalk where her imaginary fans were waiting to adore her, and she'd pump her fists in the air, screaming "¡GOOOLLLLLL!" at the top of her lungs. It was generally at this point that the neighbors would burst outside to see what the ruckus was, only to discover it was just that Frida again. They'd shake their fingers and air their grievances, and then they'd go back inside until the next time. What they didn't know was that their scorn only fueled her fire, for she had to show everyone that there would never be an opponent who could deter her.

Frida was careful to keep the agenda varied, meaning that Infant was never sure what they were up to until the plan was already well underway. For example, what was one afternoon staged as a stroll through the town's Plaza turned out to be something else entirely.

"Infant, I need you to climb into that fountain over there, and gather up all the coins on the bottom; can you?"

He wasn't sure where this was going, but he obeyed. And yes, it was slightly humiliating to be knee-deep in water trying to scrape the coins off the concrete bottom with no thumbs to facilitate the process, but he took solace in the fact that Frida would put a good twist on this, because that's what Frida did. So when his work was done, he handed her the loot, at which point she stomped across the Plaza toward the Church stairs, making every effort to draw attention to herself. First came a succession of very loud obscenities, followed by one exclamation of "Viva Zapata!" and finally, a flip of her skirt to show a passerby her panties.

When she could feel all eyes upon her, Frida approached the women who frequented the patio in front of the Church, curled up on their tattered blankets, babies clinging to their naked breasts as they chanted their alms, palms out and eyes pleading. And then she moved past them, climbing up a half dozen stairs so she'd be more easily visible to everyone, because that was the point, and Frida always had a point.

"¡Oyen, pinche cochinos! Yes, you, over there, with money enough to throw away on passing whims! This offering in my hands is for these sad women who've got no other way to survive but to humble themselves, asking for even a little bit of sympathy. What do you do instead? Indulge in selfishness and pretension, tossing money into the fountain as if it means nothing to you, coins that might've meant a sack of frijol or a bag of pan dulce for someone in need. Shame on you, pinche cabrones! You are basura!" At which point, Frida descended the stairs, squatted down to the beggars' level, and tucked the loot into the hand of whichever woman was closest. As she stood up again, she patted the arm of her chosen recipient, and then she grabbed Infant by the wrist and marched them off the stage.

Periodically, Infant would wonder why he kept getting assigned the supporting role in all her performances. Which led him to consider whether he wouldn't be better off loitering around Guillermo's studio, for when there was a break in his schedule, and they might have the opportunity to speak of "gentlemanly" matters—things like business and politics and whatever else he'd need to know to get ahead.

And yet, if he were honest with himself, his doubts about with whom he was spending his time had far less to do with his social progress, and much more to do with his growing concern that their relationship was not built on reciprocity, which, in turn, was making him feel disrespected. Oh, he adored the time they spent together, inspired by ceaseless layers of emotional complexity, wit, and a provocateur. Unfortunately, it seemed the reverse was not true.

To be fair, there had been that one occasion a month or so ago when she'd asked about how he knew her father. Initially, Infant had been shocked by her concern—even suspicious?—but if this was his long-awaited invitation to share something about himself, he was in! He explained that he and Guillermo shared mutual "acquaintances," and that Herr and Frau had encouraged him to come to México City. All the other stuff he left out.

"Why, though? What was my dad supposed to do for you?" Sprawled there on the bedroom floor, chest down, feet in the air dangling behind her, she didn't look up, continuing to doodle in her notepad.

"Mentor me, professionally." That this mentorship was unilaterally designed by Infant was not relevant here, he decided.

"Oh."

He waited for her to ask if he, too, were interested in photography. Or if he had other ambitions, or what he liked to read, or how he'd amassed such a debonair wardrobe. But she didn't.

"What do you think this picture looks like?" This time, she looked up.

"I dunno."

"It's me, silly. See?" She pointed to the figure with a bow on her head appearing to be hiding among an assortment of potted plants. "See how I'm crawling across the patio; it's because I'm trying to hide. Mami used to make me take piano lessons—I hate that stupid instrument. *'Free-dah*, where are you?' my mother would scream for me, ja ja. Over and over. So that by the time I'd finally reveal myself, my instructor was already gone. And I was saved!" She smiled, tilting her head smugly to one side.

Infant wanted to stay mad, to keep his resentment brewing for the one-upmanship she was always subjecting him to. Because why did she have to go and change the subject like that? Why, he hadn't even needed piano lessons. He was self-taught, having learned simply by observing the ghost women in the StatelySittingRoom, so there, take that, Frida! And yet, the image of a younger Frida up to her usual antics even as a small child was enormously entertaining, causing his expression to soften and his mood to grow lighter. Come to think of it, so what if right now wasn't the right moment for sharing what books he liked to read, or what the EmeraldLagoon looked like? He enjoyed her tales of chicanery, and surely there'd be plenty of opportunities to share his history another day. And you know what else, he continued his rationalization, maybe it was his own fault the conversation got switched around like that, because he was still new to this game on TheOutside, clearly underprepared to contend with humanity's sophisticated manipulation of words and actions when jealousy, frustration, and remorse were involved. Being with Frida was educational and inspiring. Wasn't that enough? He told himself to stop being so sensitive.

"Let's go over to the corner bodega, wanna?" It was one of those idle summer days a month into Infant's arrival, the twosome casually tossing pebbles at a half-buried shard of glass lying there. (Yes, a month was longer than he'd anticipated staying, but he was getting along well here, no reason to rush things. Frida was obviously enjoying his company, and Guillermo was enjoying that Frida was enjoying. Don't change horses midstream—isn't that what humans said, though he'd never quite understood what the horses were doing in the stream in the first place.) "They have comic magazines is why. We can flip through 'em for free when the clerk isn't looking," said Frida, flashing that devious smile. "Oh, you do know how to read, right, Infant?"

"Yes, Frida, I know how to read." For the thousandth time since he'd arrived at the Casa Azul, he wasn't sure whether he should be flattered by her concern that he might not be fully acculturated into her world or infuriated that she assumed she was that much better than him. He could read in sixteen languages, could she?

When they walked into the store a few minutes later, Frida pointed to where the magazines were, and then, out of tune with their plan, she scooted off in another direction, leaving Infant alone to bury his head in the adventures of Krazy Kat. Snorting and chuckling, as was typical whenever he got into this silly genre of literature, he lost track of time. She finally circled back for him, fidgety now, nudging him out the back door with sharp little prods to the spine. At that point, they took off, rounded the corner, then darted up an alley and plopped down as she began unpacking her loot.

"Whoa! Where'd you get all that, Frida?" His jaw dropped at the mountain of chewing gum in front of her.

"I took it, silly," she answered nonchalantly, already stuffing a few pieces in her mouth, then nodding her head at the pile. "Take some, we need to chew all of it for this to work," she slurred through chomps, saliva drooling down one cheek. "I coulda paid for it, you know. I got the money and everything." She paused, now wiping her cheek with the back of one hand. "I just didn't want to."

"You stole it? Why'd you do that, Frida?"

"I did it, *Infant*, because that owner is mean!" She sat up straight, swallowing the excess liquid made up of sugar and bile. "Which I know because I saw so with my own eyes! What happened is, I came in here a few months ago—before you came to town—because Conchita needed some flour, and I overheard the owner making fun of Papi. Get this, because he only has daughters! He was saying my papi wasn't a real man, uf! I was so mad! No one gets to make fun of *my* papi! And what's the matter with daughters anyway? We're just as smart as boys!" She thumped crossed arms against her chest, a sly grin appearing where once there'd been spite. "Why, I'd say we're even smarter. And I think I just proved it!" *Smack, smack, smack*, went her gum.

"Anyway, this is just the first part of my plan. Next we go over to my classmate's house—Marcos is his name. I have to give him something."

"Is it a wad of chewed gum?" She was making him nervous. Because whatever trick was up her sleeve was sounding a bit more insidious than an innocent victory celebration over a soccer match.

"This isn't funny, Infant! Do you know what he did to me? Ese cabrón called my boot ugly, in front of the whole class! You can't go around treating someone like a bug for squashing!"

Yes, you can—if you're going to eat it, because that's the way the food chain works, and the Universe balances itself out. And why was she always so mad at everybody?

"There's no way I'm going to let some schoolyard bully get away with this. We have to get him back, Infant, it's not fair what he did! People can't just be mean. Somebody has to stop them, right?" She stood up now. "So, are you coming or what?"

His knee-jerk reaction was to hightail it out of there, because he suddenly felt in over his head. This ploy of hers seemed to have a lot less to do with exposing a social injustice, and a lot more with reaping vengeance on a nine-year-old kid, which, using her own words, seemed mean. On the other hand, what did he know about "mean" here on TheOutside? Maybe he was just reading this situation wrong. After all, how could it be right to let this Marcos kid rule the playground like a tyrant? Now *that* was mean! It was settled then; he jumped up and hustled after Frida, charging through the cobblestone streets to wage this oh-so-virtuous war.

When they came to a curbside azalea big enough to hide them both, Frida ducked behind it, pulling Infant with her.

"Give me your gum." She was all business now, no room for theatrics this far in; deployment had commenced. Meshing the two gooey wads into a larger one, she continued, "I need you to do this next part, Infant. I can't, well, because I'm a cripple—as Marcos reminded me today, *grrrrr!* So take this gum, will you? And go across the street, to that tree—see where I'm pointing?" She traced the route with one finger. "And then, all you have to do is swing over to the light fixture above the door, and use your tail to lower yourself down, so you can put this wad over the keyhole, okay? It shouldn't be that hard. I know you can do it, Infant," she offered last-minute encouragement to the soldier she was sending into battle. "I can't wait to see Marcos get what he deserves!"

This time, Infant didn't hesitate. He'd wholeheartedly swallowed the call to arms—that tyrants and bullies had to be stopped. Framing it this way was not only reassuring, but it made him feel proud to be a crucial part of the solution. Off he went, across the street, up the tree, and then over to the light fixture. His heart was thumping as he lowered himself down, steadying his breath to mold the gum over the keyhole—almost done now, just a tuck here, a nip there—when he heard footsteps. He panicked, flexing his tail to pull himself back up, only to realize that the hair on his chest was caught in the gum. He was stuck.

Fortunately, Infant never left the house unprepared for situations like this. His deep-seated fascination with Sherlock Holmes had instilled in him the need to always be ready for the unexpected. Ergo, he'd adopted his fictional hero's predilection for impromptu costume change when the situation called for it. In the case of the button-swindling villain Mister Miser, for example, at one point, Inspector Infant had been forced to cast aside his plaid deerstalker cap and Inverness cape, disguising himself instead as a rag-tattered opium dealer to con his way into the thief's warehouse. And while Infant did not lug around changes of wardrobe per se, he was sure to always have on him his most essential sewing supplies so that he might doctor his dress at a moment's notice. It was, thus, the small pair of embroidery scissors that saved him from being caught red-handed that day.

He whipped out his tool, cutting around the affixed clump of fur, gasping when he felt the patch of flesh pinch and break, blood beginning to trickle from the wound. But when he considered that the blemish might one day serve as his medal of honor, he imagined himself kneeling before his Reina Frida, the most courageous knight in all the land, accepting whatever reward she chose to bestow upon him. Rectified in spirit, he catapulted himself back into the tree, out of breath but safe.

Just in time, it turned out. Because Marcos had appeared, kicking at the ground as he shuffled to the front door, disgruntled-looking as only a spoiled nine-year-old can be. Lost in thought, he put key to lock—or, better said, he tried to.

"¿Eh, qué pasa?" he muttered under his breath. "Wait, is this gum?" His face puckered in disgust as he inspected the goo on his hands. "And hair? No! Blood? There's blood and spit all over me, someone let me in, quick, I've been poisoned! Open up!"

Scattered between their street adventures were quieter moments, allowing Infant and Frida to feel safe in the privacy of each other, to act with less inhibition. It was in this context that Infant came to know Frida dreamt of one day becoming a doctor. She explained that while girls weren't supposed to pursue this profession, she was determined to do so. Infant was her most avid supporter, offering to help her study if he could. She took him up on it, the twosome retreating into her room to flip through the anatomy books she'd slipped from Guillermo's studio, alternately reciting the names of organs in a studious fashion, then pointing fingers at genitalia, wondering what purpose that thing served, ja ja ja.

On other occasions, they played "school," where she assumed the role of la gran maestra, and he, the student—always strongly encouraged to play dumb. ("I'll buy you caramelos when we're done, please, Infant?") So he'd sit there obediently, letting her lecture him on vowels and consonants, odd and even numbers, no matter that he'd mastered all of it—in what, his first hour in the StatelySittingRoom? But he really did like the candies, and imagining his small contribution in her path to becoming a civic leader made him proud.

But by far Frida's most curious pastime was her doll collection. She had over a dozen muñecas, each precisely groomed, with nary a hair out of place and always impeccably dressed—with shoes that matched purses and hair ties that matched dress fabrics. They were lined up neatly on a shelf next to her vanity. She gave them names—there was Greta in the pink dress, Petunia with the dark braids, Francesca with the shiny black patent leather shoes—routinely running down the list like she were taking school attendance, checking to be sure each was in her proper place, as if one of them might have gotten up and walked away, shattering the puzzle she'd fitted so carefully together. When one day a moth hole appeared in one of their tiny lace bonnets, Frida ran to Conchita, pleading though a face full of tears, please, could she fix it, because her baby was so sad, she *needed* that bonnet to be fixed! And when she tucked them in at night, she cooed to them with soothing words and invented lullabies. How odd, Infant sometimes thought to himself, that the rest of Frida's days were spent pushing back against social norms, and yet, there was this hidden other side, so gentle and nurturing. He wasn't sure if anyone else had been witness to this part of her; he suspected not. This fact made him feel special, because he knew her this well, and yet, enormously responsible for protecting her.

It was a few months into his stay at the Casa Azul when Infant came upon Guillermo at the patio table surrounded by the geraniums.

"Oye, Infant, you ever tried cognac? I've got a fine Cuvée Léonie right here, why don't you join me?" The first signs of nightfall were upon them when Infant accepted the seat opposite his host, the moon's crescent form slowly coming into focus as the sky turned mauve, the street's traffic dwindling to a lone car passing by every now and again, a huddle of giggling schoolchildren making the lazy walk home. It was that time of day preceding the evening meal, when work is done, and only rest and leisure remain to fill the waiting hours.

"I'm glad you happened by, Infant. I've been wanting to talk to you. Seems we rarely get the chance—that Frida sure is keeping you to herself, isn't she—well, not that I'm complaining, to the contrary . . . Which, I suppose, brings me to my point. Her mother and I want to thank you for staying on with us, you know, helping Frida. It seems you've single-handedly turned things around here; it's nothing short of miraculous what you've done for her!"

Infant's belly felt warm. "How kind, Guillermo, though I don't consider my stay here a favor. I like Frida, she's special." *It's more than that, though, words do her no justice—the way she draws you in, challenging every rule you thought was binding, merely by giving you a taste of what is possible when inhibitions are cast aside!*

"Well, she is my favorite, you know!" He was leaning in toward Infant, one hand cupped over his mouth, a feeble attempt to muffle his admission. Though it wouldn't have mattered if anyone had been within earshot; everyone already knew that Frida was Guillermo's golden child, the way he was always heaping praise on her, as if he didn't have three other daughters living under the same roof.

"Here's a little secret, *shhh*, but I used to make-believe she was my son, can you believe that? That's how badly I wanted a boy! Why, I'd go so far as to describe to the gentlemen down at the Club how different my Frida was, so much tougher and more ambitious than all the other muchachas. 'She doesn't throw like a girl,' I'd brag. 'She doesn't cry like a girl. She doesn't act like a girl. So I guess I'll go ahead then and just pretend she's not a girl, ja ja!'"

Infant had never known his own father; Guillermo was as close as he'd ever come. As such, he didn't have a lot of preconceived notions about what a "good" father might look like. But preferring a son to a daughter? Or one child over the next? As far as Infant was concerned, the complexities that defined the connection between humanity's obsession with social stratification and morality were becoming none the easier to comprehend.

"I am anxious to see how my Frida turns out. Frankly, I wouldn't be entirely surprised if she ends up president of this fine country one day! I know, I know, we still don't allow ladies to occupy that post—and between you and me, I'm not saying I think that's such a bad thing." He leaned back in again, whispering through the side of his mouth as he fiddled with one end of his moustache. "They're too emotional, have you noticed? Crying or praying for things to get fixed. Hard to be a good decision-maker when you let yourself be guided by such flimsy tenets."

Infant half-smiled in response. Just one more oddity for the books, he supposed. Spider monkeys were a matriarchal species. Mamá had been the leader of their Troop. True, she'd ended her reign in a less-than-noble manner, but that was a different story.

"But who knows?" Guillermo wasn't through. "Frida could be just the one to change all that!" He set his snifter down on the table with a *thwack*, followed by a hearty chuckle. "Now, wouldn't that be something? My daughter, La Presidente!"

"Ja ja, yes, La Presidente Frida rolls right off the tongue."

The two of them sat there in the comfortable silence that develops when the golden hour and cognac intersect, imagining Frida seated behind an oversized mahogany desk, issuing orders to revolutionary *generales* clad in decorated war uniforms, standing at full attention before her, awaiting their next directive, prepared at the drop of a hat to deliver whatever she requested.

"Enough about Frida, though, Infant. Why don't you tell me a little about yourself? What are your plans? Certainly, a bright young lad like yourself has lofty aspirations. Perhaps you could accompany me to the Club the next time—such a distinguished group of gentlemen down there, you couldn't go wrong getting to know any one of them. Why don't I put together some background notes on a few of them for you, you know, so you don't get caught with your pants down, ja ja!"

And what would be the matter with that?

"If you've any interest in banking, there's Señor Zarragoza, yes, you'd definitely want to talk to him if that's your interest . . ."

Infant's heart skipped a beat. This was it, the moment he'd been waiting for! He'd been spending all his time with Frida, so that he kept forgetting why he'd come here in the first place! *Impressive thoughts, impressive thoughts . . . I've often thought of living in Europe, Sir. Perhaps international commerce would make the best use of my particular skill set? I'm fluent in sixteen languages, have I mentioned that?*

"Papi, it's time to eat!" It was Adriana, the second oldest of Matilde and Guillermo's girls. "Infant, come sit by me, *pleasseee?* I brought down some of my pretty hair ribbons; I want to put them on you, can I? Hurry, before you-know-who gets here and grabs you all for herself!"

"He sits by me, Adriana! He's my monkey!" huffed Frida, stomping into the room. Oh, how his heart soared to be wanted. Also, Adriana was stiff and boring, and he was not interested in being dressed up like one of Frida's dolls with that silly hair stuff, *sheesh!* He might not be a full-fledged gentleman yet, but his dignity was still intact! "And you are not putting that ridiculous bow on his head!"

"Guillermo, did you hear Adriana? Join us at the table, will you?" Matilde was working with Conchita to put the final touches together, delivering dishes to the bright yellow table, shifting glasses around, refolding the napkins, the usual frenzy of last minute pre-dinner activity. Truth be told, Infant loved this time of day, all the excitement, anticipating what fine flavors he was about to sample for the very first time as his body continued acclimating to human cuisine, what adventures from the others' day would be revealed, what comically offensive retort Frida would inevitably insert into the conversation.

Guillermo raised his eyebrows at Infant, then stood up with a heavy sigh, no urgency in joining the confusion going on over at the table. In return, Infant met his gaze, trying to affect the same disappointment, because hadn't their gentleman-time just been aborted, and shouldn't he be really, really disappointed about that? But he wasn't.

Doing his best to conceal his true feelings, Infant trudged along behind Guillermo, slipping into his chair at the table alongside the others, his insides feeling comfortably warm. He adored his designated spot, this mark of belonging! So what if his setting was a bit different from the others—sans fork and knife, for example, because these were ineffectual tools for those lacking thumbs; he'd learned to make do instead with a small hand shovel previously used for potting flowers. And of course, he'd fine-tuned his table manners by now, responding with "please" and "thank you," placing his shovel neatly on the far lip of the plate when he was finished, dabbing at his upper lip with the linen napkin provided. Against his innate tendency, he'd even trained himself to suppress the release of bodily gasses until he'd formally excused himself from the eating area.

"So, Infant, we didn't have a chance out there to talk about General Carranza. I was wondering what you thought about him as a leader? Do you think the Revolution is finally coming to an end?" Despite the five women also seated at the table, Guillermo was looking directly at him, eyebrows raised as if he were genuinely curious about what some interloping monkey thought about national politics. Once more, Infant was baffled. Guillermo had just run off at the mouth about his reverence for Frida; so why was he forging comradeship with him over his most prized offspring? Because he had a penis, was that it?

"Guillermo, no politics at the table, you know that! Please, everyone, let's say grace." Matilde grabbed the hands of the girls on either side of her, closing her eyes. She ran the house, and she ran it according to strict Catholic tradition—nobody had to like it, they just had to pay lip service to her instructions, at least pretending piousness at mealtime, and then again during Sunday Mass. It was how she reinforced her value among the bunch of them, by reminding them of a mother's eternal value to her family, the selfless martyr who existed only for them and God. As all heads bowed in accordance, Matilde moved into the evening's prayer. Frida squeezed Infant's knee under the table. He opened his eyes; she stuck out her tongue. He bit his lip to keep from giggling. When he snuck another peek, Frida was picking her nose as Matilde rattled on about blessings and mercy. He'd already forgotten about his and Guillermo's unfinished business. He was exactly where he wanted to be.

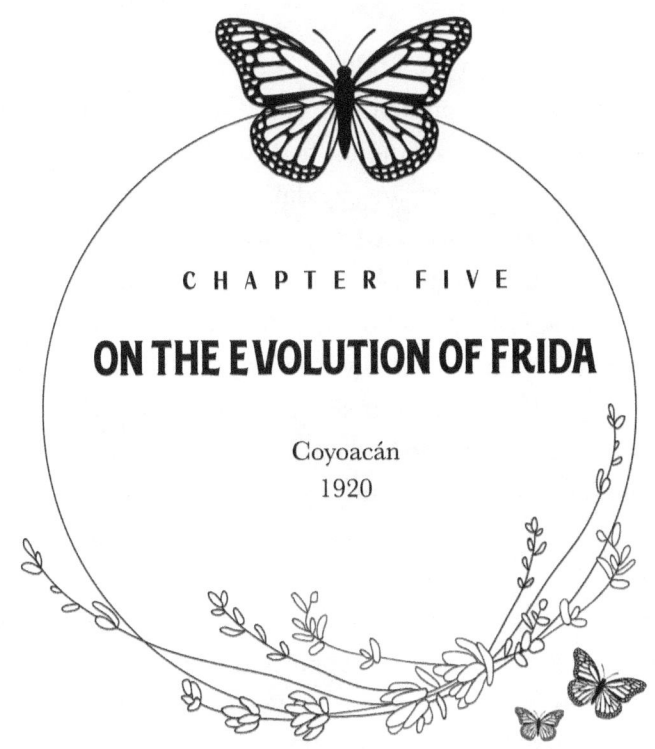

CHAPTER FIVE

ON THE EVOLUTION OF FRIDA

Coyoacán
1920

As the years went by, Infant conditioned himself to overlook Frida's shortcomings, convinced that he was the luckiest monkey on the planet, because spending any amount of time with Frida was worth it and their friendship was of the rarest and most special kind, and nobody was perfect anyway, they all were marred by at least some minor inconsistencies, right? And then came adolescence. Worse yet, human adolescence. That's when things changed.

In the beginning, Infant barely noticed the shifts, just minor things that were entirely uninteresting to a spider monkey. Sure, he was aware of Conchita's monthly grousing over the girl's bedding needing to be laundered yet again, and her underwear needing bleaching—*"¡Su sueg-*

ra llegó!" And then there were Frida's blouses that needed to be let out a few centimeters, and more buttons added to the neckline. But who liked extra work, was how Infant justified Conchita's moods.

However, when Frida began spending afternoons tucked away in her room, Infant took notice. He was accustomed to her racing home to find *him*, begging *him* to join her in whatever afternoon antic she'd planned, tempting *him* with caramelos and adventure. He didn't understand why all that had suddenly stopped, why she headed straight upstairs instead. What was so great up there anyway? And so, one afternoon he snuck upstairs to find out.

What he spied was Frida sitting at the vanity, cooing at her image in the mirror as she tried on different shades of lipstick, pausing intermittently to plump up the new mounds of flesh sprouting beneath her blouse. Why was she acting like this? His Frida wasn't like all the other girls. She didn't go for all that curtsying and flowery stuff. Perhaps she was confused, Infant reasoned. Yes, it was perfectly normal to get confused—why, it'd happened to him more than once. He smiled to himself remembering the JungleTent, the StatelySittingRoom, the butterflies, all those times he'd been unsure which fork in the road to take. So as her oldest friend, Infant decided it would be appropriate for him to provide some guidance.

The opportunity presented itself a week later when, oddly, she hadn't gone directly upstairs to admire herself in the vanity mirror. Instead, he'd found her in the kitchen, rapt in conversation with Conchita.

"Aha, there you are, Frida!" He feigned surprise. He always knew where Frida was beginning the moment she stepped in the house. "Hey, you wanna go over to the Plaza, dig up some coins in the fountain like we used to? Remember? Make people's wishes *not* come true, ja ja!"

"Not right now, Infant, I'm sorry." While her apology rang wholly sincere, that she'd said no made him go weak in the knees. "Conchita's telling me how she got to Coyoacán, all the horrible things she had to go through—and with three siblings to care for! Did you know they had to run for their lives when the ganaderos showed up one day and just took over their land? No legal claim, nada, they just took it, for their cows to graze on! Imagine, throwing a family of poor farmers off their land to make way for cattle! 'Hey, I know, how about we starve the masses so we can feed the big city ricos all the juicy steaks they can swallow!'" She was holding her arms out wide by her sides, rocking from left to right, her big city rico impression. "Ick! It makes me so mad! Oh, and I just remembered the other thing you said, Conchita, about that corrupt town council, uf, unbelievable . . ." She was rattling away now, as passionate about Conchita's story as she'd once been about an imaginary soccer match.

"So, then, you don't want to go to the Plaza?"

She stopped her ranting, turning to Infant with a blank stare. "But you understand, right? Why I can't go?"

"Yeah." But no, he didn't.

"Conchita's story feels important to me. It'd feel wrong to let myself get distracted by . . . well, by that other stuff. But you go ahead." She forced a smile at him, and then she turned back to Conchita. "What was I saying?"

"Other stuff"? That "other stuff" is what our friendship was founded on, it's what made me think I could actually fit in here, that "other stuff" inspired me to believe that underdogs like you and me had a shot at making it! And answer me this, Free-dah, why don't you ever want to hear about my past, huh? I've overcome some "horrible things," too, you know!

Infant felt kicked in the gut. Dragging himself across the patio, he came across a spindly tree he'd barely noticed. Tucked away in the corner, it looked about as lonely and underwhelming as he felt right now. Because it wasn't in full bloom, it took him a minute to realize just what he was looking at, but the tiny golden buds were the giveaway: it was a trumpet flower tree. The same one cherished by his Troop. Producer of the same bloom held by each of his Troopmates on the day of his birth, and the same sweet aroma that blanketed his Tent every evening as the sun slipped away. Now he felt kicked in the gut with the other foot.

Infant didn't care about going to the stupid Plaza anymore. Right now, all he wanted to do was climb into this tree, tuck himself away from the rest of the world, and console himself for the disrespect Frida kept throwing in his face. He scurried up the trunk, settling into a functional nook there, then reclining with his feet propped up on an opposite branch, one elbow tucked behind his head. Issuing a melancholic sigh, he crowned this spot his private oasis, a safe place where he could go for brooding and contemplation. He named it the PoutingTree.

For the next year or so, Infant was sulky, spending much of his time in the bowels of his nest. Frida had been accepted into the highly acclaimed National Preparatory School in downtown México City. ("I'm one of only thirty-five girls, Infant, fíjate! Oh, and did I mention there are two thousand boys? How ridiculous is that!") While Infant was proud of the spunk and guile that had won her admission, he felt wistful about the way her world was opening up in sequential waves of possibility (impressive!), while his was looking more like a neap tide (unimpressive!).

"I'm home!" And still, he spent every minute of the day waiting for this precise moment, when she walked through the door. For she'd gone back to her old practice of racing home to find him, to brag about her new experiences, he supposed, what with all the glamour, intellectualism, and sophistication La Prepa awarded her. He knew he was no more than the audience in this arrangement, but he couldn't stop himself from hanging on to this thread of possibility, that their time together would spark something in her, rekindle what they had, eventually return their relationship to its rightful order.

"Hey, Frida, qué pasa?" he countered with well-rehearsed aloofness, because no way he wanted to come off as needy.

"I had such a . . . culturally edifying day," she pronounced with her nose in the air, plopping her rear on a rock beneath the PoutingTree. "Do you want to hear about it?"

He knew exactly what was coming. Frida was about to relate some story about some great thing she did at school, to which he was to listen patiently, and then confirm that *wow, she really was amazing, she sure did a number on that uppity so-and-so, that sure ought to have put him in his place!* Their roles were by this point entirely prescribed: Frida was the leading lady, and he was the village idiot. As long as he did his part, the show was cleared to go on indefinitely. And if he chose to carry on his part, indefinitely would buy him time to win her over again. Despite the maltreatment he believed he was being subjected to, he clung to this thread of hope.

There was something else, though—something just as important that he'd realized recently in the countless hours he spent brooding in the PoutingTree. There was leverage in playing the village idiot. While it was his job to offer her endless support, ultimately, she'd come to depend on it. Her sense of worth depended on his praise and admiration. In that sense, it was he who got to issue the final verdict, to either approve or reject whatever prank she'd just pulled, because she was and would always be the little coja who would never be entirely convinced she was good enough. So, yeah, he continued with his part hoping she'd come around and treat him with due respect. And also, he continued with his part because he didn't want to hurt her by manipulating her sacred and rare trust in him.

As for her latest prompt, he responded, "I do!"

"Oh, good, you're gonna love this one!"

Infant could feel her eyes reaching for his. A satisfied warmth, tinged with an equal share of shame for his imperfect intentions, filled his body.

"So, I've got this one class on pre-Columbian culture, and today our lesson was on Aztec symbols and names, and how they got tangled together to reinforce communal tenets—not by coincidence, of course, because the elite are always manipulating culture to control the masses. Same story, different century." She shook her head. "Anyway, I'll skip the details and get to my point. Your name is all wrong, Infant, I mean, come on, you haven't been an infant in years!"

Something was off. Usually, her chronicles of roguery had nothing to do with him. Where was the part about the museum they visited on a field trip, and how she called the condescending docent a jackass? Or the kid whose father was in the president's cabinet, and how she scored higher than him on the math test? No, no, no, something else was going on here today; she had a new trick up her sleeve, mused Infant, as if this were another Sherlock Holmes adventure rather than two childhood friends navigating their changing relationship.

"So, what did you have in mind, 'MiddleAgeMonkey'?"

"No, silly, I've got something much more fitting."

"Go on."

"What about Nahuatl?"

The circuits in his brain fizzled.

"Oh, it's the Aztec language, there's no way you could've known that." She was straining her neck now, to check his expression, be sure he cared, condescending and pitiful at the same time.

He bit his lip to keep from barking back that yes, he did know that, because he happened to be fluent in Nahuatl, if she'd ever thought to ask!

"I was thinking we could use it as a cultural statement, a symbol of resistance to México's stupid obsession with European culture, by promoting our indigenous roots?"

The problem was, the Aztecs weren't *his* forefathers. He was from Chiapas—which was the one fact she did know about him, on account of his connection to Frau and Herr. And Chiapas was Maya territory, almost a thousand kilometers away—which she also knew! So why was he getting an Aztec name?

Noting his hesitation, Frida did a minor retreat. "Or we could just call you Nat? For short? Nahuatl might be too intimidating, you know, for those less informed," she groused. "What do you think, Nat? You like it?"

He was absolutely sure she had an ulterior motive for giving him such an inappropriate name. Off the cuff, he'd guess it was for bragging rights, to demonstrate to her classmates how radical and creative she was, that it didn't matter if they were the children of diplomats and banking moguls, she was the wittiest one amongst them. He imagined her flaunting this tale of reverse-colonization, probably interspersed with a lot of cussing for emphasis, because she had to leave her mark. *I belong here! This is my space, too!*

"Nat . . . *Hmmm.* Why, yes, I think that will work just fine," came his decree. True, it was the same old song and dance, but he'd been on her mind at school that day, hadn't he? That had to be worth something.

Concerning Nat's (née Infant) already fragile state of mind, things worsened when Frida began a courtship with her classmate Alejandro Gómez Arias. As was proper, Frida brought him home one afternoon to make the formal introductions. Which turned out to include Guillermo and Matilde. Not Nat.

Per usual, he was tucked away in his nest. Which meant he was privy to everything that went on in the courtyard and even beyond that when doors and windows were open, which was often. Well, and the truth was, even when it might've benefitted him to ignore whatever Frida was up to, he always succumbed to the temptation to eavesdrop. He couldn't help himself—he desperately wanted to know every last detail about Frida. On this occasion, he knew within a few minutes he did not care for this Alejandro fellow. Frankly, it was embarrassing to watch, the way the calculating little letch gushed praise like some fabricated gurgling fountain, complimenting the home's colonial-style décor (in truth, he hated it, as he was repulsed by imitators of European high art). He raved about Guillermo's framed photographs hanging so prominently on all the walls (they were fine; that he'd chosen to display work commissioned by the evil dictator Porfirio Díaz was highly unfortunate, however). And he applauded Matilde for her dedication to the poor through the works of the Catholic Church (he bit his tongue about the Catholic Church having done as much to rob the poor as it had to help them). Mostly, however, his flattery was heaped on their daughter (everything he said on this matter was entirely heartfelt).

"I noticed her the very first day, because she was always raising her hand and—"

"Sounds like my Frida!" Guillermo interrupted.

"I'm sorry, Alejandro, what were you saying?" Matilde shot her husband an angry look.

"Oh, well, and every time the teacher called on her, she said something cunning and wise. I haven't looked away since."

Though Nat was appalled, he knew the boy had put on a masterful performance, employing just the right dose of awkwardness to keep the adults from suspecting him of something more sinister—the way he wiped his sweaty palms together as they took their meal at the bright yellow table, or paused awkwardly to come up with the most effective way to demonstrate his deference, "yes, ma'am," "no, sir." But the second Guillermo and Matilde excused themselves from the table, the boy flew at Frida like a starved animal, pressing his body against hers, his fingers fiddling with her blouse.

"Ay, mi amor." Well, and she certainly wasn't fighting back, panting between kisses, pulling him outside by the collar, onto the patio, toward the storage shed there. "Oh, my sweet Alex, vente conmigo, no one's out here—"

"Um, I am!" Nat sniped back from his nest. Because this was where he was ninety percent of the time. Which she knew because this was where she'd sought him out every day for the last six months!

"Oh, Infant!" She startled, pulling away from Alejandro, rebuttoning her blouse, but without the haste to indicate any embarrassment for having put all of them in this awkward situation. "I forgot you were there."

Ouch!

"Wait, not Infant, what am I thinking?" she snorted, slapping her palm against her forehead. "I meant Nat—Oh, gosh, you haven't met Alejandro, have you? I'm sorry. Nat, this is Alejandro. Alejandro, Nat." She unfolded her arms gracefully in front of her to designate a formal introduction.

Grrrr! As if none of this was painfully uncomfortable for him, that she'd been half-naked a second ago, plus the fact that he appeared to be last on her list of those-I-want-you-to-meet!

"Hey, Nat, nice to know you. I gotta admit, when Frida first told me she had a pet monkey, all I could think of was you being chained to a tree and playing with your, er . . . instrument, ja ja. But then I found out there's more to you than that, you know, and how much you support each other. I really respect that, the development of this unlikely friendship."

What? Who did this prick think he was?

Sensing there might be trouble, Frida guided the conversation in a different direction. "Hey, Nat, you wanna hear what we did at school today?" She turned to Alejandro. "He loves this stuff." Then back to Nat, "You want to?"

"Always."

"Okay," she exhaled, bending over slightly and putting her hands on her knees, then looking up at Nat with the same pleading eyes he knew so well. "We set a donkey loose in the school hallway! It went wandering into all the different classrooms, interrupting lectures, making kids go wild. Oh, and then, get this, it started crapping everywhere—in the cafeteria, along the walkways! I think it took four administrators—is that right, Alex, was it four?" She waited for his affirmation, and then, "Yeah, four to finally get it off campus!"

"Ja ja, gosh, good work, guys," was all he could think to say. *Just as Marx would have foreseen it: the proletariat, the bourgeoisie, and the unfolding of class conflict. I don't remember exactly how untethering an ass on a school campus fits in there, but* The Communist Manifesto: Tale of a Donkey on the Lam *works, too.*

He waited for Frida and Alejandro to sneak off into her room, and then, for no reason other than outright frustration over his diminishing control over how things were unfolding, he snapped a trumpet bloom from the tree. He held it in front of his face, considering the crepe paper folds in the petals, then bringing it tentatively to his lips. Its mild sweetness was seductive, making him take a few nips of the nectar, feeling it melt down the back of his throat. The next thing he knew, the trees and the flowers around him began gyrating, flapping their wings of magenta and yellow and red, releasing their perfumes into the air in an orgasmic spray of dewy bliss. Odd as it was, he felt relaxed now, like his body was being swept up into the swirl around him, weightless, his worries dissipating. He could hear Frida and Alejandro making love across the patio, but the magical juice floating through his body made their noise inconsequential, everything falling softly around him.

CHAPTER SIX

LA PROSPERIDAD PUPPY FARM

Outside Coyoacán
Summer 1925

A short drive from Coyoacán, a litter of Xoloitzcuintles, or hairless Chihuahua dogs, came into the world. It didn't take long for the farmer's son to develop a special affection toward the runt, a female with a matching pair of white tufts on her head and tail. Still unusually tenderhearted for a sixteen-year-old boy, he'd served as a sort of foster parent to dozens of litters by now. But his concern for this runt was special, her fragility reminding him of his own, and so he tended to her with the utmost care, excusing himself from the table every night after dinner so he could go to her with scraps from his plate smuggled into the folds of his clothing. "The fat is the best part, perrita, I saved it for you, so you can grow big."

"*Yip*, thank you MyBoy."

The boy would wrap her in his arms, making the short hike up the hill to the jerry-built altar his mother had constructed there years ago—and continued to tend every day since, lighting a candle, dusting away any cobwebs, kneeling in two well-worn holes in the ground where her knees found temporary solace two times a day. He would take a seat just beside his mother's spot, pulling out his Bible from between the loose notches in his belt, and he would read to the pup, the same lessons his mother had imparted to him—solace for the poor, inspiration for the meek.

"But how do you know God's love is enough? How can you be so sure that He is capable of fixing all things in this world?" the pup asked on one of these evenings. "You sacrifice your own comfort to feed me, but who is taking care of you, MyBoy? I see the barren pantry, the way your mother speaks of ham hocks as if they're made of solid gold. Why does God deny meat for your table, while He graces others with such abundance?"

The boy could feel the depth of her concern. She was not being gruff nor contentious; she was merely searching for proof. And who among us has not shared doubt at some point, the boy reflected.

"He has reasons that are not for you or me to know, my pup. God has a plan for all of us. What happens today is how He prepares us for the future, so we're best suited to carry out the work he assigns to us here on Earth. I endure hunger today because I have faith that He is leading me toward my Natural Duty; that is when my plate will be full."

The runt seemed satisfied by his explanation, tucking her nose into her chest, curling her back legs into her middle, and listening with renewed purpose as his recitations started up again.

Three months later, the HombreFeo with a wad of pesos in his pocket drove out to the farm. The runt and her littermates were shepherded into a corral in front of the house, signaling the start of negotiations, the farmer leaning his elbows into the shovel he was never without, the vendor gumming an unlit cigarette as he paced in circles around the merchandise. From her vantage point on the selling floor, the runt spotted MyBoy quavering behind a tree a stone's throw away. She opened her mouth—to call out, to let him know she saw him there, that she'd be fine no matter what happened next—but nothing came out. As consolation, she closed her eyes and said a prayer that what MyBoy had preached to her was true, that God was watching over her at this very moment, and that being placed in the hands of the HombreFeo was actually a blessing, because this was part of His larger plan. While she was at it, she put in an extra plea that He take care of MyBoy. Her prayers were cut short when she felt herself being picked up by the scruff of her neck, then tossed into the back of the truck, recognizing for the first time the volatility of human behavior. She turned around one final time as the truck pulled away, to look for MyBoy, but he wasn't there.

There was no way she could have known that MyBoy would remain in hiding for two more hours, letting his despair settle over him, followed by the shame, for having done nothing, an implicit supporter in the injustices that occurred every day against the weak and the poor. When his shame gave way to anger, and finally, to resolution, he stood up, because he had to consecrate his vow. Once he shared it with someone, there would be no going back, and so he slipped out from behind the tree, and he went to tell his father what he'd decided. *From this day forward, I will take matters into my own hands. I will accomplish good things for people like us, los de abajo, no more waiting around for someone else to take care of us. From now on, I will do the honors, Papá, I will end this suffering. I lost my pup today, but I gained self-will.*

Never again did he return to the altar on the hill above their house.

CHAPTER SEVEN

ACCIDENTE NÚMERO UNO

Coyoacán
September 1925

Nat had been with the Kahlos for almost a decade on that most fateful day. Coincidentally (or not), he'd decided the time had come to take leave of the Casa Azul. Frida had Alejandro now. She'd made it abundantly clear by what little time she spent around the house in general, and the PoutingTree in particular, that she was done with him. Shit, it'd probably be days before she even recognized he was gone, that's how bad it'd become. He'd never intended to stay on this long anyway—well, to be honest, what he'd intended was to live up to his supposed specialness, but, alas, he'd stumbled a bit. No matter, though, he could still self-correct, he told himself, get back in the ring and make a go of life as a gentleman; where one door closes, another opens, or some other moronic anthropological-spiritual directive to make you feel better about passages—which it didn't, but that didn't matter anymore, because he was moving on. Today. Definitely. A quick bath, throw his things together, and then, *ciao, Frida, have a nice rest of your life*—all before she'd had time to catch the bus back to Coyoacán. Gosh, he didn't like the way he'd become so sour in spirt; he hoped that would change by the time he got to the next town.

The sun was full in the sky as he stood over the birdbath, running his fingers through his hair, then taking a deep breath intended to chase away the quiver in his throat, but the sweetness of the Pouting-Tree's flowers instead made him choke as their perfume infiltrated his lungs. When he stopped coughing, he turned suddenly melancholy, reminded of his Tent and the camaraderie and the feeling of belonging he'd once known. His train of thought was then sideswiped a second time, because given everything he'd read on pre-Colombian mysticism, he knew that a trumpet bloom emitting perfume during the daytime was the darkest of omens, reported to signal the impending death of a loved one! No, no, not now, not in the hour of his departure, he reprimanded himself, chasing away the psychic babble in his head, drying himself off, and then climbing back into his nest to finish packing.

Toc, toc, went a caller's knuckles on the front door.

A shiver of dread shot up his spine.

"Yes? What do you want?" barked Conchita through the cracked door.

"Perdón, Señora, I've come to speak to the parents of . . ." The man with the white service uniform glanced down anxiously at the paper in his hands. ". . . Señorita Frida Kahlo. Are her parents in?"

Nat dropped the bag he was holding.

"Pues, sí, pásele." Conchita turned around, her face blanched now, the air in the house turned heavy. "Señor Guillermo? Señora Matilde? Someone is here to see you!" she called out in a shaky voice that wasn't hers.

The couple shot out from separate rooms, racing to hear what it was an unannounced stranger would be calling about.

"Señores, buenas tardes. I've been commissioned here . . . well, to bring you some news about, er . . . Frida?"

"Is she okay?" Matilde's voice was trembling.

"Yes, she's going to survive." There was a collective sigh, everyone's worst fear behind them. "However . . ."

However. However. However. Nat had wanted to get away from Frida, true, but that was all. Not this, though—oh, no, no, no, he'd never in a million years wish her harm!

"Your daughter has been in a very serious accident." The communal sigh was cut short; everyone gasped. "It appears a trolley crashed into the bus she was on, and she was impaled by a railing. She's in critical condition at the hospital, but they say her chances are very good."

"Ayyyyy, nooooo!" Matilde began to weep, heaving waves of sorrow rippling across the courtyard, through the cobblestone streets, over to the Church where she prayed three times a week, causing the votive flames to leap up against the glass that contained them, their red-hot fingers reaching up in desperation, to commiserate with Matilde, acknowledgement of a mother's greatest pain.

"As I mentioned, they're saying she'll be okay. I have here the official medical report." He handed them the envelope, too stiff to contain any good news. "Again, I'm sorry, Señor y Señora Kahlo. I pray for your daughter's speedy recovery."

He didn't have the guts to tell them that Frida's spinal column had been broken in three places . . . and that her pelvis had been fractured . . . and that her collarbone was broken. As were two ribs, and her right leg and foot, and her left shoulder had been dislocated. It was all there in the envelope; they could read about it if they wanted the gory details.

"Impaled"? That sure doesn't sound very encouraging! Nat fretted, beginning to unpack the books and sewing supplies and sin pulga wardrobe

he'd only just stashed away. Because there was no way he was leaving now—not when her life hung in the balance. What kind of gentleman would he be dancing across the ballrooms of Nuremberg while his dearest friend lay crippled in a hospital room halfway across the world? *And what did that guy mean, "they say her chances are very good"? Who the fuck is "they"?*

Fully committed to his change of plans (or was it simply relief he felt?), he finished hanging up the last of his smoking jackets on the branches surrounding his nest, and then he lay down, folding one knee over the other, tucking his elbow behind his head, and snapping a bloom from its stem. To an outsider, it might've looked like he was relaxing with a fine cigar, rather than contemplating mortality, guilt, and jealousy while high on a foreign substance. The fluid melted over him, softening his frustration, resentment, and fear. Frida's face appeared to him in the sky, that familiar sparkle in her eyes, the same devious smile, and then she was turning around, skipping up a gilded path that disappeared in the clouds, wagging her finger for him to come join her, floating away now, smooth and easy.

It was already late morning of the following day when Nat came to, the sun poking through the tree branches like spiked fingers digging into his eye sockets, an aftereffect he'd come to expect when he overconsumed the flower's nectar. He dragged himself to the kitchen to look for Conchita. To find out about Frida.

"Buenos días, Conchita." What he meant was, *How is she? Is Frida alive?*

"Good morning, Nat. How are you?" What she meant was, *I didn't sleep a wink last night, worrying about our Frida. Oh, my, isn't this the most horrible thing?*

Conchita had yet to glance up, focused instead on slicing the papaya, pineapple, and watermelon in front of her. Every last centimeter of counter space was occupied by slabs of orange, yellow, pink, the previously dislodged chunks now splayed across the floor, accumulating in small heaps in the corners, so that it felt to Nat like the kitchen was getting smaller with each fell of her blade, *chop, chop, chop.*

"I'm good." Nat pawed at a sliver of papaya, working double-time to get it to his mouth, trying to appear casual but unable to refrain from blurting out the only thing that mattered. "Any word on Frida?"

"Oh, dear, Infant—er, Nat—yes, what a wreck I am. I thought I'd already shared the news with you, silly me. El Señor sent over a message saying the surgeries went well. She's out of danger, gracias a Dios." Conchita paused to bow her head, making the sign of the cross. "They think she'll be able to come home in a few weeks. She'll need months of bedrest to recuperate, of course, but she's going to be okay. The worst is over." *Kerplunk,* went another slice of melon hitting the floor, punctuating their awkward silence.

The subsequent days dragged on, heavy with nervous anticipation. Guillermo and Matilde did what was typical whenever they were overcome by grief, loneliness, or general dissatisfaction: they sequestered themselves separately behind locked doors, which left Nat and Conchita basically alone in the Casa Azul. Oh, Nat tried coaxing Guillermo out of his shell, with invitations to the neighborhood CornerBar for cervezas or some soccer on the radio over a cognac, or even just a round of canasta at the patio table with the geraniums. But this was his Frida, he explained apologetically each time Nat called on him, closing his studio door to get back to his glumness.

So Nat ended up spending most of his time in the PoutingTree, while Conchita kept herself barricaded in the kitchen. She'd long ago exhausted the household's fruit supply, having subsequently moved on to baking bread. Loaf after loaf came out of the oven, piling up sky-high around her until she was blockaded in there somewhere, or at least he thought so. When he didn't hear from her for a long stretch, he'd make a special effort to come down from his tree to check that she was still alive, hidden away behind all those brick comestibles. To which she responded, yes, she was fine. She'd been careful to stack the loaves in a manner that allowed ample air flow, a survival skill she'd picked up while living in the city's slums during the crux of the revolutionary activity in the capital.

Several weeks later, an outfit of somber-faced hospital attendants arrived at the Casa Azul carrying Frida in on a stretcher, her limbs hoisted in all directions by a web of pulleys and cords. The image brought to Nat's mind a marionette cut loose from its strings, sent crashing to the floor, splayed body parts landing in implausible positions. The mood was heavy and unsettled, because they were elated to have her home, but then again, she was so horribly broken, and what if they weren't enough to help her pull through? Nat ignored all of this, myopic in his drive to see her. So that the instant the attendants settled her upstairs—and despite the prevailing medical advice that she needed rest above all else—Nat raced to her before anyone could tell him otherwise.

"Frida?" he whispered, afraid anything louder might break whatever body parts were still in one piece. "It's me, Nat." *You do know who I am, right? Please say yes. I think I might die if you say no.*

Her response was delayed. She occupied a different time dimension now, her world moving in slow motion, prodded forward according to the perfectly administered sedation the doctors ordered. At last, she managed a woozy smile.

"Oh, Nat, hello! I guess I've been in a little crash? Perhaps you've heard? Busted me all to pieces. I still can't move a fucking bone, but they keep me high on morphine, so I'm not complaining." She tried shrugging her shoulders; her constraints forbade it.

"Anyway, how glad I am for your visit, my dear friend—though not at all surprised. It was you who kept me engaged in all those street antics during that dreadful period after the polio, after all. How lucky I am to have a friend like you, someone willing to stick by me during my darkest times." Her head wobbled and her words slurred as she struggled to continue. "Thank you, Nat. I must rest now, my eyes, so heavy . . . so . . . tired." And then she dropped back into her pillow, shriveling into her cast like a tortoise into its shell.

He felt empowered in that moment, called upon once again to help her through whatever impediments might lie ahead in her road to recovery. *"How lucky I am to have a friend like you."* That was what she'd said, wasn't it? *"How lucky I am to have a friend like you."* It felt like his purpose in life was clear again. Starting right now, he was committing himself to serving as her chief enfermero, a loyal and sensitive caretaker uniquely suited to get her back on her feet.

In the days that followed, there was a sense of trepidation tending toward exhaustion around the Casa Azul as the residents struggled to find their new rhythm in a world that had to be rebuilt from the bottom up. And yet, Nat found himself happier than he'd been in a long time. He occupied his idle hours by Frida's bedside, crocheting for her a bathing suit made from a yarn of the softest mint green (a loose relative of the color emerald, though he wasn't yet conscious of why he'd chosen the particular shade, nor how memories of lineage, family, and home always looped back, never losing their relevance despite efforts to run away from them). It was a one-piece garment, cinched at the cleavage, and held in place by two braided straps that clasped behind the neck, fitted snuggly around the torso, the short pants reaching midthigh. He dreamed about the day they might take an outing to a pool somewhere for a picnic, to chatter idly and comfortably the way they used to, to appreciate how wonderful it was that their lives had intersected so magically. So what if he wasn't chairing a banking meeting right now, or touring the Louvre. He could do all that other stuff later, no problema, there was plenty of time. Being impressive could mean lots of different things, right?

His bliss was shattered several weeks later when ThatAlejandro showed up. Nat was infuriated, because how was it that the kid had escaped entirely unscathed from the same accident that'd wreaked havoc on Frida? Not to mention, why was the little shit only paying her a visit now, all this time later? As if he had more important business to tend to before checking in on his mutilated novia? Nat scurried upstairs to eavesdrop on whatever sorry excuse ThatAlejandro was serving up to disguise his poor manners. He wasn't being jealous or vengeful, Nat reasoned. This was simply part of his job, to protect her, so she could heal faster.

But apparently, Frida wasn't looking for any explanation. By the time Nat got there, the two of them were already wrapped in each other's arms, locked at the lips. Nat looked at the bathing suit he was still holding, suddenly embarrassed, hurling it to the ground. He staggered back to his PoutingTree, snapping a flower from its stem, then gulping down its nectar, waiting for the moment of release, for the cool fog to carry him away, up past the stars, *ahhh* . . .

The next thing he knew, Frida was calling for him. "Nat? Nat, where are you? Please tell me you're down there!" What her voice lacked in force and volume was compensated for by the sense of urgency.

"I'm coming, Frida!" Concern gripped his insides, rushing in her direction despite lingering thoughts of ThatAlejandro. And despite the throbbing pain in his temples.

"I've been calling for you, Nat. I was getting worried that you'd left me, too!" He thought he saw panic in her eyes.

"You okay?"

"No, Nat, I'm not! Everything's falling apart. I . . . I can't do this anymore." It wasn't panic he'd seen a moment ago. This was despair, because whatever she'd dreaded had already occurred.

"What are you saying? Is it medicine, do you need more medicine? I'll get it—"

"No, it's not that—it's far worse than that! I wish it were just my pelvis or my leg. This time it's my heart that's been shattered. I'd rather be dead!" she whimpered.

Nat wasn't sure what to say. Last time he looked, she and ThatAlejandro were looking pretty smug.

"Alejandro came by earlier. I'm not sure if you noticed?"

"I did."

"You want to know why?"

"Ummm, yes?"

"To break off our relationship." She watched Nat turn stunned. "Yep, that's what I said. He came to tell me we were finished. The bastard tried pinning it on his parents, that it was their fault, going behind his back and enrolling him in some fancy school in Europe, and now there was no way out of it, he had to go, pobrecito! Like he's the fucking victim here! How could he do this, Nat? Shit, I can't even fight back. I just sat here like the invalid I am, watching him walk away, isn't that pathetic? It wasn't supposed to turn out like this! I'm different, Nat! My life was supposed to be exciting and surprising and full of adventure! I was going to be *special!"*

It wasn't supposed to turn out like this! The words kept ringing in his head during the weeks that followed. Because he was supposed to be impressive already, not sitting here by her bed, day in and day out, clacking his crochet needles together on the half-finished swimsuit, jumping to attention every time she made even the tiniest peep. And yet, he was undeniably happy. He liked the smell of her sweaty nightclothes, the sound of her gentle snores, the moments she had clarity and might share a rare smile with him. It seemed the more time elapsed as she just lay there, uninspired and listless, the more Nat became convinced that his presence here was imperative. *But you are special, Frida, don't let anyone tell you otherwise.*

CHAPTER EIGHT

ZOE COMES HOME

Coyoacán
December 1925

For the first couple weeks after being sold to the HombreFeo, the runt was diligent about saying a prayer every night, asking that MyBoy might soon come for her, to deliver her from the cage she'd been sentenced to. She knew her faith required patience, that God would unveil His larger plan when the time was right, but the days were tediously long, empty without MyBoy's soothing words and gentle touch. Sometimes, she'd dream her plea had been granted and she was back at the farm, cuddled into MyBoy's lap, and her heart would soar with joy—only to awaken, realize the fallacy, and sink to a new low, her appetite waning, her body growing frailer by the day. Soon, the dreams ceased coming to her at all.

By the third month of captivity, she'd turned numb to the darkness that made up her new life. Each day was like the last—first, the bumpy ride to the market, then the vendor unloading his cages, the shoppers trickling in, the man hawking his wares with no concern for whether he was making a deal with a sadist or a saint, it didn't matter. Though to be fair, by this point, the pup didn't much care either.

"Amigos, gather around, won't you?" bellowed the HombreFeo from the front of his marketplace stall on one of these otherwise typical days. "Have I got a deal for you, folks! These here are Xolo dogs. Did you know this here breed was worshiped by our Aztec ancestors? Now, go ahead and dare to imagine having one of these regal pups for your very own!" If nothing else, the vendor was good at what he did when it came to turning over his product; curious shoppers rushed in his direction.

"Why, they really are quite an interesting-looking species, aren't they?" mused an anonymous market attendee. The pup started, which was saying something, because nothing moved her anymore. At the root of her intrigue was the speaker's velvety voice, confident and poised, yes, but also imbued with something nurturing, and hence, evocative of her past and the life she'd once known under MyBoy's guardianship.

"Yip!" She was surprised at the sound of her own voice, half-wishing she could take back her outburst, because the HombreFeo forbid even a peep. And yet, she was also enormously relieved that she couldn't.

The gentleman with the velvety voice snapped around at her provocation, fully revealing himself. The pup noticed immediately that his tan bowler hat complemented perfectly his finely pressed beige linen suit and well-shined leather shoes. His moustache was precisely manicured and gelled at both ends. And yet, despite her lack of experience with this slice of fine society, there was something that suggested to the pup that behind the pretenses, this stranger was suffering—from the way his suit hung loose on his frame to the dark circles under his eyes.

"Yip." Are you okay, Señor, you look so sad.

"Might I see this one here?" asked the stranger.

The HombreFeo obliged him, stuffing the runt into the gentleman's chest before he'd had time to rethink his request. She looked up from his arms, feeling his grief-laden eyes rest upon hers. The morning sun hovered above, draping them in its soft warmness, making the pup's head tingle, her body slowly reawakening.

"Yip!" I get it now, oh, halleluiah! God has done this, brought us together. I have been praying to be released from this purgatory, and I sense you have been looking for something, too! Please, tell me what it is. Perhaps I can help? You can trust me, Señor, there is chemistry between us, can't you feel it? Oh, how beautiful is His glory!

In the end, it was the penetrating concern he saw in her gaze that won him over. He could've sworn the dog was talking to him, though he'd never admit it—ja, folks were already worried silly about him. (Later in life, he would wonder how it was that he'd never given a second thought to the talking monkey, but that a ubiquitous domestic pet could speak was absolutely out of the question. He'd reason that it had something to do with the way people tended to search for the magical in what is foreign, and predictability in the mundane.)

"I think this sweet little girl might be just what my Frida needs! I'll take her!" he sang out, touching his nose to the dog's, then slapping down a wad of cash and heading back the way he'd come, light on his feet for the first time in months.

"Conchita? Conchita, I'm back from the market . . . and with something special, I do believe!" Guillermo called out as he strode across the patio, beaming down at the runt still tucked in his arms. "The only unfortunate thing is that I've got an appointment I'd nearly forgotten about. So I must dash off again. Might you take her for me?"

"Claro, Señor, I'm coming," said the housekeeper hustling his way, wiping the masa from her hands on the hem of her apron so that she was only able to glance up at the last moment. "¡Ay!" She halted, taking one step back. "It's got no hair, Señor, did you not notice—Oh, dear, Señor, are you not feeling well? Too much stress—"

"Oh, no, Conchita, that's just the breed," he chuckled, as if he were an expert in dogs, not a downtrodden middle-aged man using his purchasing power in search of happiness. "And trust me, I'm feeling quite well today. I'll explain it all later. I thought bringing the dog into our household might be helpful for, ahem, a certain someone," he said, gesturing with a shake of his head toward Frida's room upstairs. "Anyway, would you mind? So I can tend to that business?" He extended the pup in her direction. With some trepidation, Conchita accepted.

"Enjoy, Conchita, she's a fascinating creature." Guillermo chuckled again at his ingenuity, then disappeared into his studio.

"All right, then, chiquita, looks like it's just you and me. So, let's see, what to do? *Hmmm,*" she wondered aloud. Though she was in uncharted waters right now, her life was organized around a very particular function, one with boundless applicability, it turned out. "I bet you're hungry, eh, flaquita? You're too skinny. But not to worry; you've come to the right place," she said, bursting with pride at her ability to cure all ills with a single remedy. "How about some milk, would you like that? I'll go get it. Why don't you stay here and . . ." She paused, because what did dogs do? "I know! Go play! Yes, that's it, why don't you go play!" Conchita put the pup down, shooing her with the back of one hand. But the dog didn't move.

"Go along, go play, I said." Still, the dog wasn't budging, instead settling in on her haunches, staring up at the old woman. "Do what you like, then. I'll be right back," Conchita conceded, shaking her head as she moved off toward the kitchen, dumbfounded by the curiosities that went on in this house. *A dog with no hair? Why, Guillermo?*

The problem was, the pup had no idea what it meant to "go play." She'd come into the world infirm, and more recently, been confined to a cage. She shuddered at the image of Conchita returning only to find her still sitting here like a bump on a log, incapable of fulfilling even the most basic instruction. Worse yet, what if Conchita told Guillermo? God had upheld His end of the bargain by getting her out of that forsaken cage. Now it was supposed to be her turn to fulfill her end of the bargain, to lift Guillermo out of the doldrums—surely not to loll about his property resting on her laurels! Panicked, she did what she knew best: she crisscrossed her front paws on the ground in front of her, the closest she could come to approximating the human kneeling position.

"A Dios, please help me to 'go play.'"

"What are you doing?" boomed a voice from above.

The pup froze, every muscle in her body taut with fear. Could this be happening? Was that God speaking to her? Some of the fear dissipated, replaced by excitement, that she might be experiencing this miracle of the most miraculous kind! But then again, she realized in the next moment, she was woefully unprepared—how was one supposed to address God in a face-to-face conversation? Would it be in the tú form or Usted? Oh, dear, and what if God was only calling on her because He was angry that she'd requested His assistance for something as trivial as how to "go play"?

"I *said*, What. Are. You. Doing?" the voice bellowed again.

Yep, He sounded mad. She took a solemn moment to accept that there was no way around her predicament. Sure, she could run. But she couldn't hide. This was God. Her best option was to hope to make amends, and then double down on whatever penance she was assigned. She turned her head, looking up now, to confront her fate.

She thought she saw a monkey—dressed in a silken waistcoat, but no pants? He was standing in his nest, fisted hands on hips, a scowl on his face. He paused to pick his ear with one finger, gazing off into the distance as if something more compelling might've captured his interest, before finally returning to the pup.

"So, are you gonna tell me now? What you're doing?"

"Um . . . the old woman? Pues, she told me . . . to 'go play'? But I . . . um—"

"You're stuttering, baldy." Nat dusted off the ear detritus from the shoulder of his coat with one hand, and then he wiggled down from the Pouting Tree to see what kind of creature had just entered his life. "Listen, all I wanna know is what you're doing down here. I'm not the pinche federales come to drag you away, so take it easy!"

Studying the monkey up close now, her suspicions told her this was not God. For starters, sarcasm was not His preferred tone of communication. If He had something to shame her for, she was sure He'd get right to the point the way He did to Adam and Eve and King Solomon and Peter and all the others who needed correction. And though the monkey was gruff indeed, the pup felt instantly comfortable in his presence. Which made sense, because it was he who was reaching out to her right now, in this most vulnerable state, was it not? And it was he who'd answered her prayer, no matter who "he" turned out to be.

"I was praying, Señor, that is all. The woman, Conchita, told me to 'go play,' but I don't know how—"

"*Puh-leez,* do not call me 'Señor.' It makes me feel old." Nat was standing next to the dog now, arms crossed over his chest. "I'd prefer you call me Nat, it's not my birth name, but the girl upstairs gave it to me. Speaking of whom, if you're going to be staying on here, you should meet her. Frida is her name. C'mon," he said, flipping his wrist for her to follow.

"Hey, Guillermo? I know you're tied up in there," Nat shouted at the studio door. "But I'm taking the sewer rat upstairs, to meet your daughter."

"The what, Nat?"

"Um, the new dog. I'm taking the dog to meet Frida."

"Ah, yes, thank you, Nat, wonderful," came a voice from behind the door. "Exactly as I'd wished."

"A fine gentleman, indeed. Just another soul in this house who's sorta lost at sea right now, but more on that later," Nat said, continuing his role as resident liaison, bringing them to the threshold of Frida's room.

They found her lying face-up, eyes glued to the ceiling. She didn't turn to look at them, not even when they climbed onto the bed next to her.

"Frida, look what your dad brought home. Isn't it so *ccuutteee?*" Without moving her head, Frida shifted her eyes in the pets' direction. Then she looked back up at the ceiling.

"Okay, let's try this again," Nat said, clearing his throat. "Hey, Frida! Look what your dad got! Isn't this the funniest looking dog you ever saw? It's bald!" This time, Frida turned to consider the pup; encouraged, Nat continued. "Yup, your dad got you a fucking bald dog—oh, except for these matching white sprouts on head and tail—what's that all about? Tell me, Frida, do you think it looks more like a hairy unicorn or a sewer rat?" Fortunately for Nat, in addition to "go play," the terms "hairy unicorn" and "sewer rat" were also lacking from the pup's dictionary.

"Damn you, Nat!" Frida giggled, unable to hold back the smile that went with it. "Okay, okay, I give up, show me the dog." She wiggled back against the bed frame for the extra support she needed to prop herself up and reached for the puppy, bringing it into her lap, then tracing the wrinkles of skin along its back. The seconds elapsed in silence, no rush to her undertaking, a palm reader deep at work weeding through all the supernatural dispatches.

Meanwhile, tucked there in the folds of this Frida person's nightdress, the pup couldn't help but notice the tremble in her fingers, or the halted breath trapped behind her torso cast. It was then that the runt suspected her assignment here might be larger than just Guillermo alone—perhaps God had brought her here because it was Frida who was at the center of whatever tribulations were going on?

"Tzotzil. I've decided her name will be Tzotzil."

Tzotzil?

"After the Maya. You see, the Tzotziles are one of dozens of lines of indígenas from the southern part of México. This dog's name will be a celebration of our indigenous past, kind of like yours, Nat. Sound okay to you, little Tzotzil?" she cooed, tickling the dog's chin.

The runt was confused. The HombreFeo spoke of her breed's connection to the Aztecs; why would her namesake be the Maya? On the other hand, it was clear this Frida was in poor health. Maybe she was having a difficult time making clear connections?

Nat was incensed. *Tzotzil? That dog traces its roots back to the Aztecs, for whom, ironically, I'm named. And then there's that other curious point, you know, that I'm the one from southern México! Ah, yes, but of course, even strapped to your bed, you're still up to your same tricks, aren't you, dear Frida? "Look at me! Look at me! I may be down for the count right now, but I am still the wittiest in all the land!"*

"Wait, or is Tzotzil too much?" Frida panicked in the ensuing silence. "Because we could call her Zoe, you know, a shorter version of Tzotzil?" She looked to Nat's reaction, and then she continued. "Tzotzil *'might be too intimidating, you know, for those less informed.'*" Nat rolled his eyes, mouthing along the very same words she'd used to rationalize his name choice years ago.

Despite his distaste for Frida's relentless self-promotion, Nat couldn't help but be relieved at the appearance of a crack in her shell, to know that she was still rambunctious and fiery beneath all that medical plaster. And so, to build on this minor breakthrough, and also to bring Zoe into the fold, he guided their conversation toward more lighthearted chatter. Beginning with Conchita's kitchen idiosyncrasies, the most egregious of which, they told Zoe, was that the pantry was currently stocked with roughly five thousand loaves of bread and nearly the same number of cans of dried fruit. "In case the Revolution picks up steam again," Conchita routinely explained to them, for at least they'd be well fed, should they be cut off from the outside world. *For about four millennia, ja ja ja,* they giggled amongst themselves. Nat brought up the fact that, to exorcise the anguish Guillermo felt over his daughter's poor health, he was continuously purchasing more drawing supplies than Frida could ever possibly use, but that Nat had come up with a way to incorporate the paints and shredded canvas strips into his sewing practice to hide the poor fellow's blundering. It was late into the night when Nat noticed that Frida was barely able to keep her eyes open, and so he excused himself and Zoe, and they retired to the Pouting Tree.

"As you already know, that's my spot up there." Nat nodded at his nest, then leapt with both hands onto a branch, flipped into a handstand position, then vaulted upside down, landing squarely in his nest feet-first. He exhaled to catch his breath before continuing, because if he were showing off, he certainly didn't want the newbie to know. "I don't know anything about the roosting habits of hairy unicorns, but I'm sure anything down there will be fine."

"Thanks, Nat," she said, sniffing at the space beneath the tree, searching for the right mix of texture and scent, clawing at the terrain's malleability, then circling her tail a few times and plopping down in a tight ball. She recognized that there were plenty of creatures on this planet who would've scoffed at the pile of dirt she'd selected, but they were the ones missing out—the soundness that came from knowing there were all those layers of hot silicate rock and molten iron and nickel strategically situated to support the lives that existed here on the surface, gracias a Dios, the One responsible for making it all possible. As the gratitude washed over her, it dawned on her that she hadn't enjoyed this earthly pleasure since La Prosperidad, with MyBoy . . .

It felt like a ton of bricks dropped on her chest. True, the last few months she'd been struggling spiritually, grappling with some real questions about God as she wasted away in that horrid cage. But since running into Guillermo at the market this morning—and subsequently Nat and Frida—well, she'd begun feeling alive again; her heart and soul had thawed out in a single day's time. It was beautiful—life's resilience. Except that for the first time Zoe could remember, MyBoy had not been on her mind. And though it was only a single day that had elapsed, this simple fact made her feel terribly, sickeningly guilty. Because how could she ever be truly righteous if she were so easily distracted, so fickle about keeping in mind her humble beginnings and those who'd helped her as soon as an easier life presented itself?

"Nat?"

"Yup."

"Were you asleep?"

"Not anymore. What is it?"

"I'm sorry to bother you. You've already been so helpful. I'm grateful, I hope you know that . . . It's just . . . well . . . I was wondering—"

"What is it, Tzotzil? I insist you stop this blathering you're prone to. You've already woken me up, so just get to the point."

"Okay, Nat, you're right. I need to learn this speaking up. I guess I'm accustomed to either being doted on or silenced entirely, so I—"

"Tzotzil, please! Get on with it!"

"Yes, yes, Nat, okay, I hear you." She took a deep breath, and then, "It's about where I come from, and who I left behind. You see, my family was poor, and I was born a sickly runt. And yet, I was the happiest dog on Earth, because I had MyBoy. He fed me and he sang to me and he kept me warm and safe tucked in his arms. I felt loved. I had a place to belong. There was nothing I wanted for.

"But then, the HombreFeo appeared, and he took me away from MyBoy, and I fell into such despair. Oh, I'm extremely pleased that Guillermo found me today, that he rescued me and brought me here to you. But still, I'd be remiss if I were to give up trying to find MyBoy, if only to know that he's okay. Oh dear, I'm trying to make myself heard at your request, Nat, but I'm afraid I'm no good at this, that I'm not making any sense."

Oh, but yes, you are, little friend. I have struggled with similar issues. To stay or to run? To defend one's dreams or to pursue new ones? To live more influenced by remorse or by inspiration? It never ends, I'm afraid; once we are thrust into the human world, the complexity of emotions forever blurs the choices before us.

Stunned at how much beauty and truth was coming out of the runt's muzzle, Nat bent over his nest to look down at her. Sure, she had a lot to learn, but her honesty was endearing. Not to mention that he could really use a partner in crime these days, someone to pal around with while Frida was on the mend.

"If you're asking me to help you track down this kid, sure, I can do that. And what a lucky coincidence for you that I have a prior career in the detective industry! Let's just say that Inspector Infant has been on an extended sabbatical, though I believe it's due time he gets back in the game! As it happens, my tomorrow is wide open. I propose you and me get out there and put my skills back to the test, eh, Zoe?"

But there's no such thing as "coincidence" in this life. What she said aloud was, "Thank you, Nat."

True to his word, first thing the next morning, Nat slipped on the Inverness cape he'd kept tucked away in the bottom of his nest for far too long, and then he descended from his nest to call upon Zoe.

"Time to hit the cobblestones, pal! I've already taken the liberty of doing a preliminary background check by speaking with Guillermo, who informed me that he found you over at the mercado poblano. Ergo, I say we head over in that direction, see if we come across anything interesting along the way. Oh, and here." He tossed Zoe a tweed cap that matched his cape. "It's not my finest work, but not bad given that I threw it together last night, after you fell asleep—oh, by the way, you snore, did you know that? Anyway, it's important that my partner look the part. I'm a professional; anything less would reflect poorly on my reputation," he quipped with a grin.

Zoe slipped it over her head, deeply moved that the ear holes were a perfect match for her aural appendages, and scooted out the door behind her mentor. A mood of exaggerated confidence swelled between the duo, the natural byproduct of adrenaline fused with a sharp new wardrobe accessory.

"Okay, the first thing you need to know in this line of work is you can never exclude a single possibility until it's been factually proven otherwise," Nat announced proudly, all the lessons learned in the StatelySittingRoom coming back to him. "Assumptions, past experiences, generalizations, none of it matters if you don't have the hard evidence to prove it. That's what makes Sherlock Holmes such a genius. He goes against the grain, unconcerned with what the criminal *should* look like, which then allows him to remain open-minded and keen to the proverbial wolf camouflaged in sheep's clothing. ¿Comprendes?"

Zoe nodded her head excitedly.

"Excuse me there, BigDog?" They'd come upon a large husky dog standing on the balcony of a second-floor apartment, biding his time until that climactic moment in the day when the mailman appeared. "Perchance, have you seen a boy with brown hair wandering these parts, he'd have been about yay tall?" Nat asked with hand stretched overhead. "According to my partner here—she knew him personally—he might've been singing lullabies?"

"Bark."

"Qué pena, ragtime, huh? Wouldn't have been our guy then, muchas." He turned to Zoe. "No big deal, pal. We're just laying out the pieces of this jigsaw puzzle, looking to see what we've got to work with, that's all."

On they went until they came to the corner bodega. "Oye, GroceryStoreClerk, you seen any muchachos lately with anything about them that might've suggested they weren't from around here? Maybe smelled like expired avocado byproducts?" Pause. "No, I'm afraid what you're describing sounds more like sawdust. Avocado's got more of a nutty smell," Nat pronounced, fluttering a cupped hand under his nose.

This time, Zoe's head hung on her neck like an overripe sunflower.

"Ah, come on, Zoe, don't worry. We're just getting warmed up, remember?" He stopped in his tracks. "Hey, you know what? We should play a game. It's something I came up with awhile back. I call it 'The Daffy Detective Game.'"

She lifted her head, tilting her neck askew to be able to see Nat from under the brim of her cap.

"Okay, this is how it goes. We pick a person to be our target. It can be anyone we want, someone who looks interesting or silly or smart or innocent, doesn't matter. There's only one caveat, and that is, the target must be chosen exclusively on physical characteristics. You following me so far?

She nodded, her tail wagging now.

"Okay, good. Next step is we make up some heinous crime that's been committed by our target. It's got to be entertaining; nothing serious allowed here. Life is serious; our singular objective here is to have fun. The truth is, I came up with the idea on one of those days when my spirits were dragging—you know, a little bit like yours today. You'll see what I mean, Zoe." Nat reached down to pat the brim of her cap; she pretended to try to nip his hand in response. "So back to the rules . . . Once we've concocted a hypothetical crime scene, we tag along after our target looking for clues, accumulating evidence along the way until we can credibly prove or disprove our storyline. Care to give it a go, Zoe?"

"I don't understand—no disrespect, Nat—but you were just explaining all that Sherlock Holmes stuff, about looking for the wolf dressed in sheep's clothing. Why are you suggesting we do the exact opposite? Aren't we supposed to be challenging conventional assumptions rather than adhering to them?"

"Ja, you make a very good point, my insightful little friend." He beamed at his protégée. "You are absolutely right when it comes to the real world and solving crimes. But today, lest you forget, we go rogue, allowing ourselves this much needed escape into a world of absurdism and buffoonery. For as much as I love Guillermo and Frida, I'm often overwhelmed by their behavior—whether it's her torturing a childhood classmate, or him openly declaring a favorite child, or even why there are so many wars going on—sometimes I need a break from it all. I get tired of beating my head against a wall trying to solve the crime that, plain and simple, cannot be solved. Human behavior can be baffling. Best to accept that now." Nat paused to straighten his cape around his shoulders. "Make more sense?"

"Sorta. You can't find a consistently direct correlation between human behavior and the prevailing moral coda. So you made up this game to feel more comfortable living in the space you occupy in their world? Because it makes you laugh? And it helps you feel like you're not going mad?"

"Ja ja ja, well, dear Zoe, how fast you learn! I'm impressed. Couldn't have said it better myself!" He patted her on the shoulders, thinking quite highly of himself, for his detective skills, yes, and also for the mentorship he was so graciously providing. "So, then, Zoe, shall we get started with round one of 'The Daffy Detective Game'? Why don't you go ahead and pick a target for us? Who's the bad guy the police are too foolish to notice?"

Only God can judge the good guy from the bad, Nat, it is not for us to decide. Instead, Zoe began tottering around in a circle in search of the perfect muse. She spied an older woman across the street, locking up her apartment door to go out. When she turned around, Zoe took note of her dark skirt and baggy wool sweater, age-appropriate dress, nothing out of the ordinary there. But then, what to make of those bright red lips, so heavily painted that Zoe noticed them from thirty meters away! And why did she have a stuffed toy rabbit under one elbow?

"Her!" Zoe blurted out, pointing at the woman with one paw.

"Mhmm, over the hill, but still well-groomed," nodded Nat as he stroked his pretend goatee, lower lip extended pensively. "I sense a demonstration of self-respect mixed with a predilection for child's play? So, tell me, Agent Tzotzil, what crime has this woman committed?"

It is for God alone to decree what is criminal. But again, not the time. "Well, Inspector, the toy makes me wonder if she might be a preschool teacher by day. The lipstick, on the other hand, screams that her after-hours are of an entirely different ilk. Given the indicators before me, I suspect that we have just stumbled upon a member of the city's vast underground escort service. That when the last school bell rings, off she goes to the cantina to wet those red lips of hers!"

"Provocative premise, Zoe, let us crack on, shall we? We can't let the suspect get away!"

The pets crept along after their target, until a neighborhood later, she veered off into a park, one that contained but a single bench and a modest sandbox. Lacking a gated area, tables for snacks and art projects, or equipment for more than three tots, this was definitely not part of a preschool schoolyard. Nor was there a discernible cantina nearby.

"¡Abuelita, ya está!" A young girl standing on the edge of the sandbox dropped her mother's hand, racing toward their target with arms extended. The old woman handed over the rabbit. The girl reacted by smothering her face in the doll, then reaching out for the old woman's hand and pulling her toward the sandbox, already midway into a barrage of fantastical accounts only a five-year-old can imagine and only a grandmother can appreciate.

"Aha, yes! I see now what's going on here! She's trying to fool us, that clever woman! She wants us to believe she's nothing but a harmless grandmother doting on that little girl. Bah, as if hiding behind that virtuous motherhood, marionista façade is enough to throw the two of us off track! *Pshaw*, never! I bet our target has been pilfering cash from that preschool where she works, and that she's subsequently sewn it into the stuffed animal for safekeeping. All that was left to do was stop by the park, pawn it off on her granddaughter, and then wait for the school to give up trying to recover the stolen money. At which point our target would have the opportunity to reclaim it for herself! In the meantime, off to the cantina goes our evil abuelita, not a care in the world. Yeah, well, be forewarned, we're on to you, vieja, and we won't let you get away with this!"

They cackled like wild hyenas after that one, pleased with the creativity they'd culled together to come up with such an unordinary theory. When they couldn't stop laughing, they climbed into the sandbox just for the fun of it, rolling around like toddlers, periodically tossing handfuls of the tiny gravel at one other, their amusement escalating into a cascade of guffaws so rowdy that passersby stopped to shake their heads at the commotion. On this afternoon, neither Nat nor Zoe was concerned what people thought of them or where they fit in. On this afternoon, they were the enlightened ones, uniquely qualified to pass judgement on humanity. What did it matter if their search for MyBoy had come up empty-handed, Zoe thought to herself on the way home. She'd just learned how to "go play." For Nat's part, he was glad to be back in sync with Inspector Infant. He wondered why he'd neglected his alter ego for so long. Then he wondered what other parts of himself he'd been neglecting.

When they weren't searching for MyBoy—or chasing after improbable criminals—Nat and Zoe spent their time at Frida's bedside. She might just be sitting up more easily now, sketching in her notepads or reading. Equally as significant was that she was eager to engage in conversation about what was going on outside the walls of the Casa Azul. As if she was ready to reenter the world of the living again.

"Oh, good, you guys are back! I've got a surprise for you," she announced gaily on one such afternoon.

"¿Caramelos?" Nat asked, palming small circles around his tummy. She shook her head.

"Is it a comb, so you don't have to watch me pick my navel grit anymore?" he tried again, thrusting his torso forward.

She shook her head a second time. "It's better than both those things put together! Wanna know what it is?"

The pets wagged their heads.

"Okay! Watch this."

And then, placing her hands firmly on either side of her chair, she began to push herself up. Her arms twitched. Her face turned strained, the seconds elapsing, sweat beads forming on her brow. Until she'd succeeded, bringing herself to full standing. A crooked smile threatened to expose her glee; she bit her lip to make it go away. Because there was more: she grabbed the cane that was leaning against the chair. With tiny, halting steps, she shuffled across the room to her easel and plopped triumphantly into the seat there, the sound of air cycling through her skirts—the final curtain come down.

"Frida, how—"

"Also, I've been painting while you two are out. And not just casual sketches." She dismissed her previous undertakings with the flick of a hand. "Ones I hope are good enough to sell—well, and that's the real question, if they're any good. I have to find out first."

The pets were speechless.

"I know Papi is worried about all my medical bills. He thinks I can't hear him, but guess what, Papi? My ears are two of my body parts that still work perfectly fine, ja ja. But if I can sell these paintings, I'll be able to help, ojalá!" she said, crossing her fingers. She nodded at the table on the other side of the room. "You want to see one? They're over there, behind that table. Nat, can you pull around the one I'm calling *El Accidente?*"

Nat obliged, scooting it to center with the weight of his back, then flipping it over between his biceps. The room went silent, all three of them transported back in time to that ghastly street corner in México City, where Frida's body was lying on a Red Cross stretcher. Wrapped in gauze, she looked like a mummy except that her face was exposed. A mangled bus and trolley car floated in the sky above, corpses and mourners scattered in the street. This was no ordinary accident; this was her accident, The Accident.

"So? What do you think?"

Nat wasn't sure how to respond. Maybe she was just goading him, and he was supposed to respond with effusive adoration and awe? Another listen-to-what-Alex-and-I-did-at-school-today standing ovation? On the other hand, because Sherlock Holmes was himself an art aficionado, Nat had dedicated substantial time to acquiring this same skill set, such that he now considered himself a relatively credible critic. Over the years, and while Frida was away at school, he'd been making a habit of visiting the town's scattering of local galleries as well as the single historical museum. Oh, and he'd been fanatical about attending the traditional folklórico dance festivals that occurred every third Sunday outside the municipal building. He'd even made a point to try to attend the state-organized military band parades, though these events were his least favorite given all the weaponry on full display. In sum, it was a provincial education, to be sure, but he'd done his best to squeeze out every gram of knowledge from the limited resources available. Ergo, his input had to be worth something, didn't it? It wasn't like he was pretending to be the Louvre's curator. Just some feedback from a reasonably valid source was all he hoped to contribute.

"*Hmm*, well, this is just a pencil sketch so far, and thus, unfinished. But I'm trying to imagine its effect once you've added color—you will add color, right, Frida? On the most basic level, for example, a blue sky would create such a different mood than gray." Nat paused, taking a few strides in front of the canvas, hands clasped neatly behind his back. "Right now, though, it seems, well . . . sad. Perhaps too sad? See the way you've drawn your eyes closed here? And your mouth is squeezed into a pinch on this side? I'm afraid it might be off-putting—I'm not saying it's not good, Frida—I'm thinking more of your audience, is all. What about a still-life, maybe a bowl of juicy mangoes? People seem awfully fond of looking at painted versions of the very items sitting in front of them on the kitchen sink. You got any mangoes?"

There was an eruption of glass shattering, the paint jars that had been lined up next to her easel crashing down, colorful shards of destruction strewn about the battlefield, bullet wounds in green, orange, purple spattering the floor and the hem of her skirt.

"Fucking mangoes?" she roared, a fire-breathing dragon emerging from its cave. "The suffering that goes on in this world, and you want me to paint mangoes? I don't see mangoes, Nat! I see pain. Everywhere I look, there's pain—starting with the rotting corpse I live in." She lowered the waist of her skirt to reveal tracks of scars and sutures, a road map to remember this pain by. "Look! Just look! I dare you not to look away, Nahuatl! I hurt. Every. Single. Day. And when I don't think it's possible to hurt any more, I'm haunted by the pitiful pleas of the woman living on the street outside my window. Or when I open the weekly circular, I'm punched in the gut to read about the new shantytown that's just gone up on the other side of town to accommodate those displaced first by capitalismo and then by the so-called 'Revolution'! All this suffering, it's inescapable!

"But I'm supposed to ignore all that? For mangoes, is that right, Nat? Yeah, well, you're not the first one to try to force me into a box. 'Keep your thoughts to yourself, young lady,' I've been told all my life. 'Go stitch your dreams on a pillowcase, add it to your wedding trove.' All these rules about what I'm allowed to feel, and how I'm supposed to disguise my pain to keep others around me comfortable.

"I've got one outlet for communicating the truths I see." She held up an index finger, whether to indicate the number of outlets available to her, or as a scolding tool, Nat wasn't sure. "And that's my painting. Even then, the only way I get away with it is by dipping my brush in what the 'masters' are calling surrealism, where the product is so far-fetched and so fantastical that the timid viewer can easily dismiss what he sees as fictitious, so he can sleep at night, unburdened by the pain of others. Yeah, well, I can't stop seeing the mutilated uteri, the wounded deer, the dissected hearts, because those are the images that come to me, begging to be put on canvas, so they can finally be exposed as a reality of the human experience. We suffer; this is part of life. Go fuck your juicy mangoes, Nat!"

This time, Frida threw out both arms, knocking over the easel, eyes fixed firmly on the blank space in front of her. For his part, Nat retreated into a corner, cowering there in shame. He hated when she was angry with him. He was pretty sure there was nothing worse in this world.

But his embarrassment quickly turned to self-pity, because, shit, he knew a few things about pain, too! There was Mamá . . . oh, and his thumbless-ness, and the way she'd treated him when ThatAlejandro used to come around. How come he never got to talk about his pain? He had problems, too, so why was it always about *her?*

Wait, what was he doing? Why was he comparing their pains, as if one were bigger or more important than the other? What did he really know about her pain anyway? He'd never had an iron handrail rammed through his private parts. He'd never walked the streets without the protection and respect afforded by a penis. What kind of enfermero—what kind of friend?—would judge the way his dearest patient had chosen to represent something uniquely hers? Here he was, silently condemning her for not appreciating his pain, but he'd done no better. Now he was back to feeling ashamed.

"*Uhhh,* Frida?" he sputtered, beginning to crawl out from his hiding place. "I'm sorry. I spoke out of turn. I was only trying to help." What he meant was, *Still, it was wrong of me to pretend I know everything about something I actually know nothing about.*

"Are you sure about that, Nat? That you were 'only trying to help'?" What she meant was, *More than anyone else on this planet, you know that even the most minor slight can be catastrophic to me—and especially when it's coming from you, Nat, that's what this is really about. I depend on you. I need you to support me and tell me that yes, I can.*

He was humbled, his heart crashing into his feet. Perhaps he'd acted too big for his boots (and yes, he was currently donning a dapper pair of tan leather wing tips with navy blue insets in case you were wondering), and yes, in hindsight, he'd been improper and insensitive and a whole lot of other callous things, all of which he'd take back if he could.

"I'm really sorry, Frida," he whispered, his head half-sunk between his shoulders. "The funny thing is, I don't even like mangoes." Here he affected an awkward smile.

"Okay, no more mangoes then," she smiled back. "And I forgive you."

His bowels released a slow wind of gas. So this was not to be the absolutely worst day of his life after all.

"Can we get back to my paintings now?" she began again, redirecting the conversation away from the wreckage. "I still need to find one that's good enough to get appraised. So can we just forget the other stuff? And get this done?"

And so, the threesome settled back in, putting their heads together as they studied her art, giving her the space to explain the significance behind the grisliness, how to read between the lines. She had planned to go to medical school, before the accident, she reminded them. So she knew all about anatomy and how the human body worked. And if they looked more closely at the girl on the stretcher, they'd be able to tell that she was still alive, that because there was no evidence of pooling blood or swelling in her extremities, her heart was still functioning. Did they get it now, that this was on its face a sad drawing, but beneath the surface, it was also a tale of perseverance and resilience, because yes, this girl was going to get up and walk again, and after that, she was going to paint up a storm!

Tsk tsk, Nat reprimanded himself for neglecting to search for clues beyond the obviousness that is blood and gore, opulence and grandiosity. *Sherlock Holmes would be ashamed! Alas, how quick is the tendency to overlook basic truths when one's heart becomes involved.*

Two days later, the pets set out once again in search of MyBoy. The morning was brisk and ripe with anticipation. Homeowners and shop-keepers alike, mops in hand, stepped out to do what they did every day at this same time, scrubbing their cement sidewalks until they glistened, the smell of soapy water filling the air. Corrugated metal storefronts clanged in succession as the heavy gates were hoisted open to announce the start of a new day. Bicyclists zigged and zagged seam-lessly through traffic on their way to work or school, capably avoiding straggling pedestrians, stray dogs, and bleary-eyed itinerant peddlers. Thus far, the pets' searches had come up empty, but the pandemonium bred buoyancy, and buoyancy gave them hope that this day might turn out differently.

Squeak, ping! Squeak, ping! went a sequence of shrill twangs, aborting the neighborhood's normally cordial discourse during this hour. Arriv-ing at the lip of the Plaza in that same moment, it was easy for the pets to locate the source of the chaos. In the middle of the square was a potbellied man, a red barrel organ strapped to his torso. He was crank-ing the instrument in halting, spasmic circles with one arm, producing a belching musical number that evaded any worthy title. There was an unidentifiable object perched on his shoulder, and a crowd of onlookers had formed a circle around him.

"People actually pay to listen to that?" ribbed Zoe as the pets con-tinued toward the commotion out of pure curiosity.

Nat halted.

"Oops, that was mean, sorry," she said, bowing her head in shame.

"No, no, it's not that," sputtered Nat, staring straight ahead as he moved along. Because he couldn't believe what he was seeing—such that he'd doubled-checked, and then triple-checked. But yes, it definite-ly was! The "object" on the musician's shoulder was a spider monkey! Not a howler monkey. And not a yellow-tailed monkey. He was both exhilarated and scared to death. Because what if their lives might've overlapped back in the jungle? What if the other spider monkey knew something about what had become of his Tent? Or Mamá? He was in a trancelike state now, the primal urge to know one's own history propelling him forward.

As the pets got closer, Nat noted that the other monkey was clad in a red fez cap fastened awkwardly to one side of his head, a corresponding red vest with gold twine that looped down the lapels, and white wide-legged linen pants. Not exactly what he would've chosen for himself, but then again, he had high standards when it came to fashion. The other spider monkey had reached the part in his act where he jumped down from his perch, launching into some kind of choreographed can-can dance that required high kicks and cartwheels and, worst of all, a vigorous shifting and swirling of imaginary skirts and petticoats. When the show came to its conclusion, the monkey issued a contrived bow, and then the crowd erupted in cheers and applause, circling in closer to drop odd coins in the tin cup the monkey had magically pulled out from behind his back.

Ever the empathetic creature, Zoe recognized what was transpiring. She took a step back, prodding Nat forward with her nose, then nodding at him when he turned around again for the encouragement he needed. So onward he went, centimetering through the thinning crowd, reaching the stage just as the last of the stragglers turned to go. Concurrently, the organ player snatched the tin cup from the monkey's grip, and then he disappeared into the cantina across the street.

Which meant that it was just the two spider monkeys now, standing face to face, looking back at the image on the other side of the mirror. Jaws dropped; neither said a thing. Nat considered trying to force out the words to ask about what he'd presumed he had no interest in: *What did I give up that day I left Mamá?* But when he opened his mouth, the earth began to rumble, and he shifted into survival mode.

It felt like someone had dropped a bag of marbles beneath him, his feet splaying out, then cycling in rapid motion, a colossal effort just to keep his teeth from meeting the pavement. People scurried about like ants in a rainstorm, bumping into each other, repelled, then heading in an alternative direction. The Church bell on one side of the Plaza burst into anarchical refrain, a choral debauchery that would've been banned on any other day.

Suddenly, the world went black, making Nat wonder if perhaps the electricity had gone down because of whatever this was? Then came a breeze, and an eddy was sucking him in, a steady hum in his ear. He scrambled to stay upright, but his knees were buckling. He closed his eyes, reaching out his arms to brace for the fall he was sure was coming. But no, it was as if he were being lifted from above, gently carried through the sky until, *splat!* He landed straight into the arms of the other monkey. The pavement rolled on as they clung to one another for the next few seconds, until, just like that, the rumbling ceased. The people exhaled. The cars resumed sputtering along, now honking their horns at the annoyance that had put them behind schedule in the first place. The policemen blew their whistles to assuage the cars, and the vendors hawking their wares pitched more loudly to be heard over the horns and the whistles.

"What was that?" Nat stammered, peeling himself from the arms of the other monkey. "This is so odd . . . I don't understand . . . Why, I haven't seen another spider monkey since I was an infant. Which is odd enough, but then the ground starts rolling around like it's about to open up and swallow us?"

"I never seen anyone who looks like me either. I come across lots of other monkeys—you run into 'em in my line of work—just not any like us, you know, *real* compañeros, eh, hermano?" The other monkey tapped Nat genially on one shoulder. "Oh, and that ground thing you were asking about? Nothing to worry about, just a little temblor. Earthquakes happen around here all the time."

"Yes, an earthquake, well I guess that would make sense, silly me." Nat shook his head, trying to cue up any bit of logical thought. "It just seems so . . . well, so unlikely. I mean, if we were to consider it statistically, and if we chose to measure the total number of spider monkeys in the region against the—"

He noticed a look of bewilderment on the other monkey's face. Which made Nat want to slap himself for being so singularly focused! Here he was with this rarest of opportunities to speak with another spider monkey, to explore his past, and what intersections they might share, and instead he was choosing to blather on about math theories?

"Hi, I'm called Nat, née Infant? In case that last part means anything to you?" *Does it? Please tell me it does!*

"Good to know you, NatNayInfant. My name's Bobo. Just Bobo, not fancy, but I respond to it. Gosh, you got a good name, and you got on a nice vest—no pants though, interesting choice. No way my boss would let me out in public with my stuff showing, ja ja," chuckled Bobo, thrusting his covered groin in Nat's direction. "Funny thing, the boss chases after the cantina girls like a hungry wolf, but that I might have any similar desires is strictly forbidden. Anyway, you're lucky, NatNay. Look what I gotta wear." He pulled the fez a few centimeters from his head, letting it snap back with a pop, then rubbing the spot there, as if this were the first time he'd been exposed to the laws of elasticity.

"Ah, it's not so bad," Nat lied, careful to hide his fashion elitism. Plus, he had other matters he wanted to dive into lest this golden opportunity slip away. "Oye, since we've run into each other like this, coincidence or otherwise, mind if I ask you a few things? Stop me if I'm being too forward, it's just that our little encounter here has caught me by surprise, bringing to mind some unanswered questions." Bobo nodded, so Nat continued.

"Have you ever heard of a place called the JungleTent? It's far south of here. I ask because that's where I'm from. Or what about the EmeraldLagoon?" He could feel his heart beating a million kilometers a second, frantically enough, in fact, that he wondered if Bobo could see it pounding through his pinstripe vest.

"Oh, NatNay, wow! You're gonna get a big laugh outta this one, but I never even been to the jungle, can you believe that? Ja ja ja. Bo-bo-the-spider-monkey who's never been in his natural habitat. I've been doing the performing thing ever since I can remember. I'm not exactly proud of it," he grimaced, rolling his eyes toward the fez that was now sliding down one side of his face, so that it looked like a third ear. "But it's the only life I've ever known. I hope you're not disappointed, Nat, that I'm a fraud of a spider monkey." Bobo put his head down, kicking at the pavement there.

Nat was disappointed that Bobo was unable to provide him any information about his Tent. But looking at his forlorn friend right now, what he was feeling most was ashamed. Because Nat of all creatures should've been more sensitive to what it was like being made to feel inadequate.

"Yeah, well, you're not missing much, Bobo. I'm not even sure the JungleTent exists anymore. The EmeraldLagoon is pretty and every-thing, but it's not like you and me get to swim there." He poked Bobo's side with his elbow, referencing their species's lack of aquatic skills.

"What do you mean, NatNay?" Bobo furrowed his brow.

"On account of spider monkeys can't swim?" Now Nat's brow was furrowed. "Right?"

"Like I said, I'm the only spider monkey I've ever known, ja ja ja. But I can swim just fine, NatNay." As Nat stood there stunned, Bobo got an idea. "Say, you know what we should do? You and me should go swimming! Right now, yeah, that's a great idea! I'll show you how! I know a place just a few blocks away. We'll go swimming, and still be back before my boss finishes drinking away that money I just made him! What do you say, NatNay?" Bobo looked as excited as a five-year-old waking up on his birthday.

Nat didn't say anything. How was it that he could read, speak six-teen languages, develop a budding sleuthing agency, serve as the guard-ian to a runt pup and the nurse to an ailing girl-turned-woman—even though spider monkeys weren't supposed to be capable of any of those things? And yet, he'd accepted as absolute truth that he couldn't swim?

"You know what? I'd really like that, Bobo! I need to let my friend know—she's around here somewhere. Will you give me a minute to find her?"

"No problem, NatNay! Gosh, this is gonna be a lot of fun. I never met a monkey who's been in a real jungle—oh, by the way, do all spider monkeys over there got one of them nice vests like you, because I woulda thought—"

"Monkey, what in the hell you doing over there? No fraternizing! We got work to do!" Unfortunately, Bobo's owner had burst back onto the scene, lurching across the street in their direction now. "Them quakes are good for business. Make folks wanna laugh a little, distract themselves from the scare. So let's get a move on, boy, you're wasting time!"

"Ah, rats!" Bobo's bottom lip curled into a pout. "Sorry, NatNay. I was really looking forward to that swim." And then in the next moment, his despair disappeared, replaced by that same unlimited supply of cheer. "But we'll do it some other time, okay? The boss has me going from town to town, following the tourist traffic, but when we get back here, I'm gonna find you, and you and me are going swimming. We won't let anything get in the way next time, right, NatNay?"

He was a few steps down the road when he called back to Nat. "Oh, NatNay?"

Nat nodded.

"Did those butterflies come from the jungle, too? The ones that lifted you into my chest during that quake?"

Nat's knees went weak, like the earthquake thing was happening all over again. Butterflies? No, Bobo was wrong. Nat hadn't seen any butterflies.

"Hurry up, pinche monkey! Stop slowing me down!" screamed Bobo's boss.

With a pep in his step that continued to perplex Nat, Bobo obliged, spinning back around on his heels and skipping down the street. This time, his arms danced around him with natural grace, his legs barely touching the ground such that it looked like he was floating, entirely unchoreographed and splendidly, poetically uninhibited.

Nat watched Bobo go. He could run after his new friend, ask him about the butterflies, maybe even help the poor guy get out of his current situation. And yet, he didn't. Oh, he was grateful for their encounter, for the way Bobo had reminded him of severed connections still buried in his consciousness. As well as for the way he'd unintentionally alerted him to the potentially artificial limitations he'd placed on himself. But Nat was going places. And he needn't be ashamed of the assets he'd accrued, he reassured himself. Why should he have to pretend that he wasn't a mathematical genius, capable of spouting out complex probabilities about spider monkeys and earthquakes intersecting? He had impressive thoughts, and he intended to continue doing impressive things. And that was just how it was. Period. Butterflies and monkeys in the entertainment industry might be perfectly lovely, but they were not part of his calling.

"Oh, Nat, there you are! Gracias a Dios, I found you!" His ruminations were interrupted by Zoe, clasping her front legs around his middle and resting her head there. "I was getting worried, all that shaking, and then you didn't come back, and I couldn't find you. Are you okay, Nat?" There was panic in her eyes.

"Yeah, yeah, I'm fine, Zoe. Sorry I scared you. You good?"

"Uh-huh. I hid under a park bench—that one over there," she hiccuped, pointing across the Plaza with a trembling paw. "It was the only thing I could think of—I'm so small, you know, if something were to have fallen on me—"

"Oh, Zoe, you poor thing!" He scooped her up in his arms, bringing her to his chest and kissing the top of her head as he moved over to the very bench that had only moments ago served as her safe haven. As he sat down there with Zoe tucked in his arms, it dawned on him that it was precisely because of her small size that she'd skirted danger, that a creature any larger would never have fit! Ja, and all this time she'd been viewing her runt status as a detriment!

"Oye, Zoe, I just thought of something. Answer me this, will you? Who's to say that you aren't big enough just the way you are? Sure, science can tell us that the average size of a Xolo dog is 'X,' but why have we been led to assume that 'bigger than X' is definitively better, while 'smaller than X' is definitively worse, huh? If you ask me, size is just one more inane factor a particular subset of humanity has included in its algorithm to keep itself in power. I admit that out in the wild, size does matter. The jaguar eats the monkey, and the monkey eats the bugs, and the bugs eat the moss so that new growth can emerge, which means there's a bigger food supply for the bugs, and then more bugs for us monkeys, and so on and so forth. But here's the catch: We don't have bodegas like humans do. Ergo, in the human world, size is utterly irrelevant in terms of securing sustenance. Except that the existing hierarchy is reinforced by the popular idea that the taller human with a penis is more worthy of power than the undernourished, over-worked, medically neglected—that is, shorter human with a penis. And before you say that I'm being too cynical, I can support my claim with a bibliography of some two hundred sources based on my research while serving as a resident at the StatelySittingRoom. Trust me when I tell you that 'bigger is better' crap is exactly that: pura mierda!"

"I guess I never really thought about it—"

"Well, and while we're at it, what about that 'expert' on spider monkeys out there who once upon a time declared my ilk incapable of swimming because our limbs aren't strong enough to buoy the weight of our torsos? Based on what? Some Greek mathematician's calculation in 200 B.C.? Yeah, well, what if there existed a spider monkey with atypically strong limbs developed during a childhood of extensive tree-swinging activity, the hours of which were accrued in one highly dramatic attempt to flee the felling blows of the tools with teeth? Then what? How's that 'expert' going to fit that case study into his neat little model about what spider monkeys can and can't do? Tell me, why does some human who knows nothing about you or me personally get to put us in a box with a warning label attached, 'this dog is too small,' or 'this monkey will sink in water,' huh, Zoe?" He was feeling rejuvenated as he pieced together this new truth. It had been a peculiar day, that was all. And speaking of hierarchies, he'd already forgotten about Bobo and butterflies, self-satisfied with his supreme command of human logic and the baselessness of subjective categorization. "Besides, I happen to think there's something really special about being 'less than X.'"

He stood up on the bench now, leaning against the back slats, placing Zoe on the highest bar beside him, then draping one arm over her shoulder. "Enough of that, though. How about a round of 'The Daffy Detective Game'? I could use a good laugh right about now."

Zoe nodded excitedly.

"Okay, then, I do believe it's my turn to choose," Nat proclaimed, relaxing back onto his elbows and surveying his options. "Ah, yes, see that man across the way? The one with that bony old mule on a lead? I notice the animal's got some empty sacks draped over its back, which makes me wonder . . . Agent Tzotzil, with what does the man intend to fill those sacks, do you suppose? Certainly, there's no way such a lame creature could sustain the weight of more typical loads, say, firewood. But . . . what if he was planning to fill those bags with something much lighter—paper, for example? Moreover, what if that paper was in the form of pesos taken from a nearby bank? And here's the real capper, what if he was not acting alone, but in cahoots with his lover, that devious grandmother with the bright red lips we spied at that park last spring? All she'd have to do next is sew the cash into another stuffed rabbit doll for her granddaughter, and no one would suspect a thing! Improbable perhaps, but not impossible, am I right, Zoe?"

CHAPTER NINE

ACCIDENTE NÚMERO DOS
(HOW DIEGO RIVERA RUINED EVERYTHING)

Coyoacán
1927

"Nat? Zoe? I'm home!" Frida's orthotic boot pounded across the patio with unusual urgency. "You aren't going to believe what just happened! I met him, Diego Rivera—I met *the* Diego Rivera. Diego Rivera is going to look at *my* art!"

The pets jumped to attention, digging themselves out from under piles of paperwork to hear whatever good fortune was making Frida this giddy. They'd been drawing up strategies for how they might be able to find MyBoy. *("You know an awful lot about Bibles, Zoe. Can you buy those holy books at any old bookstore, do you know? If so, I want you to find out how many bookstores are in town, and get me those addresses. In the mean-*

time, I'll get to work sewing us a couple of those book bags." He pantomimed the object under discussion, throwing an imaginary strap over one shoulder, then listing to the other side to indicate the weight he was supporting. "Like the kids carry around? It'll be our disguise, so no one suspects we're in the crime-fighting business.")

Unfortunately, while they'd uncovered critical information a week ago that had indeed taken them to the HombreFeo at the mercado poblano, he'd lived up to his name, refusing to cough up the source of his dogs as a means of protecting his supply. Which meant the pets were back to square one, and so today, they were chasing down the Church angle of the case.

"What did you say about someone Rivera?" Nat called from the stairwell as he and Zoe headed in her direction.

"Diego, his name is Diego. And he just happens to be the grandest painter in all the land. Did I mention he's going to look at my work? I'm still pinching myself! Isn't this fabulous news?" she gasped, draping both hands over her clavicle.

"Wow, Frida, that really is wonderful!" Zoe galloped across the patio, bounding into her arms and licking her face. Miracle of miracles, their Frida was starting to blossom again, gracias a Dios, qué buen día es hoy!

"Yeah, Frida, sure is." Nat tried to sound enthusiastic, but he could tell his voice came off flat. The truth was, this wasn't fabulous at all. How was it wonderful that he'd spent months by her bedside nursing her back to health, and then weeks supporting her painting endeavors, only to have her turn to some stranger for approval? That was supposed to be his job, didn't this Diego guy know that? Nat was her audience; he was the one who got to issue the final verdict. He told himself to be satisfied, because she'd made it clear that she needed him when they'd had that little scrap over *El Accidente*. And, well, he wasn't a painter himself, so going to Diego made some sense in that regard. It's just that no matter how much logic he applied to any situation, when it came to his relationship with Frida, he ended up feeling fragile and inadequate, the same stuttering jungle monkey who'd knocked on her front door all those years ago.

Staggering sleepy-eyed along the catwalk on his way to the restroom the next morning, Nat was witness to a sight so horrific, so terrifying, he thought perhaps he might still be asleep, locked in a nightmare of the worst kind. A stranger hovered there on the patio below. It was the ugliest human Nat had ever seen.

The predator was a hulking creature who easily surpassed the two-meter mark (*bigger than X,* he cringed to himself), with a tremendous girth tented up in a tweed jacket big enough to fit a small dinosaur. Its pants were hoisted up to armpits, cinched awkwardly with a belt that could've lassoed a grown bull. And its bulging eyes sagged in their sockets, melting into its cheekbones, then folding into its neck. Still, it was not the physical appearance that made Nat's stomach turn over so much as its essence, such a vile aura, a composite of something sinister and something arrogant. The worst part was that the visitor was talking to Frida. Nat ran back into Frida's room.

"Come on, Zoe, you gotta see this! There's an ugly frog-thing downstairs, talking to Frida—do we know if she has any amphibian friends? And if so, are they prone to feasting on crippled twenty-year-olds?"

Zoe sprang from her haunches, the two of them sneaking back across the catwalk, to see what Frida had invited in.

"Señor Rivera, my methodology is simple, really. I paint what I know best. And that is my pain. I know that the casual observer of this piece before us might deny that such a self-portrait evokes anything 'painful.' To which I would respond, that viewer is an imbecilic poseur."

She looked so small down there next to him, thought Nat. And yet, her personality shone so large, the way she was shaking her finger in his face, announcing her intention to be allowed into his space.

"I painted this picture for an ex-novio—Alejandro was his name—begging him to keep me in his thoughts after my accident, to reconsider our courtship. But look how I paint myself here, akin to a European princess with the neck of a swan, torso of a Roman goddess—down to my fingers, even! Just look at how long and angular I've made them. When what I really have are but stubs." She wiggled her hand in his face.

"My mother's family is from Oaxaca—Indígenas, all of them! Certainly not the palace of Versailles! So why do I insist on painting myself white as fine porcelain? Why do I negate my entire self in some desperate attempt to woo a boy? In this regard, Señor Rivera, I see my painting as so much more than a decoration for the bourgeoisie to hang on their walls. No, I see this portrait as exposing one of society's most unfortunate realities: that we women are socialized—institutionally and culturally—to employ these pathetic ends, all in pursuit of something as fleeting as a mate," she rasped through her conclusion.

"*Mhmmm,* interesting." Hands behind his back, he turned from the painting toward Frida. "Please, call me Diego, won't you? And let me say, Señorita Kahlo, I'm impressed by your candor—and I do not impress easily!" He issued a guttural snicker as he moved closer to Frida. "I don't think I've ever really sat down and considered the effects patriarchy might have on self-portraiture. I'm not sure if you're familiar with the details of my work, but class antagonism has always been my forte." He was, of course, keenly aware that *everyone on the pinche planet* knew the details of his work. "It's a fascinating perspective, one I suspect has the real potential to challenge some outdated cultural boundaries."

"Thank you, Diego. And, please, call me Frida." She smiled coyly. "Oh, and by the way, I don't give a shit about 'cultural boundaries,' I should warn you now."

His elephantine shoulders heaved with amusement at her retort, reaching out to tap her on the elbow, his hand remaining there a moment longer than was natural. She giggled up at him. Their eyes locked, and something magic sparked in that singular gaze, as if they'd each had the sudden reckoning that they'd known each other all their lives. And then he was taking her arm and ushering them toward the patio table with the geraniums. They settled comfortably into two chairs there, chatting easily, their bodies growing soft and relaxed, all of it making Nat's skin crawl.

This visitor was not to be trusted! He smelled of lechery, appetite, and conquest. What could this Diego possibly know about what Frida had been made to endure in her short lifetime? About how she'd come out of her traumas both lovely and erratic, fragile and steely? And what were the chances he'd know how to cherish the oxymoronic whole she was? If he were to shit on the guy's head right now, would that be enough to chase him away forever, Nat wondered as he trudged back to Frida's room. Because he couldn't watch one more second.

"I've already said I'm sorry, Zoe, I've never been inside a church before. How was I supposed to know?" Nat and Zoe were racing up the stairs to see Frida after another fruitless day searching for MyBoy. If either pet were honest, they would've confessed that the primary reason for continuing the search was as much about MyBoy as it was getting out of the house—and far away from the UglyFrogMan. (To be fair, Zoe did her best to keep MyBoy in her prayers, but time had the effect of fading memories.) As for Diego, ever since Frida's first meeting with el gran maestro several weeks ago, she was either locked away in her studio with the door closed, producing whatever it was he thought she ought to be producing, or in her studio with the door open, so that he could enter at his leisure to assess the quality of that production.

"Zoe, you said MyBoy was religious," continued Nat, noticing the door was open and crossing the threshold into Frida's studio. "I was just following up on a possible lead. It's not my fault that priest had never administered to a monkey before. I was asking a few simple questions, sheesh, he didn't have to get hysterical and run off screaming like I was a leper! He hurt my feelings, Zoe. *Harumph,* and I thought priests were supposed to be so tolerant!"

Nat switched gears when he saw Frida, leaping into her lap in a single bound, then draping himself playfully over her back. Oh, he disliked the UglyFrogMan, but the fact that he'd inspired this kind of dedication to her art—or dedication to anything other than lying in bed feeling sorry for herself—was wildly encouraging.

"Zoe's being a meanie. I was just trying to help. What's a guy gotta do to get a thank you around here?" From his perch on Frida's shoulder, he was pawing tenderly at the wisps of loose hair fallen over her face, trying (ineffectively) to pin them behind her ears.

"All I'm saying is there might've been a better way to convince the priest to hear you out—besides swinging after him along the apse crossbeams, that is."

"So what, Zoe! He didn't know MyBoy, which means we're never going back there. It's all good. Plus, I learned something very important today." He paused to tilt Frida's chin in his direction. "Frida, are you aware that the holy water they got in those places is not intended for the cleansing of one's genitals?" He smirked at Frida before addressing Zoe again. "I really am sorry about that part, Zoe. Can we talk about something else now?"

Zoe smiled back at him, because how could she stay mad at her broken shepherd, however irreverent he might be. All these months later, he was still willing to engage in what'd become one sham of a chase for a boy he'd never met simply because it mattered to her. Surely God would forgive the disturbance they'd caused in light of his good intentions?

"So, tell us, *Free-dah*, what's going on with the UglyFrogMan? You guys sure are seeing a lot of each other lately—which reminds me, you are aware that frogs don't really turn out to be princes, right, that it's just a fairytale?"

"Ja ja ja, Nat, very funny. And I don't have the time right now to think about Diego being anything more than my teacher." She was in one of her serious moods, gaze glued to the blank canvas in front of her. "He wants these paintings next month. That's not enough time! What can an amateur like me come up with that'd be half good enough for Diego Rivera? He's not just anyone, you know." She flopped into the back of her chair, hunched over and scowling.

"But he likes what you've shown him, Frida, he keeps saying so."

"But what if that's the extent of my talent? What if I never come up with anything else to impress him? Then what?

"Just look at all this shit, nothing but a bunch of child's doo-dles, that's all I'm capable of!" She brushed a hand over the crum-pled sketches littering the table next to her. "It's fucking blather, the mumblings of an imposter who's spent way too much time bedrid-den to have anything significant to share with the world that hasn't already been said a thousand times before! Who was I kidding?" This time, she flung her paintbrush to the ground, effectively adding the "spoiled" to the "bedridden imposter" imagery.

"Stop it, Frida!" The intensity of Nat's admonishment surprised even him, leaping to the ground in front of her, then shaking his index finger in her direction. "Just stop it! Because yes, you can! Go paint that pain you're always talking about! Shoot, go finish that pencil sketch of *El Accidente* . . . or start a new one of mutilated uteri and im-paled bloody hearts, I don't care! Just. Go. Paint. In case you forgot, you like busting down barriers, Frida Kahlo, it's in your soul, to disprove all the doctors and schoolyard bullies and society gatekeepers who try to dismiss you! So don't you dare think about quitting right now—and certainly not because you're worried about what some *man* thinks—ja, now wouldn't that be the irony of all ironies, all that preaching you do about girls being better than boys, and then you drop out of the show because, boo-hoo, Diego might not approve?"

Nat turned to Zoe. "Come on, let's go ask Conchita for some of her caldo. I'm hungry from chasing after that priest." Which wasn't true, but he needed to punctuate his threat. And find a way out of there, pronto, in case her mood turned from pathetic to ire.

In the aftermath of his little speech, Nat wasn't sure what to expect from Frida. The best he could tell, she hadn't left her studio, though whether that was because she was back to painting, or had instead pulled the sheets over her head, he'd no idea. In turn, he holed up in his nest, pretending to Zoe that he wasn't feeling well, even suggesting that perhaps the unwelcoming priest had cast a hex upon him. He would've much preferred the hex explanation to the other one, which was that Frida hated him now, because that would be the death of him.

His trance was broken a couple days later when Frida called for the pets.

"I'm sure you're curious why I've sent for you, so I'll get right to the point." Nat stood there with hands clasped before him, head slightly bowed, Zoe on her haunches beside him. "I listened to what you said, Nat, and you know what? You're absolutely right! Quitting would be wrong." She smiled. At which point a slow trickle of stomach gas spread from Nat's behind, the trepidation that had been weighing on him now cast from his body.

"I think I've finally figured out where I was getting stuck. At first, I thought it was the heaviness of my subject matter. And then, I considered that maybe I've been leaning too much on self-portraiture.

But the conclusion I finally came to was that I'm too focused on my *personal* pain. Come on, admit it, there are only so many tears one can shed over the little cripple girl before the audience gets bored! And given that there's no way I'm ever getting rid of pain as my signature mark, I've decided I'll simply have to expand on it!"

There was a frenetic energy about her that made Nat uncomfortable, like the barometric pressure was off, and she couldn't decide if she was celebratory or panicked or simply overwhelmed, so she'd opted to be all three of these things at the same time.

"And so, the solution is that my work will express our *collective* pain, that pain which we, los mexicanos, suffer, subjects of an oppressive and morally bankrupt system. I've been thinking of the way Conchita's family was kicked off their ejido land. Remember that, Nat?"

He tried not to. That was the beginning of the end, the period when their childhood shenanigans halted, and her adult life began.

"And what about the factory laborer I read about in the paper the other day? The one who had his hand chewed up in some faulty machine, and then was fired a week later because he couldn't pull the lever anymore? It's this composite of pain that I want to delve into, bring it front and center, to lay testimony to the failures of our government, and the unfinished promises of our half-assed 'Revolution.'" She spun around with a theatrical flounce, her colorful skirts flying up around her like a pinwheel, leaning her backside against the windowsill when she got there, arms crossed over her chest. Again, Nat was confused about whether she was due to burst into tears or jubilant cheer.

"The problem is, the more I thought about it, the more conflicted I became. Should I paint Conchita as a young girl fleeing her property, armed federales hot on her tail? Or would it be more effective to show her recently arrived in México City, shoeless and begging for scraps in the streets? Which, in turn, made me wonder if it was even ethical to tell Conchita's story as if it existed in isolation? Because it's not just the federales who should be blamed for her fate—what about the cycles of imperialismo that have ravished our people and our land for centuries now? Híjole, we've been locked in a cycle of exploitation since the day Cortéz's vessels touched our shores, and an endless stream of rapists, murderers, and disease were unloaded, set free to plunder the wonders that had taken centuries to create!

"And if the oppression goes back that far, well, then, it only makes sense that I'll need to include images from our pre-Colombian past—things like the great pyramids, majestic warriors, labyrinthine floating gardens!" She was back in motion, arms waving, heaving steps toward the magnet that was her easel, the sole medium capable of translating these buried truths. "All of them prime examples of the beauty, ingenuity, and strength from which our vibrant mexican-idad was born. It's ambitious, I know. But, as I've been reminded by my dear Nahuatl, no barriers have ever held me back. Nor will this be the first, I assure you.

"Which brings me to my point." And just like that, her calm was back, reseated at her easel, flattening her skirts around her as if she were a proper schoolmarm, predictable and harmless. "My dears, what do you think about sitting for me? For my paintings? Both of you are symbols of our indigenous roots . . ."

What? Zoe is from a puppy farm, not the pyramids of Tenochtitlán! And I know a hell of a lot more about statistical means than night stars' celestial messages!

"It was Diego who helped me work through all this—what a savior he is! We were discussing the current state of affairs . . ."

Nooooo! What about what Frida thinks?

". . . and as he so brilliantly pointed out, it is our obligation, as artists of the Revolution, to incorporate indigenismo into our chosen medium. As he so eloquently reminded me—he's genius, pure genius!—all those Victorian traditions and Baroque styles we continue to mimic in our architecture and our fashion are expressive of absolutely nothing related to our authentic roots. We are, at heart, indígenas, people of the earth, with close connections to the sun and the moon, the volcanoes and the rivers. Anything less than this would be a fallacy at best, and a betrayal of el pueblo at worst. And so, I say, basta to all the European bullshit! The day has come to create a new art, one that is genuinely and faithfully Mexican." She'd reached crescendo again, arms stretched overhead in triumph, then pulled back in and across her chest so she could continue.

"Anyway, I really should get back to work now. Besos, mis queridos muñecos." She blew them kisses as she shooed them out the door. "Oh, and thank you for doing the sitting stuff. I promise I'll make you both look stunningly handsome!"

The pets just looked at each other.

Nat had seen it coming from their first interaction: Frida and Diego were destined to fall in love. It was an unlikely courtship, to be sure. Diego was worldly, forty-two years old, and reputed to be an insuppressible philanderer. She was twenty-two, barely back on her feet from an injury that had almost done her in. As Nat watched their courtship evolve, he worried she might crumple under the weight of him (figuratively speaking; he forbade himself from considering the literal interpretation), or that she'd lose her unique sparkle in what was becoming an increasingly crazed quest for his approval. He cringed at the way she'd begun repeating his every word, as if nothing more profound had ever been said. She raved exhaustively about his murals, arguing that Diego was the primary force behind this next stage of the Revolution, that he was the central driver of this cultural transformation. Her reverence for him was fanatical, such that she even tossed to the curb all the starched blouses and pleated skirts that had filled her armoire for a decade now, replacing them with huipiles and indigenista wraps, because that's what Diego preferred. Oh, her beliefs remained steely strong and pointedly adversarial. It's just that they weren't her beliefs anymore as much as his.

Nat continued to tell himself that the chronic downside to his otherwise idyllic perch in the PoutingTree was that, like it or not, he was cornered into being witness to everything that went on across the patio, which, in the present, meant being the unfortunate observer to Frida and Diego's developing love affair. He winced and cringed on the occasion Frida slithered down the stairs, lips painted ruby red, a cloud of perfume hanging over her, an indigenous seductress come down from the pyramids with the intent to conquer this emperor of Mexican art. She greeted Diego by pulling his face into hers, devouring his lips, groaning with delight as she rubbed her pelvis against his. Did he like the lipstick, the perfume, the gown, she asked, and wouldn't he like to see what was beneath! He bumbled through his reply, because yes, he very much wanted to see all of it. But then came the twist, because she'd only give as much as she was sure she'd get in return. Even Diego needed to be reminded of those things which he could not control. Would he like to join her for dinner, she cooed in his ear, to which he smiled greedily. Her parents would be there, she finished the invitation, snickering at his surprise, taking his hand anyway, leading him toward the dining room, then pausing at the threshold to suggest he use his hat to cover the evidence of his, er, pleasure, out of respect for her parents. She teased, and then she tempered, making him stumble, which gave her satisfaction, that even el maestro could be made manageable. For his part, Diego found the tension deeply arousing, intoxicating even, returning for more as often as she'd let him. Before long, Diego asked Frida to be his wife. She accepted.

When Frida announced her engagement, Matilde wailed with despair, retreating to her room and dropping to her knees in search of otherworldly intervention. *¡A Dios, es comunista, no es creyente, eso no!* Guillermo was more discreet, congratulating his daughter with a warm embrace, then retreating to his studio, an exemplarily polite ostrich, taking the extra step to bury his head in private. Frida and Diego's circle of friends was warmer when the couple revealed their plans, but behind closed doors, they shrugged their shoulders. *Who knows? It could work—doubtful, though. She seems a nice girl—poor thing . . . oh, well.*

Frida knew about the skepticism swirling around her, but all it did was make her dig her heels in deeper. *You are wrong. I can control him. He loves me! And, oh, how I love him back!* For these petty gossipers didn't know what it was like when they were alone, that Diego didn't wince at her withered leg or the scars that crisscrossed her shattered torso. Why, he worshiped the way she endured her hardship, yearning to soothe it out of her, because what he uncovered was both hideous and enthralling at the same time. And she, in turn, was deeply moved by the intrigue he took in her brokenness, the way he studied every curve of her body, making her feel like her imperfections were the missing piece to the age-old conundrum of defining Absolute Beauty. His obsession with her fueled her obsession with him, the two of them engulfed in this flame of ecstasy, until she began to wonder if she'd be capable of breathing without him, awakening in the middle of the night gasping for air when she dreamed of a thousand scenarios capable of producing such a tragic loss. But, no, she'd never let him go; she would keep him close forever.

"You ready to do this?" It was the night before the nuptials. The pets had invited Frida to sit with them on the balcony outside her room, a *despedida*, or farewell party, from one stage of life to the next. Which meant it was Nat's last chance to raise some outstanding concerns, self-inspired in part, but mostly because he'd promised Guillermo (who'd promised Matilde, who'd promised God) that he'd poke around one last time. *"She'll rebuke Matilde for meddling. And, well, I guess I've never been very good at confronting my beloved Frida. Please, Nat, you're our only hope of getting through to her."*

Half a bottle of tequila down, and comical updates about Conchita's idiosyncratic culinary creations exhausted (currently, her muse was the Rosca de Reyes cake—though it was nowhere near the Navidad season—which they suspected was the old woman's last resort for dispensing of the mountain of dried fruit she'd canned back in 1925), they turned to the topic at hand.

"Diego's been married twice before, right?" Nat began, buoyed by the courage the alcohol provided him.

"So?" Frida clapped back.

"Well, and the second divorce—Guadalupe, is that her name?—has barely been finalized, is that what I heard? People are saying there've been quite a few others, behind the scenes, if you know what I mean." He winced through the last part, because, yes, it was all true, but also, he didn't want to hurt her. "You're okay with all that, Frida?"

"Oh, Nat, don't be so bourgeoisie!" She cackled, as if what he was asking was so ridiculous it was embarrassing. "Of course I'm okay with 'all that'! Would you prefer I pretend to be the virgin bride who giveth herself over to some Prince Charming? Really, Nat, all that prescribed shit around marriage, it's all so unnatural!

"Diego and I complete each other, intellectually and spiritually, as if we share one heart, one brain. That's what matters, not the number of lovers we've taken!" She paused, transitioning seamlessly from the frenzied to the collected, something she'd become quite good at, mused Nat. She leaned back in her chair, gazing up at the stars, then issuing a contemplative yet unfaltering sigh. "Oh, but don't misinterpret what I'm saying. The sex with Diego is blissful!"

And there was the segue, a calculated gesture to turn the mood toward their usual crassness, to deter them from any further discussion of the elephant in the room. *Poor Frida,* Nat thought to himself, *already defending herself, always the misfit coja.*

"So, Señorita Kahlo, it is set, then. You, my dear, shall be wedded tomorrow! A small ceremony, then a dinner with esteemed citizens afterwards, and, well, you do know what comes after that, do you not?" Nat feigned the air of some eighteenth-century advocate of the chastity force. He needed her to laugh right now, because the die was cast, and he wanted to seal off any remaining gaps for doubting herself, not to mention put to bed any tension between the two of them for the issues he'd just dared to raise. "Why, my dear girl, you must be prepared, to taketh a man into your bed! Which is why I've brought with me tonight one very special item, something customarily bestowed upon the bride on the eve of her nuptials." Continuing to pretend solemnity, Nat reached under his chair, pulling out a package, and then he handed it to her. "This, our dear betrothed, is for you."

"Moi?" she asked, landing one hand softy on her chest.

"Pour toi. Go on, I beg you to unfold it. For this is no ordinary gift—*bah,* as if anything ordinary would ever do for my most unordinary friend!" The chastity guise was cracking; he was getting emotional despite his best efforts.

So Frida peeled off the paper, revealing an ivory-colored blanket sewn in his signature sin pulga style, exactly one hundred and seventy-five heartfelt, emotive, sympathetic crocheted chain stitches, each with the same intricate, symmetrical detail. The quipping was done; the patio turned quiet. Frida ran her fingers over the soft pink roses needlepointed into the corners, then the fist-thick vines that looped prominently around the perimeter in every shade of green under the rainbow, but mostly in emerald and mint. But it was when her eyes landed on the center of the blanket that her awe gave way to an explosion of laughter.

"What? Is this what I think it is, Nat?" She snickered, pointing at the palm-sized hole in the center of the blanket.

"Pues, you are to be his bride tomorrow, Frida, there are responsibilities that come with such an arrangement. Oh, but you needn't be afraid, my child, you will have this wedding sheet to maintain some of your honor—"

"Now, this is a gift I will treasure forever." She guffawed into one fist. "I'm not saying I'm going to use it for its intended purpose, because, well, I do enjoy sex! But I promise one thing, and that is, I will cherish this blanket for life." She pulled one corner to her face, inhaling, recognizing lanolin, and the sweat from Nat's labor, and a perfume that must've come from the blooms of the Pouting Tree. And then she smiled weakly. *Yes, I'm scared, Nat. But I do love him. And you are, forever and always, my greatest solace. Thank you, Nat.*

The next day, Frida and Diego took their vows at City Hall, God deliberately left off the invitation list. It was just her parents, Nat and Zoe, and a handful of close friends in witness. The bride rejected the traditional white gown, opting instead for a beige dress with rose-colored floral insets, a well-worn green shawl draped over her shoulders, and hair pinned back in a no-fuss bun at the nape of her neck. *Presenting, Frida Kahlo, a true stalwart mexicana, soft and luscious on the inside, hard as nails on the outside. I dare you to forget me from this moment forward. You will not succeed.*

After the civil ceremony, a larger reception was held at a friend's home, attended by a frenzy of artists, avant-garde thinkers, and Communist comrades. It wasn't expressly communicated to the guests—it needn't have been, everybody knew—that all formalities were to be cast aside, the party rigged to be a blazing spectacle, flames of utter release burning down the walls. *Diego Rivera is getting married! (Gasp!)*

Again! And this time, to a feisty young vixen! And though they were Diego's friends more than hers, this was what she wanted; anything less would be a disappointment. *Take note, world. Diego Rivera has chosen me! I am his wife now. I see you laughing, because you think I'm fragile like a doe, unaware she's stumbled into a den of predators. But you don't know me! In the end, it will be me who laughs last, you pompous fools!*

When Nat and Zoe walked in the door, they were swallowed up in a cloud of haze that reeked of smoke, sweat, and want. Faceless bodies were coupled together, loose on their feet with booze, clumsily heeding the call of the tango blaring from the phonograph. Nat was certainly no prude—he'd never say no to a drink or two down at the neighborhood CornerBar, and he imbibed from the trumpet flower probably more than he ought to. But the mood here was different, making him feel dirty, like a layer of grit had gotten under his skin, making him itch, though he knew instinctively that no scratching in the world could expel this toxin from his body.

Always the protector at heart, Nat took Zoe by the paw, escorting her to an otherwise inopportune spot at such a celebratory event (under a side table, hedged in by a wall on one side and a sofa on the other), but perfect for the mayhem he was expecting. He spotted Matilde, likewise apart from the crowd, seated quietly in a corner chair, staring straight ahead, trying to see as little as possible, until the time came when she could politely excuse herself from this madhouse, back to the Bible she kept next to her bed, to pray for her daughter's salvation. And there went Guillermo sidling back to the bar to refill his drink. Though he dreaded leaving his wife's side at a time like this, the thought of having an empty glass was of equal concern.

"Híjole, that's bullshit! The stalinistas are the ones we need to be supporting! Ask Diego! He was at that meeting with me. Diego? Where are *youuu, pinnncche noviooooo?* Frida, where's that ugly husband of yours gone off to now?" It was one of their comunista comrades stirring the pot with political commentary, a phenomenon they'd come to expect during their rambunctious gatherings.

Frida halted her conversation with a guest. Because come to think of it, where was Diego? She knew infidelity was inevitable, but tonight? He wouldn't. Would he? She was suddenly consumed with dread at the possibility, her shoulders sinking low as she darted from the main room like a bull charging the torero, throwing open one door, finding nothing but coats and handbags, then slamming it shut, lunging for the next, until she'd checked every room and every closet, returning to the main room now, because somebody had to know where that bastard was!

They turned to look when she blasted through, out of breath, the hair around her face come undone from her bun, ringlets matted to her forehead with sweat. *Ahh, there he is, mi Diegito.* Her face relaxed. She exhaled with a snicker, because she'd panicked was all, he was right there. But wait, who was that he was cozied up to? No, it couldn't be. Was that his ex-wife, Guadalupe? Y esa puta, was she daring to pull up her skirt, to show off her bare legs to Diego? In front of their wedding guests? And was Diego daring to notice, even relish, what lay before him? It wasn't fair! Frida touched her mangled limb in consolation, never good enough, mi pobrecita piernita.

"You see these, Diego? You want these fine gams wrapped around you in your bed? Or do you pretend to prefer the feeble ones across the room?" Guadalupe threw a scoff in Frida's direction, pulling her skirt higher still, the party's attention now focused on the spectacle she was creating. "Tell me, Diego, who will it be, that child over there? Or voluptuous me?" She lowered her face down to his, wobbly from drink, barely keeping herself propped up there with one knee against his side.

The room went quiet, everyone waiting for Diego's response.

"Ja ja ja!" he bellowed. "Quite a show, my dear—"

Frida's reaction was primal, the way she ran at him, shrieking, then pounding his hulking chest with her too small fists, her words steeped in venom. She was humiliated and ashamed. How could he do this, she wailed, throwing verbal daggers far more dangerous than her tiny frame looked capable of. The mariachi band went silent, making haste to throw their instruments into their cases, then vanishing through the back door. The guests followed suit, slipping out under the cover of the night's shadows, leaving the newlyweds alone on their first night as man and wife. Nat and Zoe waited until the coast was clear, and then, they, too, made a run for it.

The Casa Azul was painfully quiet the next morning. The only evidence of life came from the kitchen, the aromas of huevos rancheros and café de olla enticing Nat and Zoe to greet the day even if their first instinct was to stay tucked away out of self-preservation.

"Buenos," Conchita acknowledged them tersely, a no-nonsense formality for conducting business on this day. She slid over two plates, followed by a pitcher of fresh papaya juice. "Well? What are you two waiting for?" she prodded them when they'd yet to sit down. "You should eat, while it's still warm. The others will come . . . Well, who knows when, but your food is ready, you should eat . . ." Her voice trailed off as she retreated to the comfortable isolation that was her kitchen counter, all of them inhabitants of a city under siege, risking their well-being whenever they left the safety of their private domains.

The pets settled into their respective seats at the bright yellow table, Nat just dishing up a bite for Zoe with his garden shovel when Diego walked in. It was a reprehensible sight, the way his lower eye lids sunk into his jowls like someone had put a hammer to his face the night before. He still had on the same sleeveless undershirt, boxer shorts, and brown dress socks from the night before. Zoe spit out her half-chewed eggs.

"Conchita, get me a tequila, will you? A little morning-after elixir to get the blood flowing," he said nonchalantly, as if whatever unfortunate events had transpired last night were harmless, unworthy of mention by today.

"Nice party," said Nat. Which they all knew it hadn't been.

"Frida up?" He ignored the provocation, aggressively spearing his food with his fork. He gave an appreciative grunt when Conchita returned with his tequila. "Hell of a good cook, that Conchita. You two should eat up." He commended the old woman like she wasn't standing right there, bits of spittle and eggs pooling at the corners of his mouth.

The sound of an exasperated sigh made them all look up. It was Frida, leaning with her back against one side of the doorway. Her hair fell over her shoulders, dark and wavy, no indigenista façade this morning, no political posturing, just lovely Frida in her natural state. Wearing a mid-length white nightdress with billowy sleeves and a crocheted neckline, she looked to Nat both brilliant and innocent at the same time.

"Good morning, Diego."

"Good morning, corazón," he managed between bites, tapping the space next to him. "Come, sit here, my blushing bride."

"Nope, I came down to get some juice is all." She puckered up her face before continuing. "I've got the foulest taste in my mouth— I'm not sure what from, though I do have my suspicions. In any case, I'm desperate to be rid of it." She poured herself a glass, and then, with a calmness unbefitting of the situation, she left again.

None of them said anything as Diego continued feasting, no indication he was at all affected by the tension hanging over the place thick as the fog that so famously settles over the Sierra Madres. When he was finished, he stood up, pushing his empty plate to the center of the table and rubbing his belly.

"Riquísimo, Conchita," he shouted toward the cooking quarters.

And then to the pets, "Pues, amigos, I'm off to the studio. An artist's mind never rests. Con permiso."

"What?" Zoe squealed when Diego was gone. "To the studio? Like there's nothing weird going on? No apology? The UglyFrog-Man should be down on his knees begging for forgiveness!"

Fortunately, Nat was a step ahead of his friend. As he'd sat there through breakfast (perhaps a subconscious effort to escape the slobbery, snorting crudeness on display before him), he'd let his mind transcend the passive-aggressive punches being thrown around, discovering a rare moment of clarity. *Impressive thoughts, impressive thoughts,* he'd guided himself, *stay away from the cliff, Nat, you can do this.* Though he'd come to accept fury in all its variations as a force that might occasionally be used for a greater good, Nat's basic instinct was still to avoid mean-edged reactions, to rise above the itch to do others harm. And more important still was his basic instinct to protect Frida, which, as of yesterday's nuptials, meant not antagonizing Diego.

"You're right, Zoe. The brute has shown no effort to make amends. *Hooowevvverrr,*" he dragged out this last word, lifting one index finger, "I do believe there's something you and I can do for Frida, since it is she we are concerned about and not her frogman husband. How about you and I give her that wedding present we've been working on, see if we can cheer her up a bit?" He didn't have to wait for Zoe's response; she was already halfway up the stairs when he sprinted after her.

They retrieved the gift from the cabinet where she kept her doll collection. (*I know, let's hide it here. She hasn't checked on her "babies" in years—too busy trying to make real ones with the UglyFrogMan, ja ja ja.*) And then they hustled into her studio, finding her standing in front of the window there, arms folded across her chest. She didn't turn around when the pets entered.

"Good morning, Frida," he began, using his most subdued voice. "Zoe and I got you something, for your wedding." Timidly, he moved forward, slipping the gift from behind his back, then handing it to her. "We hope you like it."

"My wedding, ja! Fue un fracaso, what a mess that was!" she snorted back. "On the other hand, I guess I deserve at least something for going through with it." She was shaking her head at the recollection of the night gone awry, but also smiling at the pets' gesture. "Let's see what you two have been up to."

What the pets had gifted her was the mint green bathing suit—the very one Nat had been sewing all these years. As Zoe's contribution, she'd insisted that the gold-plated collar Guillermo had given her as a pup should be integrated into the garment, to be repurposed as an amulet between the breasts.

"Oh! You guys!" she exclaimed, some of the color returning to her cheeks as she held the suit up to her frame, then turning around to admire her reflection in the window there. "This looks like it might've come straight out of one of those fancy fashion magazines!" she gushed, running her fingers over the hem lines. "This is a masterpiece—a worthy-of-preservation-in-a-museum kind of masterpiece!"

"Well, we're glad you like it, Frida. Oh, and just so you know, we tried to make swim trunks for the UglyFrogMan, since this is a wedding gift, so it probably should include something for both of you. But alas, try as we might, we were unable to secure sufficient fabric meterage for a creature of his, er, particular physique."

"Ja, good one, Nat!" Her laugh was warm and real, a crack in the plaster she hid behind whenever she felt slighted. "You know what? Ya, enough pouting! The weather is spectacular, I've got a couple of my best friends right here, and a new swimsuit I'm dying to try out. I refuse to let Diego ruin another minute of my life. I think we should go swimming, and I happen to know the perfect spot. What do you say?"

Physically speaking, the quarry Frida took them to turned out to be wholly unremarkable, nothing but an artificial body of water hedged in by heaping limestone slabs. Not to mention that the trek down to the water proved particularly arduous for a crippled woman, a runt dog, and a monkey anatomically constructed for treetop travel. But so what? He wasn't going to let anything bother him today. He smiled when Frida dashed on ahead of them, ripping off her extra clothing and plunging into the pond.

"The water is glorious!" she shouted when she came up for air. "I can't even remember the last time I did this, went swimming. Which is a shame, because water is a true friend, the way it turns my body weightless, and the most basic movements become suddenly natural and unstrained." As if to prove her point, she swam out a bit further, turning over to float on her back, reaching one arm over her head, letting it slide back into the water behind her, then pulling herself forward with the other, feet fluttering, all of it so graceful, so anti-co-ja-ish.

For much of their relationship, Nat had pitied her, because of Diego, and her lack of a penis, and her physical limitations. Right now, though, he felt inspired by her. Because once upon a time, someone said, *You'll never walk again after that bus crash, prepare yourself now.* And someone else said, *Cripples can't compete, they're invalids, you know.* Then one more chimed in, *You've no formal training in painting, what makes you think you've any talent?* And the most evil of them all said, *Diego will never love you, he'll take another lover the moment you look away, just wait.* And still, she forged on, defying them all.

This was her day to make peace with an awful yesterday. He'd no intention of trying to take her place onstage. It's just that her courage was infectious. And the doubt was pressing: If Bobo the other spider monkey could swim, why couldn't he? Frida had proved that she could walk and paint and stand up to the UglyFrogMan, so why shouldn't he be able to float? Zoe was safely curled up on a low hanging rock, so why not give it a try right now?

And so, Nat wandered down to the shoreline, taking a step, then pausing to squeeze the mud between his toes, to notice the way the water and gravity played off his body, to appreciate the feel of the wet rocks and mossy shallows around him. He ventured forward another few steps, feeling the water surge around his kneecaps, spreading his arms out on either side of him for balance. He chuckled to himself, because he wasn't sinking like a lead weight, no, he could do this, and took another step.

"Ay, chíngate, fucking cliff!" Simultaneously running through her mind was, *esas malditas piernas, you damned legs, failing me yet again!*

Nat looked up to see Frida slipping down the opposite bank. He froze, cursing himself for being so preoccupied with the merit of Archimedes's principle that he'd failed to notice that she'd swum to the other side of the quarry, already halfway up the rocky slope when she'd lost her foothold. Thankfully, she'd stopped her slide after a few meters, but it was still unclear how much damage she'd incurred.

"You okay, Frida?" He was back on solid ground now, cradling his body around Zoe's, as if his power to protect was so easily transferrable, that to comfort one from his inner circle extended to all. "Maybe you should come back? I think Conchita put some tres leches in our basket. It's your favorite, Frida, yum! Yeah, why don't we eat."

"No, not yet." Her response was unequivocal.

And then she was back at it, culling up every gram of strength to finish what she'd started, shimmying back up the cliff, past the spot from which she'd just slipped, hoisting herself onto an overhang when she'd reached her destination, and then standing.

"You think you should be up there?" It was Zoe's turn to take a shot at it.

"I do. Because I want to show you guys something; it's important to me." Her voice wavered; her actions did not. Her feet padded in place, toes groping for traction, their last connection to solid ground, and her arms were held tightly by her sides. She closed her eyes, letting her feet be still now. And then she took an extended inhale before leaping from the ledge, arms outstretched in a V formation. It felt to Nat like she was gliding overhead for longer than was humanly possible, making him wonder if perhaps the best and the worst of his dreams had just come true, that she'd sprouted wings, and now she wanted to use them, because she'd realized it was indeed possible for her to have a life of lightness and freedom, and now she was gone forever, chasing her dreams. But in the next instant, there came the sound of a small splash, Frida slicing seamlessly through the water's glassy surface. Nat was relieved and disappointed.

"'Smooth as a Monarch Princess'—that's what Papi used to say." She came up with a sparkling smile, slowly stroking her way back toward the pets. Nat and Zoe were standing up now, grateful she'd survived, but still anxious from the danger she'd just put herself in.

"I'd just gone back to school after the bout with polio. Little did I know the hell awaiting me. My classmates were horrible, calling me things like 'coja fea' and 'pata de palo.' Most of it I just ignored, because the last thing I wanted was for them to know they were getting to me. But then came the day I was called to the chalkboard at the front of the room, and the biggest asshole of them all stuck his foot out when I was passing by. Intentionally stuck his foot out, that is. And I fell flat on my face. Everyone burst out laughing, hee-hawing, and pointing fingers, while I just lay there sprawled out on the floor, humiliated. Eventually I pulled myself together and went back to my seat where I tried to make myself small and invisible, just waiting for the day to be over.

"On my way home that afternoon, I decided I was going to hack off this pinche leg. Oh, how I hated this thing, for never leaving me alone, always reminding me that I was less-than. In retrospect, I realize it was a monumentally stupid idea, but I was a kid—an embarrassed and angry kid, remember, incapable of sorting through her own feelings at that age."

Are you implying you're an expert at sorting through your feelings now, Frida? Nat bit his tongue.

"So I went straight to the kitchen, grabbed a knife, and then went upstairs to proceed as planned." She'd reached the shore now, climbing out of the water and finding a seat on the rock nearest the pets, pulling her knees into her body and wrapping her arms around them for warmth. Or was it consolation?

"Honestly, I probably wouldn't have had the guts to go through with it, but that turned out to be irrelevant. Because Papi walked in right then—well, you guys know how he is, always fretting over me."

The pets nodded awkwardly, because yes, they were familiar with Guillermo's preoccupation with his daughter. But not yes to this tragic tale she was telling.

"When I explained to Papi why he'd found his seven-year-old in possession of a meat cleaver, he suggested that we go out for a while, that perhaps some fresh air would do me good. Next thing I knew, we were driving out here, to this very spot, and then we were in the water and swimming to the other side, the same way you just saw me do.

"But when we got to that cliff, he got all serious. He confessed that he'd brought me here for a reason other than simply 'fresh air.' No, we were here because he wanted me to dive off. I remember his exact words. 'At the end of the day, we can endure much more than we think we can.'"

Frida smiled at the recollection, softly stroking the hair on her shins, spellbound by the silky comfort of the memory she'd stumbled upon after all this time. But then she remembered the story wasn't over yet, she was still stuck on that cliff, and so she stiffened her back, sitting up tall to resume her account.

"At first, I was petrified, but that quickly turned to rage, because why was Papi torturing me like this? Before I could arrange my confused thoughts enough to argue with him, he'd launched into this soliloquy about how the thing that set me apart from everyone else was that I never dodged a challenge, and so of course some landings were bound to be rougher than others. But he said if I stopped getting up when they knocked me down, then soon I'd forget how to bounce back. And they'd have won. I think it's because Papi was always flattering me or taking it easy on me—both of which I interpreted as pity—that I took the challenge seriously.

"Pues, so I did it, I dove in. This next part is going to sound dippy—so much that I'm embarrassed I'm saying it—but jumping off that rock was metamorphic for me. Because for those brief moments, everything below was . . . inconsequential. What I mean is that it didn't matter that I'd been the laughingstock at school, or even that polio had mangled my body. It was like these weighty facts ceased to exist during my great leap of faith. The only thing I could feel on my way down was the adrenaline rushing through my veins, merging my mind and body into this omnipotent force, and I knew I would survive.

"When I tried explaining the sensation to Papi later that night, he said it sounded like what I was describing was my superpower, and wasn't it amazing that not only had I overcome polio and schoolyard bullying, but I could fly! He warned me I'd have to be careful, though, because there are always villains out there dedicated to destroying superpowers. So I'd need an alias right away, before anyone figured out my identity. He's the one who came up with 'Monarch Princess.' He said it was fitting because I'm always transforming myself, appearing fragile one moment—but only as a cover, because what I'm really doing is using that time to hone my skills—and then exploding back on the scene, making the world gasp at the majesty I've turned myself into!

"I promised myself that I'd reimagine that dive every night before sleep for the rest of my life, so I could keep alive that same sense of wonder and power. But you know how things go, you get distracted, things come up, and you just kind of push some memories to the side until they're nearly forgotten." She looked down at her hands in her lap, fidgeting with her thumbs, then jerking back to attention. "On the other hand, what a lucky thing that today I've been reminded of that glorious afternoon! Shit, maybe there's a silver lining to the humiliation I endured last night. Because here I am today, getting to resurrect the Monarch Princess after all this time, and in front of you, my little muñecos!" She smiled. It was an easy, unrestrained smile, thought Nat, the kind that turned her facial features soft and delicate, free from ulterior motives or making impressions.

"We should eat!" It was a change of topic, but not awkward or abrupt as can be the case when one is trying to avoid an uncomfortable conversation. This felt more like an invitation, to punctuate and celebrate what had just transpired among them. "Weren't you saying something about tres leches, Nat?"

The sun was sinking behind the pines on the other side of the quarry as they climbed back up the hillside to find comfort in the remaining pool of sunlight there. Without speaking, they worked together to spread out the goods from the picnic basket Conchita had packed for them, and then they feasted to their hearts' content. Lazy with satisfaction, they reclined on the warm rocks, quiet again, savoring the afternoon's pause to begin privately unpacking the day's lessons.

Nat turned on to his side to look at Frida, her hair spread out in a tangled web, the curves of her body contrasting with the flat surface of the rock there, her supple flesh captured perfectly in the swimwear he'd created. It was reassuring, to watch her here, away from the Casa Azul, to be reminded that beyond the fragile coja married to the gran maestro was the Monarch Princess planning her next move, a pendulum in perpetual motion.

One rock slab over, Zoe was also deep in thought, lamenting the fact that she hadn't been doing a whole lot of communicating with God lately. Well, and she'd been lacking a little in the conviction department when it came to locating MyBoy. It's just that his image was becoming more of a blur than a tangible figure at this point. On the other hand, she was helping Frida. Which was the work He'd commissioned for her, right? True, she'd been remiss in her prayers, but how else could she describe this feeling swelling inside of her but one of love of the purest kind? Here were the three of them, the perfect example of friends helping friends, prodding each other to become better versions of themselves. Wasn't that exactly what God wanted for his flock?

"*Ahhh,*" Frida said, breaking the silence some vague amount of time later that no one could identify because that's exactly what total fulfillment does to you—time stops being a dimension and immediate presence supersedes all else. "I haven't felt this refreshed since . . . *hmmm,* remind me, when did I meet Diego? Speaking of *whommmmm,*" she said, raising her eyebrows and starting to put their dishes back in the basket. "I probably should go figure out what to do about that." The pets didn't say a word; best to savor the gifts the afternoon had brought them.

The threesome was exhausted by the time they got back to the Casa Azul, intent on heading straight upstairs and collapsing face-first onto Frida's bed. But their plan was thwarted by a drunken Diego waiting at the patio's bistro table with the geraniums. He was slumped over in his chair, lower lip sagging into his chin, clinging to the empty bottle resting in his lap. It was not lost on Nat that the pendejo still hadn't changed out of the undershirt and dirty brown socks he'd worn to his wedding.

Frida turned to Nat and Zoe. "I'll meet you upstairs." And then to her husband, "Diego."

"Frida, querida, where have you been? Is this my punishment? Leaving until I'm sick with worry? Please, Frida, you are my light and my soul, what else can I say to make you believe me? I know I am flawed." He looked down at the bottle in his lap, turning it over in his hands. "But none of the others matter. I don't want Guadalupe. I don't want anyone else. I want only you as my wife, Friducha."

Frida's expression turned pained. And then, somewhat haltingly, she held out her arms to him. Because his suffering was her suffering—why, she loved him enough to carry both their burdens if necessary! Diego stood up, nestling his cyclopean head into her chest. She tussled his curls with one hand, patting circles gently on his back with the other.

"Oh, Diegito, my dear, tortured genius." She kissed one side of his neck. He bent down to kiss her on the lips. She let him, and then they moved off into the downstairs bedroom.

And so, exactly sixty seconds after they walked in the door, the pets' spirits were dashed. They were left wondering if any of it had been authentic, or just Frida's next move in this larger game of chess she so efficiently masterminded. *But you're stronger than that, Monarch Princess! Fly away, now, before it's too late!*

CHAPTER TEN

ON SURVIVAL OF THE BRASHEST:
THE NEWLYWEDS HOLD COURT

Coyoacán
1929

So on their second night as husband and wife, it seemed Frida and Diego had reached a détente. Oh, the underlying tension persisted, but following Frida's lead as they always did, the Casa Azul hummed along as if everything was fine, just a minor hiccup was all. As for the newlyweds, they played their parts to a tee. They appeared attached at the hip, arm wrapped around the other's back as they glided through the hallways on their way to market, or to a new art installation, or trip to the cine. Maybe it was all an illusion, to put the gossipers to bed. Except there was a certain tenderness in their treatment of each other that couldn't be denied. The way they got locked in one another's gaze when they thought no one was looking, the way he touched her lower back when the pain in her pelvis became unbearable and she needed help to her room, and the way he beamed with delight when she regaled their guests with vulgar tirades against the capitalist pigs who were ravishing México.

As a gesture of conciliation, Frida reached out to Guadalupe—though, to be fair, it wasn't an entirely altruistic appeal. The truth was, she needed Diego's ex-wife to teach her to prepare his favorite dishes. She'd have to be able to satisfy his many appetites—not wholly, that was widely known to be impossible—but to keep him sated for as long as possible. *Ja, I will keep him sated forever, you fools, I will never let him go, you've no idea of my powers!* So Frida invited Guadalupe into the Casa Azul, asking for lessons on how fine to dice the jicama, when to stir the olla, how much constituted "a pinch" of cilantro. It turned out that despite the women's initial clash at Frida and Diego's wedding, Guadalupe was extremely gracious, passing on every bit of wisdom she'd accumulated over the last six years, teaching her successor to hold back on adding the chiles until that moment just before the onions turned translucent and how to toast the tomatoes until they were evenly charred before adding them to the salsa to bring out the smoky flavor Diego fancied.

"Did you hear me, Frida?" she asked a week and one bottle of shared tequila into their kitchen lessons. "He won't change his philandering ways. You know that, right?"

"Yes, I heard you the first time. And thank you, Guadalupe, for your help. Really. But I think we're done here." She was unfastening her apron, her back turned to her guest. "I'm planning to treat my husband to a feast of the senses tonight, and I'd like to have a bath before then. Should I have Conchita see you to the door?"

Guadalupe smiled at her protégée, so fierce in her belief that she was the sole miracle worker capable of domesticating him. In the end, sighed Guadalupe to herself, they were victims of the same fate, comrades in a war that could not be won. The women hugged good-bye, and then Guadalupe let herself out.

"¿Te gusta, mi amor?" Frida was spoon-feeding Diego at the bright yellow table later that night, her knees pulled up beneath her on the bench beside him, upper body draped over his. She'd adorned herself in as many tehuana garments as her small frame could carry, arms thick with bracelets in jade and obsidian, hair twisted up into an ornate knot above one ear. (Later, she would reveal to him that she'd foregone her underclothes, so she'd be that much closer to feeling the ripples of his pleasure upon consuming what she'd prepared for him. And that he oughtn't be surprised, because she cooked like this, too, touching herself as she added the flavors, imbuing her dishes with hidden indulgences for him to enjoy. *I am domesticated. And I am entirely not, mi Diegito.*)

"Riquísimo, Frida, you do amaze me!" He kissed the top of her hand resting on his elbow. "Thank you, Friducha. Guadalupe is a good person, you'll see. You just got off to a bad start is all." Frida winced, turning away. He reached for her chin, gently spinning her face back in his direction. "She's a part of my life, and the mother of two of my daughters. I cannot pretend she doesn't exist, Frida, you understand that, no? Remember it is you I love, for your passion and your grit. You must believe me when I say that you are the one I want." Her eyes had been cast downward, but now she looked up at him, brushing her cheek against his hand.

"You know what we should do? We should have a party! A cause célèbre! So I can show off my beautiful bride. We'll invite everyone we know, and we shall throw an event that will get talked about a generation from now!" It was the closest he would ever come to apologizing for his epic blunder on their wedding night, by proposing a do-over. He pulled her more tightly into his side, jostling her playfully.

"A party, *hmmm,*" she mused, tapping her fingers sequentially on the table, biding her time—enough that she could feel him growing anxious in the pause, unsure what she was thinking, afraid that she might refuse his gesture, and then how much time would he have to devote to winning her over again? He had work to do . . . When she sensed this vulnerability, she sprung to her feet.

"Okay, then, Diego, you want a party? Well, then, a party it shall be!" It was the closest she'd ever come to accepting his apology. "But Coyoacán has no idea what they're in for! Behold the magic my Diegito and I are capable of creating! Why, we'll bring them to their knees, mi amor!" *Take that, world! You were wrong about us! Diego and I cannot be torn apart, our wedding night was an aberration, that is all. Come and gawk at us, oh, dubious ones. I will prove you wrong. I will make you weep with envy over what I am capable of!*

"I'm going upstairs now, to get started with the planning." She was already dashing off, her energy turned electric, ideas whirring in her head. She was halfway up the stairwell when she halted, skirts balled up in one hand, because there was that other thing, the final act in tonight's performance, push-pull, seduce-repel. "But don't be too long, mi amor. I have something to show you—underneath all these uncomfortably heavy skirts." She flashed him a peek, and then she was gone, leaving nothing but a cloud of perfume to remind him of her proposition.

For the next few weeks, Frida barely sat down. She'd temporarily set aside her artistic endeavors to focus on the party. Because she wanted to make him happy—no, no, no, she *needed* him to be happy, so he'd stay, *please stay,* carving out her niche as irreplaceable to him, of which she would remind him at every opportunity, that he was happy precisely because she supported his happiness, whatever he wanted. *You want a party, Diego? No problem, anything, mi amor, dime, I'll do it.*

She drew up a guest list, and then she went back through and crossed off the names of the women she saw as a threat and added those who she knew would look dull next to her. She hired an army of gardeners to come in and tend to the grounds because, like her husband, she was a supporter of the indigenista movement and all things rural about her homeland, fully at home in the selva or the llano or the montaña or the desierto, no me importa, for she was a true lover of the land and the Universe's many treasures.

None of this attention to detail should've suggested to anyone that she had forgotten about her wedding night. Because she would never forget about that. *You'll have your party, mi amor, but for a price. I'm nobody's fool!* It was the same strategy she'd used to captivate him in the first place: she had to keep that bastard unsteady and on his toes. It was her only chance to match him in this battle of love.

"Conchita, you have a minute?" Frida burst into the kitchen one day, list in hand as she worked through dinner possibilities. It was one week before the party. "I'm afraid I'm going to need your help."

Conchita refrained from issuing the sarcastic retort that was burning in her throat, because did the girl even know the difference between a carving knife and a paring knife? Not to mention cooking an entire pig!

"I've been dreaming about those chiles rellenos. The ones in that heavenly walnut sauce. You used to make them at Christmastime, do you remember those? Gosh, I'd look forward to those all year, did I ever tell you that?" *Not entirely true, but they were delicious, and I really need you to say yes.* "I know how much work they are, which is why I hesitate to ask, but do you think you could make them for my party?"

Conchita gritted her teeth. Eighteen hours in total, not including visiting five separate mercados to secure the ingredients. She nodded her head and affected a smile.

"Oh, mil gracias, Conchita! You're the best, I knew I could count on you! Oh, one more thing: Guadalupe's mole, could you do that, too? Over chicken, I thought—shoot, or whatever you think, pork is fine, too, I'm not picky."

Conchita took a deep breath, moving around Frida planted there, reminding herself that the poor child had suffered so much. "Claro, dear, como quieras," is what came out of her mouth.

"Oh, thank you!" She flounced over to Conchita's side, hands clasped in the prayer position in front of her chest. "We'll need rice and beans, too, if that's okay, I mean, how could we not, 'viva la patria' and all that stuff. Oh, shoot, one last thing, flan for dessert? And that's it, nothing else, I swear. I wouldn't be requesting all this, Conchita. Except that I have a personal stake in this party, you understand, right? They're all watching me. I need them to see that I'm in control here, that I can satisfy Diego Rivera."

"Yes, Frida, I understand." So what if it was a little more than she might've liked to take on? She was impressed by her jefa's fearlessness. And, well, she wouldn't be disappointed if Diego's gang of creídos with their noses in the air got a little bit of comeuppance. "I'll get started—"

Frida lurched toward Conchita, embracing her in a bear hug, then resting one cheek on the old woman's shoulder, inhaling her familiar smell, evocative of fond childhood memories, of the warmth and comfort Matilde could never give her. She realized in that moment that she felt tenderly toward the old woman, and that one day she would pay her back for all the nurturing she'd bestowed upon the Casa Azul. Just as soon as she got through this party, gosh, the whole thing was turning out to be more of a headache than she'd expected.

"Well, I should go now. I still have the flowers to figure out." *Calla lilies or marigolds? For the two convey such different messages. A hostess must consider every detail, you see, for she is transformed into a hypnotist while the guests are under her roof, capable of masterminding any trance she desires.*

Later that afternoon, in the lull of the golden hour when México rests, Nat went looking for Frida. She'd been perpetually in motion since she'd taken on this hosting feat, but the party was upon them, and he had something to give her. He found her tucked in a garden corner, puffing away on a cigarette, legs outstretched in front of her on an elevated flower bed, tapping one ankle nervously against the other. The trance was broken when she heard him approach.

"Well, hello there, Nat," she smiled through a mouthful of smoke. "What brings you down from your nest this afternoon?"

He was comforted by her playful tone. One could never be sure these days.

"I heard you're throwing a party? And given the commotion that's going on around here, I'm supposing it's going to be a large, rather important party?" he returned her taunt, hands tucked behind his back as he rocked back and forth on his heels.

"Why, yes, I am, indeed! How quick of you to notice."

"Thank you. I pride myself on my investigative skills. Anyway, I'm here because a hostess of your caliber will need to look the part. And I do believe that I have the very item to lend you that extra-something to make the guests turn green with envy. Wanna see?" She nodded. He untucked his arms from behind his back, extending them toward her. It was a peineta, or decorative hair comb. "It's a little something I made, to acknowledge the grand debut of the Monarch Princess. In case the party turns sour, you'll need to fly away, won't you?" *I remember that afternoon at the quarry. Do you, Frida?*

She hurried to snub out her cigarette, reaching over to accept her gift, taking it gently into her palms. The shaft was covered in black velvet, then embroidered with a series of walnut-size butterflies in splashes of purple, red, and yellow that popped out against the dark background, as if about to take flight.

"Butterflies! I love butterflies!"

For a moment, Nat paused to consider that he'd chosen to embroider butterflies specifically. But he'd only done so in honor of the Monarch Princess, he reminded himself. Yes, yes, that was it. It had nothing to do with *his* past. No, of course not. That was then and this was now.

"How I do so adore you, my dear, dear monkey. Thank you, Nat!"

Frida tucked the comb safely into the folds of her skirt, and then she reached out with both arms for him to climb into. It seemed to Nat like she held him there for a particularly long time, but he wasn't complaining.

So exactly one month after their previous attempt, Frida and Diego hosted a party, this time, under her tight control. A row of meter-high talavera vases had been positioned symmetrically along either side of the entrance and continuing across the patio, sprays of birds of paradise, bougainvillea, and sunflowers guiding the way. *Exotic, but highly incongruous in the same vase. It's symbolic, you imbeciles, you will never figure me out.* Diego was there to greet the guests, offering them a drink, then encouraging them to explore the patio grounds as he tended to the next wave of arrivals. The life-sized papier-mâché Judas dolls Frida had commissioned stood watch at different stations across the patio, hulking figurines in purple, green, and red that made the guests laugh at the out-of-place caricatures, and then wince at the ghoulishness. The bright yellow dining table was awash in a hundred twinkling votive candles, lace doilies running down the center, a setting of Frida's mother's fine china at every chair, the aromas from the chiles rellenos and the pollo en mole (and also the puerco en mole, because she *was* picky) making the air seductively thick.

You find me entertaining; I can tell. Go ahead: stare at my limp, then cringe at my scars. You won't be able to figure out if you pity me or adore me, if I amuse you or frighten you. I laugh at you—the way you're so easily confused. Ja, you're like children, really! And this is your greatest weakness! I've been watching your condescending type since I was a schoolgirl. I know you already, though you haven't a clue about me!

But the truth was, the party didn't begin in earnest until the leading lady made her appearance. Tucked away in her bedroom upstairs, Frida waited. She occupied herself by reapplying her trademark red lipstick, spritzing herself with her favorite Italian perfume, pacing back and forth along the window that looked down on the party. Only when the last invitee had arrived did she open her door with a calculated thud, so that all eyes rose to meet her. That's when she began her descent down the basalt staircase, slow enough to give them the opportunity to take in every detail about her, but not so slow they might think her at all daunted by their presence. After much stormy deliberation *("The other one, Conchita! The blue one makes me look like I'm trying too hard. Please hand me the green one already, will you?")*, she'd decided on a red cotton huipil with an embroidered yellow U-shaped inset over the chest. Her floor-length skirt was maroon with tiny white floral imprints, a fashion choice some might have derided as a clumsy clash of patterns but that Frida made look positively glamorous. A lattice malachite necklace hung around her neck, chandelier earrings dangling to her shoulders. Her fingers were awash in bands of jade and amber, and her hair was piled up in thick, coiled braids, a red ribbon woven into the plaits with a magenta hibiscus tucked above her left ear. The crowning touch, the peineta, was pinned prominently at the back of her head. The princess arrived at last to the ball.

"Buenas noches," she said, offering a kittenish smile when she got to the bottom of the stairs. "Thank you all for joining us. Diego and I are so pleased to have you." She could feel their eyes on her, sizing her up, bewildered, because how could someone like her be the ruler of this most peculiar castle?

Why, just look how the little cripple-girl-turned-dishonored-bride has pulled herself together! And that outfit is something, isn't it? Absolutely gorgeous . . .

Her ears were on fire, she couldn't miss anything, because starting right now, this was her dialogue to manage.

"Did I overhear you saying that you liked my blouse and skirt? Mil gracias, I'm beholden to our pre-Colombian forefathers—or should I say, foremothers. For I am both indígenista and feminista after all." She placed one hand gently to her chest with a wink. *Were you fools enough to think your little revolutionary cadre was exclusive? Bah, I will carve out a place for myself in your Bohemian pantheon by the night's end!*

"And let me just say how humbled and honored I am to be wearing these pieces. I've selected them as a celebration of our indigenous past. Oh, did I mention that I personally purchased this huipil and skirt? I make it a point to travel regularly to the most rural markets, you see. Which is how I've come to know this particular tehuana dressmaker—¿como se llama? Well, I can't remember her name right now, so you'll have to trust me that she is a lovely woman. And a true beacon of our people's strength."

Once again, Nat was privy to all of this given his tree's location. Sure, he might've retreated to the bowels of his nest to avoid whatever shenanigans were sure to go down given the crowd in attendance. Instead, he'd created a makeshift booster out of his books, and then he'd climbed atop the structure and sat down to watch. It was Frida's last words that caught him off guard, because what she was saying was simply untrue. He'd been with her at the marketplace that day when she'd bought the huipil and skirt under discussion, and he could attest to the fact that she'd been outright belligerent while bartering for it. He remembered it distinctly, how the viejita with the knobby hands and the leathery face had cited her asking price, at which point Frida had gasped, throwing her bags on the ground and firing back, "No, not one more peso, or I walk right now! Are you a fool? Do you want my money or not?" Which sure didn't sound particularly "beholden to our foremothers."

And yet, Nat knew perfectly well what she was up to. He didn't like it, but it was predictable. Frida had an audience, and it was a very special audience. She needed them to see her value to their larger whole, to accept her claim to belong amongst them. If the way to do so was to promote her unorthodox nature and political savvy, well, then, so what if she amended her story to fit her intention? Ultimately, what was concerning to Nat was not that Frida was being devious, because she'd been pulling stunts like this since she was a child, punishing the schoolyard bullies or the frivolous ricos. No, what bothered him this time was that she wasn't advocating for others; she was only advocating for herself.

Meanwhile, the party raged on, Frida continuing her pretense as the grandest social debutante ever to be presented, Diego regaling the guests with the latest news on the postrevolutionary struggle in Russia. The guests circled around, desperate for the rogue gossip.

In the short run, Frida was happy to cede the floor to Diego. She was proud of his fame. Not only had he lived in Russia, but he'd spent time in Paris among the world's most promising artists and thinkers. *Ja, let the fools gather around their gran maestro,* she chuckled to herself. *It pleases me so to watch, the way even the Coyoacán elite fall to their knees when an idol presents himself, behaving just like the Catholics they condemn for their blind allegiance.*

But she could only let it go on for so long. When she sensed the scales tipping, it was time. Because she'd drawn a line in her mind's eye on the night Diego had humiliated her in front of their wedding guests. Never again would she allow him to monopolize center stage at her expense. They were a couple now. It was due time this overgrown toddler learned to share! She'd let her easel gather dust while she orchestrated this event, but it came with a cost, for nothing was free in this world. *Tsk, tsk,* he should've known better.

"Oh, my Diegito, always working so hard." She halted his sermon, sidling up to him, touching his cheek with the back of one hand. "My lover doesn't sleep, dear friends. And he only eats because I must hand-deliver his lunch to the scaffold where he works. That is why I interrupt now, to propose a toast. To no more discussion of Diego's work for just this one evening? I want my love to enjoy a brief respite from the weight of his artistic burdens, este pobrecito." She jiggled the flesh of his cheek between her fingers as if he were a pudgy-faced kid. "Besides, I'm trying to throw a party here—you people are supposed to be drinking and getting lost in the ambiance," she remarked, swiveling her hips. "Certainly not talking about armies and war plans, for crying out loud!

No, camaradas, tonight is about indulgence! For the next few hours, let us all be cast free of the world's woes!" She held up her glass. "And so, Diego, dear guests, here's to an unforgettable night—pues, or a forgettable one." She shrugged her shoulders. "Whichever comes last! ¡Salud!"

The guests roared back, eager to heed her call, to rid themselves of their inhibitions for tonight, to sample from this provocative buffet she was dishing up, one in which exotic beauty, radical politics, and cultural revelry blended seamlessly together, the perfect embodiment of what they were convinced was the only force capable of saving them from the evil políticos and greedy capitalistas. They felt themselves sinking into the night's darkness, losing track of time and conversations, but laughing—always laughing—and also, singing and dancing and eating and all the verbs in the universe until the sun's first rays peeked over the horizon. Only then did they feign embarrassment for having stayed as long as they had, bidding their hosts farewell as they staggered out the door.

Frida shot up in bed early the next afternoon, all the glory from last night's performance still rushing through her veins. She wanted more, *more, MORE!* The thrill of winning them over was exhilarating—naïve fools that they were, blind to the pitfalls of foregoing any semblance of moderation, so convinced by each other's company that nothing could ever touch their goldenness! She hastened to pull on her night jacket, scurrying downstairs to find Diego. Because she needed to confirm that he was as defenseless as they in this regard, that her magic had worked on him, too. She had to know if his craving for self-pleasure and the smugness that came with it was as insatiable as theirs.

She found him at the bright yellow table, sketching ideas for his next mural. She slid into his lap, kissing his neck. He smiled back at her with a guttural snort, pecking her on the lips. When she told him she wanted another party, he assented.

"I know better than to try to keep you from something you want, my Friducha."

Ah, Diego, it is indeed true that any attempt to stop me would be futile. But, oh, how little you know about what I want. I want you more than I want life itself. And I will not hesitate to do whatever it takes to keep you clutched to my breast for eternity, mi amor.

She flew back into action, rushing around like a madwoman trying to outrun her own shadow, wild-eyed and driven by a source called pain. She lived according to a rigid measuring stick she'd created for herself long ago, one that demanded improvement at every step, lest she fail. Which meant this next party would have to be better than the last, more preposterous or baccalaurean, it didn't matter, as long as her victims feasted on her potion. None of this disarmed her in the slightest; she relished a challenge. She could walk, couldn't she? She could fuck Diego Rivera until he begged for rest. Who else dared boast of such feats?

Come to think of it, she realized one night, locked in her room, cigarette in one hand, bottle of whiskey in the other, throwing a party was a little like embarking on a new painting. For what lay before her was an endless stream of possible color schemes and imagery dancing through her consciousness, no final project worth conjecturing about at this point, because she wouldn't know until she got there. It was this journey of finding her way through the greens and the reds, the angular and the fleshy, bit by bit, quadrant by quadrant, that both tormented and enthralled her, turning her into a creative genius with little connection to the real world for the time it took to bring the project to fruition. And it was this fine line between passion and repulsion that fanned her life's work.

Ultimately, she decided the crowning touch to her next event would be to turn the patio into a sort of animal sanctuary. México was at its core an agrarian society, no? And no call to revolution would ever garner enough popular support unless the campesino in all of them was rekindled, no? So she'd have to reeducate her guests; that wouldn't be impossible. She envisioned her new pets slithering and flapping and padding around the property, issuing their native calls, emitting their natural pheromones, staking their ground with grunts and excretions. Not only would such a project serve to reintegrate the countryside into their urban cosmology, but simultaneously, she'd be creating an environment where embarrassment and inhibition disappeared, because primal urges ruled the land. *Pure genius, Frida, brava, ja ja ja!*

When she'd first mentioned her plan, they'd all laughed at her, because "the imprudence, Frida, really!" She'd responded by laughing right back, because fretting about things like clean floors and manicured gardens was nothing but bourgeois frivolity! Had they turned reactionary on her, is that what they were doing, she'd asked point-blank. To which they'd had no response, suddenly self-conscious and meek. Triumphantly, she moved forward, bringing in a parrot, a peacock, two roosters, and a baby deer. *"Squawk-squawk." "Bleat-bleat." "Cock-a-doodle-do." "Baaaa."*

Nat was wholly nonplussed by her decision.

"What, does she think *I'm* gonna be the one to take care of them? That it's my duty to make sure this place doesn't get run into the ground? Yeah, no thanks, I'm not interested." He didn't care about "manicured gardens" either, but, *sheesh*, he wasn't exactly keen on cohabitating in one giant dung heap. He was supposed to be watching over her, not running a zoo. And then there was that other nagging concern, the one that mattered a thousand times more than the first. Which was, what if he were no more important to her than the latest round of imports, as replaceable as a potted geranium, a bird bath, or some other garden toy? What if he wasn't special? Evidence pointed to the contrary, but still, he wondered. He always did.

His first line of defense was to ignore the other animals, as if by turning a blind eye, they didn't exist. Or at least that they were so insignificant, they barely existed. To this end, he overcompensated, walking around with his nose in the air, a book from the StatelySittingRoom tucked under one arm, crisp in his silk waistcoat with the paisley print. No, he was not like the others, bah, nothing at all! But precisely because the other pets had come into the Casa Azul an anarchic bunch, each with his or her unique set of operating rules, they grew unignorable, increasingly bickering and impatient with each day that passed. Ultimately, Nat's inclination to protect his ego at all costs was superseded by his need to assuage his nerves.

"Oye, Paulina, sweetheart, I'll just come straight out and say it: You need to shut up! I'm sorry, that came out harshly; it's just that I've reached my breaking point. I can't take any more of this! You talk too much—has anyone ever told you that? I mean, you've barely shut up in the two weeks you've been here. I'm not asking for perfect silence—I'm a fair guy, you'll see—but the nonstop squawking has got to stop! Not sure what you're used to back in Parrotville, but here at the Casa Azul, afternoons are properly reserved for siestas."

"Paulina wants a peanut! Paulina wants a peanut!"

"Now that is exactly what I'm talking about! I think everyone here is more than aware you'd like a peanut, so why keep repeating yourself when it's gotten you nowhere the first hundred times?" If they were all this dumb, Nat wondered, what had he been worrying about? Proof in point, you better bet he was special! "Truth is, you're lucky no one's given in to your pleas. Because then you'd be dead. Peanuts are toxic to parrots. You know that, right?"

Nat's assailment was followed by an awkward silence. The gravity of their collective situation was sinking in, well beyond the isolated case of Paulina. No, the time had come to choose sides, prepare for war, define the balance of power out here on the patio. There existed no charter to follow, no rules of conduct nailed to the wall. And now this monkey was trying to take charge? Unilaterally imposing order upon their diverse selves? Telling them when it was permissible to squawk and bleat? What next? They'd be required to produce their bodily waste in designated spots according to a schedule? What about their individual preferences and innate tendencies? Did those not matter anymore? Oh, and another thing: Did they really want a leader who got all dressed up like a human but refused to wear pants? What was that about?

"Is that true? That I could've *(gulp)* . . . died?"

"Yes, Paulina, I'm afraid it is," replied Nat, standing over the lip of his nest to gaze down upon the others. "Look, I don't want to be a bully, really. But there's a lot going on around here, and Zoe and I have found that a little peace and quiet in the afternoons does a lot to soothe our anxiety levels. MyDoe, you're fine, I got no problem with you—oh, except leave some moss for the resident bugs, will you? As for you roosters, GalloUno y GalloDos, you guys have to stop all that squabbling! It just adds one more layer of stress to this already boiling pot with that peck-peck-pecking you do. And, dear god, LordPeacock, you're lovely, but that screeching of yours makes my skin crawl."

The pets were silent, absorbing their respective slaps on the claw, wing, and hoof. That is, except for LordPeacock, who chose that moment to reveal for the umpteenth time since he'd arrived the majesty of his train. The colors fanned out before them, a hypnotic display of downy glitter in turquoise and teal and purple, a thousand watchful eyes on perpetual alert. It was a finely spun act of resistance for having just been treated in a manner inferior to what his title suggested he was worthy of.

"I will have you know, Mister bossy-monkey, that I do not 'screech.' Screech sounds barbaric, and I assure you, I am none of that! The sound I emit is referred to as a 'scream,' okay? Which implies greater intention and a higher consciousness. Not only am I nice on the eyes, but I'm highly civilized. And you should also know that the scream you so rudely referenced is highly useful in the wild. For it enables the male to draw a predator's attention away from his mate, to protect her, a noble endeavor indeed! I just thought you should know," boasted LordPeacock, now strutting circles around the PoutingTree, neck stretched to its natural limit.

"Well, if that's true, LordPeacock, then perhaps we've all been saved! Maybe we can sic you on the UglyFrogMan, you know, fix this giant mess we're in!" Nat was peeved with the peacock and frustrated with the pets' general tendency toward pandemonium. But he also recognized there was a larger evil to confront. "Because Zoe and I can tell you that bastard has zero understanding of protecting *his* mate!"

"Oh, no! Is someone in danger?" gasped MyDoe, breaking from her standard pose—which was silently staring at the nose on her face.

"Yes, yes, someone is," Nat sighed. "It's our dear friend, her name is Frida, she's the one who runs this place. Unfortunately—and I mean of the most unfortunate-unfortunate kind here—she's taken on a horrible mate called the UglyFrogMan. And this guy, *whoaaa*, this guy makes my bowels turn loose! He's a horrible, insensitive bastard, which, to make a long story short, has put our dear Frida in jeopardy. Zoe and I are very worried about her."

Again, the patio fell silent. This time, it was because their native inclinations had been reawakened by Nat's speech. Socially, they'd been preprogrammed to cooperate with their respective genera, as a means of survival in the wild. Hence, neither bickering nor divisiveness was inherent to their primary familial unit. And since the bossy monkey sure was coming out of this looking like a loyal guy, the way he was so concerned for this Frida person, would it be terribly wrong if they went ahead and put aside some of their genus-specific concerns? Maybe agreed to a few of his ground rules?

"I digress though. Let's get back to how we might be best able to manage ourselves out here. I'd like to clarify that I'm not opposed to all screaming—well, and whatever other odd behaviors the rest of you are genetically programmed to engage in, that's okay, too. All I'm asking for is that we respect each other's presence, try not to get in each other's way."

The newbies had gathered together in a semicircle around the PoutingTree, shooting each other furtive glances, casting silent ballots, because it was getting down to the wire: did they or did they not want to place themselves under the guidance of the bossy monkey?

"Excuse me, Nat." It was LordPeacock stepping in, figuratively and literally, because he'd moved a body-length in front of the crowd of pets to be heard. "About this Frida person? Please let it be known that, henceforth, I do solemnly volunteer the services of my magical train to distract the UglyFrogMan upon your request. Consider me armed and ready!" he squawked, stepping back to his position among the others.

"Yes, me too, I can help! I know how to look deceivingly innocent."

"Count me in! I'm going to teach myself how to spray peanuts from my beak like bullets—without swallowing nary a one of them, of course, ja ja ja!"

"*Bleat!*" "*Peck!*" "*Scream!*" "*Yip!*"

Nat was surprised by the way his heart swelled at the outpouring, that it touched some part of him he hadn't even known was there, because he'd been too red in the face over the other pets impeding on his domain to notice the possibility of camaraderie right in front of his nose. He chided himself for being too quick to pass judgement, for constructing boundaries to separate himself from them, all to prove that he was more important to Frida than the rest of them. It didn't have to be a zero-sum game, now, did it? They all wanted the same things—peace on the home front, the triumph of good over evil. And so, Nat dubbed them the PatioPets, a battalion of ragtag fauna come together with the noble mission of rescuing Frida from the evil clutches of the UglyFrogMan. Had he not been so delighted by what had just transpired, he might've wondered from where he'd learned this drive towards social stratification. But otherwise preoccupied, the thought didn't cross his mind.

"Pancho, have your crew distribute the animals the way we discussed, will you?" It was the day of the party and the PatioPets' grand unveiling. "Natural, remember. It needs to feel like the patio belongs to them as much as it does to you or me, all of us living here together in synchrony, creatures belonging to a larger whole—oh, no! Not there, Alfonso, what are you doing?" She'd been preaching one vision when she'd noticed something gone awry on the other side of the patio, rushing off in that direction now to correct the workers who were arranging the candles along the raised flowerbeds, because they belonged along the staircase outside her room, for when she made her grand entrance! Hadn't she made that clear? So much work to do, she sighed to herself. Couldn't anyone get a single thing right?

Only when the sky turned mauve and she'd quadruple-checked that her stage was impeccably set did she move upstairs to prepare for her role in this upcoming performance. Taking her time, she slipped casually into the tehuana gown she'd so carefully laid out, then twisted her hair into knots and buns with pins and ribbons and scarves. She paused when she was done, raising her snifter of vodka as she looked into the mirror. A sly grin spread across her face. *Facíl, there's nothing to this.* And then she pulled up a chair by the window, and she watched them come in.

And, oh, how it was worth every grueling hour she'd put into this project, watching their faces soften when they spotted placid MyDoe and then fragile Zoe. And their jaws drop in wonderment when Lord-Peacock unfurled his full beauty. And also, their egregious chuckling as they observed the Gallos pecking fruitlessly at the cement ground. But by far the most fulfilling was watching their surprise upon noticing Nat, debonair in his handmade silk smoking jacket and matching top hat as he stood leaning with one shoulder against the PoutingTree, ankles crossed and arms folded neatly over his chest. (She'd had to goad him into coming out of his nest for the evening, arguing that his presence always put her at ease—knowing full well that he'd be unable to refuse her.) When Frida had seen enough, she moved downstairs to relish what she'd so carefully concocted.

"Oh, my goodness! That isn't a real monkey in that tree, is it?" wondered a blond woman with a finger waves hairdo and large hooded eyes. Nat had lived up to his end of the bargain by serving as part of the welcoming crew, having subsequently retreated to his nest.

Come on, lady! No, I'm a stuffed doll! And for your information, not only am I a "real monkey," I'm a master sleuth, a brilliant philosopher, and an important mentor for all the other pets here!

"Why won't that parrot take this peanut?" asked another befuddled guest. "I thought parrots loved peanuts. So why does this bird keep hissing at me? What, is he stupid or something?"

That parrot is named Paulina, and she happens to know a hell of a lot more about avian toxicity than you obviously do, you moron!

"Yes, the monkey is real," Frida intervened with a commanding voice, then placed one finger over her lips. "*Shhh*, he's my favorite of all the pets. He's been with me since childhood. Such a dear. Seen me through some very difficult times," she cooed up at him, nodding her appreciation. "All the shared history, all the trauma we've endured together. Which is why I'm very protective of him. That monkey means the world to me. And I am *never* letting him get away," hissed Frida with clenched fists, closing in on the blond with the hooded eyes, then glaring right through her. *I've seen the way Diego looks at you, you whore! And also, I've seen the way you return his furtive glances. But he is my husband, so keep the fuck away from him!*

"Oh, interesting fact!" She changed her tone. "When he first came to us, I found it perplexing why he was spending so much time tucked away up there in his nest. Was he frightened in his new landscape? Was he lonely for spider monkey companionship? What was it that was so captivating up there, I wondered. In search of answers, I retreated to my library, and I began digging around for everything I could learn on animal behavior. Now, friends, cover your ears if what I'm about to reveal is too risqué—which it shouldn't be, or you'd be better off at one of those dull, polite-society events with starched white napkins and discussions about the weather forecast!" She paused for the uncomfortable laughter to die down.

"Well," she continued, "it turns out that my lovely Nat and his brethren are quite fond of the self-pleasuring practice," she smirked. And then she turned around briskly, because they'd have to stay on their toes if they hoped to follow her argument. "But then again, I'm not one to believe something simply because the literature says so . . ."

Nat jumped to his feet. Yes, he should've smelled it coming! Frida was twisting things around, to catch them with their pants down! *¡Eso es! Brava, Frida, trapping them in their hypocrisies and preconceived notions!*

". . . because that would be the lazy way out, an unsophisticated interpretation of a much more complicated reality. The truth is, my Nahuatl here cannot be reduced to an encyclopedia entry, one that simplifies him into some primordial, underdeveloped, urge-centered beast."

Oh, yeah! You tell 'em, Frida! Nat thought, swinging one arm across his torso victoriously.

"What I came to realize is that all the reading I did had less to do with spider monkeys in particular, and more to do with the male condition in general. Why is it, I ask you, that we pass judgement on the monkey for being unrefined and raunchy? But for those of you in pants here tonight who happen to share these very same qualities, do we not applaud you for flaunting your virility? Unfortunately, I've no answer to my own question, and I've accepted that. In fact, you might say that I've learned to live quite comfortably in this world where a man's sexual drive makes the earth spin round. Dare I say, I've become exceptionally skilled at taking care of the male drive under my rooftop." She winked at Diego. And then she turned around to glare at the blond with the hooded eyes.

Kerplunk, went Nat's heart, sinking into the pit of his stomach, alternating images of ThatAlejandro and garden tchotchkes flashing through his mind. *But I am more than an encyclopedia entry, Frida! Tell them! Tell them about my multilingualism and my tailoring prowess!*

"Ja ja ja!" went the guests, their hostess's erotic nuances opening the night to deeper, more forbidden possibilities.

When the uproar died down, one of the bravest stepped forward, swallowing his fear and daring to toss his hat into the ring of immodesty she'd created.

"Say, Frida, maybe you should get that horny little monkey a pair of pants? Maybe that would solve the problem?" he posited, hands clasped proudly in front of him.

"He doesn't care for pants," is all she said. *Have you missed the whole point? I was talking about you, you bastard, about human patriarchy and misogyny! Not my monkey! Shush with your unimaginative wisecrack! This party is not about you. This party is mine!*

"Now, about the parrot. Please, follow me into the dining area, won't you? So we can be seated for dinner. I'll tell you what I know about her, which isn't much, unfortunately. She's relatively new here, you see . . ." her voice trailed off as she entered the house, a flock of guests trailing behind her.

As Nat turned toward the comfort of his nest, where he intended to minister to the ego-whipping he'd just suffered, he noticed that the guest who'd just tried to insert himself onstage with Frida hadn't gone inside with the rest of them. Instead, he was seated there alone on a bench off to one side of the patio, shoulders slack, hands tucked under his thighs. *Oh, the endless wake she leaves behind.* Nat shook his head one more time before leaping face-first into the darkness of his nest.

Within three years, Frida had won them over. It was all they talked about anymore: when was the next event, what novelty would be unveiled, who would be there, what would she wear? In the beginning,

they adored her, for being in her company was nothing short of enchanting, like her presence cast all the colors of the rainbow onto an
otherwise black-and-white frame. But then, they began to envy her.
Because she wasn't the fragile doll they'd once assumed—quite the
opposite, in fact. They hadn't seen it coming, the way, quietly, steadily,
she'd grown her stature, continually becoming more alluring, more unorthodox, more tawdry, until she'd amassed everything they wanted.
Only then did they realize that they resented her—*that bitch!*—which
was fine by her. It was one thing to be a novelty, an on-loan exhibit
passing through their museum of alternative wonders. It was another
entirely to be promoted to crown jewel, placed on a marble pedestal.
Whether they liked her or not was inconsequential; she only cared that
they were paying attention.

She chewed them up, spit them out, because it was their hypocrisy
that led to their demise. Their devotion to the hierarchy-less hierarchy,
comrades in arms; all that other lofty talk was baseless. For their credo
was doomed to shatter the moment one of them transcended the parameters they'd so carefully and strategically erected around their little
circle to forbid others from entering. Their jealousy made them fanatical, desperate to know more about her so they could be closer to her
somehow, to the power she had amassed when they'd stopped paying
due attention. They reduced themselves to boorishness, if that's what
it took—sneaking into the kitchen in search of the magical ingredients
that went into her cooking, studying her jewelry so they could seek out
similar pieces, attentive to the way she moved her hands, her eyes, her
lips, anything to garner something more about her, something to take
home with them, to try on in front of the mirror later that night.

But by far what pleased Frida the most was that Diego noticed the
attention she'd garnered. For he, too, was greatly impressed by attention. She was aware that he'd already begun taking lovers—she wasn't
happy about it—but so immense was his pleasure at the limelight she'd
designed to land on both of them that he rushed to be by her side for

every one of their appearances. Frida and Diego loved each other, to be sure. They also loved being loved. Which love was more potent remained to be seen.

And then the state of affairs was thrown into chaos when Diego was commissioned for several art projects in the United States, the scope of which would require he be gone a few years. Initially, Frida had balked at joining him, because why should she abandon all the celebrity she'd masterminded here at home? On the other hand, it would allow the rest of the world a peek at Diego's exotic bride, expanding her reputation—well, and also, disproving the baseless gossip abroad that she was no more than "the young Mexican girl" who "hung herself on el maestro's arm." No, such idle chatter could not go unchecked! She'd have to go, prove them wrong, just like she'd done here at home. She knew her enemy was ubiquitous, sprouting new heads when she thought she'd destroyed them. But she was not afraid. She welcomed the challenge.

Oh, and there was one more impetus for going. The real one. She didn't trust Diego to go alone. Every time she imagined all the lonely, art-collecting wives of wealthy industrialists he'd be meeting with, and all the female intelligentsia with their provocative flair who frequented the art gallery scene, her stomach twisted in knots. Yes, he would be unfaithful no matter their living arrangement, but she needed him to return to her at the end of the day, as proof that she mattered, that he loved her as deeply as he professed. That she was special, different from the others.

And so, she packed up her tehuana gowns, huipiles, and rebozos, shoving them into an oversized trunk. And she'd need her lipsticks, perfume vials, and nail polishes. Plus, her obsidian necklaces, onyx earrings, and decorative hair scarves. She would be the antithesis to those manufactured bourgeoisie bitches, spotlighting their blandness through the telescope of her erotic, colorful sensuality and her roguish wit.

"Pablo, get this last bag for me, won't you? I've got one last thing to do." It was the morning of their departure.

"Frida, we're late already! We can't—"

"Please, Diego," she said gravely. "It won't take long."

He nodded his consent. She gathered her long skirts in both fists and hurried down the stairs to the PoutingTree.

"Nat, I must speak to you, please! It's important!"

He was hesitant to jump to attention. He was sore with her. All these weeks of planning the trip, and not once had she come by to discuss it with him. She'd checked with Guillermo and Matilde, then Conchita, and finally, the lead gardener about whether they thought her going was a good idea. But never had she checked with him. And worse yet, she'd given no indication that she might miss him. That she was coming to him in the eleventh hour felt like insult to injury. He considered feigning his own absence. But then again, he'd never been able to tell her no. He poked his face cautiously over the lip of his nest.

"Oh, good, you're there." She bowed her head, shaking it with relief. "Zoe, you too, please, I have something to say—well, and all of you PatioPets, I want you all to hear this." She clasped her hands together just below her waist, fingers fidgeting. "I'm sorry," she hiccuped through this first part. "I don't even know all your names yet. It's embarrassing, really. I've been so sidetracked lately, which is why I've come to you now."

She looked up at Nat with the same pleading eyes of her youth, so desperately seeking his approval.

"I'm here to say goodbye. And to let you know that when I get back, I'm going to make a real effort to do a better job of prioritizing you pets. Because I do care, though it might not seem like it right now. Nat, I wanted you to know that I'm taking this." She tilted her head to one side so he could see the peineta pinned in place, a timid smile on her face. "In case this Monarch Princess lands in a scrap and needs a way out." *I'm scared, Nat. I'm really, really scared. It's so far away from the Casa Azul, from Conchita, from you! Whatever will I do?*

"*Free-dah!* Vamos, we have a train to catch, querida."

"I have to go—but I'll write you, I promise! Ciao, my loves, take good care!" Her fingertips were shaking as she blew them kisses, then dashed across the patio, Diego meeting her halfway to prod her forward without further delay.

If she'd stayed another moment, she would have seen in Nat's eyes what he was aching to tell her. *I'm scared, too, Frida. I'm scared you're suffocating under the pressure of trying to keep him content, and that you won't have any support so far away!* But she was already gone.

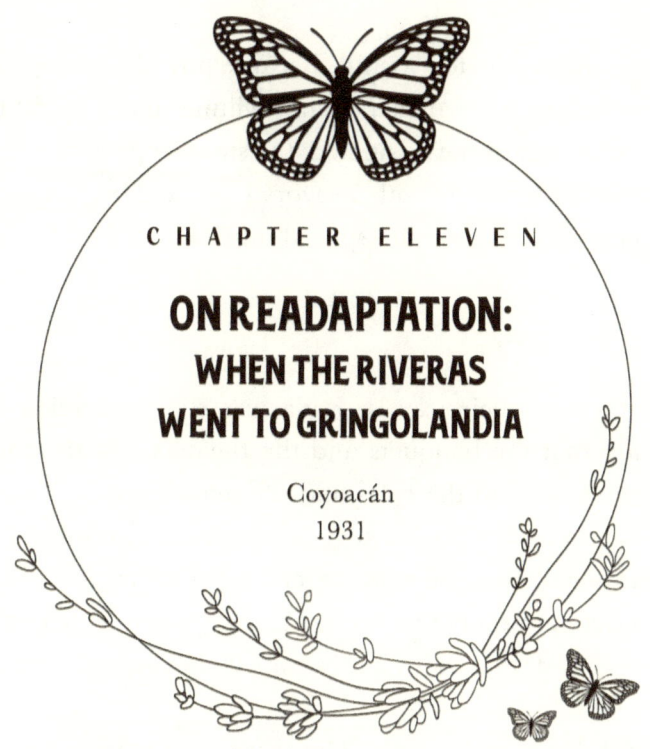

CHAPTER ELEVEN

ON READAPTATION:
WHEN THE RIVERAS
WENT TO GRINGOLANDIA

Coyoacán
1931

The house was eerily quiet without her. Gone was the weekly caravan of delivery wagons that used to pull up to the curb, an army of helpers leaping out to unload the milk and the meat and the produce she'd ordered for her upcoming event. As were the daily visits from the elderly flower vendor, whom they warmly called LaFlorona, with her waist-length gray hair twisted into braids as thick as a grown man's knuckles, a smile as wide as she was tall, an armload of gladiolas so robust she had to lean to one side to stay afoot. Without a party to throw, there was no need.

Nat had expected to find relief in the suspension of the raucous gatherings; instead, he felt wistful. Because now the house was too still, stagnating in its own silence and wilting under its drabness. The scent of her perfume dissipated, the stove stopped hissing with dollops of oil portending another savory feast, and the flora refused to show their buds without her special touch.

Two months into their travels, Frida was still pretending things were grand, that the banquets and the theaters and the cabarets and the art shows and the cafes and the manufacturing tours and the public parks were fascinating, unimaginable, futuristic, alluring, inspirational. Because it would crush her father to know. And just as importantly, there was no fucking way she'd let her enemies know, why, they'd drag down her carcass if they sensed even a hint of weakness.

Nat and Zoe knew, though. This was because Frida had set up a private correspondence for just the two of them, via the mailman Luis, who'd been instructed to pass on her mail directly to them and only them. As such, the fact that Frida was miserable was privy to Nat and Zoe alone.

She wrote long-winded letters explaining that Diego was too busy with work to have much time for her, which left her feeling terribly alone. It's not that she was unfamiliar with loneliness *("shit, I've spent half my life in bed")*, but this time felt different:

I imagine that I've been kidnapped, dragged to an abandoned factory warehouse, and the world I occupy exists solely in black and white. It's dusty and cold, but also heavy with grit and silence. I'm strapped to an unknown piece of machinery that spins around and around, slowly though, so I can make out remnants of what this place used to be—rusted metal crates, blueprint pages crumpled on the ground, inoperable wires hung up hap-

*hazardly, spiderwebs. Around I go, the spinning never ceasing, making me
wonder if I'm doomed to this existence. It horrifies me that no one knows
I'm being kept here. Or worse yet, that no one's realized I'm even gone.*

Making things worse, Diego was having an entirely opposite
experience. He basked in his celebrity status, of course, but he was
also smitten with the wonders of industrialization, fascinated by
the cogs and wheels and machines that she so despised. Oh, how
she maligned the artificiality of the steel scaffolding all around her,
and the sunless streets boxed in by skyscrapers, and the relentless
soot that caused her coughing fits! And, oh, how she missed the way
the magenta bougainvillea exploded against the patio's indigo blue
walls, the sounds of her father sifting through boxes of clunky cam-
era equipment in his studio, and the smell of Conchita's simmering
caldo with the mysterious ingredients she refused to divulge, because it was her ancestors' ancestors' recipe, and it was their knowledge of village secrets that still flowed through her veins alone.

The heaviness weighed on the pets, oftentimes sending them
into the streets to wander aimlessly after reading one of her letters,
circling around until the pads of their feet turned raw and they
were too weary to feel her pain anymore. For better or for worse,
they'd begun making ritual stops at the CornerBar on their way
home after one of these meccas of doom. Though they knew alcohol was only an illusory cure, they longed for the tingle in their
bellies that came with the first round, and how, after a few more,
they became enveloped in a glowy warmth, reassured in each other's presence that things were bound to turn around soon.

Nat was leaning with his back against the wall, one ankle tucked
over the other, while Zoe relaxed on her haunches next to him, just

a monkey and a dog anxious to hear how things were going over there in Detroit or New York or San Francisco or wherever Frida and Diego's travels had taken them. Good fortune struck that day: Luis the mailman arrived with a letter in hand.

"I have something here addressed to . . . a Nat . . . and a Zoe? Is that you?" smirked Luis, referring to their shared secret, including the fact that this same thing occurred often.

"Thanks, Luis. See you tomorrow." Nat tipped his hat as he tore off one corner of the envelope with his teeth *(pinche thumb-less-ness)*, shaking the contents into one palm, and then rushing to read her words:

Nat y Zoe,

Estoy embarazada.
Yes, you read correctly. I'm with child. I'll write you more soon. In the meantime, reciben mis abrazos fuertes,

Tu Frida, XOXO

Nat and Zoe were speechless, each waiting for the other to say something, or burst out crying, or laughing, or run for the hills without looking back, so unsure what sort of response was warranted. How Nat wished for Frida's happiness, but given her medical history, he knew the chance of the fetus surviving was unlikely. And that regardless of the baby's health, a pregnancy was sure to wreak havoc on her already fragile body. Plus, there was the father to consider. So, no, this wouldn't have been his first choice—getting rid of him altogether was his first choice. But if this was what she wanted . . . Flustered and confused, Nat could think of nothing else to do but start working on a bonnet for the baby. He decided on green—he wasn't sure why, perhaps because it seemed more neutral than blue or pink?

Days went by, and then a month, then one more, without a word from Frida.

"Do you think she's had the baby yet? It's been more than fifty days!"

"I'm afraid the human gestation period is a bit longer than the canine's fifty days, though sometimes I do wonder if their offspring might emerge a little more benevolent if their process were more like yours or mine, ja ja ja! Anyway, looks like we're about to get an answer. Here comes Luis!"

"Hey, kids! How's your day?"

Nat wasn't in the mood for chatting today, grabbing the letter from Luis, barely squeezing in a terse "thank you" before turning around, tearing open the envelope, skipping over any pretense of formality to get right to its contents.

"It says, 'I want to die right now . . .'" He paused, rereading the opening line, then scanning through the rest.

"What? Tell me what it says!" spat out Zoe.

"Oh, no, she lost the baby! She says, um . . . she was feeling okay . . . and then she hemorrhaged . . . 'It was like a dam opened between my decrepit legs, the blood spewing forth like a broken faucet.' This is horrible, 'the sinewy fiber that was my placenta slid to the floor, returning to the ground from which it was sprung, useless now, just like me.' This is too much, Zoe, I can't." He didn't want to read anymore; nor did Zoe want to hear anymore. They got the gist of it.

Nat went straight to the PoutingTree, taking out the baby bonnet he'd been working on, pulling the stitches apart with his needles, huffing and puffing as he worked to undo everything he'd worked to do. He loathed that silly bonnet! And he loathed the shade of green he'd chosen. Mostly, he loathed that he was finding it so easy to loathe these days.

As if that weren't enough, while Frida was recuperating, her mother died. It was a double-whammy, an uppercut to the jaw when you're already bent over at the middle clutching your gut, neck snapping back in utter disbelief because how could this happen? No child, and now no mother. It was true that Frida had never been particularly close to Matilde, but she was her mother. Whether Frida chose to follow along with her mother's direction or veer a hard right, her choices were, at least indirectly, in response to the foundation Matilde had provided her.

As much as it had been Frida's intention to keep her parents from finding out the truth about her state of mind, Matilde's death, in conjunction with the miscarriage, proved too heavy, and she'd relented to sharing her personal news with her father, widening her circle of confidants from two to three. In an attempt to lighten her load even if it meant further burdening his, Nat promised Frida he'd try consoling Guillermo.

"Hi, Guillermo," Nat said, standing in the doorway of his photography studio one day. "Mind if I join you—while you work, of course, I know you're busy." Which obviously he wasn't. The only evidence of activity was a half-finished bottle of whiskey on his desk and a rumpled blanket tossed over a chair in the corner.

"Yes, of course, Nat, please do. I'm afraid I might be poor company, though. I'm putting together a proposal for some photographs I have in mind." He scattered some papers around on his desktop with the palm of one hand in a futile effort to support his claim. "*Errrr,* let's see, can I offer you a drink? I've got some whiskey here somewhere . . . where . . . ah, yes, there it is." He picked up the bottle sitting in front of him, raising it in Nat's direction.

"Sure, please, why not?" Other than it was ten in the morning. Nat hopped onto the desk, taking a seat there on his bare bottom, letting Guillermo slip a snifter between his palms. "How're you doing? You know . . . what with everything that's been going on?" He took a giant gulp of his whiskey, hoping a little fortified courage might help him get through the awkwardness.

"Oh, Nat," he sighed, folding into his chair, smoothing back his hair with one hand. "I've been better. I loved Matilde—a woman tightly wound, yes, but she was a good mother. And she kept our household intact. Nothing is perfect, you know, but I really did love her." Then came a stuttered sigh. "But it's Frida I grieve for now. The loss of a child she'll never hold is one thing, but pile on top of that Diego's inability to remain loyal even as she suffers? She must be demoralized. My poor Frida is too young for all this pain!"

"Maybe there's something we can do? Or I can do—I know you're busy, with deadlines and whatnot. Just tell me. I'll do it, Guillermo."

"That's very kind of you, Nat. If only I knew how to make that happen. Once upon a time, I welcomed a young monkey into my home, and then a lovely little dog, because I thought it would make her happy. But bad luck seems to follow that poor girl everywhere." He leaned into his elbows on his desk. "Just keep in contact with her, will you? She loves me—I don't question that. But it's you she confides in."

"Okay, Guillermo, you have my word."

But it's you she confides in! But it's you she confides in! Yes, the conversation had been somber, but Nat left the studio feeling like he was on cloud nine. Sometimes a little pick-me-up was all a guy needed to keep on being impressive, he smiled to himself.

Meanwhile, Frida's letters to the pets grew increasingly desperate. It was as if she'd discovered a corollary to her painting, a sanctuary in written words, such that she felt comfortable laying bare her most vulnerable vulnerabilities, a sacred space her enemies did not have access to. One such correspondence described the pain she'd felt when her younger sister, Cristina, was born, for Matilde had taken Cristina to her teat, handing over eleven-month-old Frida to a wet nurse.

My mother never loved me like she did Cristina. From the moment my sister came into this world, I was demoted to second best. Then there was Alejandro who cast me aside after the accident. And, of course, now there is Diego, who pierces my heart every time he takes another lover. Am I not worthy of love? If I'd been blessed with a child of my own, how I would have poured my passion into that baby, to reverse the negative flow that has defined my entire life, to pass along unwavering love to the one with my blood.

Unbeknownst to anyone, Nat was deeply and personally affected by her words, making him wonder about his relationship with his own mother in a more profound way than he'd ever allowed himself. Sure, there'd been that brief interaction with Bobo the other spider monkey, but that proved fleeting. He was glad about the life decisions he'd made—on this point, he was clear. And yet, he itched to know what had happened to Mamá and to his Troop-mates, and most important of all, what "unwavering love" felt like. And though he knew Frida was in a dangerously despondent state, he sat down and he wrote a letter to the only one who might understand.

He started off with the basic formalities: sending his heartfelt condolences and gracefully acknowledging that while he couldn't possibly understand her grief, his thoughts were with her. It was at this point that he moved on to his personal angst, that after a deep dive into the works of Sigmund Freud, he'd come to suspect that his premature separation from Mamá had left him without proper closure. He'd long ago separated from her physically, but emotionally, well, that was a different story. He believed that because of this stunted stage in his development, he'd been forced to seek out connectedness and acceptance to a degree far out of proportion with reality.

I've come to believe that childhood without a mother, emotionally or physically, is a chronic disease, as the symptoms of self-doubt and betrayal never let us rest. In one moment, I see myself as a gentleman savant—an intellectual wizard with poignantly clever wit. But in the next, that all too familiar feeling of self-consciousness seeps back in, and I'm a groveling fool, begging for scraps of approval like a street urchin. My dear friend, I lay bare here my tender soul, for you alone, because it is you with whom I feel this most special connection. As such, I am placing my heart in your hands for safekeeping. Please, take haste and write me soon, will you promise? I fear I won't sleep until I hear back—

He slammed his pen down in shame. What was he doing? She'd never shown any interest in who he was before arriving at the Casa Azul. So why would she now? Or worse yet, what if she laughed at his confessions? And yet, he longed for her words, for any comfort she might be able to impart, for more details about the maternal slights she'd suffered, so that they might compare notes, commiserate toward healing. He knew he'd be taking a risk. But he also knew he had to try. And so, with shaky paw, he signed his name, and then he handed the letter off to Luis.

Time passed, and no word came from Frida. Nat did not take it well, cutting himself off from the PatioPets, neglecting his physical presentation (wearing the same seersucker jacket for twenty-five days straight, for example), and even passing up Conchita's famous caldo (instead, consuming the bugs that resided in the PoutingTree in an effort to recall any repressed memories from his days in the JungleTent).

Zoe tried drawing him out—inviting him into the streets for a round of "The Daffy Detective," or to the dulcería for a bag of his favorite candies. But he always had an excuse for why he couldn't: his throat was sore, a sweater needed hemming, his belly button was due for a cleaning, anything to stay tucked away in his nest. Zoe posited that perhaps Frida's return letter had gotten lost in the mail, or maybe her pen had run out of ink. But Nat would have none of it.

Zoe grew concerned. It wasn't like Nat not to participate in life. No, Nat was supposed to be at the center of it, impelling them forward with games and jokes and wisdom. And so, she made a unilateral decision to share with the PatioPets what was going on with Frida—and as a ramification, Nat's downslide—with the hope that, together, they might be able to distract him, because she'd never seen him like this.

"Maybe," she told them, "our broken shepherd needs a little shepherding of his own this time."

"Nat? Zoe? We'd like to call a meeting. We know it's not our place, that you guys have seniority and everything. It just, well, it just seemed . . . important?" LordPeacock was standing at the base of the PoutingTree, the other pets fanned out behind him. It was exactly as Zoe and the bunch of them had planned it.

Nat had been face down in his nest for days now (yes, in the same seersucker jacket, going on thirty-eight days now), ruing the day he'd let Frida go to the US, and even more so, that he'd put that silly letter in the mail. He'd become disturbingly preoccupied with an event that had occurred years ago, when he and Frida had gone for a bicycle ride in the neighborhood (of course Nat could ride a bike—the way the vehicle's chain worked was, in fact, quite similar to tree swinging in regard to the relevance of the law of inertia), and she'd popped a tire. Ever the dramatist, she'd dropped to the ground in a puddle, hands over face, whining like her toenails had just been systematically peeled off. Thankfully, Nat had with him his sewing kit, which included a precut patch that he subsequently applied to the tire, and voilà, off they went again. On the one hand, it was a poignant story of friendship. On the other hand, it was also a poignant story of the imbalance in the aforementioned friendship. Nat felt like that popped tire right now, deflated and empty. And nobody was coming to his rescue with a patch to put over his punctured heart.

"What is it, LordPeacock? I'm terribly busy up here—researching . . . on how to make myself into a gentleman . . . so I can go and do impressive things." He winced at the fallaciousness of his alibi. *Sheesh, all this gentleman has taught himself recently is how to sleep comfortably in his own excrement rather than face the day.*

"I'll make it quick then. The gang and I have been talking . . . about Frida . . . and all the bad stuff that's happened to her. Zoe told us." Best to avoid the truth, that the PatioPets were more worried about Nat than Frida. And because they knew Nat would be too proud to accept charity, the PatioPets had agreed to use Frida as their guise.

"Oh?" He shot a glare in Zoe's direction. "I wasn't aware Zoe had taken the liberty of sharing that news with you. I'd thought the two of us had been sworn to keep it under wraps."

"Yes, well, she told us, which seems fair, no? We had consensus, remember? When the rest of us pets first arrived, and we were trying to figure out how things were going to work around here? And the one thing we could all agree on was dedicating ourselves to helping Frida?"

"Yes, well, I suppose this is true. Go on, please."

"Well, we think we might've come up with a way to help." Lord-Peacock was nervous. They'd made him their spokesperson, which normally was a role he'd have leapt at, but he liked Nat, and he didn't want to step on his toes. Especially not now, when he was letting himself wither away up there in that nest, disengaged from the world he once commanded. LordPeacock took one deep breath, exhaling slowly, and then he delivered the plan the pets had concocted.

"What if we were to come together and do something nice for Frida, to welcome her home, whenever that may be? One collective show of sympathy? Obviously, a party is one option, but considering Frida's, how shall we say, destructive tendencies surrounding parties, we were thinking maybe a piece of theater would be more fitting? Or an operatic rendition of some sort?" The patio fell silent, waiting for Nat to respond, because the whole plan depended on what came out of his mouth next.

Though Nat wanted to stay mad at Zoe for going behind his back, his interest had been piqued. He began by wiping a week's worth of sleep from his eyes, then shaking off the dung stuck to his rear end, and finally, pulling himself to standing position. "Yes, I hear you. Continue."

"I wanna be Puck! I wanna be Puck! Can I be Puck?" Paulina blurted out, ruffling her feathers and puffing herself up, a diva with the stuff to prove it.

"Uh, Paulina? I think you're getting ahead of yourself." LordPeacock laughed nervously, afraid he was losing control of his troop already. They'd discussed this, that they couldn't force anything on Nat. It was imperative that he believe that it was he who was behind whatever plan they decided on. "Nat, I'd merely suggested to the others that *A Midsummer Night's Dream* might be an interesting choice if we were to decide upon theater. And that's a big 'if'—though of course I would gladly offer my humble services as director, if that's the route decided on."

"I like what I'm hearing, LordPeacock," said Nat, launching himself from his nest in a single sweep, then shimmying down to join the others. "That you've thought of a comedy is commendable, for her mood will surely need lifting," he continued, this time with the regular haughtiness they'd once assumed they disliked, but realized in this moment was enormously comforting. "But I worry about the farcical treatment of marriage in *A Midsummer Night's Dream*. Zoe, what are your thoughts on the matter?"

"*Hmmm,*" she mused, giving herself the necessary time to feign that all of this was news to her, pretending that she and the PatioPets hadn't already come up with a backup plan, the script for which was now in her hands. "While I like the idea of theater in general, the problem I see is that when the curtain goes down, the gift has expired. What if we were to create something tangible? Perhaps something we make for her, with our hands and our claws and our hooves?" She gulped in a mouthful of air and held it there.

Nat nodded his chin at her, flapping one hand to entice more detail.

"Well, as I think about it," she said on the exhale, "we happen to be in the presence of a master tailor—one who, I hope, might be willing to oversee a project of this nature?" When she looked at Nat this time, she saw the hint of a smile, so she hurried on. "Yes, and under Nat's supervision, what if each of us was given a square of cloth, to embellish as we saw fit, with the goal of making it emblematic of who we are as individuals? So Frida can get to know us—she did say she wanted to get to know the rest of you, remember?"

The other pets wagged their heads, not so much because the idea itself set their hearts on fire, but because Zoe was handling her part of their plan like a seasoned pro. Nat was really eating it up.

"And then, what if we stitched all those pieces together into a single patchwork quilt, one she could wrap herself up in and think of our friendship?"

"Yes, Zoe, I like that idea! And yes, I'd be honored to take charge of such a meaningful endeavor!" Nat had begun pacing in front of the group, arms tucked behind his back the way he did when he was thinking through a puzzle. "Let's see, we'll need needles and thread—oh, and oodles of thimbles—trust me, getting started can be rather tricky—or should I say, pricky, ja ja ja!"

"Ja ja ja!" It was a horrible pun, sophomoric in a way that made him cringe. But they all laughed anyway. Because it was laughter, and Nat had initiated it.

"You know what? Why don't I dash out right now and gather a few items? We should get started right away! There's no telling when Frida might be returning, and we'll need to give ourselves plenty of time. The sin pulga is not a simple stitch to master, be forewarned, and my expectations will be high. Yes, that's it, I'll head out right now, be back in a jiffy," Nat babbled on through his mental list of supplies as he strode toward the door.

"¿Oye, Zoe? Will you ask Conchita to bring us a bottle of tequila?" he called back over his shoulder from the doorway. "It's about time we had some fun around here, wouldn't you say? All of this for Frida, of course."

"Yes, Nat, for Frida," the others sang back in a single voice.

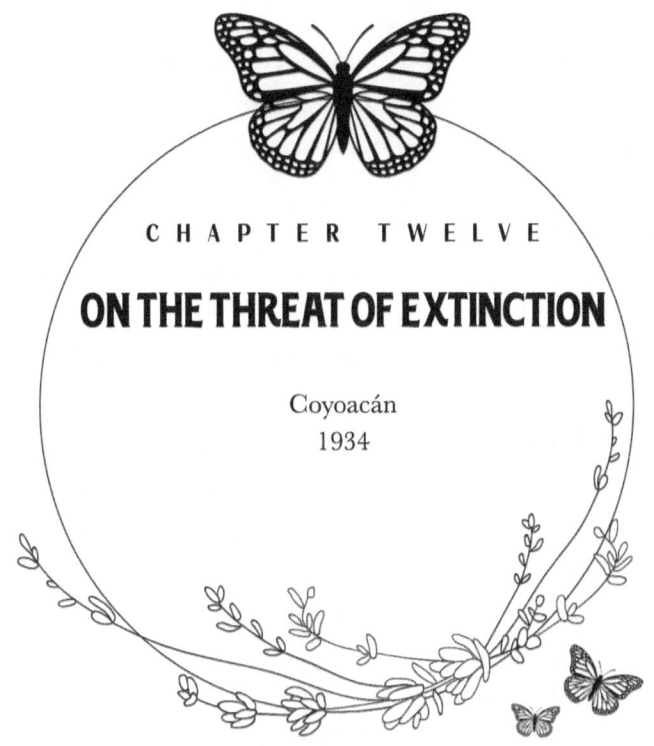

CHAPTER TWELVE

ON THE THREAT OF EXTINCTION

Coyoacán
1934

After three years abroad, Frida and Diego returned to Coyoacán. Guillermo, Conchita, Frida's younger sister Cristina, and her two children were there to greet them. Everyone wore black out of respect for Matilde, heads bowed, the normally boisterous bunch of them unusually staid on this occasion. For in addition to losing the matriarch of their family, they were also mourning Frida's miscarriage. Oh, and less directly, Cristina's move back to the Casa Azul to escape her abusive husband. It was as if the weather had been cued, an ominous cloud cover planted directly overhead, odd peals of thunder crackling in the distance, the wind making the tree limbs scratch out eerie pleas along the windowpanes.

"Get inside, before it storms. I'll get us something to eat." Conchita took the stern, guiding them to safety once again, the bright yellow table the family's most trusted refuge no matter the tension outside. "Frida, dear, you choose. What dish have you missed most while away?"

"Is that even a question? Why, your caldo, of course! I don't care if your secret ingredient is a bat wing or a newt leg; all I know is that soup always fixes whatever ails me." She smiled, a small gesture of reassurance, that, yes, she'd be fine, she was working through it, lest they begin probing, which she was not in the mood for.

"¡Claro, cariña, cualquier cosa! I'll get right on it! In the meantime, Pancho, get their bags, won't you? Take Frida to her room, and then Diego to his? So they might freshen up before we eat?" (As was not unusual among couples of that day, Frida and Diego maintained separate bedrooms. It should be noted, however, that depending on the state of their relationship, as well as the state of her body, they frequently shared a bed for the night.)

"Yes, that would be nice, Conchita, that sounds like a good idea. Thank you, Pancho."

Helllloooooo! What about me? Aren't you gonna say anything to me?

As Nat watched Frida go, he was panicked by a sense of heart-rending déjà vu. Because hadn't he lived this very same moment a decade earlier? On the day Frida came home from the hospital after the bus accident. He'd been drowning in worry that day, too—not just for her health, but for himself, too, because he so achingly doubted his relevance beside her. It was this same overwhelming wave of incertitude that befell him now. He knew it was inappropriate and unfair, that she'd only just walked in the door after days of travel and her body was still healing. But he couldn't stop himself. He had to see her, racing up the stairs when the crowd dispersed and there was no one to stop him.

Toc, toc, went the back of his hand tapping lightly on the doorframe. He peeked around the corner, spying her sitting on the side of her bed, holding a blouse she'd just pulled from the bag next to her. "Is this a bad time?" He hoped she didn't notice the quiver in his voice.

"Oh, Nat! Never, not for you! Get over here!" She beamed, dropping the garment and holding out both arms to him. He flew into her embrace, tucking himself into her chest, both of them home at last.

"How I've missed you! And Zoe, of course, well, and the Casa Azul, all of this—the smells from the kitchen, my garden, all of it so rich with flavor and life—the antithesis to that pinche gringolandia! How easy it is to forget what's important until you no longer have access to it. Such a simple lesson. Might do me well to keep that message a little closer to my heart." She grimaced in self-deprecation.

It's called taking something for granted. And, yes, that would be nice.

"Anyway, on to the happy stuff, please! Nat, tell me what's been going on around here—and you better not leave out any of the juicy details!"

What Nat wanted to say was, *Worrying about you.* Or maybe, *Waiting for an answer to that letter I sent you.* What came out of his mouth was, "I'm sorry about the miscarriage. And Matilde."

"Thanks. Honestly—because I can confide in you, right?"

He nodded his head—he was her confidant!—swallowing the thrill in his throat to keep it contained.

"Honestly, I'm miserable, Nat, nothing but a shadow of my former self." She inhaled, holding the breath, then exhaling, long and heavy. "Did I write to you about my tipping point, when I realized I'd left my dress outside overnight?"

"No." There were lots of things she hadn't written him about.

"It was my favorite tehuana gown. I'd hung it on the clothesline outside my window to dry, but then I forgot about it. So when I pulled the curtains the next morning and saw it there—limp and weighed down in all that gruesome factory grit—oh, how I despised myself! For my negligence, because rather than paying attention to what mattered, I'd been wallowing in self-pity—I don't remember exactly why, maybe Diego hadn't come home the night before, or so-and-so had given him a come-hither look at some gallery opening. Whatever it was, the perceived slight became my sole focus.

"I know it sounds ridiculous, that I would punish myself over a dress. Except that someone made that dress! Someone carefully embroidered all the detail and symbolism, devoting hours and hours to reviving her cultural history, fine-tuning her story by guiding thread with bare hands. You understand what I'm saying, right, Nat? You're a tailor. You can appreciate all the passion and the breadth of emotions that must go into every stitch, no?"

How long had this game been going on? Where she drew him in by making him feel special? Well, it still worked; he was hanging on her every word.

"I imagined the old indígena behind the loom. I didn't know her, of course, but I had an image in my mind—of her sitting on the dirt floor of a flimsy wooden hut, working around the clock to finish the dress in time for the village's patron saint day celebration, wondering whether the income it brought in would be enough to buy her grandchildren shoes. I couldn't shake the impression, revising it throughout that morning, adding in a dwindling pile of dry beans in one corner, then a sick villager being ushered in for the old woman to cure with something from her wall of ancient recipes of herbs and brews. And yet, she remained calm as she managed through life's hardships and interruptions. I was overcome with admiration for this woman I'd created in my head, for her commitment to family and village, for surely it was this ethos that begot such strength. Which made me disgusted with myself, for behaving so contrarily, for my fickleness in adhering to the credo I've built my whole image around.

"And still, I didn't rush to retrieve the dress. I just sat there, staring at it, wondering if the old woman was still attached to it somehow, if the threads she'd given life to were like an uncut umbilical cord stretching across the continent. Did she know that I'd abandoned it last night, left it there defenseless, for strangers to heckle its 'otherness' and for the natural elements to try to dismantle what she'd so painstaking-ly created? Oh, Nat how I loathed gringolandia—that part I already knew. But now, I loathed myself, too, for not being able to protect what I professed to cherish most, for abandoning the things that really mat-ter when life gets in the way."

Are you just talking about the dress? Or is there something else you're trying to apologize for? I'm all ears if there's something you'd like to say!

"Ugh, but enough woe is me. Let's get back to you! Regale me with tales of scandal around these parts, my dear monkey! You've al-ways been so good at cheering me up." She smirked, pushing one palm playfully against his closest arm.

"Let's see . . . Oh, I know, LordPeacock tried to get us to put on a play while you were gone. Seems he's an aficionado of all things Shakespeare. He thought *A Midsummer Night's Dream* might be a good start for the novice thespians among us. But as I—"

"Are you fucking kidding me? Another reenactment of something Shakespeare? Haven't we seen enough of that dead man's work al-ready? How difficult can it be to come up with a single piece of theater that is not bogged down in European bullshit?"

Oh, hallelujah! Go ahead and throw your stake in the ground, Frida! This time I don't mind one bit! Go ahead and pronounce yourself the savviest, the artiest, the most avant-garde across the land! Because you're still alive in there somewhere, Fri-da, you're going to be okay. And I will be right here to applaud you with all the zeal in the world if that's what it takes to pull you out of this abyss you've fallen into.

But that lone glimmer of hope quickly fizzled, and then it went dark altogether. It didn't take long. Diego wasted no time reacclimating to life in Coyoacán, hopping into bed with some new model or bene-factress, convinced that his ongoing war against capitalism merited a sampling of life's simple pleasures between battles. In response, Frida spent most of her time locked away in her room, refusing visitors, her appetite dwindled to nothing but whiskey and cigarettes. Even Nat seemed unable to get anywhere with her. *"No, Nat, I can't. My head is throbbing, I need to be alone, don't you get it?"*

But then one day, with no discernible provocation, her mood shifted. Seismically. Just like that, she came dancing down the stairs, all made-up, decked out in the textiles and the heaping stone accessories she'd been letting gather dust.

"The muse has struck," she interrupted Cristina and Conchita's discussion on the merits of yellow plantains versus the riper, dark ones. "I've decided it's time for one of my famous parties! I'm done mourning; let us commence with some rejoicing."

"But Frida, honey, perhaps take a few days to think about it? See how you're feeling? It's been such a long time since you've taken on a feat like that. It might be healthier, after everything you've gone through —"

"I know what I'm doing, Cristina!" she snapped. "Please, just stay out of it if you're not going to support me. Because *that* would be unhealthy for me." *Do not tell me that I cannot. Because yes, I can!* She turned and walked out the door, no word about where she was going nor when she might return. Neither Cristina nor Conchita said a thing, both women bowing their heads in shared concern.

Frida had a new mission to carry out, and she set to it by unharnessing all her passion and also, all her fury. She hired a work crew to come in because she wanted a replica Tenochtitlán pyramid built along one side of the patio. *"So what if you've never done anything like this before. If the Aztecs could do it with their bare hands, no luxuries like trucks and electricity at their disposal, then what's your problem, eh?"*

The workers set forth with the specs she'd put before them, hastening to accomplish the impossible, racing against the clock to assuage the Señora, all hands on deck around the clock.

"Excuse me, excuse me," she griped, elbowing her way through the crowd of workmen spread across the courtyard, making her way toward the scaffolding that would become the pyramid. "Gentlemen, you'll have to pause your work for a bit. Pablo, get them out of the way, will you? I need this area quiet right now."

"But Señora, if we are to finish by the date you have requested—"

"Did you not hear me the first time, Pablo? Get your fucking crew out of here! I'll tell you when you can come back in. I'm the one paying your wages, have you forgotten that?"

The men scurried away, petrified, but also laughing on the inside, because this one was turning out to be a real chiflada! Meanwhile, Frida moved through the scaffolding until she discovered a footstool, at which point she climbed atop her new podium and she began quoting Aztec poetry, arms outstretched in theatrical display. On and on she went, playing with different volumes, annunciations, tones, until at last, she was satisfied, and she had the workers ushered back in. She would repeat this same exercise the next day, and then the day after that, because practice makes perfect, and you better bet your ass this performance was going to be perfect, pinche Diego! For their part, the workers grew accustomed to their jefa's idiosyncratic behavior, opting to take their lunch breaks tucked behind the plants and the flower beds so they could watch her most curious display, but always outside of her line of vision, because to unleash her wrath was unthinkable.

The days leading up to the big event weren't any smoother, everyone tiptoeing around the property, dutifully carrying out their assignments, but trying to make themselves invisible. For the first time Nat could remember, Conchita wasn't humming along to her favorite ranchero songs that typically blared from the kitchen radio she kept on the windowsill there. LaFlorona, the familiar flower vendor, had taken enough verbal beating at this point that she'd simply stopped calling at the Casa Azul. And when Frida's doctor came by amidst the party-planning fervor to explain the severity of her recent liver test results, which was why it was imperative she slow down, she chased him out of the house. Later in the day, she had the doctor fired.

On the morning of the party, however, she awoke with a sense of calmness. She'd birthed the idea, then she'd nurtured it to fruition, and today she would show it off to the rest of the world. She reached under her nightdress, feeling her body stir to life, lingering there, finding her pleasure. When she'd wholly satisfied herself, she lit a cigarette and lay back in bed, wondering if Diego would find as much amusement in what she had planned for tonight as she'd had putting it together. In that moment when her physical and emotional passions converged, she thought herself indomitable.

How much I love you. And also how much I hate you—in equal parts, mi Dieguito, and with all the passion in my heart! For dragging her across the hemisphere, letting her wallow in her fruitless body with minimal consolation, then diving into someone else's bed the moment they returned, always bent foremost on what was best for him, that bastard! Because if he was so cavalier as to venture elsewhere to fulfill his desire, well, then, starting tonight, so would she.

Later that night, when the curtains went up, a new Frida revealed herself. She was sexier, rawer, slithering across the floor, sweat and perfume coming off her body in a hot cloud. She was still indigenista but no longer a tame tehuana princess—hell no! She was a malinchista now, a traitorous vixen with a predisposition for sex with the enemy, no urge taboo. She was exotic, an Amazon warrior, embracing the hair above her lip and between her brows, letting it grow wild and masculine. She stacked the braids on her head half a meter high, adorning them with barrettes and jewels, silk sashes, crowns of flowers, a tropical rainforest in full bloom. Gone was the poised performer they were accustomed to, the way she'd once held her head high and floated amongst them discussing monkey and parrots, or huipiles and feminismo. No, she was coarse and indelicate now, crouched over as she stalked the jungle floor for flesh ripe enough to bite into.

An hour into the party, she corralled her guests toward the miniature pyramid. She insisted on silence. When this end was achieved, she climbed the steps to the top of the structure, and she launched into her Aztec poetry presentation, limbs flying around like she was an octopus in distress, chanting tales of bloody sacrifices, insatiable gods, tribal warfare, and celestial destiny, her very own one-person theater, no room on the stage for her scoundrel of a husband this time. The guests issued a round of applause when she was through; they were afraid not to. Which was just as she'd hoped.

For it was this fear that made their bodies tingle with dangerous excitement. They were flirting with the perilousness that is unpredictability, and the primitive allure was too strong to deny. It was as if tonight's landscape were a giant chessboard, her versus them, a game in which she was right now tempting them in one direction, though they couldn't be sure if she was bluffing. She quivered with delight at their hesitation, their clumsy hands fumbling in pant pockets pretending to be useful, or nibbling on their manicured nail tips with childish unease. She kissed Diego on the way to freshen up her drink, because she hadn't forgotten him—ja, she couldn't if she tried! But the night was young, there was plenty of time, a little exploring wasn't off-limits.

She sidled up to one of Diego's comrades, asking for a cigarette, flaunting her cleavage as she leaned down to accept his light. She extended her neck to one side on the exhale of her first drag, feeling him ravish the bareness of her décolleté with his eyes. Later in the evening, she returned to his side, offering to show him her art studio.

"I'd appreciate your opinion on that one piece we were discussing earlier? I promise, we'll just be gone a minute," she cooed in his ear, grabbing his forearm and pulling him upstairs. He didn't resist, making small talk to calm his mind, because was he making a pact with the devil?

"It's this one," she said, facing her easel as she leaned her pelvis against the back of the chair there. It was a self-portrait, one she'd labelled *Very Ugly*. Perhaps the painting's title was a self-inflicted punishment for not being enough to keep Diego satisfied. Or maybe it was a plea for public affirmation. In the end, there were no clear answers for what it was Frida intended. He moved in behind her, his front glancing across her back, making her turn around with a jerk, so that she was facing him now, separated by mere centimeters. He leaned down to kiss her; she rebuked the gesture, turning her gaze to one side. And then, for no other reason than because she could, she took his hands, placing them inside her blouse, under her brassiere.

"What do you think?" she asked matter-of-factly.

He scanned her face for a signal. But then again, he was hungry, he had urges, and she was stoking the fire, bringing them up here, all alone like this, right? He leaned down again, this time to kiss her neck. She pulled back, slapping him playfully on the chest.

"Well, you certainly haven't been much help! I ask you up here for your professional opinion, and all you do is flirt with me?" she giggled. "Come on, we better get back to the party."

If Diego can do it, so can I!

She went to bed with Diego at the end of the night, thrilled when he groused about her provocative antics that evening—including the way she seemed to have skipped out for parts, where had she gone off to, by the way? She teased him about his jealousy, exciting herself in the process, and then she slipped into his arms to celebrate her victory. *You want to taste me, I see it in your eyes. I look delectable, I know. But I will singe you with my acrid bite, make you hurt until you cry out for a truce. Go ahead and chase me, but you will never truly catch me, for when I'm done with you, I will fly away.*

On that first night, she'd only teased, to test the reactions. But that Diego had taken notice? Nothing could have pleased her more! *Nothing!* And so, she set herself utterly free, nothing off-limits anymore, the more carnal, the more titillating, then the more she yearned for it.

From his vantage point in the PoutingTree, Nat could see all her sneaking around, slipping into the bathroom with the curious blond woman with the hooded eyes one night, and then behind the shed with the pseudo-art critic on another. Man, woman, Mexican, foreigner, she wasn't particular. Yes, to increase her allure. And yes, because she loved sex. But mostly, to punish Diego. *Fuck you, you bastard! I am irreplaceable, do you still not hear me? And I will never let you forget it!*

Unable to sleep one night because of all the turmoil swirling around the Casa Azul, Nat snuck upstairs to look for his sewing kit, hoping his craft might help him relax. Because Frida had gone to bed downstairs with Diego that night, he'd be safe starting in her room, rooting around through the skirts and blouses strewn across the floor, shaking his head at the extent of her wardrobe, but mostly at the carelessness with which she treated it when no one was looking. So much for the harrowing experience back in New York when she'd left the tehuana gown on the clothesline overnight. *Pshaw, just another one of her performances,* he lamented. Well, it certainly wasn't the first time he'd been had; he shook his head, turning the corner into her art studio.

What he saw there was so disturbing and so repulsive that he fell backwards, collapsing on a nearby steamer trunk. He didn't move at first, collecting his breath. Ultimately, however, out of both morbid curiosity and a yearning to know every last, minutia-like detail about Frida, he pulled himself up and returned to the source of his alarm.

It was a portrait of Frida—well, sort of. It was actually a portrait of her adult head—shaved bald, though, and eyes closed—emerging from a woman's bloody vagina. The "mother" appeared to be dead, as suggested by a white sheet covering her face. Above the gruesome scene hung a picture of a weeping Virgin.

He wanted to run. And also, he didn't want to run; oh, how he wanted to stay! Because years ago, Frida had coached him to look for a painting's hidden meaning, that the blood and gore in *El Accidente* carried messages beyond simply blood and gore. That if you opened your consciousness, looked for hidden clues, you'd notice that the girl on the ambulance stretcher was alive, that her heart was still functioning, and that the sketch was a testament to resilience and hope.

And so, Nat did his best to practice what he'd been taught, standing there before the painting as the hours elapsed, periodically switching his position in case a different angle might trigger something revelatory. What did it mean? Mothers, death, coldness. Coldness, death, mothers. And then, as heavy as his bewilderment had been weighing on him, the onus was suddenly lifted, and the answers were all there! In the painting, Frida had depicted a daughter in the stillborn uterus, and a mother laid to rest behind the white sheet, and a Catholic in the picture of the sobbing martyr. And what value was a Mexican woman if she were none of these three things? Sure, Frida rejected societal norms, but she was steeped in that society, nonetheless. The way Nat interpreted it, Frida viewed herself as a failure when it came to fulfilling her duties as a daughter, a mother, and a Catholic!

On the other hand, he mused, the painting was evidence that she was taking a stab at untangling her complicated relationship with Matilde, no? In which case, wasn't it also possible that she might carry repressed interest in the points he'd raised about Mamá in his unanswered letter, assuming she read it, of course? And if the answer to both these questions was yes, then mightn't he consider this painting the response she never wrote to him while abroad? Moreover, what if she *wanted* him to see this painting, or she had the intention of showing it to him at a later date? Nothing for certain, Nat would admit that much. But it was possible. Which was all that mattered, because perhaps she hadn't shunned him after all. She'd been burdened by too much too quickly; she just needed some time, that was all. She'd reach out to him about this source of her discontent when she was ready. Poor Frida, vitriolic in her claim to Diego, perhaps, but so very fragile on the inside.

"Get the hell out of here, you fucking bastard!" she shrieked, chest heaving between verbal punches, fists clenched by her sides. "And don't you dare come back, you piece of shit!" Diego didn't make a single plea; he simply let himself out. When the door closed behind him, Frida crumpled into herself, burying face in hands.

"You okay?" *Thank goodness the Pouting Tree is so central to everything!* he admitted to himself for the very first time, foregoing all pretenses that he was the victim forced to watch. For on this day after he'd discovered *My Birth,* he was enormously glad for this excuse to race to her rescue.

"No, I'm not! You want to know who she is? Who he's sleeping with now? Guess, I dare you, try and guess who my husband is fucking now!"

Silence.

"Well, too bad, because I'm going to tell you. It's Cristina. Yep, you heard me, my baby sister. Diego is sleeping with my sister."

For the next few weeks, Frida stayed sequestered in her room, a premature recluse engulfed in the kind of anguish that comes from only the most intimate acts of betrayal. Nat declared a patio-wide moratorium on "frivolous activity" while she recuperated, firm in his belief that her recovery demanded the same level of mental intention as was paid after the bus accident all those years ago. The pets could still work on their portions of the quilt, but they were to do so without undue cheer. Out of respect for the victim.

Twice, Diego came to the house asking for Frida. Both times, Nat raced to the door to get there first. He was still flying high from having seen the *My Birth* canvas, continuing to tell himself that the artwork was an invitation from Frida for the two of them to finally explore their complicated histories. That he might've been imagining his own relevance to the painting was one thing; what mattered was that his presumptions heightened in him the need to protect her. Which meant keeping out the UglyFrogMan at all costs. The first time Diego came by, Nat was outwardly cordial, explaining that Frida was otherwise occupied, trying to piece back together her shattered heart. *"I'm sure you understand, she's suffered the unimaginable."*

The second time, when Diego arrived with a cottontail rabbit tucked into one elbow, an intended gift for Frida, Nat's hackles went up. Did he really think the cute little bunny was going to fix this? *That's all she gets? In exchange for sticking your appendage in her kid sister?*

"Oh, Diego, it's you again," he said with undue authority, crossing his arms over his chest. "I'm afraid Frida still isn't ready to see you." Which was untrue; he'd neglected to mention Diego's visit—on either occasion. "She can explain it all when she's up to it, which, as I've already established, is not now." He started to close the door, only to pull it wide open again.

"Hey, since I have you here, though, this might be a good time to share some of my thoughts on your art. I'd invite you in, where it'd be more comfortable, but, well, as I've said, you're not exactly welcome here. We can just continue this conversation as we are, I hope you don't mind."

Diego wondered, first, what it would feel like to squash this busybody little jungle rat with his hulking miner's boot, and second, whether the bloody remains would leave a stain on the patio floor. Because he certainly didn't need any more trouble with Frida. For some reason he'd never understood, she really liked the thing.

"After studying your murals, my principal concern is that contrary to all the publicity you like to generate over your so-called allegiance to indigenismo, your artistic depiction of el pueblo comes off as so . . . well, so narrow." Nat pinched up his nose at "narrow." "I mean, every one of your indígenas looks exactly like the last. Which leaves me unclear about whether you are, in fact, promoting respect and appreciation for la mexicanidad? Or if the exact opposite might be closer to the truth? On the one hand, I do admire your portrayal of the proud Aztec warrior—the angular face, protruding muscles, bronzed skin. However—and this is a big 'however'—they seem to lack unique personalities, has anyone ever pointed that out? I'm referring to the way you make their eyes glazed over, staring back at the viewer like wind-up toys, put there to do a job they've no emotional connection to. What an improvement it would be if you paused to really get to know your subjects, perhaps delved into their personal situations, histories, uniqueness, you know what I mean? I'm no expert, mind you, it's just one opinion coming from outside your regular circle of sycophants. Oh, and I'll let Frida know you came by. See ya, Diego."

There, he'd spoken his mind. He closed the door behind him, shaking his hands clean. He had no intention of mentioning any of it to Frida.

Frida agreed to a reconciliation with Diego several months later. Nat had done everything in his power to prevent it, even creating a schedule amongst the PatioPets so that one of them was always sure to be watching the door. But there'd been that one afternoon when the rain wouldn't let up, and their ground nests had flooded, forcing them to seek temporary refuge in the only unoccupied bedroom, which, unfortunately, happened to be furthest from the front door. And that's when the UglyFrogMan managed to slip in. So that when the weather dried up by early evening, and Nat shepherded the pets back to their rightful place in the patio, his worst nightmare had come true. Diego was sitting at the table with the geraniums, Frida sprawled across his lap.

"Diego, dear, you haven't been taking care of yourself—you're too thin! I'll have Conchita fix you up something special. All this painting is wearing you down." She stood up to rub his back, noticing Nat as she did so.

"Oh, Nat, buenas," she spat through gritted teeth, refusing to look up from Diego's shoulders, bracelets jangling around her wrists like a ring of dungeon keys. "Are you surprised to see that Diego is here, Nat?" She paused to kiss the top of Diego's head. "Or not?"

Now she looked up. He barely recognized her, the glowering, icy glare, like a dagger driving a hole through his heart, the cry for help he thought he'd gleaned from *My Birth* smothered in that single moment. This time, he didn't have to worry whether she was mad. What he had to worry about this time was whether she'd ever forgive him. *It was your sister, Monarch Princess. Where, oh, where have you gone?*

First thing the next morning, Nat was summoned to Frida's room.

"Not you, Zoe. Just Nat."

He put his head down as he followed her upstairs—the chivalrous hero tragically sentenced to the guillotine for a crime he did not commit. Over and over, he'd rehearsed his plea, that he was innocent, he'd only been trying to protect her.

"So, about that little encounter with Diego the other day? I suppose you have something to say for yourself?"

"Um . . . yeah, yeah," he stuttered, trembling in her frigidness. "I think we had a mostly constructive discussion about his work. I'm not sure if he passed on my suggestions—"

"No, he did not. As I recall, he was too infuriated to get much out—oh, except that he wanted to rip your head off. Which he would've done, incidentally, if I hadn't been there to stop him! Let me be absolutely clear, Nat. Diego is my husband. I love him more than my own self. He and I have our issues, I won't pretend otherwise, but it is none of your business, do you hear me? Don't you dare interfere in my life again, Nat. Because I will not defend you a second time."

After staring at his feet through the tongue-lashing, Nat looked up now, searching her face for any indication that she wanted to say more, to speak to him without words the way they'd once done so effortlessly and instinctively, to let him know that she was giving him the abbreviated version right now because she was so tired and broken. But there was nothing there. He might as well have been looking at a stone wall. He'd lost her entirely. This vicious new Frida had finally succeeded in consuming the old one. There was no turning back now, Nat was sure of it.

For the next few years, Nat drank too much. Zoe accompanied him on his escapades, to console him, but also to protect her broken shepherd from himself. She understood that he needed someone to listen to him unload about the pain Frida had inflicted on him, and how he was convinced his heart had degenerated into a pulpy mass that no longer functioned properly, and that because of this, he was soon to die. But because the duo had begun frequenting the CornerBar on a daily basis now at Nat's insistence, and because Nat tended to get so inebriated that he couldn't walk, Zoe went along to protect him. It was not uncommon on such an occasion for her to have to use her teeth to clamp down on his tail and drag him through the streets, back to the Casa Azul. When he'd come to the next morning, only to discover his body covered in bruises and flesh wounds from being pulled along the cobblestone roads, Nat didn't care. In fact, it was as if he welcomed the physical disfigurations, self-flagellation for refusing to steel himself against her charisma, or abide by the law of "survival of the fittest." For having loved Frida too much.

During this dark period, Nat lost all interest in reading and sewing and crime-solving. The PatioPets tried encouraging him to get back to working on the quilt, even offering to sneak out for a different shade of yarn or cut of cloth if that'd provide incentive. LordPeacock volunteered to direct one of Sor Juana's plays, because wouldn't the sixteenth-century feminist nun serve as the antithesis of anything Sir William Shakespeare? Zoe begged him to join her on their bench in the Plaza. But he refused them all, preferring to hole up in his nest to drown out the world.

As for Frida, she fared no better. That there existed an even deeper place to descend to seemed unimaginable. And yet, she found it. On the one hand, she and Cristina had made peace, and her marriage to Diego had been saved—if only because she'd once again begun turning a blind eye to his infidelity. On the other hand, some damage can never be undone; even when the sting dissipates, a throbbing ache far deeper and more pervasive takes its place. She screamed bloody murder for her pain medication, because on top of it all, her body was falling apart.

The unfortunate truth was that she trusted no one now. Everyone was her enemy, a suspect in the crimes against her. The culprits were far and wide, not just her husband anymore. No, her sister was a betrayer, as was her trusted monkey . . . well, and the gossiping public, and her shattered pelvis, the list went on and on. This next time, though, she'd be ready! Never, ever, *ever*, EVER again would she let herself be ambushed like that! It didn't matter that she was collapsed in her bedclothes on the floor of her room right now, because that was fleeting. The next time she stood up, she'd gather her weapons to her chest, and she wouldn't dare put them down for even a single second until she'd unleashed her havoc. *You think you've won, don't you? Ja, it's only an illusion, I was never yours to begin with, I have already flown away.*

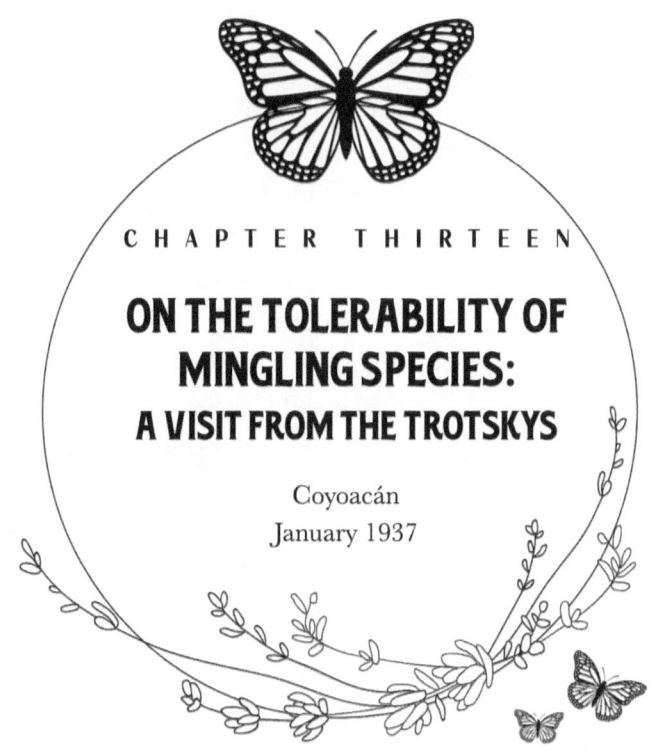

CHAPTER THIRTEEN

ON THE TOLERABILITY OF MINGLING SPECIES:
A VISIT FROM THE TROTSKYS

Coyoacán
January 1937

Their lives changed forever on the day Russian revolutionaries Leon Trotsky and his wife Natalia were granted asylum in México. It was an arrangement Diego helped to orchestrate, and, per his love of public attention, he'd even offered to put them up at the Casa Azul. No matter the danger involved—the stalinistas were in hot pursuit of the Trotskys, having already murdered most of their family and friends—he'd have round the clock security, rest assured, everybody, "the problem was solved!" Diego had called a meeting of the home's residents and staff to explain the situation.

"We owe them a warm welcome, to show our gratitude for what

they've endured in their quest to—"

"Well, I, for one, am honored to be granted this distinguished opportunity to help my comrades in need." It was Frida.

Their heads spun around in confusion, because she rarely showed herself anymore. Just to scream at someone. Or bewail the state of the world in general. And yet, here she was, an explosion of unstable energy descending the staircase, headed right their way.

"I'm sure you all feel the same, no? That it is we who are lucky to have the Trotskys in our house?" She nodded cheerfully at the bunch of them circled around Diego, now assuming her place next to him. She extended one hand to take his, then reached up to kiss him briefly on the lips.

"Sí, Señora, eso es, we are the lucky ones!" *Has anyone here checked to see if the windows will be boarded up, because are we sure this is such a good idea?*

"Claro, Frida, it will be my greatest honor!" *I can endure the crazy lady, but international assassins lurking outside these walls isn't really my thing.*

"Well, then, how nice we can all be in agreement." She did a half-bow, as if issuing proclamations from her palace balcony. "As for my reclusiveness, that is over now. I'm done being injured. By which I mean I prefer the subject not come up again. Understood?"

The crowd nodded timidly.

"Okay, then. We have work to do, and I suggest we get right to it. The linens must be laundered, pressed and perfumed. And the floors scrubbed down, please. We'll need to send a couple of cars to the market so we can load up the pantry and ice box—oh, and don't forget flowers while you're out. That fickle LaFlorona—or whatever you people around here call her—well, she's stopped coming. How's that for loyalty? Anyway," she clapped her hands a few times, "let's get going, folks. The Trotskys are coming, and we must make them see that México stands beside them in this international crusade!"

Despite the threat of stalinistas bent on hunting down the Trotskys, the staff was enormously loyal, and seeing Frida inspired like this gave them a glimmer of hope, that maybe she was really pulling through this time. *"Maybe she really is okay. Her cheeks are rosy, that's a good sign, right? She's not breathing fire, right? Or is she just high? Well, anyway, she's not wielding a battle-axe, so that's good."*

Nat's reaction, however, was quite the opposite: he smelled a rat. He'd been the victim of her ire, he'd felt the cumulative depth of her abomination for every one of her assailants, a list he supposed had no end. So it didn't add up that after being down for the count ever since the Cristina fiasco, and then, suddenly—just as this tidal wave of political controversy and social puffery was about to descend upon the Casa Azul—she shows up all sunshine and roses? Yeah, highly unlikely. Based on their long history together, Nat presumed that she was acting out of pure panic, desperate for the limelight and chatter that would surely come with hosting the Trotskys. He also assumed that there was another, even more important reason behind her miraculous recovery: Never in a million years would she allow Diego any more of the prize than she took for herself.

"And, Diego, mi amor," she said, turning to face him, taking his other hand, so that now she held both, reassuming her place center stage, her choreography impeccable. "I come to you now, to reassure you that I am still, and will always be, your loyal comrade. I love you with all my heart." *And I hate you with all my heart, mi amor, for twisting my insides until I can barely breathe.*

He chuckled, grabbing her by the waist and then picking her up, pulling her into his chest.

Ah, you stupid, stupid fool! After all this time, and still so naïve. She half-kissed him on the neck, her thoughts jumping ahead, because she was already considering her next move.

A week later, Diego and Frida returned from Veracruz where they'd gone to meet the Trotskys' ship. Conchita and her staff were respectfully positioned at the front door to formally receive their guests, first taking their coats and luggage, then nudging them toward the bright yellow table where dinner would be served.

"Mil gracias, Conchita, you are a godsend—well, that is, if god existed, which he does not. Let me rephrase, ahem, Conchita, your presence here is . . . invaluable." *I am witty, too, you see? Before long, you will look right past the almighty Diego Rivera. You will realize that it is I who runs this machine.* "And will you please bring us some of that rare vintage Spanish wine I treasure so? We despise Franco, but his grapes we cannot do without!" Without looking up, she handed Conchita her shawl, sliding into her seat at the table with a satisfied sigh.

"Oh, I almost forgot. Nat? Are you up there?" She craned her neck toward the PoutingTree, simultaneously reaching for the tequila bottle in front of her, always one step ahead of the others, moving the pieces forward in this game, to keep them from noticing there were no rules anymore.

"Oh, I almost forgot. Nat" . . . Yeah, well, I almost forgot you used to have a nice bone in your body! So there, take that, bitch!

"Can you come down here, Nat? I've just learned on the drive home that spider monkeys aren't found in Russia, you see, and our guests are curious to meet you." Then back to her guests, "A drink, anyone?" already filling their glasses, continuing to plead with Nat as she did so. "Please?"

He wondered briefly what would happen if he refused to comply, but then he considered that she interpreted any rejection nowadays as pure provocation, which, in turn, had the potential to provoke Diego. Who wanted Nat gone, Frida had made that clear. Oh, and also, he didn't know how to tell her no, that was the other thing. So down he went.

"There he is, my Nahuatl," she cooed when he appeared by her side. She felt warmly toward her monkey just then—was it gratitude, perhaps, because of course he could see through her little act right now, he always could, the only one. And yet, he'd heeded her call.

"She has a monkey, Leon! What an amusing choice!"

Frida wasn't meant to hear Natalia's whispers, but her ears worked wonders on occasions like this, when she was taking over command in a new setting, luring them in before she locked the door and threw away the key. She shuddered with delight, that even someone as sophisticated as Mrs. Trotsky might fall for her tricks.

"Friends, please meet here another innocent victim of capitalismo." Her emotionalism toward her pet was short-lived. She had a job to complete. "Alas, este pobrecito was chased from the Lacandon forest by the British lumber industry . . ." She knew the speech by heart, including how to draw in her audience, captivate them with tension, so that when it came time to deliver her final words—"and he never saw his mother again"—she had them practically in tears.

Practically in tears of joy in Nat's case! She'd read his letter! She knew about Mamá! She knew about his exodus from the jungle! He'd never mentioned any of it to her in person, so it had to be the letter! He was elated, hopeful, dizzy that this crack in her armor existed, that perhaps she did care! Maybe he had interpreted *My Birth* correctly after all, and maybe she really was planning to reach out to him? Had she been waiting for the right time? He held his breath, wondering what she would say next, something about mothers, maybe?

"Señor y Señora Trotsky, I'd like to make a toast, in honor of your arrival, of course, but also, to christen this house an asylum. Let the Casa Azul be a place of solace for those afflicted by the tyranny and oppression raging around the world, separating mother from child, citizen from homeland. May my house serve as a refuge for the victims of imperialismo. And may we continue to struggle against the evil forces intent on eliminating the beauty and justice we around this table risk our lives and reputations to sow." She picked up her glass, raising it above her head, nodding for the others to join her. "¡Qué siga la revolución! ¡Salud, camaradas!"

"¡Salud!" they trumpeted back, followed by a wave of praise for Frida's oh-so-compelling words, and then, on to a discussion of the commonalities between early twentieth-century Russian serfs and the Lacandon forest's spider monkey population, speaking of those affected by tyranny and oppression.

Yep, she'd read his letter alright. And gone ahead and turned it into another one of her tricks! She didn't care about Mamá; she was using his pain to further her own agenda. That was it, he was sick and tired of being batted around like a kitten's catnip. He didn't have to take this! He could march out of the Casa Azul right now and have no regrets! Well, and for starters, he was marching out of this dining area this second and going back to his nest, let's see how they liked that!

As he scanned the table one last time on his way out, he realized that nobody was looking at him. Already, they'd forgotten about him; he was that discardable. He couldn't help but notice the way Frida had succeeded in solidifying her position as master of ceremonies, having by now pulled from her repertoire the tried-and-true chronicles of "The Life of Conchita." Diego was leaning back in his chair, arms clasped proudly over his paunch, basking in the glow of his wife's performance, which, as he saw it, he was ultimately responsible for—he was the one who'd discovered her and brought her into the circle, wasn't he? Nat wasn't surprised that Leon wasn't paying him a gram of attention—his children had been murdered by the stalinistas, and his life was cold and bleak, so why would he give a fig about someone's house pet? What was perplexing, however, was the degree of interest the old man was showing his hostess, almost gawking at her through those glass-bottle eyeglasses, hanging on her every word as if never had such a fascinating tale been told.

And then there was Natalia, who, unlike the rest of them jockeying for position, sat there quietly, steadfastly congenial in the attention she paid to others as they spoke. Nat felt oddly stirred by her presence, letting his eyes wander over her neatly coiffed, ashy blond curls, then settle on the softness of her face, moving down to admire her upper frame, so prudishly disguised behind the fitted woolen jacket. He must've been staring, because she noticed him, smiling when their eyes made contact. His heart skipped a beat.

Despite coming up on the second half of his expected lifespan, what was happening to him right now was entirely new. He knew ardor—a lustrous, satiating lifetime of ardor, albeit partnerless and confined to the privacy of his nest. But this response was steeped in something deeper, something that stirred his insides, like orange-hot metal coils were spinning around in his tummy. The heat was too intense to be contained, spreading like wildfire, down his legs, into his arms, his fingers, the tips of his nails, until his whole body was pulsating with desire. He knew he shouldn't have these yearnings—she was much too old for him. And yet, he wanted her. Oh, how he wanted her! Overwhelmed, he dashed out of the room, thinking only of relieving himself without being found out.

"What're they like, Nat? The Trotskys? Huh, Nat?" begged the PatioPets, waiting for him outside the kitchen door, then chirping after him as he continued full speed ahead for the PoutingTree. "Do they have pets? Do they like Sor Juana?"

"Hard to tell much of anything yet," he conceded, hoisting himself up into his nest. "There's a lot of posturing going on right now. I suspect it'll take some time before they show their true colors." There. He hoped that was sufficient, because he needed desperately for this conversation to be over—right now. "Siesta time, good night, friends."

Resigned to the fact that they weren't getting any more information out of him, the PatioPets took their cue and retired to their respective nests. Only Zoe had noticed the heat coming off his body. She waited for the rest of them to doze off, and then she approached his tree.

"Nat, *psst*, it's me." She waited until he showed his face. "*What* is going on?" she whispered testily. "Tell me, Nat, I know there's something!"

"It's a powder keg in there, Zoe. An epic explosion is due our way, I can feel it. A bunch of big heads angling for top dog position—no pun intended, because, trust me, there's nothing funny about any of it. The oddest thing though, Zoe . . . It's Natalia I'm most concerned about. I can't explain it, but I'm captivated by her." And then he disappeared again.

Zoe shook her head. *Oh, dear, my broken shepherd is at it again, bringing another wounded lamb into the flock. I hope he knows what he's doing, because it feels like this ship is already going down. I don't know if we can support one more lost soul.*

Once Frida was sure the Trotskys were comfortably settled, she was back in motion. That is, she began preparations for her next party. Their neighbors and other prominent artists in the larger México City area were hankering for a chance to mingle with the Trotskys, to get an inside peek at what international drama and intrigue looked like. The world would be watching; her very survival depended on getting this right. She'd been caught off-guard too many times in her life. On those rare occasions when she felt she might be losing her edge, she made a point of picturing in her head those instances of humiliation and betrayal, until bile rose in her throat and her insides seethed with fury, and she felt properly hardened once again. She'd begin per usual, wooing them to her side, but this time, she'd wait until every last victim had taken the bait, for there could be no survivors. This time, she was determined to bring the whole house down, no matter the casualties, no matter if *she* was one of the casualties. As long as Diego went down with her, she'd have won. Nothing extraneous to this objective existed in her world anymore.

Though wholly out of practice, she didn't miss a step spinning her usual magic on the night of the party. The guests were treated to fine tequila upon arrival, moving on to potato vodka served with patas de pollo stroganoff as their main course, then washing it down with French wine and beet flan, the perfect blend of international flavors to celebrate their international revolution. They sang the Communist International in Russian, then in Spanish. They were hopeful and self-congratulatory, imagining themselves guardians of underdogs everywhere, puffing up their chests, sure their way was the right way. By the time the clock struck midnight, and they stumbled on their words, they got out the phonograph to speak for them, cracking open another bottle of whatever was within reach, because they weren't close to being done—they had a revolution to carry out! When their vision turned blurry and their lips turned loose, they lost interest in the communalism that had brought them together in the first place—alas, they were only human after all, and their individualism could only be kept under wraps through so many copas and tragos until they became boisterous about what was most imperative, each of them thinking themself a bolder visionary than the next, the most capable to guide this movement forward. *Me, myself, I, yo!*

It was at this point that Natalia got up from the table, politely excusing herself and thanking her hosts, explaining she was still exhausted from her travels. She thought it better to spare them the truth, that the rancorous banter that had cropped up was making her head pound, that she longed to get back to her room, to be alone, perhaps soothe herself with poetry and a cup of hot tea. And so, with heavy shoulders unbefitting her tiny frame, Natalia padded back across the patio to her room, shaking her head at all the acrimony she'd witnessed in her lifetime.

From his perch in the PoutingTree, Nat watched her go, a parched desert traveler searching for an oasis. Perhaps it was the aura of loneliness hanging over her that he empathized with, because he, too, understood what it was to be an outsider. Why had her husband not accompanied her to her room, he wondered? How could Leon just disregard the grief that should've been his to share? Why wasn't anyone comforting her or reassuring her? Why was the world marching on when there was so much carnage right there in front of their faces? What was the matter with people, why didn't anyone care? And so, with the compassion of a true gentleman (and also, the passion of a monkey in his physical prime), he went to her.

"Señora Trotsky? It is I, Nat, the house monkey?" He tapped lightly on her door. "We met briefly, on the afternoon you arrived, though I understand if you don't remember. Anyway, I thought it polite to stop by, see if there's anything you might need?" When she didn't respond, he crouched down, peeking through a gap in the door's curtain. He spied her sitting in a chair next to the bed, knees pressed neatly together, legs crossed at the ankles, fingers interlaced in her lap. Instinctually, he grabbed his male part, redeemed in his compliance with the no-pants rule.

"¿Alo? ¿Señora Trotsky? Zdravstvujtye, are you there?" he tried again.

Realizing at last the summons, she shook her head, dragging herself back from the reverie, images from childhood, the only safe place that existed in her world anymore.

"Yes, yes, here I come." A smile spread across her face when she opened the door. "Well, hello there, Nat! Zdravstvujtye! Of course I remember you, dear. And how thoughtful of you to learn my language."

His heart skipped a beat and his breath caught in his throat. *Of course I remember you, dear."*

"Señora Trotsky," he responded once he remembered to breathe again. "It's a pleasure, though I'm afraid I know very little beyond the basics." The truth was, he'd been studying up on Russian ever since word of the Trotskys' asylum had first been announced. (And no acquisition of new language could come without the proper cultural backdrop, so he'd committed himself to a deep dive into Dostoevsky, Tolstoy, Pushkin, and Lenin, all of his knowledge coming full circle now as he sought to charm this lone flower shipped to him from the Siberian tundra.)

"I realize it's late. Maybe you'd prefer I came back another time? I'm happy to accommodate your schedule."

"Whatever are you talking about, Nat? This is a fine time. Please, do come in." She pulled the door open wider; he entered, following her to the foot of the bed where she took a seat. Which was a conundrum for Nat, because the bed was the only piece of furniture besides the chair she'd been occupying when he'd first spied her, which left him unsure what to do next, where to sit, what to do with his hands, what to say—

"I suppose I owe you an explanation," she began awkwardly.

And though he never would've wished her any more reason for worry, whatever she was about to apologize for did have the benefit of easing his own self-consciousness given his lack of experience pursuing a romantic interest.

"Aren't you wondering why I've retired so much earlier than the others?"

No, I would have done exactly the same thing. They're a bunch of self-promoting narcissists.

"They're all such fine people, really, so intelligent and so . . . important. Oh, Leon and I are extremely grateful for all the hospitality that's been extended to us. It's just . . . well, I'm not entirely fond of crowds, truth be told." She was looking down at her lap, fumbling with her thumbs. "Perhaps it's because, for so long now, my family has been like hunted prey. It's gotten to the point that I've even begun suspecting that the person seated next to me at a dinner party might be my assassin. I know that might sound crazed, but you can see, can't you, how frazzled my thinking has become?"

He saw no right way to answer that question, so he kept his mouth shut.

"Anyway, rest seems my only cure. And as lovely as everyone is, they're not exactly prone to restful conversation, have you noticed? What unsettles me is the general perception that it is the crassest, loudest, most fevered language that trumps all others, each person thinking himself wiser than the last. Where is the humanity in that, I sometimes ask myself. It can be so conflicting, Nat, to be a part of this greater, glorious comradeship on the one hand, and then to wonder how it is that we can each view kindness and goodwill in such different ways." She turned to look out the window, as if catching herself for saying too much to someone she knew so little. But being afraid could be so exhausting, locked up in one's head. No, this was good for her, she reassured herself. "One thing I've learned over the years is that unchecked anger serves no good end . . ."

Not only was she beautiful, but Natalia was articulating his exact thoughts. *Yes, the anger! I know exactly what you mean! Frida has become so angry, Natalia, I worry that her love for Diego has turned sour.*

". . . It's like a cancer, the way its seed gets planted—so seamlessly, at first, that you don't even notice it's there. Until one day, you wake up, and the only thing you can think of is how to carry out your next vendetta, who must be taken down, how many lives shattered. So that you can no longer remember the softness of a baby's skin against your cheek, the sound of your lover's voice when he walks in the door, or the taste of his hungry kisses. Because by then, it's too late, the disease has spread, and the anger has consumed you."

Yes, yes, yes! I understand, Natalia!

"Oh, dear, what a gloomy hostess I must seem! You've so graciously called on me, and here I've gone on about myself this whole time!"

Have you met Frida? I've had a lifetime of practice, Natalia!

"Let's you and I have a proper visit, shall we? It's been such a long time since I've had polite conversation." She put one hand on the spot beside her on the bed, patting it lightly. "Come, sit with me, Nat."

Pitter-patter, pitter-patter.

"That is, as long as you promise not to talk over me about how Lenin missed an important nuance when he signed on to the Communist International, ja ja."

"Not to worry, I know very little about world politics. I'd be a fool if I even tried discussing such matters." *Actually, I could talk all night about Lenin's appreciation for and deconstruction of the most revered Russian literature of the day, and how the aristocracy's leniency toward that very genre allowed him the space to create his own political manifesto. But what I'm more concerned with tonight is that you have a shoulder to lean on.* And so, he climbed on the bed next to her, not too close that he might seem forward, but close enough that he could relish the exhilarating aroma of dust, talcum powder, and sweat-stained wool that enveloped her.

"First things first, you must call me Natalia." She raised her eyebrows at him. He nodded back. "Okay, then, tell me about yourself, Nat. I want to know where you're from, and what you like to do. And however did you end up at the Casa Azul, of all places?"

His jaw dropped onto his chest; he pulled it back into place so as not to look the fool. No one had ever asked him any of these things. No one. Well, there was the one time Frida had wondered how he'd come to know Guillermo, but then she'd changed the subject before he could answer, so that didn't count. Nat felt like he'd just been offered a way out of the pit of self-despair his life had become, to find his voice by letting the complexity of his identity be exposed for the very first time. So he could, at last, get on with being impressive. It was a glorious feeling. And so, he told her everything. Well, almost everything; he opted not to tell her about his association with the ghosts in the StatelySittingRoom. He'd need to get to know her a little better first.

As he spilled the part about his separation from Mamá, as well as his assorted confrontations with Diego, he tried to keep his tone neutral. He thought it best to shelve some of his darker thoughts about humanity if he had any chance of winning over this damsel in distress. Interestingly, he spoke minimally of Frida, sharing just the basic framework of their cordial relationship. This was not intentional on his part; Nat simply had other things on his mind as he sat there beside Natalia, her compassion palpable as he unveiled his past.

And she was, in fact, genuinely touched by his honesty and his tenderness, at one point lifting him to her bosom, then stroking his head, to coax him through his emotional purge. The truth was, it felt refreshing to feel needed again, beyond simply being a notetaker for her husband, or a body to keep warm by at night.

From across the patio, a scratched phonograph was repeating the same stanza, provoking an exasperated sigh from Natalia. Nat took advantage of her emotional reaction, using the opportunity to sink more closely into her bosom. Her body was slight, but comfortingly fleshy, the warmth of her sagging breasts exciting him. If he could, he would run away with her, to an island far away. He would build her a castle where he would adore her for all that she was: loyal, kind, demure. Every night, climbing into bed beside her, he would remove her clothing, layer by layer, until he'd exposed her in all her mature brilliance, and he'd look down at her with pure love and hungry desire, and he would come to her—

"Um, I should be going . . . there's something I must do," he sputtered, pulling his sweater down past his hips, hustling toward the door. "I had a very nice evening, Natalia, thank you. Perhaps we can do this again sometime?" And then he scurried back to the PoutingTree, so he could mop up the mess along his sweater's hemline before anyone saw.

In Nat's mind, the subsequent two weeks with Natalia—more significantly measured to him as fourteen nights—proved to be no less intimate than their first encounter. Every evening, after Natalia had had enough of the dinner table's political scrapping, Nat appeared magically at her door, hoping she'd say yes to continuing their conversation. And Natalia came to look forward to their time together as her favorite part of the day. She was curious to know everything about her odd little friend. At what point in his sewing career had he introduced pigments and dyestuffs, she wanted to know. Did he know much about the kind of tree he'd built his nest in, or about the beautiful flowers it produced? What touched him most, though, was that every night, just before they parted ways, she begged him for just one more story about the JungleTent. *"Tell me about the jungle, Nat, about the EmeraldLagoon and the AgoraCanopy and*

the foraging escapades. Tell me all of it! Help me escape to that faraway place, to be reminded that beauty still exists." Frida had never shown any interest in his past; Natalia wanted to know everything, each morsel an important piece of who he was. Which made him feel special, and his affection for her grew with each day that passed.

"Buenos días." He'd arrived promptly at Natalia's doorstep that morning, hair on his head slicked back after meticulously preening himself at the birdbath, boater hat and striped vest dusted off and steamed, respectively. (He'd considered foregoing the vest in favor of suspenders, but given the lack of pants in his wardrobe, he'd stuck with the vest.) Today he was taking Natalia on a trip to Xochimilco, the famed floating gardens established by the Aztecs centuries ago, and more recently transformed into a popular water park.

"Shall we, m'lady?" He offered her his elbow, snapping it back a second later, clasping it there admonishingly by his side. *Nat, you fool! She'd have to get down on her knees to accept your arm, you naïve jungle monkey—*

"What fun we shall have, Nat! I could barely sleep last night just thinking of it!"

So what if he only reached her waist? This could work.

They climbed into the car Nat had hired for the day, Nat nodding in acknowledgement to the bodyguard in the front passenger seat. (Because unlike Diego who professed his love for Frida, and then invited Stalin's bait into the bedroom next to hers, Nat was determined to protect the woman he loved, a knight of the most chivalrous rank.) They made their way through the neighborhood streets, Nat commenting on the landmarks around them. It's not that they passed by anything particularly noteworthy *("That's the bodega that sells the best Krazy Kat comics in town—oh, and also chewing gum, it turns out. And that's the Church where the priest hates monkeys")*. But it allowed him the role of sophisticated city-dweller, the kind worthy of her companionship. An unexpected extra was that it also provided him the excuse to wiggle in closer, hanging over her shoulder to point out the next sight, and at one glorious point he was sure he'd remember forever, resting lightly against her breast.

When they arrived at their destination, Nat was the perfect gentleman, informing the bodyguard of their itinerary to ensure they'd be protected at all times, then helping Natalia from the car. In the calm voice he'd been practicing, he explained that, though neither of them was keen on crowds, they would have to weave their way through the frenzy of tourists to get down to the dock where the trajinera boats were stationed. But she shouldn't worry, because he'd be right there beside her. He took her hand, offering a final smile to comfort her by, and then he ushered them forward.

A barrel organ was blasting out the standard cacophony of squeaks and pings. A toddler screamed with rage when his mother refused him the balloon he'd set his sights on. Street dogs with protruding ribs and glassy eyes skittered about in search of anything edible. Tourists jostled from all directions, no respite from the madness, vendors going against the current to peddle their wares. And still, Nat and Natalia forged on, holding fast to each other, surprised when they made eye contact and burst out laughing, *"because what are we doing?"* then leaning in together playfully, two adults giving themselves over to the childish euphoria that occurs when innocence and amusement intersect.

By the time they reached the river's edge, they were out of breath with giddiness. The crowd had thinned out, so that there were no more than a couple dozen people along the docks. The late morning sun was warm on their backs. And the rhythmic sound of the water curling back and forth against the shore played like a lullaby of the purest kind. The smell of the river was evocative of mermaids and treasure boxes. Natalia closed her eyes, lifting her face toward the sky.

"Oh, Nat, this place is magical! I feel like I've been transported in time, as if the year were 1500, not 1937. And I'm an Aztec princess, not a fifty-five-year-old exile!" She opened her eyes, checking his face for signs of ridicule, always on the lookout for her Judas. Nat was nodding at her to continue. "Promise not to laugh, Nat? I'm trusting you." He nodded a second time.

"Okay, I imagine that I am to be married today. My eyelids and my cheekbones are painted with beautiful streaks of charcoal, and there's a wreath of feathers woven into my hair. I'm young and voluptuous, on my way to shop for the freshest fruits I can find, for I have promised my betrothed a plateful of the highly prized pitaya fruit, sacred to our people, which I will serve to him with my bare fingers when we're dismissed to our private chambers after the ceremony tonight." She shook her head, causing a few odd curls to bounce around her face, making her look far younger, mused Nat, someone who still had dreams and believed in fairytales. "Oh, dear, you must think me a fool," she recoiled as the deep-seated fear crept back in.

"That is hardly the case, Natalia. Seeing you excited like this is a gift to me."

"Oh, thank you, Nat," she blurted out, relief pouring over her once again. "I don't know how I can ever thank you, for reminding me what it feels like to imagine . . . to hope."

Well, there is this one thing . . .

"Would you be interested in this pontoon here? I can give you a very nice tour, Señor, for you and the Señora." Nat might've been bothered the trajinera operator was interrupting this most provocative moment. However, the fact that the guy seemed to consider his and Natalia's outing together nothing unusual overrode that concern. As such, he accepted the guide's offer, steering Natalia in that direction with his hand on the small of her back.

Theirs was a turquoise-framed trajinera, the *Rosalina*, the letters painted in vibrant yellow and red script along the vessel's front archway. Below her namesake were two child-sized orange doves on either side of an indigo heart, held in place by a fuchsia sash between the birds' beaks. The boat's floor was painted in alternating, meter-long triangles of turquoise and red. The effect was at first dazzling, and then dizzying, which Nat found appropriate, since it was exactly how he felt whenever he was around Natalia.

The two of them slid into seats along a bright red bench, shaded by the turquoise canopy, the boat gliding out into open water. There was a bottle of tequila sitting there—on a bright yellow table. Which made Nat think of Frida. And then, *bammo*, the images from another life were flooding his consciousness—of the Kahlo sisters, Matilde, and Guillermo, all of them crowded around the other bright yellow table, Frida taunting him with her elbow. He bit down on his tongue, to punish himself for his mental laxity, chasing away the memories, because he didn't want to be thinking about any of that right now. He reached for the tequila, pouring two glasses, to bring focus to the time and place he'd been dreaming of for days now.

"Salud, to life!"

"Yes, Nat, to life!" she echoed back, sitting up straight, reaching her head high, the light breeze breaking across the deck, making her cheeks flush and teasing her curls again. The mood was light as they settled back into their seats, chuckling when they came upon a group of children squealing with delight as they tried catching the boat's wake with their fingertips. As they glided along, they bent their heads together, pointing out the details of the banksides' lush flora. They clapped heartily when a boat of mariachis performed a particularly festive set that made all those within earshot tap their feet and clap their hands. And so elapsed the next couple hours, sipping tequila, savoring the ambiance, letting the serenity of life away from the Casa Azul wash over them.

"Compadres, excuse me, but may I draw your attention to that doll over there? You see it?" interjected their guide, pointing to the child's toy nailed to a tree on the nearest chinampa, or island. "I wouldn't have interrupted, but everyone who comes out here wants to hear the story behind it. I figured you'd be the same?" He waited briefly, in case there was any objection. The truth was, he'd never been hired by a monkey before. Hell, he'd never even *talked* to a monkey before, and he'd heard they could turn vicious when provoked.

If he'd stayed on task, Nat would've protested. Today was supposed to be a joyous occasion, not one haunted by a maimed doll. But just as occurred when he'd first taken note of the boat's bright yellow table, so, too, did the doll send his thoughts reeling back to the Casa Azul . . . He thought of a younger Frida cradling the disfigured toy, first bathing it, then gussying it up in a white cotton dress and matching bonnet, and how, after that, she'd probably tuck it into bed alongside the others she so dutifully tended to—*yes, that would be just like her!*—Nat smiled to himself, continuing not to hear the guide's dramatic rendering of the actual doll's fate. Not the part about the toy having belonged to a girl who'd drowned right around this very spot, nor the part about the kind hermit who'd come to pay homage to the deceased on the next day, only to discover her body gone and the doll in its place. And certainly not the part about the panicked hermit then nailing the doll to the tree in order to fend off the girl's evil spirit—which, as legend had it, still haunted the canals today!

"Oh, that's a horrible story, just horrible!" Natalia cried, shrinking into Nat's side and startling him back to the moment.

Natalia was right, it was horrible! That he'd wasted even one second thinking about Frida's pinche doll obsession was horribly horrible! He wanted to slap himself silly for being sidetracked like that. Why couldn't she just leave him alone? Was it so she could make him as miserable as she was? Because he wasn't giving up that easily! He looked around for a distraction—*something! anything!* He had to get back in control of the situation, to save this day. That's when he noticed a jewelry vendor paddling by.

"Oye, joven, pull up your boat, will you? Show me what you got there." Nat knew he sounded gruff, and that the "joven" to whom he was speaking was easily twenty years his senior. But sentimentality was a slippery slope—one misstep, and suddenly, you're tumbling down that mountain, *smack* into a bright yellow table or a fucking dollhouse!

"¡Claro, para servirles! One hundred percent real silver here, Señor, I got it straight from Taxco." Effortlessly, the vendor slipped his vessel right up alongside the *Rosalina*, reaching for his case with the midnight blue faux-velvet interior, then rearranging the display slightly to prioritize what years of experience had taught him about what certain kinds of customers tended to be most interested in. Which turned out to be futile in this instance. *Wait, is that a monkey? I'm selling jewelry to a monkey? Oh, well, you got all kinds out here, that was for sure. And if the monkey had the money . . .*

"Or I got amber—maybe you are someone who prefers amber? And turquoise, only the best quality here. Which one does the Señora like?"

The image of Frida rehabilitating that dismembered doll was still haunting him, but at least Natalia seemed to have rebounded, hovering over the boat's edge to peek at the vendor's collection. Which helped Nat to relax a little, because maybe the day could still be salvaged. The sun was beginning its slow descent, turning the water a darker, murkier shade of green as the shadows crept over the canals. There was something primal about this time of day, when the traffic was reduced to a trickle, all the commotion humanity brought with it halted, just the calming sound of oars slicing through water, a lone boat of straggling partygoers laughing downstream, the crickets warming up for their evening serenade.

"May I see that amber ring, please?"

The vendor stood up with the piece, leaning over to hand it to Nat. Nat reciprocated with the required pesos, the significance of the moment coming into focus now, because this was really happening, fumbling the ring nervously in his hands as he returned to his seat next to Natalia. Loose-lipped from the tequila, but still too jittery to look in her eyes, Nat began his declaration. It wasn't the way he'd imagined it, but then, this certainly wouldn't be the first time his life was unfolding in a way he couldn't have predicted.

"Did you know, Natalia, that amber is a capsule of carbonized truths? That up to this point, its contents have remained a secret? Were we to crack it open under a microscope, perhaps we'd discover an insect wing containing genetic details about when it inhabited this land. Or maybe we'd find a strand of hair from an Aztec child, carrying with it hints about a civilization that sailed these very canals centuries ago. Like the resin in my hands, I, too, have a secret, Natalia—one I'm afraid I can no longer keep hidden. Natalia, I must confess to you that I have fallen—" He lifted his head, leaning in with his lips, to consecrate their unlikely courtship.

But she'd fallen asleep, woozy from the tequila, her head resting against the side of the boat, a gentle snore dashing his hopes.

"It's not a big deal. I told you, nothing happened." He was explaining to Zoe where he'd been all day. "Natalia could use a friend, is all. Since when's a little compassion such a bad thing anyway? Humanity's not exactly overflowing with it, in case you hadn't noticed!"

"I just don't want you to get hurt, Nat. She's married. And if Diego finds out—"

"Diego's not going to find out, Zoe!" Nat was in a bit of a snit, cursing himself for having continued pouring the tequila—poor Natalia, it was his own fault his amorous gesture hadn't been received the way he'd hoped. "Anyway, the UglyFrogMan's barely here anymore. Sure, he turns up for the parties, but then he's gone again in the next minute—not that I'm complaining. My hunch is the brute is too busy making notches in his bedpost to notice what anyone else is up to.

"Come to think of it, I haven't seen a whole lot of Frida lately either. *Hmmm* . . . when was the last time? Tuesday maybe? Or was that

Wednesday? Well, whenever it was, she sure was in a state, stomping around here like some kind of deranged army sergeant. What was her problem again? Oh, yeah, she couldn't find her Russian dictionary. She needed it to transcribe some notes for Leon. 'Yeah, Frida, I stole your Russian dictionary because I enjoy watching you act demonical! It's such fun!'" he mimicked disdainfully. Because he really didn't care what day it'd been. Nor what she'd been up to. He wasn't in any mood to be worrying about Frida, not when he had the evenings with Natalia to look forward to.

What Nat didn't know was that Zoe had reached her tipping point. The way she saw it, Nat was on the precipice of disaster, and she had to find a way to help. For starters, it didn't sit well with her the way Nat was flirting with danger, chasing after Natalia like a dog in heat (no offense to her own genus). But what concerned her infinitely more was that Nat was acting like Frida didn't even exist. Though Frida and Nat's relationship had frayed over the years, he'd still actively fretted over some look she'd shot him, or how many hours had expired since the last time she'd acknowledged his presence. The point being that whether the two were on speaking terms or not, Nat had always and without question been obsessed with Frida's impression of him. That is, until now. And it was this egregious change in behavior that sent Zoe into action.

She called together the PatioPets, pleading with them to double down on their efforts with the patchwork quilt, because Nat's love of sewing was deeply rooted in the history of his life, and maybe seeing the finished product would jog his memory. The PatioPets had responded with an outpouring of enthusiasm. GalloUno y GalloDos concocted a way to press the colorful dyes from the patio's flowers by using their nibs against the stones, subsequently creating a spectrum of new colors so rich and deep that the pets could swear they had flavors and smells. And

MyDoe agreed to do the covert runs up to Frida's bedroom, rummaging through jewelry boxes for odd trinkets and embellishments they might use, because who would suspect her of such deviousness? The resident spiders hunkered down to provide an extra supply of silk should it be needed, and the birds on the property offered their musical services as entertainment for the hardworking crew. For her part, Conchita was quick to bring them trays of nuts (without peanuts) and fruit to support their endeavors.

"Hurry! Keep going," Zoe urged them. "I don't know how much time we have left!"

"Oye, Nat, have you seen my petticoat?" Frida called out from below his nest.

The hour was much too early for a creature who'd pretty much become nocturnal since the Trotskys' arrival. Despite that awkward moment in Xochimilco a week earlier, he and Natalia had continued with their late-night rendezvous. (She had no memory of what had gone wrong that day; ergo, there was no reason for him to be burdened with shame.)

"The one with the lace. I thought it was hanging on my armoire." A pause, and then, "Nat, are you listening to me?"

He succumbed to her badgering, laboring to pull himself up to standing, then working out the cricks in his neck, resigned to confronting the day, because she wasn't going to let this go.

"I need it for a self-portrait."

Ah, yes, here we go! "Sorry, haven't seen it."

"It's to wear around my face."

He shook his head. Not because he was confused by whatever odd connection existed between a petticoat and her face—he didn't care enough to be confused. It was because some things never changed, and here she was back to goading him again. *Best to get it over with,* he told himself. *Go ahead and accept the stale bait she keeps tossing you.*

"But Frida, I thought petticoats went *under* one's skirts?" he posited with exaggerated curiosity.

"Normally, yes. But you know how much I subscribe to 'normal.'" She shot him the same coy smile that generally accompanied these little acts. "Since you asked, though, let me brag—just a little, between friends? Because I think this next project of mine is going to be *geeeennius!*" she exclaimed, looking to the heavens as she melted slightly into her knees, fists clenched by her sides.

Nat searched her face for any sign of who she used to be—that she was mocking herself in some small way, or that the coja who got pushed around in the schoolyard was scared, and if she could just get his approval—shit, at this point he would've taken either. However, what he saw was a smugness brimming with bitterness so audacious that he had to steel his bowels for the extra control he needed right now. Oh, yeah, she was definitely up to something. Whatever it turned out to be, all he could hope for was that it didn't turn the Casa Azul upside down.

"I need to give you the backstory first, though. It makes more sense that way."

He did his best to nod.

"Okay, so it happened during colonial times. Apparently, a European ship got lost at sea, and a woman's wardrobe from the sunken vessel washed up on the Oaxacan shore. Chroniclers say it was recovered by a group of Tehuantepec villagers, who were greatly amused by the garments inside, trying them on like costumes for a play that had no script. But when they got to the petticoats, they were particularly perplexed, what with no buttons or clasps to identify how they were intended to be worn. Ultimately, the group decided that the women would wear them as headdresses in the upcoming local festival. And guess what? The villagers went so wild with excitement that the elders decreed that the petticoat-as-headdress would henceforth be adopted as a staple of their wardrobe. And you know what else? The Tehuantepec women still wear those petticoats around their faces even today!" she huffed through her conclusion, catching her breath as she pressed the folds of her skirts into her form.

"And that, my dear Nat, is the tale of how the Tehuantepec women appropriated Western culture for their own ends! By turning Eurocentrism on its head—literally, ja ja ja. Which is exactly what I'm about to do, too—ugh, as soon as I find that damn thing!" And then she was done with him, already heading across the patio to look for Conchita, she was always a good listener.

He watched her go, contemplating a brave retort like, "But Tehuantepec is a mouthful, 'might be too intimidating, you know, for those less informed,' isn't that how you put it, Frida? How about we just call them 'Huante' women instead?" But he presumed she'd miss his point. *And that, my dear Frida, is the tale of how an egotistical debutante appropriated Tehuantepec culture for her own ends!*

"Why so sad-faced, Nat? You okay?" It was Natalia, coming upon Nat grumbling from his nest. "I'm on my way to the kitchen for some coffee, if you'd care to join me?"

"You know what, I'd like that very much." He shimmied down from the PoutingTree, loping over to her side. "It seems you've caught me on an off day, is all. A cup of coffee sounds nice."

"Glad I came across you, then," she said, patting him gently on the head in the same friendly manner she always did. "Tell me, what's happened that's upset you?" They were in the kitchen now, Natalia pouring two cups of coffee, then carrying them over to the bright yellow table where they took seats opposite each other. The French doors had been left open to let the freshness of the late morning air come in off the patio, broken rays of dusty sunlight trickling in through the garden's foliage.

"Well, I don't usually speak poorly of Frida." *What goes on in my head is another story.* "She's done so much for me since my exodus from the jungle." *Mostly, break my heart and fill my head with self-doubt.* "But lately . . .

well, I don't know how else to say this, except to come straight out and say it . . ."

"Yes, Nat, what is it?"

"Sometimes I feel like Frida doesn't appreciate me. It's like she only calls upon me when there's something I can do to further her agenda. Oh, Natalia, I know I sound ungrateful—"

"Actually, Nat, it doesn't sound ungrateful, not at all. I think I understand." She rested her elbows on the table, blowing on her coffee and then taking a short sip, her gaze fixed thoughtfully ahead. "I, too, live with an artist—perhaps not an expert of forms and colors like Frida, but one of words. Leon asks a lot of me, which I'm eager to do most of the time. I believe wholeheartedly in his work, and I know firsthand the obstacles he's had to overcome. But it's come at a price for me, having to resign myself to being the one who transcribes his work, or irons his trousers, all the tedium that goes on behind the scenes. I'm going to let you in on a little secret . . ."

A secret? I, too, have a secret I've been wanting to tell you! You go first, then I'll reveal mine!

"I'm a writer myself. Everyone speaks of Leon's accolades, but I've also produced some influential manifestos. It's not my intention to be boastful or remorseful here, but to share what my experience with an avant-garde thinker has been like, to let you know that I can empathize with the sacrifices you've surely had to make in order to help someone else's dreams come true.

"Well, and then there's that complicating factor—namely, that our two artists have quite the egos. Oh, how Leon and Frida love to be loved, don't they?" She issued a half-hearted chuckle. "Sometimes I wonder, though, if perhaps they've no choice but to be so self-centered? Their foe is formidable, after all, and their critics relentless. Maybe they have to believe they're larger than life, inflate themselves beyond reproach, so they can persevere with their work. My advice to you, Nat, is that if Frida's only asking you to praise her outfit or a sketch she's done, then, really, there's no harm done, right? I mean, no one's getting hurt, at least. Sometimes it helps me a bit to frame it that way."

He nodded excitedly, a wide-eyed child receiving life-changing moral instruction. He could feel his lower lip begin to tremble because, on the one hand, she was providing a rational explanation for Frida's erratic behavior, but equally so, because Natalia cared enough to listen.

"Rather than stew in anger, I've made it my mission to try to consider Leon's idiosyncrasies as purely harmless affectations, nothing we can't overlook for the greater good. Come, now, Nat, cheer up, why don't you! You're such an important source of light around here. Why, just look how much joy you've brought into my life! Miracle of all miracles, sometimes I even laugh now." She smiled at him before putting her cup down and standing up. "Unfortunately, I must excuse myself. Duty calls! Leon has requested a rare manuscript from the city, and so, off I go. We'll talk later, of course. Do try to enjoy the rest of your day."

On a different day, Nat might've been jealous that Natalia was still under Leon's spell. Or that her "secret" had turned out to be something as dry as a curriculum vitae. But on this day, he was too invigorated by her admission that his presence brought her joy to let anything else matter.

When the day's light was fading, Nat was decided on his next move. He'd had a change of heart since his conversation with Natalia earlier in the day, reminded that Frida had been under attack since the day she'd contracted polio—well, and even before that, when you thought about it; more precisely, since the day she was born, because she had ovaries. As such, she had to be self-promoting, and she had to be willing to push people (or monkeys) out of the way when necessary. He could be disappointed by her behavior, sure, that was fair. But as her friend, the best he could do was sympathize with her for all the pain her otherness had caused. He reminded himself that her pain belonged solely to her; she got to determine how she expressed it. Plus, it's not like she'd ever really hurt anyone, right? She wasn't carrying out crimes against humanity. She was sad and she was mad, that was all. How much damage could she do anyway? Embarrassed by his lapse of judgement, but also liberated by this new clarity, Nat headed upstairs to look for Frida's petticoat, to make a go of this new beginning.

"You up here, Frida?" He tapped lightly on the door as he reached for the doorknob, because he could've sworn he'd seen her go out earlier. But it was already too late. The door had swung open of its own accord. And Nat was looking straight at Frida—or rather, her two splayed thighs. Pressed on top of her was Leon Trotsky, panting, his bare buttocks thrust out. The smell of sex hung in the air, a noxious cloud that reeked of bitterness, betrayal, and above all else, unbridled callousness. Without turning around, Nat started backing up, staring straight ahead at the spectacle in front of him but no longer seeing anything. As if it mattered, he closed the door behind him.

He raced down the stairs, grabbing Zoe by the paw. "Can we get out of here?" He was pulling her now, because what he was proposing was not debatable.

"Where are we going, Nat? It's late, what about the other pets, we've got something for you—"

No, Nat, wait! Let me explain! Don't go!

During his frazzled exodus, he thought he heard her voice coming from the upstairs window; was she calling to him out here on the street? No, that couldn't be, Frida didn't apologize. The neurons in his brain were fizzling, his thoughts being pulled into a thick murkiness where emotion did not exist. He was operating on pure instinct now, picking up the pace, not moving toward anything as much as away from everything, he had to get away.

Nahuatl, please! Just listen to what I have to say! DON'T LEAVE ME!

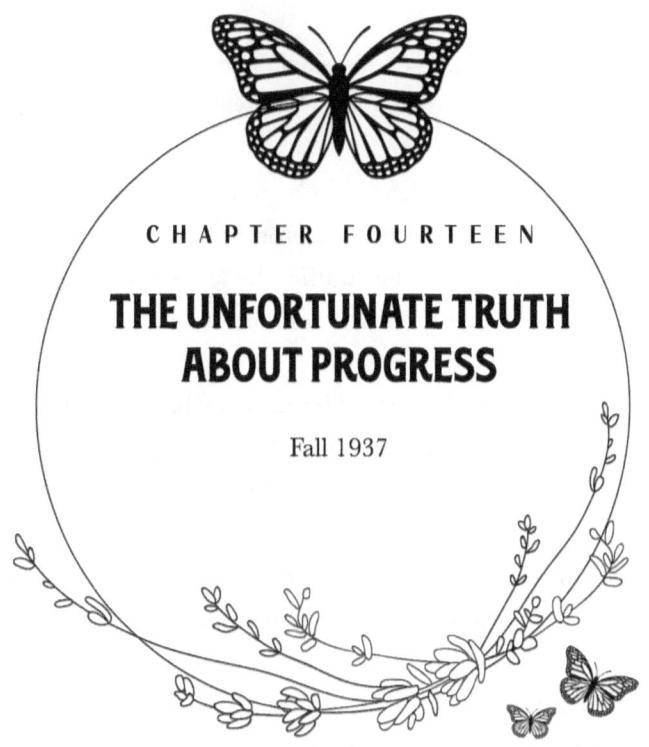

CHAPTER FOURTEEN

THE UNFORTUNATE TRUTH ABOUT PROGRESS

Fall 1937

"Ouch! I think we might've overdone it a little at the CornerBar last night," Zoe remarked, rubbing her temples. The pets were huddled together on their bench in the Plaza, the sun beginning its slow ascent. "Hey, I was thinking, and I get you might not like this idea, but you know what we should do?" she tried again, a little louder this time, because why wasn't he responding? "Sneak back to the Casa Azul? Take advantage of a warm meal and a big, soft bed? We don't have to talk to her, just in and out, as soon as we're feeling better?" She was holding her breath, expecting a barrage of sharp refusals expressed in the crassest of terms. But there was only silence.

"Nat? Did you hear what I just said?" Because worse than that barrage of sharp refusals was his lack of response. Zoe had just proposed that they return to the home of the single person he hated most in this world, and he wasn't even flinching? "Nat, what is going on with you?" She tugged on his arm now.

"A monkey! I see a monkey!" Zoe's panic was redirected toward a preschool-age boy careening their way. From the way he was plowing indiscriminately through pedestrian traffic, she knew the kid had to be a troublemaker, one of those tykes who runs around half-cocked from sunup until sundown.

"Nat, I need you to wake up!" Her urgency had escalated, shaking all of him now. "We got a big problem! Nat, *WAKE UP!*"

The child skidded to a stop in front of the bench. In time to overhear Zoe's plea.

"Hey, and it's a talking doggie? A monkey and a talking dog! Oh, wow, this is the best day of my entire life—wait, who brought you guys here? Where's your owner?" The boy's eyes turned into menacing slits, a devious grin spreading across his face. "Oh, you're callejeros, strays, ja, so that's what this is! I'm going to ask my mommy if I can—"

"No, kid you don't understand, my friend here is very sick . . . A very bad thing has happened, I think that's what's done him in, we need to find help."

The boy crossed his arms over his chest, tapping the five fingers of one hand precisely against the five fingers of the other.

Zoe wondered how someone so new to this world had managed already to develop such a psychotic countenance.

"I can help him, little doggie, don't worry—"

"Juancho, Dios mío, how dare you, running off like that!" The boy's mother, Dolores, arrived on the scene in a huff, jerking her son's arm toward her side with an irritated grunt. "It's time to go. Your father is waiting." She turned with son in tow, but the boy wouldn't budge.

"No."

"What did you say?"

"I said, no, I'm not coming. Unless . . ." The same calculating smirk reappeared on the boy's face. "Unless I get to bring the monkey and the dog. I want to bring them home with us."

Dolores could feel the crowd gathering around them. Her head was reeling. How could Juancho do this, putting her under all this scrutiny? Where was her husband, by the way? Why was he never around to help his own wife? Why did he always have to be focusing on los de abajo, sacrificing his own family to help the world's underdogs? Unbelievable! Dear God, she wished she could vanish into thin air . . .

(What she would've done to go back in time, back to her exemplary life of serving Church and family, when her name appeared proudly in the neighborhood circular every edition. But then that bastard husband of hers had gone and ruined everything, deluded into thinking his law degree meant his fellow licenciados were the only "true revolutionaries" capable of carrying out unfinished reform. She'd been patient—why, she was the prototype of what a wife was supposed to be, didn't he ever pause to appreciate that? But when he went after the Church, well, that was just too much, and their marriage had begun to crumble. They'd never divorce—oh, heaven's no, not in a million years!—but the love between them had since been exhausted.

"Do I need to tell you again how my mother used her bare hands to build that ramshackle altar behind La Prosperidad? About how I spent my childhood watching her pour her heart into that thing, as if lighting another candle would put food on our table? Do I, Dolores?

"And do I need to remind you how God rewarded her for that dedication? How our land was overrun by bandits, and our avocado farm went under? Her efforts were for naught, Dolores! That's what your God gave her!")

The crowds were closing in, sealing off her escape routes. She felt like she was standing alone in a bull ring, defenseless, the crowd's anticipatory silence foreshadowing the cheers of scorn soon to be pelted down upon her, a doomed torera backed into a corner by the bull, eyes red with rage, its preschool embodiment no disguise for the fury it was prepared to unleash upon her.

"Okay, Juancho, bring the animals, but we're leaving now," she hissed. She ran her fingers through her hair, forcing a smile, and only then turned around to face the crowd, for everyone to see that all was well, she'd solved the problem. *What child didn't long for a pet? It wasn't that big a deal, now, was it? These things happened,* she'd counter when the questions began to fly later that day.

"Thank you, Mommy, here I come," chirped the boy, capable of playing to the public just as effectively as she. He swept the pets into the air by the napes of their necks, then clasped them to his chest as he waddled after his mother.

"*Psst,* Nat, what are we going to do?" Zoe whispered in his ear, untucking her leg from the back of his knee, then his tail from around her middle. "The ImpBoy has us, Nat . . . He's carrying us somewhere." She poked him in the back with the leg she'd just freed. "Nat, you have to do something! Nat? *Nat!*"

"Shhh! You don't want to make Daddy mad, trust me!"

"Finally! Where the hell have you two been? We're late, hurry up!" hollered the boy's father when he spotted his wife crossing the street in his direction, his son's smaller frame tucked in behind her. The man shook his head, collapsing into the driver's seat, his form too heavy with despair for his mere thirty years on Earth.

"Sorry, Daddy." Juancho had arrived at the car's back passenger door now, waiting for his mother to let him in, pets wrapped in his arms where his father had yet to notice them. "Guess what? When Church was over, and me and Mommy were coming back to find you, I saw a monkey and a dog—"

The father snapped his hand off the ignition, infuriated by his wife's continued blind obedience to Catholic doctrine, not to mention her spineless acquiescence to what he suspected his son was about to reveal.

"What?" he barked.

"Don't be mad, Daddy."

"For crying out loud, Juancho, don't play games with me!" he screamed. He hopped out of the car, marching around the back to assess the situation. "No, Juancho, no pets in our building, you know that! We've been over it a thousand times! There are rules to follow—rules that are actually fair and just this time, but you can thank me for that when you're older and can appreciate the sacrifices I've made to be sure of it. The point is, you don't get to pick and choose which rules to obey based on personal whim; that's not how a republic works. What the—" He was standing in front of his son now, agape at what he was looking at. There was the monkey—wearing a finely starched guayabera shirt, but no pants?—with a dog tucked into his lap, her tiny face straining to peek out from between his arms.

"*Yip.*" *Can you hear me?* She had to try something; Nat wasn't helping.

The father's heart skipped a beat. Was that the dog . . . talking? No, of course not!

"*Yip!*" *Gracias a Dios, you can, I can tell by the look on your face. Please, you must help us, my friend is unwell, and we're in a predicament.* Zoe paused, because even with all the pandemonium spinning around her, there was something familiar about this man. *Wait, do I know you? Have we met? Was it at the CornerBar? Or in the Plaza? Ay de mí, where was it?*

The man prided himself on being a master of rhetoric, twisting around words and ideas to create illogical logic, to convince the court that his arguments were superior to those of his opponents. For the greater good, of course, always for the greater good, to bring justice for all, the way he'd promised his father, may he rest in peace. And yet, he was at a loss for words in the presence of this dog. He had the sudden and inexplicable urge to sample from that unknown dimension his law books failed to account for, where the irrational and mystical exerted influence over everyday life, reaching out one hand toward the dog now, touching her snout. A jolt of electricity shot up his arm, making his lip tremble and his eyes moisten.

You felt it, too? I knew it! Yes, we know each other somehow, this is more than mere coincidence, Señor—

"What is happening?" He couldn't contain himself, the words spilling out, fiery, acrid bits of matter released at last from the purgatory where they'd been held hostage since childhood.

"Daddy? Are you talking to the dog?" More smirking from the boy.

"¡Juancho, callate!" The man returned instantly to his highly practical demeanor, for he was a survivor, damnit, a hard-nosed prosecutor. "I'm taking the monkey." He gritted his teeth. He wouldn't take the dog just yet. His mind was spinning, wandering back to La Prosperidad, the day he'd cowered behind the tree, a bystander in his own life, all the anger and the shame slapping him in the face again. Yes, he'd figure out what to do with the dog later. For now, he'd get rid of the monkey. *What the fuck, Dolores? This thing belongs in the jungle. What is the matter with you?* He snatched Nat from his son's arms.

"Yip!" *No, my friend is sick, Señor, we need your help, please, you can still do good in the face of evil!*

Juancho dropped to the ground in tears, wrapping his arms around his father's ankles. "Don't do this, Daddy, don't take my monkey!"

Please, I'm begging you! "Yip! Yip! Yip!"

In a single movement, the man bent down to pry his son from his legs, and then he stood up again. Any hesitation now would be an admission of weakness. He'd had to grow up fast to get this far in life, and he wasn't about to throw it all away now because of some fleeting childhood memory. He knew firsthand that getting too attached to any living creature was a recipe for disaster. Best for Juancho to learn that now; it was due time his son toughen up a little anyway.

"I'm sorry, Juancho, but rules are rules. It's how justice is accomplished."

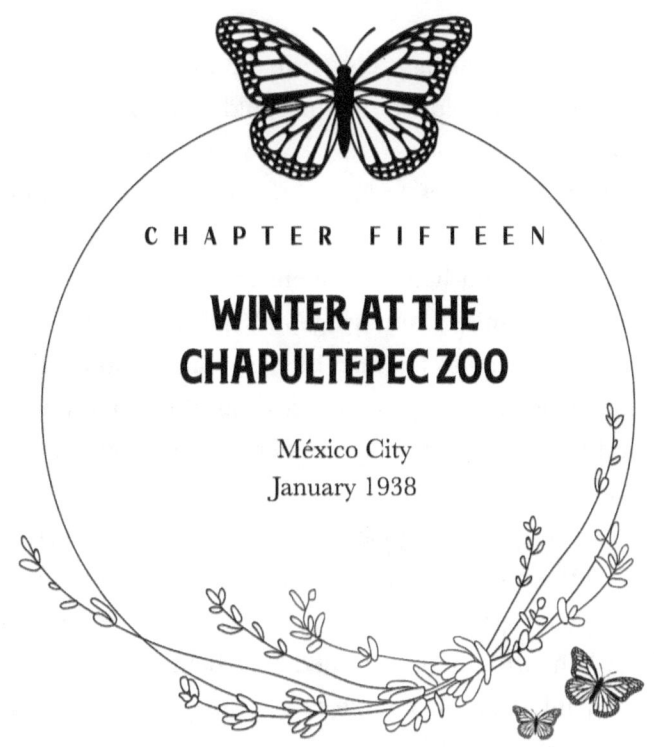

CHAPTER FIFTEEN

WINTER AT THE CHAPULTEPEC ZOO

México City
January 1938

Juancho's father headed straight to Chapultepec Park. He was still shaking, furious about his wife's feebleness and his son's manipulation—well, and his interaction with the dog had certainly caught him off guard! He didn't have time for all this nonsense. Why should he care if he knew the dog or not, because the fact remained there were *no dogs allowed in their building,* and that was the only thing that mattered when it came down to it. There was no need to go down memory lane, digging up all that nostalgia and sentimental stuff, nope, he was done! The dog was as good as gone as far as he was concerned. He'd make a call and have her taken away before he even got home, yeah, now that was a good idea, he'd do that! He forced a smile, tightening his grip on the steering wheel, increasing pressure on the gas pedal, soothed when the scenery faded into a blur so that he could imagine he was in some other day that wasn't this one.

It turned out the zoo was ecstatic about hosting the spider monkey. The steady development of the logging industry had made the species nearly extinct, so what a happy accident this was! They'd take good care of him, they promised, removing Nat's guayabera shirt, prodding around his private parts to confirm his sex, combing through his fur for fleas. But Juancho's dad couldn't have cared less. He was already halfway out the door by the time the staffers turned around to see if he had any other concerns.

Once deemed to be "in good standing," Nat was hauled over to the far side of the property, and, per the curator's insistence that the African animals be grouped together, housed in the cell next to the Bengal tiger. When the door slammed shut behind him, Nat looked up briefly, noticing the artificial tree cast in the center of his cage, and then he looked back at the ground.

"*Yip!*"

Nah, there was no way. Maybe he was already dead, and this was what the afterlife looked like.

"*Yip*, hi, Nat, it's me!"

But no, it was Zoe all right, slipping in between the cage bars.

"I snuck in through the car's back window, when the dad was lecturing the ImpBoy about laws and justice, in case you were wondering." She was speaking clearly, but her insides were quivering. *Come on, Nat, please be okay, stay with me, pal.* "And here's the best part, Nat, you're going to love this. I realized that if I'd been any bigger, I wouldn't have fit through that window, and I wouldn't have been able to come after you—I would've lost you, is what I'm saying, Nat! It's like you're always telling me, about 'bigger than X' not necessarily being better, remember? Well, you were right, Nat, I believe you now! I am the perfect size!" Her size, plus the fact that she'd gone with her gut instinct, hopping in the car without asking God for direction. It'd only dawned on her later, tucked away in the back seat on the ride over, that if she'd taken the precious time to do so, the opportunity would've passed her by.

"Nat?" *Please, answer me, Nat.*

Stirred by the sweet timbre of Zoe's voice, Nat's words began coming back to him. And though his compromised mental state made him unable to grasp all of what she was saying, he was aware that she'd come for him, and that she'd defied great odds to do so. He wiggled his finger for her to come closer, pulling her into his chest, the warmth of her body stoking the small flicker still alive in him.

Two weeks later, Nat was still locked away in his cell. He barely stirred anymore. He didn't flinch when children flung peanuts in his direction, enticements to "roll over" or "make me laugh." Interestingly, he didn't refuse their demands out of self-dignity—he had no self-dignity anymore, because he didn't care enough to have any—but because peanuts made him think of Paulina. And he didn't want to be reminded of anything from the past. All he wanted was to close off the rest of the world, so he could forget.

Zoe's situation was entirely different, however. Because she wasn't a "registered guest," she was able to move about under the zoo administration's radar. Further, the fact that she was "smaller than X" meant that she could slip between the cage's bars as she saw fit. Fiercely loyal, she spent the nights by Nat's side, but she couldn't risk being seen in the light of day. (The possibility that humanity might be foolish enough to label Xolo dogs as, say, Antarctic creatures, petrified her—such frigid temperatures would be intolerable for a hairless creature such as herself!) So, each morning, she slipped out to while away the hours, exploring nearby neighborhoods, in search of inspirational stories, of earthly wonders and human decency wherever they could be found, so that she might have tales to share with Nat at the end of the day.

On this particular morning, Zoe happened upon a quiet street lined by jacaranda trees in full bloom, their lilac boughs bent over from the flowers' weight, forming an enchanting makeshift canopy. The trees were aflush with a soft scent that reminded Zoe of the grape soda she and Nat used to buy at the neighborhood bodega on hot summer afternoons, gulping it down, and then practicing their eructation skills through snickers and snorts. She smiled at the recollection, turning in that direction, letting herself be pulled into the ambiance of this other world that was antithetical to the steel and brick labyrinth that defined city life. Several blocks later, two giggling children zipped by, nearly cutting her off, so immersed in their game of tag that they'd barely noticed her. Zoe wasn't mad; rather, she marveled at the way they were able to embrace the adrenaline and joy pulsing through their veins, fully engaged in the moment, and temporarily free of daily burdens. This, too, made her smile, feeling like she'd stumbled upon something good today, and she wanted to keep this nectar flowing.

She continued along, veering from the current street when the jacaranda canopy bent in that direction, then taking a sharp right, and then another right, followed by a quick left, all of it according to the magical maze unilaterally determined by the jacarandas. At some point—she'd lost track of all her twists and turns, the height of the sun indicating she'd been at this for some time now—she came upon a table of elderly men outside a café, taking their morning coffee over a game of chess as they clattered on about politics, their knights and their pawns pushing on in friendly competition. Basic things, life's daily activities. She stood there for a few minutes, unflinching, letting the revelation sink in that perhaps there could be good things that come out of "rivalries," that maybe competition didn't have to be a zero-sum game that ended in tears, illicit love affairs, or wars. Maybe there were peaceful—dare she dream, even joyful—outcomes that resulted when two parties were pitted against each other, because each was pushing the other to do better, be wiser, think more strategically as the parties negotiated forward toward the game's end. Yes, Nat would have to take pleasure in the stories, right? How could he not?

The problem was that Zoe was so enjoying herself that by the time she finally paused, she was lost. She scolded herself for not being more mindful, that there was no space in her world for living with her head in the clouds and chasing jacaranda blooms, sheesh! She had more important things to tend to: Nat was still locked behind bars.

When she looked around in search of any kind of recognizable landmark, her eyes landed on a fantastical church located on the neighborhood's central plaza. The edifice was constructed entirely of stucco, its white-washed walls radiant in the afternoon sun, making her raise one paw to shade her eyes from the glare. The only break in the building's sheer exterior was a green and turquoise archway framing the front doors, a thousand fist-sized geometrical and floral inlays pieced together like tiles in a mosaic, a brilliant display of architectural dissonance that had the net effect of being mesmerizingly alluring. None of this should have affected her, because every neighborhood in México had a church, what was one more? Well, and not to mention that she couldn't remember the last time she'd actually been inside one. Except that this church was unlike any other she'd ever come upon: this one resembled a castle, like in fairy tale lore, more apt to be floating in the clouds than anchored to the ground. She couldn't contain the urge to know more, and so she went in.

Zoe was shocked when she walked in. For she was not immediately besieged by throngs of pain-stricken martyrs with bloody wounds staring down at her with pitiful eyes. Nor were there any suffocating confessionals shrewdly disguised in delicate latticework to entice guilty sinners looking for solace and a way out of the hell they'd taken one step closer to. There were no gilded urns or brass candlesticks or grandiose pipe organs. Why, there weren't even pews; instead strategically placed piles of pine needles stretched horizontally along the floor. Gathered around the needles in small, intimate huddles were worshippers kneeling in prayer, crouched over half-empty pulque bottles, fresh flowers, tattered photos. Along the back wall was a small stage upon which stood an olive-skinned priest with oversized spectacles and a knee-length, black woolen vest worn over white pants. He was chanting in a language Zoe didn't recognize, sprinkling holy water as he began pacing back and forth across the limited range awarded him. It smelled of piñon and myrrh, evoking primeval forests and supernatural remedies.

And while everything about the place was unfamiliar to her, Zoe felt entirely comfortable—no, it was more than that. Because not only did she feel comfortable, but she felt inspired, as if she'd been jolted awake from a deep spiritual slumber. For suddenly, she could smell His goodness in the earthy mustiness that hugged the cement floor. And she could see His love in the golden flecks of sunlit dust floating in the rafters. And she could hear His joy in the priest's off-count incantation, euphoria spreading through her body, making her feel lighter, until she imagined she was floating above the ruckus.

Just then, an inexplicable gust of wind swept through the building. The pulque bottles toppled over, releasing their final lamentations in small puddles around them. The congregants stopped their prayers, rosary beads dropping to the floor. The priest let go of the dish he'd been holding, its spiraling rotations the final countdown in a world gone suddenly silent. And then, just as suddenly, the stillness was broken, chaos bursting forth as panicked parishioners rushed for the door.

The door was closed!

There's no wind outside!

What in God's name is going on?

How do I explain what just happened?

Slowly, Zoe moved toward the door behind the rest of them. She wasn't frightened; she had felt His presence, and this had reignited something in her. She didn't understand God's reasons for bringing her here today, or for causing the wind. God had His reasons, and she was willing to follow. In retrospect, it was the only glimmer of hope she had left.

Upon exiting the church, rather than dashing off like the rest of the flock, Zoe paused on the small patio at the top of the stairs there, reclining into her haunches.

"¿Es Usted, Dios? ¿Qué quiere?" she pleaded toward the sky above.

No answer. The minutes elapsed. Still nothing.

Zoe was flummoxed about what to do next. She could wait patiently for God to respond, but who knew how long that might be— not that she was complaining, of course, He had so many important things to tend to. Or she could return to the zoo, and regale Nat with tales of her most perplexing day. She exhaled, watching the world go by below—there was a school-age boy peddling newspapers, and a pair of lovers cuddling under a gazebo, and a satisfied businessman twirling his cane in one hand, and a young man ordering lunch from a tamal cart—

I wonder where he's going? She was shocked by the pivot in her train of thought, how she'd gone from theological ruminations to whimsical detective play. Also, she was shocked about why she'd zeroed in on the tamal customer rather than any of the others. Most of all, though, she was shocked as to why was she thinking of "The Daffy Detective Game" right now—it'd been years since she and Nat had chased after grandmothers with bright red lipstick and cargoless mules.

Even after all this time, Nat's love of the game still felt essential to her, like she'd be letting him down if she didn't pursue the suspect. So off she went, tagging along behind the young tamal patron as she considered the evidence at hand: relatively young, overstuffed book bag on one shoulder, portfolio case in other hand. *I bet he's on his way to the university, where he studies law, so he can learn to use all the fancy legalese to challenge the argument that sent his moonlighting grandmother with the bright red lipstick to jail all those years ago!* She smiled to herself, imagining Nat's reaction when he heard such an improbable profile.

A few blocks later, her target came upon an acquaintance. The two men stopped to chat, cordial in their interactions—a friendly embrace here, a pat on the back there. But something changed when the target put down his things and pulled out a poster board from his case. The second man examined it. And then he bent over at the middle like a tree snapped in a windstorm, hand over mouth to smother his cackles. "Holy fucking shit!" he spat out once he'd contained his howls. "No way! Holy fucking shit!" And then he repeated himself twice more.

What was so provocative, Zoe wondered. What had shattered the veil of decorum and turned the two young men into a cursing spectacle? She had to know, centimetering closer to peek at the source of the outburst.

Gasp!

Shiver.

It was a portrait of Frida. Painted by Frida. Actually, it was a reprint of the portrait, but its message was what mattered. The content provided sufficient evidence to generate, at the very least, public commotion from those who didn't know her personally, as the two men in front of her had just proved. At worst, the portrait carried weight enough to cause a catastrophic blow to those who knew her intimately, as proven by Zoe's reaction, feeling herself suddenly pushed from behind, then down a dark tunnel, somersaulting into blackness as she tried to sort through what she'd just witnessed.

In the painting, Frida's hair was arranged in a stack of braids, flowers woven neatly into the plaits, the princess with her campesina crown staring back at her audience, staid and unflinching. Which was all harmless enough. No, the controversy stemmed from the very color in her cheeks, flushed with a peachy, sexual charge. The inflection was not lost on Zoe. She looked to Frida's hands, one holding a small bouquet of wildflowers, the other a piece of paper.

It was the piece of paper that blasted Frida's façade of innocence sky high. Specifically, the words on the paper.

It read: "For Leon Trotsky, with all my love, I dedicate this painting to you."

In other words, she'd gone ahead and insinuated her illicit love affair for everyone to see. To spite Diego. And despite Natalia.

"You did this, Lord, didn't you?" she hissed at the sky. "You brought me here to see this! You set this trap, playing on my empathetic tendencies and religious doubts, placing one crumb after another in front of me, so that I'd end up right here! And what is it exactly You'd like me to do with this knowledge? Oh, tell me, Almighty Sir! Would You like me to hand deliver the painting to Natalia, so she'll see what a bastard Leon is and run straight into Nat's arms for one giant happy ending? Or would You prefer I push my target off a bridge, artwork wrapped in his arms, its message buried in the sandy bottoms, Frida's secret forever hidden from public eyes?

"Yeah, well, You know what? *It doesn't matter!* It doesn't matter what I do, or what Nat does . . . or even what You do! She's determined to destroy everyone in her path if that's what it takes to get back at Diego and a world that's never stopped disrespecting her! It's unfixable, the mess she's made. Leave. Me. Out. Of. It! Let me go back to the zoo and live out my final days in that pinche cage, but don't trick me into throwing myself under a steamroller just to wash Your hands clean of responsibility!"

Zoe didn't care about the stupid game anymore; she darted off in a mad rush. Though she'd been lost, the magnetic force that held Nat and Zoe together was that powerful, pulling her back to the zoo without her awareness, back up the matrix of streets established by the blooming jacaranda trees, back into the mayhem of city life, noticing nothing now, because the only thing that mattered was getting back to Nat, to soak up his goodness or his infinite wisdom—that is, if he had any of those things left to spare. When she slipped into the cage out of breath, Nat sensed her agitation.

"What?" he asked, opening his eyes but barely lifting his head.

"How could she?" Zoe had begun pacing the length of the cage. "How could Frida be that fucking cruel?"

Nat lifted his head. Zoe was cussing. Zoe never cussed. Something was horribly amiss.

"It's unbelievable, Nat! How could she do that?"

Not Frida, not now, I don't want to hear another word about her, please! And still, Nat loved Zoe, even if he no longer loved himself.

"Zoe, tell me what happened, please. I want you to tell me."

Zoe looked at Nat. In his darkest state, he was reaching into the deepest part of himself to try to ease her pain. She hesitated to add to his burden, and yet she desperately needed his guidance. She needed her broken shepherd to make sense of what had occurred today, and then to point them in the right direction. Ultimately, she took a gamble that his strength was greater than his self-contempt. And she let the words spill out, a repugnant tale of the blatant disrespect Frida had inflicted on those nearest and dearest to her.

Nat remained calm, listening to Zoe's story unfold. He didn't rush her through it, nor did he become enraged. He thought of Natalia—of her reaction when she learned about Frida and Leon, imagining her collapsing on the patio ground, utterly alone now, not even a melancholy spider monkey to watch over her anymore.

"Oye, Tzotzil, we can discuss what you've just witnessed, but first, over there, by the elephant's cage? See where I'm pointing?" Zoe turned her head in that direction, nodding. "There's a trumpet vine somewhere over there. I can't see it, but I sure could smell it this morning, sweet as a summer's rose. Grab us a few nips, will you?" Zoe was halfway to the elephant's cage when Nat called out again. "Oh, and would you mind getting us a few more than you think we'll need? You never know." He attempted to smile playfully, because yes, he was aware that it was daytime, and therefore entirely antithetical—if not ominous—that the scent should be accessible at this early hour.

Zoe couldn't help but notice that his lips were twitching like a frayed electrical wire crackling its end-of-life message. And why had he turned suddenly chipper, she wondered. Oh, well, the news she'd just revealed had been shocking. Who wasn't feeling frazzled right now? When she returned with the bouquet, Nat snatched the bunch from her paws, scampering into the tree's highest branches.

"Sheesh, that sure wasn't very gentlemanly behavior for a gentleman-in-training!"

"Gentleman? Are you fucking kidding me, Zoe? I'm no gentleman," he raged back, his demeanor changed again. "Or, I'm sorry, had you not noticed my colossal neglect of everything noble? I mean, come on, just look at me!" His bottom was covered in feces and his face was matted in drool.

"But you know what? I don't fucking care! Turns out being a gentleman isn't what it's made out to be. I've thought impressive things my entire life, and nothing impressive has come my way—no Europe, no palace, and now, no family. Ironic, isn't it, that it's taken me this long to finally realize that to be 'impressive' you gotta turn your back on everything good. Survival of the fittest, just like Darwin and Spencer predicted," he shook his head, already sucking on his second flower, the familiar warmth spreading through his body. "Basta ya, I'm getting out of here."

"Wait, *w-w-what* are you saying?" she stammered, aching to be wrong about what he was implying. Or had they come to that fatal juncture, that most unfortunate intersection of time and circumstance, where they'd both lost faith in the exact same moment, neither one of them able to rescue the other?

Nat's head was purring, his extremities tingling. He shoved a few last flowers into his mouth before his hands went numb, releasing the last of them from his grasp, the petals floating around him into the giant void of nothingness, individual entities now at the mercy of currents larger than their mortal selves, nothing without the roots that had tied them to Earth.

As his mind drifted off, Nat thought of Mamá, the Troop, and the EmeraldLagoon. How he'd spent most of his life running from his past, but something buried deep inside him had always wondered what it was he'd left behind, and if it had been as idyllic as he recalled. Then he wondered if it was possible for an idyllic place to even exist in the first place.

He thought of the finca, the thatched huts, the StatelySitting-Room and Social Darwinism, of the racial and cultural exploitation that determine one's destiny. Of how capitalism caused two continents to collide, irreconcilably, because the system's very definition requires that one side always be stronger than the other, eternally appropriating and consuming, no matter the families torn apart in the process. He'd witnessed firsthand the incursion of the lumber industry and the corresponding German finca, including the resulting displacement of monkeys and indígenas alike. What he was unaware of, but sensed now in his dreamy state, was the small farmer who was seduced into thinking he'd found a niche in the avocado market, only to have his livelihood pulled right out from under him, unaware he'd never really had a chance in the first place, because there is always a predestined winner. Humanity has fated it so.

He thought of the Mexican Revolution, Catholicism, and the struggle for justice. Of how humanity was prone to creating institutions that bred inequality, which inevitably boiled over into war, out of which new, similarly unfair institutions were built. He reflected on the cold-hearted lawyer responsible for dispatching him to this abominable cell in the zoo, a man who, once upon a time, might've been a compassionate little boy with a predisposition to do the right thing, but who was defeated by the very system he'd hoped to reform.

He wanted to keep floating through time, because he felt so good right now, having his load lightened at last. His thoughts were uncoiling so smoothly, like silk thread purling from its spool, wave after wave of relief—

Wait! What was *she* doing here? He didn't want her here—shit, all he wanted was to get away from her, so he could finally rest in peace! But there was Frida, blasting into his dreams—or nightmares, whatever this was turning into—taking center stage, of course she was. There she was with ThatAlejandro bragging about their La Prepa pranks. And there she was scolding him for confronting Diego about his artwork.

Go away! he muttered under his breath, culling together flickering bits of mental energy to force the images from his mind, so he could get back to the obituary he was writing himself. But she refused to leave, this time turning toward him with her other face, the nice one, the one with that playful sparkle in her eyes, the one he'd never learned to say no to. He saw himself leaping into her arms on the first day they met. And sitting on her bed sketching out pranks, mocking the bourgeoisie with the foulest language they knew. He saw them sitting on her balcony on the evening he'd given her the wedding sheet. How they'd both known, without words, that it was another of the many olive branches they would pass back and forth over the years, gestures of everlasting friendship despite the obstacles ahead.

And then, he saw The Light. It was exactly as all literary reports described it—that is to say, it was appropriately indescribable. The hallucinations were coming faster now, clouds of emerald green, pale mint, and cobalt blue marching through his consciousness, evocative of the lagoons, rivers, quarries, and skies that had marked his time on Earth. Well, and come to think of it, also the walls of the Casa Azul, Frida's bathing suit, the vines framing Frida's wedding sheet, her unborn child's bonnet. His life, summed up in a palette of blue and green, welcoming him home. He reached out both hands toward the space in front of him, desperate to touch their coolness. He'd be alright, yes, if he could just collect the colors in his arms, wrap them tightly around himself . . .

Yip, did you really think you were gonna lose me now? I followed you to the zoo, remember?

He stopped seeing in blue and green for the moment, overcome with joy—and just a little bit of wonder, but not too much, because logic would make a mockery of you if you wasted too much time defending it. But of course! He would take Zoe with him; it was the perfect ending, he thought to himself, strapping her to his chest in preparation for their flight ahead. They would chase the blues and greens that inspired him most, follow them over the horizon and into that other reality where he presumed tranquility abounded, where there was no need for logic or probabilities, just smooth sailing ahead.

And, so, Nat reached out for a vine he couldn't see, tightening his grasp around its absence, pulling them up, catapulting them out of the cell, across the zoo, and into the open sky, a veil of foliage tendrils unfurling before them for Nat to grab on to, one after another, hand over fist as he moved them forward. They sailed over México City's line of budding skyscrapers, the colonial-style plazas with their corresponding churches, the neighborhoods painted in vibrant and contrasting colors just like the oils lined up next to Frida's easel.

It was when they passed over the Volcán Popocatépetl that the fervency was extinguished, and the landscape transitioned into farm plots of beige, red, and grey. And yet, as Nat gazed down at the earth he was prepared to leave, he noticed something more. He could've sworn he spotted Paulina's face woven into that farm plot, could that be? With her beak marked off by the wheat field on that one side, and her face wedged between that adjacent corn field and the alfalfa? Oh, and, ja, the tip of her tail was dipping into the peanut field on the far end, *good one, Paulina!* Wait, and there were GalloUno y GalloDos in the bean fields, with the tomato crop serving as their dangles. *Clever guys!* MyDoe was more difficult to find, but ja, there were those two incredulous eyes in the irrigation's watering holes. *LordPeacock, oh, LordPeacock,* Nat snickered to himself, woven into the agaves, the plant's green leaves with purple edging serving as the perfect medium for his glorious train. In the middle of it all? Zoe, defined by the mountain range they were currently passing over, the snowcapped mountains the matching white tufts on her head and tail.

Yip, that's me, Nat. And all the PatioPets. It's the project you were supervising; the rest of us got together to finish it. For you, Nat, we got together to finish it for you. Remember how it was gonna be a quilt? For Frida? Well, we were thinking, what if we used it as a tablecloth, to put over the bright yellow table, for one of our big family meals? With all of us pets and Frida and Conchita and Guillermo? Everyone we love should be there.

He was supremely touched, imagining all of them crowded around the table, Conchita unloading arms full of steaming dishes, LordPeacock discussing the virtues of Shakespeare, Paulina lecturing them on the merits of sunflower seeds, MyDoe asking for extra moss on her hominy, GalloUno y GalloDos using their beaks to punch holes in their napkins out of nervous habit, Frida laughing at the friendly chaos . . .

But no! He would not allow himself to be overcome by sentimentality! For the first time in his life, he was determined to follow through with the plan he'd set out for himself, watching as the pets faded into the background, pleading with the Universe to speed up the scenery change before the temptation was too great.

When he spotted a dash of green along the horizon, an emerald and turquoise carpet of the softest velveteen unfurling before him with each new swing, he knew he was in luck. That, at long last, he'd arrived at the oasis he'd been looking for, one with trees and thickets and vines sprouting from the ground in a cornucopia of fertility and lushness. The cool breeze kissed his face, blessing him with all the glorious flavors of his past—of loam and damp wood and an olio of floral bouquets and a gamut of animal pheromones and all the Universe's gifts to this Earth swirling together, his life coming full circle. It was when he noticed the prisms of color rippling across a smooth surface that he prepared for landing.

Look, Zoe! It's the EmeraldLagoon! It's real, I wasn't sure anymore, so much has happened—

"I said *now!!!*" interrupted a voice in his head. "I have a letter here from Presidente Cárdenas! So you better move your asses and release my pets right now! Give me any trouble, and I'll have the federal army in here yesterday—and I assure you, they'll be putting their bayonets in places you'll be glad you can't see!"

In that same moment, a thousand kilometers away, sailing above the famed Lagoon, the pets' flight came to an abrupt halt, like they'd run smack into a glass wall. Nat tried grabbing at the space in front of him, even kicking his feet to generate momentum, to keep this flight in motion. But they were stuck in idle, a couple of flailing marionettes with no recourse.

Vamos derecho, derecho, straight ahead we go . . .

And just to add one more aberration to the madness, it was the flutter of monarchs shooting down from the heavens, hurtling back into Nat's world half a lifetime later. He was surprised to see them; but what surprised him most was the tremendous wave of relief rushing over him, realizing only now how protected he'd always felt in their presence, the burden no longer his to carry alone. He stopped jerking at the space in front of him, surrendering to the uncontrollability that is magic.

The flutter proceeded to loop around him and Zoe, once, then twice, then a third time, until they were swaddled tightly in a humming blanket of butterfly energy.

Ya! went the matriarch when the moment had arrived. *Homeward bound! Vamos derecho, derecho, straight ahead we go!*

That's when they were thrust backward.

Wait! Excuse me! We're going the wrong way! What about the "home of my bisabuelos"? **This** *is my home, I'm supposed to be here, noooooo!*

Dear Infant, said the matriarch, separating herself from the flutter to come to him as always, *it is time you know the whole truth, that you were born destined for great things. It was the Universe that set that in motion. But it was our job to assist you here on Earth. We are the ones who led you to the State-*

lySittingRoom, so you could prepare yourself for the human world, because we knew you were destined to join it, that you alone had the potential to soften their sharp edges. And we are the ones who led you to Darwin and Spencer and ultimately, Mr. Holmes, for his insistence on looking beyond the obvious. Because as you became immersed in the human world, you'd have to be reminded of what your Jungle Tent had always known, that life's true beauty lies in the blank spaces and hidden nooks, where that crucial something that floats apart from what we think we know can be discovered. Only when we thought you ready were we willing to bid you farewell at the train station, confident that your deeply personal search for meaning and truth would bring comfort to those who needed it most.

But when you became overwhelmed with self-doubt upon suffering at Frida's side, we tried to reorient you by putting Bobo in your path the day of the earthquake, to remind you that your personal history matters, that sometimes it haunts you, while on other occasions, it inspires you. But to ignore the significance of where you come from makes you a shell of your full self, and, it turns out in your case, highly vulnerable to the human emotion of jealousy, which as you've witnessed in those around you, is the gateway to self-destruction whether you're a monkey or a human being.

And though it goes against protocol to intervene in this late hour, we come to you today to ask you—to beg you, really—to consider how much of what you knew then, you've since forgotten? We are here asking you to try to remember, Infant. And when you do, to believe in it. And then she flitted off again, leaving him in a roaring silence of confusion.

He wanted to be mad, a knee-jerk reaction to having his final plan thwarted—and his aptitude called into question, suggesting he'd forgotten the basis of who he was. Because he knew who he was, a sad jungle monkey, that's who he was. A sad jungle monkey who'd been kicked in the face one too many times by Frida. What exactly was the matriarch proposing? That he should've stuck around, assisted Frida in putting her clothes back on that afternoon he'd found her with Trotsky? Helped her realize why it was a bad idea? *Pshaw,* no way! He'd tried saving her a thousand times. And all she'd ever done was shit on him in return. If the question was, was he affected by that, did it knock him off balance from time to time? Perhaps a little . . . but who wouldn't be? At least he wasn't vindictive! Nah, he was nothing like Frida. Maybe he'd never accomplished impressiveness, but he was loyal and doting and—

Uh-oh! A deluge of images invaded his consciousness, snippets of their years together, in uncontrollable succession, stacked dominoes going down, one felling the next, until the mess is complete, and the only thing left to do is either to walk away, never looking back, or to collect the tiles and start again, this time putting them back in some new order, one that takes stock of failures past, in hopes of making the next one better.

Yes, he was a very good monkey, perhaps with a heart too big to serve him well in the human world. And yes, he was hurt and terribly angry with Frida, for rejecting him, and for retreating into an emotional space he had no access to. She'd locked him out. And though he'd had every intention of rising above the maliciousness humanity engaged in, to stay true to his altruistic tendencies, and though he'd reaffirmed to himself a thousand times that he was indeed the best enfermero a girl could ever ask for, it struck him like a blow to the gut that he'd bitten into the kind of apple you could only get on TheOutside. And that he was a hypocrite. Of the very worst kind.

He was angry and judgmental about Frida's inability to see any other purpose in life except hurting Diego. And yet, hadn't he gone and done the very same thing to her, because wouldn't running away serve as the perfect punishment? She needed him. She always had, and she always would, no matter the year or the circumstances. The little coja with the wooden boot depended on him. And he'd betrayed her trust. Worse than what he perceived his own mother had done to him, or Frida's mother had done to her. She trusted him, and he had acted against that trust out of vengeance.

He knew in that instant he had to find her. He thought about screaming, to ask the flutter to turn around. On second thought, he knew there was no need, that they would be one step ahead of him, because they always were. And that going backward was, in fact, exactly the right direction.

What transpired that afternoon in 1938 was nothing short of a miracle, the way the flutter pulled the pets out of the jungle, back across the patchwork quilt of the countryside, into the urban landscape, and, finally, to the zoo's cement tree.

You're home now, Infant. She's waiting for you.

Once more, the butterflies disappeared before he could thank them. On this occasion, however, Nat wasn't sad, because all the evidence fell perfectly into place now, and he knew they felt his gratitude, and that they would never be too far away if he remembered to look for them. He reached for Zoe's paw, feeling it close around his, and then he turned expectantly toward the ruckus that had brought them back here in the first place.

"I need to speak with Nahuatl—he's my monkey—to tell him I was wrong, that I'm trying to fix things. I love him, he's the only one who understands, the only one who knows all of me!"

It was Frida, marching up and down the length of the cage, stomping her good leg for effect, billowing skirts of fuchsia and green flying out around her in a mad flush, her caterpillar eyebrows knit together in fury, a trail of cigarette smoke in her wake. From his perch in the tree, Nat noticed the peineta in her hair, the one he'd made for her before her debut as master hostess. The one with the embroidered monarch butterflies. He smiled at the realization, just one more reminder of the endless ancillary and veiled ways the flutter was embedded in his life. The clues had always been there; he'd just forgotten where to look.

"Shit, why am I telling you any of this? Just get me my damn pets, will you? And what the hell is my dog doing in that tree?"

"Yip, yip."

"Bleat, cock-a-doodle-doo, Baaaa, squawk."

"Caldo, anyone?"

"Care to share a fine cognac with me, Nat?"

SELECT BIBLIOGRAPHY

I. Frida Kahlo Paintings: These are the paintings described in *The Monkey on Frida's Shoulder*.

- *Self-Portrait in a Velvet Dress.* 1926. Oil on canvas, 79 x 58 cm. Private collection.
- *My Dress Hangs There.* 1933. Oil and collage on masonite, 45.7 x 49.5 cm. Hoover Gallery, San Francisco.
- *Self Portrait—Very Ugly.* 1933. Fresco mounted on masonite, 27.4 x 22.2 cm. Private collection.
- *My Birth.* 1932. Oil on metal, 30.5 x 35 cm. Private collection.
- *Self Portrait Dedicated to Leon Trotsky.* 1937. Oil on masonite, 87 x 70 cm. National Museum of Women in the Arts, Washington, DC.

II. The Inspiration: These two books are the impetus for *The Monkey on Frida's Shoulder.*

- Herrera, Hayden. *Frida: A Biography of Frida Kahlo.* Harper and Row, 1983.

This biography provided me with a thorough and comprehensive historical backdrop for Frida's life. The movie *Frida* (starring Salma Hayek, directed by Julie Taymor, and distributed by Miramax, 2002) is based on Herrera's book and was a further source of inspiration given the film's ability to bring to life the colors and sounds that made up Frida's life.

- Mujica, Bárbara. *Frida: A Novel of Frida Kahlo.* Overlook Press, 2001.

This novel built on what I'd gleaned from Herrera's trove of information by adding one giant infusion of magical realism. Specifically, Mujica's spellbinding book tells the story of Frida's life and times from an alternative perspective: that of her younger sister and closest confidant, Cristina. As a trained historian, I found this book deeply rewarding for its fresh, speculative approach.

III. The Grand Unveiling of 2004: Fifty years after Frida's death, thousands of handwritten letters, photographs, garments from her illustrious wardrobe, fashion accessories, and medical apparatus were released from a bathroom at the Casa Azul where they'd been kept private per Diego Rivera's request. Most of the books listed in this section are direct products of this unveiling, though I've taken the liberty of including a couple others for their unique inclusion of family recipes or contemporary pictures that help shed additional light on the Casa Azul's charming ambiance. In particular, *Self Portrait in a Velvet Dress,* which offers a close-up look and aesthetically pleasing photo compilation of the wardrobe pieces retrieved from the bathroom in 2004, is a must-see. Included is an image of the mint green bathing suit I've tried to recreate in my novel.

- Grimberg, Salomon. *Frida Kahlo: Song of Herself.* Merrell Publishers, 2008.
- Olmedo, Carlos Phillips, Denise Rosenzweig, Magdalena Rosenzweig, Teresa del Conde, Marta Turok, Graciela Iturbide (Photographer), and Pablo Aguinaco (Photographer). *Self Portrait in a Velvet Dress: Frida's Wardrobe: Fashion From the Museo Frida Kahlo.* Chronicle Books, 2008.
- Pinedo, Isolda. *Intimate Frida.* Cangrejo Editores, 2006.
- Rivera, Guadalupe, and Marie-Pierre Colle. *Frida's Fiestas: Recipes and Reminiscences of Life with Frida Kahlo.* Clarkson Potter, 1994.
- Trujillo, Hilda. *Frida Kahlo: Her Photos.* Editorial RM, 2010.
- Wilcox, Claire, and Circe Henestrosa, eds. *Frida Kahlo: Making Her Self Up.* V&A Publishing, 2018.

IV. Magical Realism and Other Ideations: This list provided the inspiration for daring to tweak history as a means for creating an alternative version of the life and times of Frida Kahlo.

- Braverman, Kate. *The Incantation of Frida K.* Seven Stories Press, 2002.
- Delahunt, Meaghan. *In the Casa Azul: A Novel of Revolution and Betrayal.* Picador, 2003.
- Drakulic, Slavenka. *Frida's Bed: A Novel.* Penguin Books, 2008.
- Haghenbeck, F. G. *The Secret Book of Frida Kahlo: A Novel.* Atria Paperback, 2009.
- Hill, Laban Carrick. *Casa Azul: An Encounter with Frida Kahlo.* Watson-Guptill, 2005.

V. All the Rest: And here are a few others, both nonfiction and fiction, that don't fit perfectly into one of the above categories but have proven helpful in my search for information about Frida's life.

- Ankori, Gannit. *Frida Kahlo.* Reaktion Books, 2013.
- Deffebach, Nancy. *Maria Izquierdo and Frida Kahlo: Challenging Visions in Modern Mexican Art.* University of Texas Press, 2015.

- Franco, Jean. *Plotting Women: Gender and Representation in Mexico.* Columbia University Press, 1991.
- Griffiths, Jay. *A Love Letter from a Stray Moon.* Text Publishing, 2011.
- Herrera, Hayden. *Frida Kahlo: The Paintings.* HarperCollins, 1991.
- Kahlo, Frida. *The Diary of Frida Kahlo: An Intimate Self-Portrait.* Translated by Barbara Crow de Toleda and Ricardo Pohlenz. Introduction by Carlos Fuentes. Essay and commentaries by Sarah M. Lowe. Abrams Books, 1995.
- Kingsolver, Barbara. *The Lacuna.* HarperCollins, 2009.
- Petitjean, Marc. *The Heart: Frida Kahlo in Paris.* Other Press, 2020.
- Stahr, Celia. *Frida in America: The Creative Awakening of a Great Artist.* St. Martin's Press, 2020.
- Wolfe, Bertram D. *The Fabulous Life of Diego Rivera.* Scarborough House, 1990.

ACKNOWLEDGMENTS

While the presence of a talking monkey in the narrative represents a strong clue, it should still be said here that this is entirely a work of fiction. Which is to say, *The Monkey on Frida's Shoulder* is *loosely* based on the life of Frida Kahlo, as I have taken my fair share of liberties in all aspects of the story. The bibliography lays out where I've gathered my background information in terms of names and dates and other essential facts. Everything else has been fabricated. For example, while it is well documented that Frida and Leon Trotsky were intimately involved, I made up the part about Nat assuaging Natalia Trotsky's general melancholy with a trip to Xochimilco. Other than the quote about "enduring more than we think we can" during the quarry scene—which are real words taken entirely out of their original context—no dialogue is factual. Nor are the letters sent between my characters. I am trained as a Mexican historian, but this book was created precisely because I wanted to let go of all the factual paradigms my studies had taught me so I could set my mind free to wander and play as it pleased.

I have spent many days as an adult within the blue walls of the Casa Azul, and every time I enter, I feel like a six-year-old again, as if I've just entered a giant-sized dollhouse for grown-ups, where magic abounds and color, smell, and texture are living organisms with secrets to share and a thousand provocations for how to lead a more authentic life. As I laze on the raised stone flower beds in the courtyard, I imagine Frida slowly and deliberately making her way down the basalt staircase after an afternoon of being holed up in her studio, then floating across the garden, stopping to greet a couple of her favorite pets and to pinch a dead flower blossom from its stem, finally disappearing into the yellow and blue tiled kitchen, the sound of her voice making dinner suggestions to her staff echoing across the yard. It is this feeling I wanted to capture, put in a box, and take home with me, that abundance of pleasure and beauty when, as adults, we are prodded to engage with our imaginations. As much as I revere the formal discipline of history, it provides little leniency for pure speculation, much less the possibility of magic.

Perhaps Frida doesn't always come out looking so great the way I've designed her in this novel. But this should not detract from the fact that she was a visionary in terms of her use of imagination in both her personal and her professional life, and it is exactly this quality that has inspired me to believe that magical dollhouses really do exist for grown-ups and that a historian can indeed conjure imaginary events while still maintaining some of the story's integrity.

I want to thank first and foremost my awesome husband, Steve Waters. This book started as a wrinkled and underdeveloped nugget of an idea. You found the soil and the sun and the water to help me grow it with your reading of the entire manuscript too many times to count and your pep talks when my spirits sagged at different points. As the story grew, so did I. I thank you for both these things.

I had many readers and supporters who got pulled onto this rollercoaster ride with me, providing both invaluable feedback and constant encouragement: my sweet adult "kids," Elena Barrera-Waters and Alex Barrera-Waters, who not only read and commented on the manuscript but didn't laugh at me when I couldn't remember my "codes" or how to log into assorted accounts; my cheerleader mom, Susan Barrera, who never ever put down her pom-poms; my soul sister-cousin Melissa Guenther; my neighbors and friends scattered across the country, Lyn Denend, Carolyn Carlesimo, Alicia Isaac-Cura; my professional writing pals Jon Weisman and Sarah Peterson Pittock; and my historian family here in Austin, Luis Murillo and Paul Hart. Thank you all. Though he is long gone from this world, my dad, Francisco Barrera, served as a prototype of intellectual curiosity during my formative years, routinely drawn to those things he didn't know and determined to find answers. He showed me that this was not work, but an exercise in joy. A special shout out to my technology support team led by Naw Wah Na Mu, as well as my grassroots Latina trifecta of marketing genius: my daughter Elena and the wonderful Sanchez sisters, Mikayla and Liana. Thank you.

Incredibly, I ended up being represented by my dream agent, Leticia Gomez of Savvy Literary, who recognizes that there are still too many deserving titles missing from bookstore shelves and works ceaselessly to change that. And lastly, to TCU Press, thank you for taking a chance on me. I am so grateful.

And finally, to my graduate school advisor, Ramón E. Ruiz (1921–2010). As fads and trends pushed the field of history in new directions, it was he who reminded us (relentlessly) with that signature stern shake of the head and tweak of the moustache not to forget that it was the essence of the people of Mexico—their respective stories and the passion they invoked—that mattered most.

ABOUT THE AUTHOR

Catherine Barrera holds a BA from Stanford University and a PhD in Latin American History from the University of California at San Diego. She has taught in colleges and universities from southern Minnesota to the California Bay Area. A lifetime devotee of Frida Kahlo, she has spent too many days to count inside the Casa Azul savoring the magic that unfolds there. With her debut novel, she is finally able to merge her academic expertise with splashes of magical realism and absurdism. Catherine currently resides in Austin, Texas, with her husband and their dog, Pepino.

www.ingramcontent.com/pod-product-compliance
Lightning Source LLC
Chambersburg PA
CBHW030638030726
47497CB00006B/1842